Introducing the first Distinguished Rogue...

"Are you interested in Louth?" Jack attempted to back away, but Constance curled her fingers into his dark waistcoat to keep him still.

"Good gracious, no. What a ridiculous idea."

"It's not so ridiculous. He is a good man," he assured her.

Jack's waistcoat slipped from her grip, but Constance caught it and held firm. "His name is not on the list. You said I shouldn't waste time."

Jack swayed forward. "So, you're keeping strictly to the list?"

"What other choice do I have?"

"There is one other option you haven't considered, Pixie," Jack whispered.

She peered up at him. No one had voiced an alternative to marriage. If he had a suggestion, she certainly wanted to hear it. "Tell me?"

HEATHER BOYD

CHILLS

Distinguished Rogues

The characters and events portrayed in this book are fictitious. Any similarity to real persons, living or dead, is purely coincidental and not intended by the author.

CHILLS
Copyright © 2011 by Heather Boyd
Edited by Kelli Collins

Dedication

———◆———

For the men in my life—both real and imagined.
You Rock!

Chapter One

———◆———

London
Spring, 1813

Constance Grange tucked a stray dark curl behind her ear and stared at the numbers on the page until they blurred into meaningless shapes. "This simply must be a terrible mistake?"

She liked the indistinct blobs far better than the appalling amount of debt accumulated since her father's death. No matter which way she looked at the single sheet, her small family was in a precarious position.

"As far as I can tell, this is the bulk of your extravagances," Mr. Medley assured her.

Constance gripped the page until it bent to fit the contours of her fingers. Medley, her family's man of business, had followed her to the Marquess of Ettington's London residence to demand payments she did not have. She had come to visit Virginia, not to deal with another parental mess. She wished he had waited to deliver his bad tidings on her return home. Could he not have waited a mere six days?

He placed a leather-strapped box onto Constance's lap without her pardon, smiling in a way that hardly reassured. It sat awkwardly on her knees, but she opened the lid to examine the untidy stack of papers contained within.

To Mrs. Peabody of Sutton Place, one thousand pounds, Faro. The bill dated February 20.

She prayed the stiff paper would turn to dust once exposed to light. When it didn't, she set the bill aside and read the next.

Mrs. Brampton of Currant Place, five hundred and five pounds, Whist. This one dated January 16.

Constance laid the promissory note atop the first and delved into the stack of papers. Aside from debts to her mama's so-called friends, there were outstanding bills to almost every tradesman in Sunderland. The tally was a huge blow. Constance could not afford the luxury of visiting with Virginia now. At the rate her mama was going, they would need to sell their home to repay even half the debt.

When she reached the bottom of the box, Constance stared at the fine timber grain before methodically returning each sheet of parchment. She closed the lid tightly and pressed her hands flat over the smooth timber.

The embarrassment was overwhelming. She could not meet Virginia's gaze. "You said there might be more?"

"It would be useful if your mother had kept a record. I've often requested prompt notice of her spending, but she has never obliged me in that regard."

Since the beginning of this interview, there had been an undercurrent of hostility in Mr. Medley's tone. She studied his pallid countenance now. The smirk twisting his lips confirmed he very much enjoyed his errand.

Her stomach churned. "I thank you for bringing this matter to my direct attention. You can be sure we will provide the funds as soon as possible."

Constance attempted to return the box to his hands. As the family's man of business he would normally see to any payments, but he shook his shiny head.

"There is only one more bill for your attention." Mr. Medley pulled a folded sheet from his inner pocket and placed it on top of the lidded box. "That one I would appreciate payment on as a matter of some urgency."

He pulled a second paper from his other pocket and placed it on top without a word.

"What is that last bill?"

"It is not a bill for payment, Miss Grange, it is my notice. In all my years in business, I never entertained the notion that I would have two such frivolous women in need of my services. You are both horrifically excessive in your tastes and should be heartily ashamed of yourselves for squandering a fortune such as you were granted. Debtors' prison will teach you to curb your—"

"That will be enough." A chilling voice cracked across the room, halting Mr. Medley's tirade mid sentence.

Constance dropped her gaze to her lap. Of all the mortifying events that could occur today, this interruption ranked the highest. Why couldn't the Marquess of Ettington still be busy elsewhere? Today wasn't a good day for him to interrupt a private conversation when he had done his best to be unavailable for civilized discussion during the past week.

Constance didn't dare look at her former guardian, so she opened the last of the papers before her. True to his word, Mr. Medley was breaking his connection with her family. His harsh wording brought tears to her eyes. Constance dropped the note as if it burned.

She drew in a shaky breath, tasting cinnamon on the air. When a long-fingered hand crossed her line of vision and picked up that derogatory note, panic threatened. But at least here was one man to whom her family was not indebted. They were free of the marquess' interference in their lives.

There was a long pause as the marquess read the note, and then the harsh sound of parchment being torn into pieces.

"Get out, and do not show your face again," Ettington demanded. "You will get your funds soon enough, but if I hear slander of the Granges' reputations, I will personally see to it that no one will employ you again. Is that understood?"

Constance experienced a moment of divine pleasure when the fish-skinned bully looked ready to cast up his accounts at Ettington's threat. The whole world knew to fear the cold-hearted marquess' displeasure.

"Yes, my lord." Medley fled.

The fair-haired marquess advanced and, once Medley was beyond the drawing room doors, turned to the hearth to consign the rudely penned note to the flames.

As firelight reflected off the large diamond cravat pin

Ettington always wore, Constance struggled to control her envy. Lack of money was a problem Jack Overton, Marquess of Ettington, would never have. He could easily afford the expensively tailored coat and breeches that defined his lean form. And if memory served, he'd commissioned yet another carriage he couldn't possibly need just this last week.

The absurdly handsome man, blessed with more wealth than Constance could comprehend, paused before the fire. He watched the paper burn with one booted foot perched on the hearth, and then he sauntered out the door. Was he born knowing exactly how to draw attention or had someone taught him?

As Constance drew in a full breath, she realized that the marquess' twin sister Virginia, Lady Orkney, had said nothing during the exchange. Embarrassment flooded Constance's cheeks with heat, and she turned to find Virginia white-faced and shaking. Concerned, she set aside her problems. Virginia's nerves were never very sturdy on the best of days. The display of aggression from the men appeared to have frightened her considerably.

Constance crossed the room and grasped Virginia's hands to rub some warmth back into them. The pale beauty's breathing slowed, but then a great shudder jerked her hands from Constance's grip.

"I'm sorry. I overreacted again, didn't I, Pixie?"

Constance smiled at the use of her nickname. "I told you your nervousness doesn't bother me." But she bit her lip to keep her anxiety under control. "Do you know I pity your brother's intended? He can truly be terrifying when he's displeased. I almost felt sorry for Medley."

"Medley doesn't deserve your pity. My brother is nothing but hot air. Though I agree with you—Jack's wife will have a hard time keeping him happy."

"That she will." Constance shuddered. "Would you like some tea?"

"I have already requested tea," Ettington replied, strolling into the room as if nothing unpleasant had occurred a few minutes earlier.

Given the rate her heart was beating, Constance could not understand how the man could appear so placid. Perhaps beneath that elegantly expensive exterior he really *was* a hard soul who gave no thought to the distress of the lower classes, as her friend, Cullen Brampton, claimed. Cullen thought the marquess insufferable.

Constance did her best to give the appearance of looking at Ettington, but avoided meeting his gaze. Although his familiar arrogance irritated, being at complete odds with her friend's fragile state, she had no wish to resume their old feud in front of Virginia.

Virginia's smile returned. "Thank you, Jack. We would like tea very much."

When Ettington sat beside the box of unpaid bills, Constance squirmed. She had left the overall figure refolded on the cushion, but the final bill for her past man of business' services was face-up for him to view.

Ettington glanced to the side, appeared to read the amount, and then turned a bland face their way. "So how was your morning?"

Virginia answered promptly and the marquess soon had her chatting about their conversations as if it were the height of entertainment. Constance gritted her teeth. Ettington had a knack for managing his sister's mood, but if he ever treated Constance as such a brainless ninny, she would dump the contents of the teapot on him.

"The tea is taking too long, sister, could you hurry the servants along? I really am very parched."

Like a marionette at a traveling play, Virginia hurried off to do his bidding. When his sister was out of sight and earshot, Ettington stared hard at Constance. She met his intense blue gaze nervously.

"I apologize for my sister's response to your plight," he told her in a low voice. "She doesn't handle confrontations well."

"Your sister cannot help but react as she does. She is trying."

Ettington's weary sigh rattled though the room. "You mean unlike me? Did I step on your toes again, Miss Grange? Should I have allowed that overpaid oaf to insult a woman under my own roof?"

Her heart thumped. "What do you mean overpaid?"

Ettington unfolded the paper and ran his finger over the scrawled figures. "His bill holds some inaccuracies that he should be taken to task over. I do hope he hasn't cheated you of more than just this one amount. He has either done it in a very clever fashion, or it is an excellent example of incompetence."

Constance leapt up and snatched the note from his fingers. "I will go over them all myself."

"There are a great many papers in that box," he remarked.

Did he think her first glance hadn't terrified her enough?

She didn't care for his interest, so she grabbed up the box and moved it away. "Then I may ask Virginia to assist me. I'm sure that between the two of us we can ferret out any further inaccuracies."

Ettington's deep, rumbling laugh chilled her, but she'd not let him cower her. She glared at him until he stopped.

He wiped his eyes. "Surely you're not too young to remember the last time Virginia tried to fathom the exact distance between your home to ours. It took her a week and, judging by the headache I acquired as a result, I fear she will not volunteer to tally sums again."

"Oh, what a terrible thing to say about your twin. I doubt you suffered."

"My sister has many talents, but mathematics is not one of them. She outshines me in many other, far more important arenas. One of them includes having an acknowledged, warm heart."

Constance fidgeted. Secretly she thought his nickname, the Cold-Hearted Marquess, well deserved. But hearing him joke about being cold-hearted, and challenging her to deny it, made her extremely uncomfortable. "One of them also includes having the tact to stay out of other people's affairs."

Ettington leaned close. "My, my, have your affairs become interesting?" He held her gaze. "What has changed?"

Constance bit her lip. She had not informed her friends of her recent attachment. Not that the decision should interest Ettington one way or the other. But she'd held her tongue to avoid upsetting Virginia when her health remained delicate.

Unfortunately, Constance had never been a proficient liar, and was usually unsuccessful with Ettington. The marquess would hound her until she confessed. It would be best to get the discussion over and done with. "I am engaged to be married."

The marquess' face whitened. "Good God. To whom?"

Constance clenched her hands into fists. "There is no need to sound so surprised at my good fortune. Cullen proposed before I left home, and I was very happy to accept. We will be married in a month."

The marquess rose to his feet. "I forbid it."

Constance stumbled back a few steps. "How dare you? You have no right to an opinion on my engagement. You might have Virginia under your control again, but not me. I am not your responsibility."

The marquess took a step forward. His jaw appeared to be locked in place. She hoped he kept it that way. When Ettington stopped a mere pace from her, she had to raise her chin high to keep him in view.

"You will not marry Cullen."

Heat stung her cheeks. How dare he attempt to bully her? Well, the marquess could go to the devil for all she cared. She'd not listen to him.

Constance turned her back on him. "The date is set."

Ettington gripped her upper arms tightly, restraining her when she would have moved farther away. "We will continue this discussion later. Alone."

Constance shivered. "No, we will not."

Luckily, footsteps clattered across the marble entrance hall. Ettington released her as Virginia swept into the room, followed by a maid bearing a tea tray. Constance sank into a chair, still shaking from the marquess' touch. She didn't know why they could never remain civil. It wasn't as if he was truly cruel, but he was bossy and opinionated. She just needed to learn how to better ignore his pronouncements.

Fearing Virginia would sense her additional distress, she raised her head, determined to defy him silently. The marquess' lips curled into an unfamiliar smile as he sank into his chair like the grand pasha he aspired to be.

———— • ————

Despite the smile, Jack Overton's pulse raced with shock. Who the devil was brave enough to take on Pixie as a wife? And how in hell had they slipped past his spies to get so close to the chit? Jack gritted his teeth then let out a slow breath. He would see an end to this disastrous misalliance the minute Virginia was occupied elsewhere.

Pixie scowled at him and, despite his anger, he softened a touch. For all her headstrong ways, she was a good girl. As his ward, she'd given him few problems that a stern warning hadn't solved. But she wasn't under his control now, as she asserted. His guardianship had ended last Christmas, but old habits die hard. He would expect to hear everything, and then he'd end her engagement.

Virginia sat beside Pixie, smiling a little nervously between them. Had she heard the discussion? Pixie had been here for five days and hadn't said a word about this Cullen fellow. Was Virginia as upset as he was that Pixie had not confided in her?

Jack couldn't question her while his twin was nearby, but he didn't often get his former ward alone anymore. Without the role of guardian to give him reason enough for privacy, Virginia tended to hover.

Yet Virginia continued to worry him, too.

The depression of her spirits had continued far longer than he'd expected. As a widow, society expected a period of sadness, but the real reason for her fears was known only to a few. It was a nuisance to live on pins and needles, but with luck and time, Virginia improved. She had already taken great leaps since Pixie's arrival. Now he just needed to get her out of the house and back into society where she belonged.

Jack shifted in his chair and his hand nudged a piece of parchment that Pixie had left behind. Supposing it was the grand total of debt, he picked it up and, while toying with the top edge, caught another glare aimed squarely at his innards. While his sister filled the void with nervous chatter, he let the paper slide between his fingers. Across the room, Pixie bit her lip, but he thought it an attempt to keep her annoyance with him in check.

He stifled a laugh. Her nickname was fitting. Small, dark-haired, and always emotional. Pixie had grown beautiful, but now was not the time for trouble. Given the wild flare in her eyes, she would like nothing better than to grasp a spear from the wall with which to run him through.

He let his gaze drift over her gown. Mrs. Grange wasn't running up bills of sale on Pixie's behalf. He hoped the new gowns ordered would get here soon. Pixie looked like a schoolgirl in all that pale, high-necked muslin. According to Madame du Clair, Virginia's dependable French modiste, she would resemble a princess when properly dressed. She'd better. He'd paid the modiste extra to deliver them promptly. He wanted Pixie fit to accompany his sister into society soon. Her impending marriage interfered with his immediate plans for that.

Jack lowered his gaze to her feet. Sensible shoes did not hide the curious turning of her ankles. As he watched, her feet fidgeted. He slowly, ever so curiously, raised his eyes back to her face. Fury blazed in her eyes. Jack enjoyed the gooseflesh that raced down his spine as she held his gaze.

"Jack, are you paying me any attention?"

Jack chuckled. "Forgive me, sister, my mind wandered onto a vexing topic."

Pixie's face pinked.

"Hmm, I was just suggesting that you should help Pixie straighten out those papers. Will you?"

When his sister put herself out to ask him to do something, he invariably did as she bade, but on this matter, he paused before answering. He wasn't Pixie's guardian any longer. He had no right to get involved in her financial affairs again.

But perhaps helping her sort through this mess would convince her to trust his instincts about this marriage. Although he couldn't recall this Cullen fellow, Jack doubted he could be the right man for her. Any fellow who'd let her out of his sight for longer than two seconds had no idea what he was getting himself in for.

Although Pixie might come to resent his renewed interference in her life, he did want to know the size of the mess she and her mother had made of their finances in so short a time. Their affairs had been secure when he'd had the management of the estate. Pixie should have had a comfortable life ahead of her.

Jack gave Virginia his most charming smile. "As long as Miss Grange has no objections, I would be happy to offer my humble assistance."

Chapter Two

———— ✦ ————

Constance was thinking of poisons. Not poisons to kill, but poisons to make the marquess very, very sick. She could not understand why he took such perverse pleasure in tormenting someone so far beneath his notice.

She struggled not to clench her fists. Virginia would notice her anger if she conducted herself as she wanted. The term *box his ears* had always rung with resounding finality, and Constance longed to do precisely that to the insufferable man. Maybe she could just blacken the eyes that skimmed so insultingly over her gown.

It wasn't possible for everyone to be as well dressed as the Marquess of Ettington and his elegant twin sister. Virginia did not notice the extent of her shabbiness, but Constance was uncomfortably aware of how outdated her wardrobe had become. The new gowns were supposed to replace it, but now she had no means to pay for them. She would have to pen a note to the modiste to cancel her order. With luck, Madame had not commenced work already.

Seeing no way out of the awkward offer, Constance turned a sunny smile on the marquess. His smug smile slipped.

"If his lordship has the time, I'm sure I could find something for him to tally."

Such as the number of occasions he thought himself better than others. That could keep him busy for hours.

Virginia rose, excused herself with an assurance she did not normally show, and made her way from the room.

Left alone with the arrogant man, with only a self-effacing maid as chaperone, the silence was deafening.

The marquess stood and held out his hand. "Shall we adjourn to the library?"

Constance looked the impeccable marquess over as insultingly as she could but didn't get the response she was after. He looked pleased.

Botheration.

Ignoring his outstretched hand, Constance stood and preceded him from the room, grumbling under her breath at how easily he got what he wanted. His low chuckle followed her, but she ignored him, placed the box on the long reading table, and lifted the lid on the catastrophe.

Lord Ettington edged close and unfolded the paper he held. The scent of cinnamon wafted over her again, and she struggled to ignore the impulse to inhale deeply.

"Sweet, merciful heaven," he said. "Did you read this?"

"Of course I did. Do you believe me incapable?"

"I commend your acting skills. One would think that a woman, faced with almost certain disaster, would react in some feminine fashion. Fainting springs to mind."

Absurd comments like that reminded her why she didn't like him. She turned to deliver a retort, but found him untidily slumped against the table devoid of his usual satisfied expression. "I don't faint."

Constance snatched the paper from his lax grip. He retaliated by dragging the box across the smooth table surface. At the loud screech, they both glanced down at the ruined wood, but the marquess dismissed the long scratches with a shrug in favor of turning out the contents of the box.

After an hour of sorting, Constance was numb. With the notes spread thick across the dark mahogany tabletop, the scale of debt looked worse. "Where are the December bills?"

"What is that one?" the marquess queried, squinting at the paper Constance held. "A tradesman's bill or another gambling debt?"

"Gambling."

"Just put it right in front of you." Ettington suddenly straightened. "Good God, how can one spend eighteen shillings on a single pair of gloves when in the country?"

"Show me that." Constance moved to his side and scanned the bill. "Ah, I remember. They were to match a lovely gown of Mama's. I'm surprised you didn't object to the price of the silk stockings, not to mention the number."

Ettington tugged the note from her fingers slowly. "I had hoped your mother would have sent at least a few of those in your direction. I certainly couldn't complain about that, since I'm partial to touching silk stockings."

Constance stared.

The marquess clenched his jaw, and then shook his head as if tossing the comment away. He lowered his gaze to the paper as if the shocking words had never passed his lips.

Constance was relieved, because when the marquess spoke of personal matters she had no idea how to answer. Part of her wanted to continue the discussion, the other part blushed. She hated blushing, so she retreated to the window to keep from asking him how he had gained such strong opinions.

All afternoon, she had suffered through his highly improper comments on their expenses, but he seemed fascinated by the fashionable purchases. Constance wasn't particularly interested in fashions. She'd had the worst time with the modiste a few days ago. Rifling through fashion plates and trying to imagine wearing such stunning creations was so hard that she had asked Virginia to approve the final choices.

But it *had* been the best thing for Virginia. She had radiated with animation and purpose, almost her cheerful self again. Constance couldn't remember what dresses she'd ordered, but she did know how much they were going to cost.

China clattered behind her back and then boot heels tapped in her direction. She braced herself for yet another argument, but the marquess' arm curved around her, presenting a cup of tea. The scent of cinnamon swamped her again, and she allowed herself to be lulled by the delicious smell.

"Relax a moment. There are still a lot of papers to go through."

Constance accepted the cup and sank into the nearest chair,

relieved for the distraction from her problems. Ettington joined her and they sipped tea in silence. At a loss for something to say, Constance kept her eyes on the bustling world outside the window.

London astounded her. She'd never visited Virginia in London before and, after close to a week of watching, the variety of unfamiliar sights hadn't lost their appeal. An orange seller's cart rolled past the townhouse, its ragged owner calling out her wares, "Oranges, cheaper by the dozen, or five pence a pair." She almost dug in her pocket for the coins.

The marquess cleared his throat. "That is a very rude habit you have acquired. Have my features grown so fearsome that you cannot meet my gaze? I do hope you will behave better when we are out and about in society."

Constance blinked at the rebuke. He knew. She turned her gaze away from London's busy street to find him smiling at her. Smiling? What on earth was there to smile about on a day like today?

"Much better."

"Do my manners really matter so much when I will be leaving, my lord?"

"You are not leaving."

Constance shook her head. Of course he would demand she stay. When word circulated that the Sunderland Granges had pockets to let, society would think she was the marquess' charity case. She could not bear that.

"My sister has made great progress since your arrival. I need you to extend your stay for at least a month—possibly longer."

"You cannot be serious. I am to be married next month."

Ettington set his cup aside. "About that. I fear you will have to give me further particulars about Mr. Cullen. I don't believe we are acquainted."

Constance considered laughing at his mistake, but thought better of it. "Of course you know Mr. Cullen Brampton."

The marquess shook his head. "The details, please."

Constance bit her lip to hold in her protest. How typical of the marquess to forget anyone without a rank to match his own. It must truly surprise him to remember her name. Although, he had forgotten the nickname he gave her. She couldn't quite remember when he'd ceased using it either.

She shook her head. "I was only to stay for two weeks. Virginia never gave any indication in her letters that anything was wrong with her at all."

Ettington shrugged. "Virginia has not been herself for a long time. I would not worry too much about the content of the letters. Please stay. She needs your company."

Constance glared at the unusually insistent lord, but her annoyance dimmed at his expression. He was pleading. He must truly be worried about his sister.

"Ah, there you are, my dear," Ettington exclaimed as Virginia rejoined them. "Did the housekeeper give you any trouble today?"

"Heavens, yes. I don't know how you tolerate her absentminded ways." Virginia's face scrunched in irritation. "She never remembers from one day to the next that you do not like fowl. She's always trying to slip it somewhere into the menu."

The marquess stretched for his teacup, eyes flickering to Constance as if to promise the discussion wasn't over. "I'm sure you cleared the misunderstanding up. Miss Grange was just telling me of the sights she wanted to see in the coming week. It sounds as though there are a great many places she wishes to visit."

"Oh, what places were they?" Virginia's voice trembled.

Constance scrambled to think up something suitable and nonthreatening to put her at ease again. "Well, I must take Falentine riding in the park soon or she'll grow so fat from idleness that your brother will take her back. And I long to see the theatrics of Astley's Amphitheatre."

"Hopefully we'll not find you perched on one of the performing horses," Ettington murmured softly. "You mentioned attending the Huntley Ball? Since they are part of your mother's set, they will expect your presence for at least a short time."

Constance blinked. Was it too late to box his ears? She couldn't argue with him about staying in Town in front of Virginia, and he was right about Lady Huntley's expectations. "Mama will have written them about my stay in London. She will look forward to Lady Huntley's letter mentioning my attendance. May we go, Virginia?"

Constance left the decision in Virginia's hands, but from the way her toes tapped beneath her gown, her friend did not want to agree. Constance felt wretched, but it was not right that Virginia hide from society.

Across from her, Ettington closed his eyes while they waited on his sister's answer.

"I suppose we should attend," Virginia murmured. She gave a half smile, then rose and hurried out again.

Constance didn't watch her exit. She was fascinated by the marquess' reaction. He carefully moved his cup to a table and raised one hand to caress his chest. She had never witnessed the twins sharing pain before, but she was almost certain that's what she was witnessing now.

The way his long-fingered hand rubbed against the stark black of his waistcoat to disappear beneath the coat edge mesmerized her. His lids cracked open and the blue of his eyes flashed bright within his pale face. He caught her gaze and the misery in his pinned her in place.

"You're in pain?" she whispered.

"It's not as bad as it once was. Your influence has lessened the intensity."

"What is it like?" Constance asked incautiously.

He dropped his gaze. "Like nothing I can explain."

Ettington stood, gestured for servants hovering at the door to clear away the tea, and then resumed his chair with the debts laid out before him.

Uncertain of what to say next, Constance waited until the maid removed the tea things. All was quiet except for the scratching of Ettington's quill.

"I apologize. It's none of my business."

———— ◆ ————

Jack lifted his pen from the page and thought of a way to respond. Being twins meant sharing more than most siblings— they experienced the other's pain, and other sharp emotions, too.

The week he had spent avoiding the house had done him some good and given him a brief reprieve from Virginia. Pixie, however, had no idea of the strain Virginia's distress caused him.

But Jack needed her to stay in London. "Have you ever read a particularly gripping novel? A story that made your blood fire, your soul weep, and happiness shake you from your ennui? It is similar to that experience, without the ability to close the book and walk away."

Jack didn't bother to turn when Pixie gasped. She had a vivid imagination and a great love of popular novels, judging from the bills before him. She would understand.

The good thing about sharing his concerns with Pixie was that she would never betray them. She would never risk hurting his sister.

"So you will stay?"

Pixie sighed and approached him. "As much as I wish to be of help, I am to wed next month."

Not if he could help it. "I am so happy you broached that subject again. Virginia needs you. I cannot even convince her to ride in Hyde Park without me as she used to. I cannot be everywhere with her and society already knows you as my ward. They will accept your longer presence without a ripple of interest."

Constance raised a hand to her throat. "But I am not your ward anymore."

"No," he admitted. "But the assumption that you still rely upon me for guidance will lessen speculation about your longer stay. Together, we can watch over Virginia until she is herself again, and prod her to do the things society expects. Please."

Jack's plan made perfect sense from his perspective. How her intended would feel about the delay was quite another matter. With luck, the blighter would go away and marry someone else.

"You know I want to stay and help Virginia in any way I can," Pixie agreed. "But Cullen and Mama—"

"Your mother should stop associating with Lord Clerkenwell," Jack cut in to change the subject, squinting at the note in front of him and changing the subject. Pixie may not have agreed wholeheartedly to support his plan but if he continued as if she had she'd be mad at him for only a little while. Relief that he had succeeded in extending Pixie's stay for an indeterminate length of time was heady. Jack fought not to smile. She did not appear to trust him when he did.

"How can I stop Mama from talking to her dear friend? I am

not her keeper."

"Insulting people works for me. Perhaps you could try that?"
Jack turned to catch her reaction. Fire burned in her eyes
again. He glanced around the room and judged that there were
no sharp objects nearby. There were heavy ones, but she might
not be able to lift the marble bust of his father too easily. It was
life-sized, after all.

"You are suggesting I insult the very people who have made
Mama's grief bearable? She was so lost after Papa died. Lord
Clerkenwell and his sister were so concerned for Mama that they
called every week, regardless of the weather. I take it you don't
have many friends left, my lord. You must be able to count them
on one hand."

Pixie's response pleased him for its accuracy. True friends were
hard to come by but easy to retain. That was the reason she was
here. Lord Clerkenwell and his sister would not be his choice for
close associates. "And now that her grief has gone, they will
deprive her of everything else."

"That's ridiculous."

"But the facts are right in front of us. Most of her gambling
losses are to him." Jack indicated to the pile of papers set to the
side. Pixie rushed to flick through them.

When she slumped against the mahogany for support, Jack
had to ask one more question. "Does she never win?"

"Mama's luck has deserted her," Pixie whispered.

Jack ignored the impulse to stand, to give her comfort. He
didn't think she would react well to that. "Luck has very little
patience with people. She needs something more complex to
occupy her time."

"There is very little to do in Sunderland until the summer
months. Maybe we should consider moving somewhere more
exciting. Cullen says that Bath has all sorts of diversions. She
might be happier there."

Jack frowned. "Remind me who this Brampton fellow is?"

"Lord Clerkenwell's heir."

Jack grimaced when he put a face to the name. "Ah, the
sniveling pup is still nosing around, is he? I thought I had dealt
with him. No, I am in earnest—you will not be marrying him. I'll
have papers drawn up for your signature today. But while a move

to Bath might be good for your mother, I fear you will be bored out of your mind."

Pixie appeared to grow an inch taller. Her back stiffened to an alarming degree. "I can find happiness anywhere, my lord. Don't start on about Cullen again. He has been my close friend these past years. I won't stand to hear a bad word spoken against him."

Steel had crept back into Pixie's voice and Jack stilled at the tone. "You've long known my opinion of Mr. Brampton, but I am surprised to hear the young pup speak so fondly of Bath. I'm led to believe Bath is the last stop on the trip to heaven for the old and infirm. Do you wish to spend your days listening to the ailments and remedies sprouted by old gentlemen in search of their missing teeth?"

"I suppose you would know about old and infirm. It must be difficult to drag yourself away from Bath."

The soft smack of Pixie's hand covering her mouth echoed through the room. She did not need to throw a thing. She had more cutting power in her tongue than anyone he knew.

Jack let the silence stretch. He tilted his head, fighting to contain the response that begged to be unleashed. Was she too old to bend over his knee or send to her room?

Once his breathing slowed, he counted to ten before standing and walking from the room.

———◆———

As the stiff-backed marquess left the library, Constance wished her words had gone unsaid. She had overstepped her bounds. She couldn't say the first thing that came into her head as she had when she was younger. No doubt he was now wishing he had not just begged her to stay. Given her provocation, Ettington had probably gone to pack her things personally.

Constance dropped into the chair he had just vacated. She had neither meant to insult him about his age nor to hint that he was infirm either. But his assessment of her disaster itched under her skin and left her maddened. Cullen had promised the marquess would become a cold, overbearing monster once he gained the title. Could Ettington not show one glimpse of compassion for her plight?

Moving Mama to Bath was going to be torture. But the greater problem would be how Cullen would feel about not living at Thistlemore when they married. He'd been so looking forward to the day he could move in to lighten her load by managing the property properly.

As much as she didn't want to live in a place where the moment she set foot out the door, she would be forced to speak to someone who was not part of her household, she feared they couldn't keep the Sunderland property.

Moving to Bath might be the only way to avoid debtors' prison.

This week in London with Virginia and Jack, enduring the suffocating presence of servants at all hours of the day and night, was enough torment to last her a lifetime. She had so little privacy and it would be the same in Bath.

Constance lifted the page in front of her and grudgingly admired Jack's penmanship. His lines were neat, his figures legible. He was a man obsessed with doing his best.

And he had thought she was best for his sister. Constance dropped the page and hid her face behind her hand. Oh, she was in so much trouble now. How could she look at him without remembering the horrible thing she had said today?

Actually, today had been a series of horrible conversations with him. It was amazing that she was still standing. According to her mama, the marquess was ruthless, intent on exacting the last penny or pound of flesh from his enemies.

Well, she was his enemy now. She fretted over how she would pay for her impertinence.

Chapter Three

————◆————

Constance lifted her silver spoon to her lips but hesitated to taste the soup. She quite liked hare soup, but was afraid that the marquess had tainted her portion with something terrible in retribution. After all, she'd done it to him long ago. An occasion she no longer remembered in precise detail—a little girl's disappointment over a broken promise soon fades. But she did remember sprinkling a lot of salt onto his breakfast tray one morning.

Taking a sharp breath, she steeled herself as the soup coated her tongue and passed down her throat. Encouraged that she didn't feel the strangulating clenching of her air passage, Constance risked another taste. Nothing.

Could she be so lucky that Ettington would ignore her earlier impertinence?

"Is anything wrong with the soup, Pixie?" Virginia's quiet question echoed around the vast chamber. "I was sure it was a favorite with you."

Constance jumped. "The soup is delicious. I was simply savoring the taste."

How could she think the marquess would extract revenge at his table? No, he would wait until she was away from his sister if he was inclined to retaliate in any fashion. She risked a glance sideways, but his gaze was on his meal. Since he had left the library, Ettington had neither spoken to nor looked at her. It was exactly what she deserved.

Constance raised her eyes to the walls and repressed a shudder. How could anyone find eating enjoyable when faced with the trophies of past hunting conquests?

Jack and Virginia's father had liked nothing better than to hunt, play cards, and drink to excess. And despite his title and affluence, the late marquess had preferred the company of Constance's father while he indulged his many expensive vices. As a result, Constance had often visited with Jack and Virginia when she was younger, and unfortunately became the Marquess of Ettington's ward.

Across the table, Virginia frowned. Unable to bear the tense expression, Constance forced herself to make conversation. "Do you think the weather shall hold tomorrow, Virginia? We should take advantage of the warmer temperatures and stroll around the square."

Virginia leaned back in her chair. "We could do that, I suppose."

Constance forced an excited smile to her face. "If we go early enough there is hardly anyone outside. I was looking about this morning and noticed how lovely the park is. We should definitely take a stroll." The marquess wanted Virginia to go outside more often and this was the start of Constance's plan. Even if he tossed her out tomorrow, they would take that walk first.

———— • ————

Jack covertly watched his sister throughout the meal. The occasional twitch of tension raising her shoulders set his heart racing. Although her awareness of the servants going about their duties shouldn't concern her, the subconscious sway of her body away from them proved they still did. However, unlike the first months of her despair, she resisted the urge to make a sound.

They didn't eat formally for every meal, but Jack was determined to help Virginia conquer these irrational responses by degrees. There was no one remaining that could hurt her again—fate had seen to that. But Virginia had to regain her confidence before she went about in society.

After the dessert course was placed before them, Jack sent the servants away, poured more wine for the ladies, and cleared his throat. His news would be another hurdle for Virginia to overcome. "Lord Hallam sent a note, announcing his intention to visit London, Virginia. He will arrive the day after tomorrow."

Virginia dropped her glass and the ruby red wine flowed across the white linen.

"Oh. I'm sorry. I'm so sorry."

Cursing, Jack circled the table as Virginia attempted to sop up the wine with her napkin. He should have waited until her glass was firmly down before he spoke, but there was never a perfect moment to mention Hallam.

He drew Virginia away from the mess. "There is nothing to be concerned about, Virginia. Hallam will stay in the green suite, as he always does when in London. He will have his head buried in a book within an hour of his arrival most likely. You won't have to deal with him any more than you normally do. Just send his meals to the library at regular intervals, and leave him to his own devices."

Virginia fussed. Her panicked state remained thick around her. Unfortunately, Jack was at his limit in dealing with her distress. He glanced at Pixie for the first time this evening.

She nodded as if hearing his unspoken plea.

Pixie crossed to them, slipped her arm around Virginia's back, and led her from the room. On the threshold, Pixie turned back.

He thanked her with a tight nod, and she graced him with an actual smile.

The warm affection in her expression almost knocked him off his feet. Jack hadn't seen that smile for what felt like an eternity. He waited until they were well beyond the stairwell before he returned to the library. There was nothing more he could do.

Returning Virginia to full health was beyond his abilities. As much as he might wish it could be otherwise, he needed help.

Pixie's help, and possibly Hallam's.

Jack sank into a chair, disgusted by the mess before him, but thankful for the distraction of Pixie's debts. They provided a balm to his battered nerves. Judging by the rate of progress he had made through the papers earlier, he would be up all night. He didn't mind in the least—the longer the distraction lasted, the better.

Light footsteps crossed the threshold but he didn't bother to raise his head. Despite her earlier smile, he wasn't going to be the first one to bring up Pixie's insulting comments. He didn't pay much attention to his age, but it appeared she thought him ancient. He was barely eight years older than Pixie. Only just approaching thirty, for God's sake. It wasn't as if he really needed a cane to steady himself.

"What happened to her?"

"Didn't she tell you?" Jack didn't want to talk, so he kept his eyes firmly on the next bill.

"No. She hasn't explained anything, and I am too afraid to bring the matter up myself. I don't like that she is so timid."

"I cannot break my sister's confidence. Even for you. She will tell you when she is ready."

"Why is she afraid of physical contact?"

Jack ground his teeth. She wasn't going to apologize for her ridiculous comment about his age? How typical. "She was hurt."

"By whom?"

"I cannot explain without breaking my promise." He had hoped that after a week, Virginia might have confided the secret herself. But it appeared his plan hadn't worked so well, after all.

"The housekeeper doesn't forget that you don't eat fowl, does she?"

Jack sighed. "Of course not, but the housekeeper says she does every week. It makes the discussions livelier than they would normally be."

"You are a very good brother."

"Flattery? Why thank you. Any day now, I will have you calling me by my first name again. But then the world will stop turning." And according to Pixie, he'd be too old to enjoy it. Jack grimaced.

Pixie moved to stand behind his left shoulder. "Where does the tally now stand?"

Even as the light scent of roses reached his nose, one delicious enough to salivate over, he shook himself back to the task at hand. "The debt stands at a little under nineteen thousand pounds, but I still have the last two months to include. I should be able to make a guess at the missing months' regular expenses."

"Nineteen?"

The fact that Mrs. Grange had managed to hide and delay the

revelation of these accumulated debts irked him. He should have known the harridan would play fast and loose with Pixie's future in retribution for his refusal to marry the girl. But Mrs. Grange's behavior would ruin Pixie so that no other acceptable gentleman might consider her for his wife. "I fear so. It is a sickness your mother has. I hope you are not afflicted with it."

"No, I do not gamble, Ettington. Luck does not hold."

"I am glad to hear it." Actually, Jack was not just glad—he was overjoyed. When Mrs. Grange eventually passed, Pixie would not have to contend with this issue once the current mess was dealt with. But her mother needed a tighter leash to control her gambling habits or they would enter Fleet before Pixie reached two and twenty.

Thinking of anyone he knew in that horrible place made Jack's blood boil. He threw off his coat and waistcoat, and then loosened his cravat, pacing to rid himself of his agitation. Grabbing a bottle of whiskey from the mantelpiece, he stalked back to the long table, pouring as he moved, then tossed it back before pouring another.

He downed the second glass, and then looked across the room. Pixie's eyes were about to fall out of her head at his undressing. He smiled, and a bright flush of color swept over her cheeks. Her gaze locked in the middle of his chest, then swept upward to his bare throat. As he removed his cravat entirely, Pixie swallowed.

Jack found her reaction fascinating. Despite the sharp tongue, Pixie was still innocent. Yet she didn't turn away or berate him as usual. It was almost as if she had never thought of him as a man before.

The idea was supremely lowering. He'd been appointed as her guardian, not her grandfather.

Jack cleared his throat to draw her attention upward to his face. "Perhaps you should retire for the night. There is a great deal left to contend with and I would prefer to be comfortable to do it."

"I cannot leave you here alone to sort out my problems."

Jack rolled up his sleeves. "Why not? I did agree to help."

"Help, yes, but not do everything." Pixie turned her back to him and fussed with the papers. Her flustered reaction improved his mood considerably.

"Tallying the debt accurately is only a minor matter. Deciding how you are going to make reparation is a much larger issue." Jack took a step that placed her face in view. "Or has that pup you intended to marry acquired a fortune? You also need a plan to deal with your mother's spending habits. She cannot continue this way without causing you significant embarrassment."

"I was trying not to think of that."

When her eyes closed, Jack allowed himself to admire the tiny woman before him without fear of offending. She was very pretty, after all, with dark hair and winged brows that heightened every emotion expressed by her green gaze.

Jack turned away as an unexpected response to her beauty stirred, giving him a problem that would be inappropriate and embarrassing if noticed. He didn't need that kind of complication in his life. He glanced to the doorway where Parkes and a maid stood, trailing behind Pixie as they had all evening. Servants made very poor chaperones. Had Pixie realized she was essentially alone with an unmarried man? Probably not. Jack suffered the blow to his ego with as much fortitude as he could bear, but there were limits to his patience. Her outburst before dinner had forced him to retreat, lest he prove he wasn't infirm at all.

"I suppose I will have to sell Thistlemore," Pixie said abruptly.

Jack winced. He had hoped to avoid this conversation. Their discussion had been headed in this direction before Pixie had disparaged his age and hinted at infirmity. She was not going to be pleased with his news about her home.

Jack waved Parkes and the maid away, then set the quill aside, closed the lid on the inkpot, and methodically straightened his work. He drained his glass and turned to face her.

"Did you hear me, my lord? We shall sell Thistlemore and use any remaining funds to lease another house in Bath. We should be able to manage with lower expenses. What do you think of that plan?"

Pixie loved her home, and he doubted she'd really thought her decision through. She would be bereft to leave Thistlemore—so it was lucky she couldn't carry out her plan. "Then what shall you live on? You will need to draw an income."

"Oh, I hadn't thought that far ahead." She pouted, the little frown reminding him of the amusing child she had been.

Jack touched her shoulder and squeezed. "It would have been a good plan…if you still owned the property."

Pixie took a step away from him. "What?"

"You don't own Thistlemore any longer," he told her softly, letting his eyes convey his regret.

Pixie's skirts snapped around her legs as she advanced on him. "I cannot believe you uttered such a malicious lie to my very face. Mama was right about you. You are beyond cruel!"

"Thistlemore passed from the control of your family seven years ago, I'm afraid." Jack looked her in the eyes as he spoke the truth, and horror crossed her pretty features. He could strangle her mother for withholding this information for so long.

"Who owns Thistlemore now?"

Jack struggled for a way to lessen the impact of his reply, but there was nothing to do but tell the truth. "I do."

Silence, deafening and complete. "You monster!"

The amusing child of his memory vanished in an instant until a raging harridan stood in her place. No other woman would dare speak to him as she did. A marquess was deferred to and respected. Pixie gave him none at all.

"Seven years ago," he repeated. "Your father lost it to mine through gambling years ago. When I inherited four years ago, I found the property title amongst his personal papers. That is also when I learned about the guardianship, and I came to Sunderland to straighten things out. I had not known before then I swear."

She pressed her fingers to her temple. "Why wasn't I told about this?"

Jack grasped her arms just in case she was of a mind to faint. "I don't know. At first I assumed the arrangements, along with the guardianship, was common knowledge in your family. But when I approached your mother to discuss improvements I thought were required, she hindered my every move. She protested, quite often that I was not welcome."

"Is that why she despises you? Because you wished to take over the property? Tell me, how fast did you wish for us to vacate so you could tear the house down?"

Actually, Mrs. Grange despised him for another matter altogether, but he was not going to mention her scandalous claim that his family had ruined them financially so he could *have* Pixie. "I didn't ask her to leave. You will never have to leave. I came to formalize a lease that didn't exist until I had one written. I don't need what little income Thistlemore produces."

Pixie slipped from his grip. "I don't understand."

Jack glanced at his empty hands. "Neither did I, at the time. It seems my father never offered yours a lease for the property, and through excessive gambling, Grange further deprived you and your mother of a comfortable future. When I discovered the extent of my father's involvement in your situation, I made arrangements to see you never went without. All the expenses of the Thistlemore property are paid by me, servants, maintenance. Everything. As things stand now, you and your mother remain as tenants of the property indefinitely and can never be evicted by my heirs."

Pixie bowed her head, and then stumbled across the room into a chair. She dropped her head to her hands. "How could Mama let me come to London and not tell me we were so indebted?"

He didn't have an answer. All he could do was help her make the best of a bad situation. She must be as deeply shocked by the news as he had been.

Jack grabbed up the bottle of whiskey and poured her a small amount. The amber liquid swirled around the bottom of the glass as he stepped toward her. He dropped to his haunches, offering the glass.

She stared at his hand but took the drink. When she tipped the contents down her throat too quickly, she spluttered, and he pounded on her back until she stopped. He let his hand rest on Pixie's shoulder, sure she was still very much affected.

She spun out of the chair and away from him. "I want to see proof that you are not lying to me."

Jack sighed. "Of course. You shall have it directly."

———— • ————

A thick wad of parchment burrowed its way beneath Constance's door and wiggled at her in greeting. She slipped off the chaise and crossed to the documents, afraid they could savage her.

Yet when she had them safely in her hands, she hesitated to open them.

These would either prove the marquess a liar or condemn her to debtors' prison.

The parchment crackled as she settled near the bracket of candles. Lifting the first sheet, she scanned the note from the marquess. He apologized, but requested the return of the documents for safekeeping on the morrow. If she desired authentication, he would make them available when she needed them.

The marquess' fair-mindedness unnerved her.

The first paper was the lease agreement for the Granges to remain at Thistlemore indefinitely. She read the terms in astonishment. The marquess was not charging rent, and any income remained in their possession. Constance swallowed over his generosity and set it aside.

The last paper was yellowed with age and handling. Inside was a promissory note from her father to the late marquess, detailing the extent of the Thistlemore estate and the furnishings contained therein. Constance swallowed over the horror at seeing her home listed, including the very bed she slept on. Her father had gambled away everything.

Constance turned the page and read the figure this surrendering of her family holdings had repaid. Seventy thousand pounds more than covered the value of the property. She didn't believe it was worth nearly that much even now. The late marquess had been cheated. She had always thought him a wise man, but this was folly. Why had he paid so much for a property that had seen better days when her father had the management of it?

She peered at the signatures and didn't doubt that the old document was legitimate. Her father had lost everything. She'd been blissfully unaware for the last seven years.

Jack had already known her true situation this morning, and still her plight hadn't affected him to show any emotion other than anger over her engagement. She had no money. She had debts she could never pay. She had a beau expecting a nonexistent dowry.

Constance had to deal with this mess on her own. She knew

better than to suppose her mama could pull them out of this situation. After all, Mama acted as if the estate had unlimited funds and in some way they had. The marquess had become their only source of income. But now Constance knew the truth depending on him couldn't continue.

Only Jack's generosity had kept a roof over their heads.

She wallowed in self-pity for almost an hour, cursing her parents for not protecting her better and the late marquess for encouraging her father's vices. Life might have been better if Papa had kept to his own level of society and not aspired to remain as the late marquess' confidant.

She also gave a silent thanks to Jack for not yelling at her for doubting him. She should be ashamed of herself, but truly, too much had happened today for her to make sense of it all.

But there was one thing she absolutely had to do. She had to protect Cullen from the mess she was in.

Shadows danced across the room as she lifted the candlestick and moved to her writing desk. Although tears streamed down her cheeks, she made a passable effort on her letter. It was messy and tearstained, but Cullen Brampton must be released from the engagement. She couldn't drag him or his family down to her level. The plans they'd been making for their future at Thistlemore could never come to pass now.

Chapter Four

———◆———

Constance rushed into the library of Ettington House, anxious to learn her exact situation before she and Virginia went out that day. She made it as far as the table before she realized the mahogany surface was bare of clutter. When she looked around, she could not spot a single paper, or the chest that should contain them. Disappointed, she retraced her steps to the marquess' study door and knocked. There was no answer. Vexed, she turned the knob but found it locked.

"There you are, Pixie. Good morning," Virginia sang out.

Constance turned, caught trying to open the door to a private room she had no permission to enter. She tucked her hands behind her back. "Good morning to you, too. Have you seen your brother?"

"If that door is locked, Jack hasn't risen yet. Perhaps he was up late?"

Supposing that could be true, Constance let out a deep breath and joined Virginia.

"I'm glad Jack isn't here this morning, because I wanted to apologize about yesterday. I was not very much help and I should have been. I'm so sorry." Virginia's voice wavered.

Constance held out her hand and took Virginia's in a tight grip. "There wasn't very much to help with unless you like looking at ruin."

"Is it very bad?"

Constance steered her friend toward the front door and the privacy afforded outside the mansion. As they gained the little park, Constance raised her face to the weak sunlight and warmth. She missed country weather—seeing the storms race toward their house, the sound of rain lashing the windows, and the familiar scrape of branches against her bedroom wall at night. London weather consisted of rain with few glimpses of sunshine and a dirty breeze she didn't want to welcome.

She sighed. "It is the worst it can be. Any day I expect debt collectors to pound on the door. If Mr. Medley could approach me here demanding payment, others will too. I cannot imagine what my mother is thinking to be gambling as she is."

"Now that Jack is aware of your situation, he will keep you safe," Virginia promised, her voice clear of any doubt. "He'll know exactly how to solve your problems."

"That is very kind of you to offer your brother's protection, but such a burden cannot continue. I suppose you've known all along what he's already done for my mother and I."

Virginia nodded quickly. "My brother and I have few secrets from each other."

Constance blushed. "He's been imposed upon too much already."

"Of course he'll continue to look after you." Virginia frowned. "What possible reason could he have for turning away from you now?"

Constance winced. "We disagree when you're not around."

Virginia shrugged. "The pair of you have butted heads for as long as I can remember."

Puzzled, Constance stopped. "Why should he concern himself any more than he has? He is under no obligation now. He's no longer burdened by the guardianship."

"While it is true he is no longer your guardian," Virginia cupped Constance's cheek, "my brother is your friend too, don't forget. He also has considerable influence. If we sponsored you for the season, the right man would look past your lack of dowry and try to win your affections for their very own. I know you refused a season years ago but think of it now. With our support, you could be married before the month was over and be free of difficulties. Jack will be happy to lend his support to any match that will make you happy."

She couldn't find a word to utter in response.

"Just think, if you married a wealthy peer we could spend every season together here in London. Wouldn't that be perfect?" Virginia continued.

Constance held her tongue. Jack wouldn't help her with this. He'd think it beneath him to help her try to snare herself a wealthy husband. "No. Absolutely not."

Virginia frowned. "I've never understood your aversion to marriage. Please, Pixie, let me help you find the right husband. Someone who deserves you and will cherish you for the rest of your days."

Constance's heart squeezed. Cullen had promised her the very same thing, and her letter to end their engagement had already been sent. She wiped her damp eyes. "I don't know what to say. Who'd want to marry a penniless woman?"

Virginia caught her hand and squeezed. "Many a man would marry you to gain just a few words in Jack's ear. You don't yet realize how valuable your connection to our family could be."

"Virginia, that's revolting. I could never condone a marriage begun on such a circumstance. Besides, your brother considers me an annoying pest to be managed."

Virginia chuckled. "My dear, you have more power over my brother than you realize. Just never let him discover that you know. It is unfortunate that he's engaged already. You could have set your cap for him. He dotes on you, and we could have been sisters."

Constance couldn't have been more shocked by the turn of their conversation. She wasn't fit to be a marchioness. The idea was preposterous. "Your brother is a bully. I'll never marry without affection."

Virginia shook her head. "Then we will find someone to love you as we do."

Although Virginia's "we" included Jack, he didn't love her. Constance was an annoying fly buzzing into his life too soon after he'd gained his freedom from the unwanted guardianship. She'd sensed his reluctance to help yesterday. "What if there isn't someone for me? I had thought to marry once, but…" Constance couldn't continue. Tears threatened to fall again. She'd not make a spectacle of herself in public. "Let's return to the house."

"An excellent idea. We can compile a list of suitable gentlemen."
Constance groaned aloud.

"Shush, Pixie. We can make a list for you to consider as a
starting point," Virginia offered. "Is there anything that you
particularly want in a husband?"

"I've never seriously considered this before." That was a lie,
but Virginia was nowhere near as good as Jack at detecting them.
Constance didn't think he had told his sister about Cullen
because, so far, Virginia hadn't brought the subject up. If she did
know something, she'd want to know everything. "I always
thought I would meet someone agreeable and he would propose.
I have never contemplated what might make a suitable spouse."

"Well, tell me what you don't like in gentlemen."

"Arrogance," Constance blurted, then shook her head as the
image of the Marquess of Ettington popped into her mind to
illustrate the point. She couldn't bear to be wed to a man like
him.

"What else?" Virginia squeezed her arm to encourage her to
continue.

"Not a gambler. That is what got us into this mess in the first
place," Constance continued. "A man my mama might fear to
cross. Someone who can deter her from excess."

Virginia nudged her shoulder. "Wouldn't arrogance come in
handy when dealing with her?"

Constance rubbed her brow. "I suppose a little, but he
shouldn't be that way with me."

"We must be practical. If I was in your shoes, I would have
taken to my bed and let Jack take care of everything."

"Virginia," Constance chided gently. "You give yourself far too
little credit. I remember a time when I was afraid to cross *you*. I
cannot remember what precipitated the argument, but you
rounded on Lord Hallam like a fury and he never knew what hit
him. It's the only time I've seen him speechless. I never told you,
but you were magnificent. Even Lord Hallam appeared
impressed."

"I impressed Lord Hallam? I should have liked to hear about
that earlier. The man deserves a good scold for the way he
neglects his responsibilities. Can you believe his mama hasn't
seen him in a year? He sends letters at the end of term but rarely

leaves Oxford."

Constance looked up at her friend in alarm. That was quite a diatribe considering how quiet Virginia had become. Lord Hallam really would change the atmosphere of Ettington House when he arrived tomorrow.

Virginia stopped suddenly. "You should marry Hallam."

Constance choked. "You cannot be serious."

"He would be perfect for you. He practically lives at Oxford year round, so you wouldn't have to listen to the pompous idiot spouting his nonsensical ideas. His mother is sweet and never leaves Parkwood. You could live there and we could see each other every day."

As enticing as Virginia made the match sound, Pixie had never felt comfortable with Lord Hallam. He was far too serious a man to encourage more than the barest affection. Acceptance, perhaps. She accepted that he was large enough to make three of her, he could argue in circles until she had no idea what the original point had been. He made her head hurt.

No, not a good choice.

The happy zeal drained slowly from Virginia's face until she was frowning again. Constance moved to support her, as she'd done all week, and Virginia smiled brightly again, shrugging off whatever bad thought she might have had.

"As much as I would love to see you every day, I doubt Lord Hallam and I would suit," Constance confessed. "He is far and away more arrogant than even your brother."

"Well, there is nothing else for it. We shall have to make sure you marry for money *and* love. Surely there is a well-positioned man somewhere you could feel more than just a passing affection for." Virginia's exhalation sounded a little relieved to Constance.

"Let us hope so." Constance prayed for that.

"Come, I want to write that list of names. At least you can be armed with a little information before we begin our search."

"Virginia, I didn't come to London to find a husband. I came to see you."

"And I am very happy you are here. It was good of you to spend your holiday with me."

"Well, I'm glad you persuaded me to come," Constance assured her as they climbed the front steps. Constance had missed her friend so much over the past years. Her letters had left her aching for more than the stilted conversations of hurried notes. But given the marquess' bad mood over the guardianship, she hadn't wanted to press for a visit to Hazelmere.

"How did I persuade you? You're always welcome."

"In your letters. Don't you remember begging me to come to London with you?"

"My letter?" Virginia frowned and then she shook her head. "Oh, of course I remember now. Pixie, would you excuse me for a moment? I have forgotten something that requires my attention upstairs. I will join you in the drawing room as soon as I can."

When Virginia hurried off, Constance stripped off her pelisse and handed it to the waiting butler. She watched the stern retainer and amused herself by wondering what Parkes might look like if the bushy brows he sported suddenly caught fire. If the butler ever wore an expression that wasn't entirely proper and respectful, she would probably faint.

———— ♦ ————

Jack glanced up as the door to his bedchamber banged open. "Sister, what an unexpected pleasure."

"Tell me you didn't do what I think you did."

The startling fury in Virginia's voice surprised him. Jack tugged the ruined cravat from his neck and tossed it onto the dresser. "What, specifically, is it you think I did? The list could be very long."

Instead of chuckling, Virginia strode toward him and stopped a bare inch away. "Did you or did you not write to Pixie as if you were me."

"I may have. You would need a man of experience, expert in the art of detecting forgeries, to prove it though. Our handwriting is remarkably similar."

"Only when you make the effort to copy mine," Virginia hissed.

He shrugged. As they had aged, Jack's handwriting had remained similar to his sister's. All it required was a little effort on his part and the use of the correct phrases in order to make a convincing replacement. The truth was bound to come out sooner or later. But did his former ward realize he'd been corresponding with her as Virginia these last years? She wouldn't be happy when she learned she'd been deceived in that too.

Yet he couldn't be sorry. Appearances had to be maintained.

His sister scowled. "You deceived my best friend. How could you, Jack?"

"Very easily. You needed her here." Inviting Pixie to London had been one of his better ideas, if her presence could transform his sister into this hissing viper. God, he had missed Virginia. "Is Miss Grange aware?"

"Oh, will you stop calling her that. I know you remember her nickname."

"Yes, of course I know her name, but I won't be using it. Does she know I wrote the letters?"

"No. And I'm certainly not going to tell her but you should. She's going to be so embarrassed when she discovers the truth."

Jack relaxed. "I will inform her when the time is right." He didn't need another reason for Pixie to be irritated with him this week. It would be better to let her ire subside before she got any other distressing news. "In case you have failed to notice, Miss Grange is not particularly pleased with me of late."

"She said you were arrogant."

Old and arrogant. The list grew daily. "She has a right to her opinions, Virginia."

"But you could change her mind."

Jack raked his fingers through his hair, suddenly uncomfortable that the subject had switched to him. "Leave matters as they are. She is your friend, and she is here for your comfort. How she feels about me is beside the point."

Virginia scowled but there was a look about her eyes, as if she was assessing him and his current state of happiness. He hoped she didn't consider him for too long. He was not very good at lying to his twin, especially if she questioned him point blank about why he hadn't done his duty and married to produce an heir. He was trying very hard to avoid that subject.

Virginia snatched up his cravat and hurled it at his head. "Don't think I shall forgive you for this, brother. You owe me."

Jack caught it. "I look forward to it."

Virginia's swift exit left him with a sense of relief. He almost had his sister back, and all it had taken was one visit from a very small Pixie.

———•———

Constance glanced at the drawing room clock again and grimaced at how late it was. Surely the marquess wasn't going to sleep the day away. He really was a beast—a cold-hearted beast. She hated calling people names, but the man deserved it. He must know she was anxious to learn how large the debt really was.

"Well, there it is," Virginia announced as she sanded the paper she had just written, holding it for Constance to see.

The close-written sheet held a lot of names.

She took the list and read each one. She didn't know any of the gentlemen listed after the first one. To her considerable discomfort, Virginia had ignored their earlier conversation and started the list with Lord Hallam's name.

"This is just the beginning. If you are to make a good choice, you need to learn as much as you can about them all. I shall make sure to introduce you to as many of the gentlemen on the list as I see at the Huntley Ball. And we can add or subtract other names after each entertainment."

Now that Virginia had a purpose ahead of her, she was embracing her return to society with great enthusiasm. Unfortunately, Constance had lost hers. Panic filled her as she contemplated marrying for money. She had always despised the women who did. "I don't understand how my life could get any worse."

"Why such maudlin thoughts so early in the day, Miss Grange?"

The marquess slid into the chair next to Constance and she glanced across at his gleaming boots. Was the man always perfectly turned out? She didn't bother raising her eyes to his, but glanced back at the list. "Some of us started our day hours ago."

"Ah, well, you will soon get used to Town hours. Everyone fresh from the country has trouble adapting at first."

Constance gritted her teeth at the condescension in his tone, struggling to keep a rebuke behind her teeth. She really didn't want to argue with him so soon. She had many more problems ahead of the marquess' little irritations.

"Are we hosting a party? It looks like quite a guest list."

Constance folded the list without comment. He didn't need to know what she planned. Given how hard his sister had been pursued before her marriage for her dowry alone, Ettington had a well-known scorn for fortune hunters. With horror, she realized she was now of that same class of scoundrel. Albeit, the female kind.

"When is it to be?" The long-legged man settled himself more comfortably, seeming excited by the prospect of entertaining.

"Oh, there isn't a party in the planning, brother. The list is for something else entirely. Pixie has thought of a way around her financial difficulties and has asked for help. Actually, since you owe me a favor, you shall help with our scheme as well. We will need your expertise."

Constance hadn't wanted to involve the marquess with this plan to save herself. "Virginia, I'm sure you shouldn't waste your favor on me. You should make sure you get a greater benefit than this."

The marquess twisted to face Constance. His knee brushed briefly against hers as he turned. "I shall admit I am intrigued. What is going on?"

Embarrassment flooded Constance's face with heat.

Virginia chuckled. "Give him the list, Pixie. Let us see if my brother can work it out on his own."

Constance's hands shook as she turned the paper over and over between her cold fingers. She didn't want to show him. He would laugh. She started to shake her head, but his annoying, long-fingered hand snatched the list before she could stop him. He stood, opened the paper, and began to read. He took a few steps toward the window, and then his lean body grew rigid.

Constance closed her eyes, waiting for him to say something cutting that would embarrass her, but the silence grew deafening. She risked a peek. He stared out the window, but one hand clenched and unclenched over the paper.

She switched her gaze to Virginia and found her pale. What was it she could see from her position?

The marquess raised the list, now crushed in his fingers. "This is utterly unacceptable. How could you involve yourself in this folly, Virginia? I thought you had better sense."

Virginia's chin dropped. "It is the only way. With your support, her lack of dowry will not matter and men will flock to propose."

Constance stood. "It was my idea, not Virginia's. Kindly direct your venom toward me."

The marquess advanced, bristling with rage. He tossed the list onto the table between them. "So you've finally tossed out the notion of marrying Brampton, in favor of marrying for money. How practical of you. Enjoy your list, but bear this in mind. It takes a very wealthy man to afford you. There are only a handful in Town who have sufficient funds."

He stalked out, slamming the door behind him.

She spun back to face Virginia, but her friend's expression wiped away her rage over the marquess' rudeness. Virginia's hand fluttered at her throat, panic evident in the gesture.

Constance crossed the room and managed to get an arm around Virginia before the older woman burst into tears.

Oh, the marquess was a horrible, cold-hearted monster.

When she realized Virginia was not going to stop crying anytime soon, Constance turned her and held her close as she sobbed against her shoulder. It felt strange to be the one to comfort Virginia. It had more often been the other way around when she was young.

"Dearest, don't cry. He's angry with me, not you."

"You don't understand." But Virginia said no more than that. Perhaps a good cry was what she needed. So Constance held her, soothed her, and let her have her cry. When her sobs had lessened, she fished in her pocket for a handkerchief and pushed it into Virginia's hands. All the while, however, Constance planned exactly what she would say to the insufferable brute about his temper.

A prickling up her spine warned her they were no longer alone.

She glanced around Virginia toward the door and saw Jack standing there.

He stared at Constance, and her unease increased. Yet, she knew that Jack felt his twin's distress very keenly. They were so close that they always knew when the other was in pain.

Despite her own feelings on the matter, she nodded, ready to call a truce until Virginia calmed.

As Jack reached them, Constance turned her friend into his embrace. When he spared her a brief glance with unspoken thanks in his eyes, his eyes had darkened to an intense blue. Shocked, she took a pace back.

Goodness, he was moody.

She looked on as Jack apologized, speaking a jumble of words she didn't fully understand. She caught the odd French word, some Italian, and perhaps Latin but soon gave up. What the twins shared was private, but Constance had never felt disturbed by how close they were.

Jack scooped his sister effortlessly into his arms and strode from the room. Constance followed along, wanting to be of help. She lagged behind on the stairs, unaccountably fascinated by the sight of Jack's leg muscles outlined by his tight-fitting breeches.

The marquess was as well-made a specimen as any man she'd imagined. But she blushed at thinking of him that way. He'd been her guardian—a role so close to that of parent that she'd always tried to please him. Thinking of the limbs beneath his clothing was simply scandalous.

Jack strode through Virginia's sitting room to the bedchamber and settled his sister on the bed. As Constance dampened a cloth at the washbasin, she struggled to suppress her ridiculously inappropriate thoughts about her friend's brother.

Once steady again, she crossed to the bed and handed Virginia a cloth to press to her face. When the cloth was warm again, Virginia handed it back.

Jack had settled on the bed edge, holding one of Virginia's hands, a frown creasing his face. "Are you all right?"

"We overreacted," Virginia whispered.

"The fault was mine," he replied. "All forgiven?"

"Perhaps," Virginia replied. "If you'll help me see Pixie settled."

When Jack raked his hand through his hair and growled, Constance returned to the washbasin.

It was a great pity the twins hadn't come with instructions. She had no idea how to prevent this discussion without upsetting Virginia again. Perhaps she could talk to Jack later and convince him she didn't need his assistance.

Constance took her time rinsing the cloth in more cool water. When she turned back, Jack had leaned forward until his head touched his twin's.

Watching them together reminded her of their earlier conversation about marriage. At least Virginia had no surprises to contend with when Jack took his bride. His arranged marriage was a longstanding agreement, without love as far as she knew. Constance steeled herself that she might have to accept such a situation.

"Will I see you later?" Jack asked.

"Yes, as we planned."

With a last look and squeeze of Virginia's hand, Jack stood. When he approached Constance, his broad chest blocked Virginia from her view. His closer-than-usual proximity startled her.

He touched her sleeve, but then his hand swiftly fell away. "Will you stay with her, Miss Grange?"

"Of course. I won't leave her."

Constance raised her gaze past his waistcoat, past the mathematical knot in his cravat, to his frowning face. The glassiness of Jack's eyes brought instant action. She settled her hand flat over his heart. There was so much uncertainty in his blue eyes that she lost her anger with him. He only wanted to protect his sister from scandal and foolishness. She couldn't fault him for that.

The superfine of his waistcoat was smooth beneath her hand and she rubbed to soothe him. Cinnamon swamped her, smooth as velvet to her senses, creating a moment of peace amid the chaos. Prickles raced up her arm and warmth spread with it.

In a moment so slow, Jack's gaze dipped to where her hand rested, and then he covered her fingers with his.

Blushing as tension sizzled through her, Constance snatched her hand back, dropped her eyes, and curled her fingers into her palm.

Jack moved and was gone long before Constance's gaze had risen again.

Chapter Five

———◆———

Virginia stared at her reflection with a mixture of fear and disappointment. At nine and twenty, she should have felt more confident than she did. She tugged at the neckline of her gown and grimaced at the small scar, a constant reminder of pain etched on her skin. Her marriage had changed her, turning her into a weak woman—constantly afraid of exposure as a victim of violence. Her actions and reactions were still controlled by her late husband, a supposedly meek and mild gentleman who had turned the tables as soon as the wedding guests had gone.

Orkney had fooled her as he had fooled everyone. But his memory should not retain the power to manipulate her from the grave. During the four years since his death, he had kept an iron grip over her life, and she chafed at his continued influence.

She repositioned her neckline, smoothed her skirts, and thought of the way she used to be. Pixie was right—at one time, she had been fearless. But as Virginia tried to recall her life before she married, the memories skittered away behind a smothering blanket of pain.

The harder she struggled toward them, the heavier the blanket grew. Visions of strangling bed linen surfaced to blind her, and she gripped the bedpost to steady herself. Perhaps she didn't need to remember the past now, but one day she vowed to. She would not remain a prisoner of her fears, left gasping at the memory of fresh linen sheets pressed over her face.

Determined, she left her chamber then made her way down to breakfast. It was too early for Pixie to be up, but Virginia had to regain her life—and especially her confidence.

As the footman lay dishes on the sideboard, silent, efficient, and above all else, respectful, his gaze flickered to where she stood waiting.

Approaching the array of dishes, Virginia stepped close to the tall footman and waited as he reached for a plate. The servant moved slowly, holding her plate while she picked out the food she liked, doing his best not to startle her. The poor servants had endured far too much of her skittishness.

When heavy footsteps paused at the door, she repressed the urge to turn. She would not overreact today. It would only be the butler, assessing the footmen going about their duties.

But the soft swish of skirts turned her around. Pixie had dragged herself from slumber earlier than usual, yet the tense set of her shoulders spoke of unease and a poor night of rest.

"Didn't you sleep well?"

"Not particularly, no," Pixie replied. Her tired eyes turned and she waved away the hovering servant.

What could have preyed on her mind?

Then Virginia remembered yesterday's argument. "You didn't lose sleep over my grouchy brother, did you?"

"He was very angry," Pixie said. "Perhaps I had better go home."

"Pish posh. My brother might be marginally older, and a marquess, but he is not my master. We had that particular argument out when we were seven. I give you leave to ignore him when he becomes unreasonable. I am going to help you, with or without his approval."

"He won't like that," Pixie promised.

Jack could go to the devil. Virginia grasped Pixie's cold fingers and squeezed. Really, Jack should be ashamed of himself for causing her friend distress. She should have protected Pixie from him yesterday, and silently promised to do better by her from now on.

"Pixie, he is just like any normal man. Once he cools down, he will behave as if nothing has happened. Trust me on this."

———— • ————

Wind whipped through Jack's hair as he galloped through parkland in a bid to clear his head. He shifted his weight and drew back on the reins, gently at first, and then with more insistence as his horse tried to ignore his command to slow. Lucarno, the finest stallion he'd ever owned, snorted as Jack used firmer pressure on the reins to drop them back to a canter. He couldn't ride forever.

But he wanted to.

Lucarno tossed his head but broke to a trot, and then a walk. The exuberant horse hated moving slowly so Jack thumped his glistening neck in gratitude for his patience.

He had a lot to think over this morning.

First and foremost, he was ashamed to have lost his temper with Virginia. He never yelled at his sister unless she was shouting back at him, too. He had crossed a line yesterday and hoped he'd not affected her recovery. Jack hadn't meant to blame her for the damned list, but he couldn't have acted out his first impulse. He had chosen what he'd thought was the lesser of two reactions.

The second, and most puzzling, was his reaction to that list. By the time he'd read the third name, he'd known what it was meant for. Pixie was hunting a rich husband. Fury, unlike anything he'd known before, had lashed at him. He had held back from throttling her by the skin of his teeth.

Yet Jack had forced himself to read the rest of the names, to be sure he had not misunderstood. All of them were single gentlemen, wealthy—and all younger than him. Lord Hallam was the only exception, and his name graced the first line. Virginia had put him there. When Hallam found out, he'd be furious.

Jack, to his considerable horror, was angry because his own name hadn't been anywhere on the damned list.

Old, arrogant, and unwanted.

Fury built anew and Lucarno sidestepped in agitation as Jack sent mixed signals to the horse.

Cursing under his breath, Jack gentled him and set off for home, still no closer to understanding his reaction. It wasn't as if he was ancient. And despite what Pixie thought, lots of gentlemen married at an age older than his—most marrying young things barely out of the schoolroom.

What was he thinking?

He didn't want to be a target for any young miss bent on catching herself a wealthy husband. He'd decided long ago that marriage wasn't for him. After seeing what Virginia had gone through, courtesy of her loathsome spouse, he had no wish to make a match.

Jack didn't need to be on that list, but a part of him—the stupid part, obviously—thought his name should be there. He could amply afford Pixie. Her debts wouldn't cause a ripple of distress for the estate. The sooner he could take control of her life and gain the right to dress down Mrs. Grange, the better.

Jack let loose a string of curses. He did not want to marry Pixie. But that foolish part of him thought it was the best idea he had ever had. He did find her more attractive than he should.

He kicked Lucarno into a gallop, attempting to run from that very thought. He liked his life as it was. There was no need to take a wife yet.

Damnation. Eternal damnation.

There were plenty of good reasons not to marry Pixie. She thought him old and arrogant, most likely thought of him as a parent figure, too, thanks to the guardianship. He grimaced. Virginia had hinted he could change Pixie's mind, but he wasn't going to change anything. He liked their little discordant rubs. He liked that she'd stopped being agreeable.

Jack imagined the dressing down Pixie was waiting to give him when she got the chance. With luck, Virginia would be occupied elsewhere long enough for the sparks to truly fly. He could imagine the little woman's aggressive scowl, lightning-quick fingers flashing to illustrate her point.

Perhaps she'd touch him again. The sensation of Pixie's fingers rubbing against his chest had affected him. That touch had sparked something else. Something he hadn't wanted to admit to at first. A reaction, if he was honest with himself, he'd been fighting for quite some time. He lusted after the pint-sized woman.

His Pixie—he'd even given her the nickname.

Shocked at his own thoughts, he pulled on the reins and stopped again. Dear God, he couldn't want Pixie like this.

"What the devil are you doing?"

Jack glanced up. A rider on the ugliest mount he'd ever viewed regarded him from the nearby stand of trees. He narrowed his eyes and recognized Lord Hallam.

He groaned. "Riding. What are *you* doing?"

"Waiting for you to stop talking to yourself in public and move your horse in a forward direction. Are you aware that you have been riding in circles for the last half hour? Lucarno is going to throw you if you don't start paying attention."

Jack glanced around at the same park scenery.

Hallam chuckled. "Must be a large problem you're contemplating. Are you going to return home now? Lucarno looks to have exercised enough for one day."

Annoyed by his preoccupation, Jack shook the reins and joined Hallam under the trees. "Yes, I'm done for now."

Hallam tapped Jack's boot with his riding crop. "Good. I thought for a moment someone was going to have to die before you stopped."

"Not yet." But close enough, if he listened to what his body wanted. Pixie would surely be the death of him.

Luckily, Hallam didn't ask what problem he'd been wrestling with. Their simple conversation blocked out his disturbing thoughts until they were crossing to the house from the stables. Virginia and Pixie stood in the garden. He slowed his steps, cursing his lack of planning. He had no idea what he was going to say to Pixie after yesterday's outburst. How could he explain his reaction without appearing an utter fool?

Virginia straightened at the sound of their booted feet crunching across the gravel. She scowled when she saw Hallam. Then her shoulders squared, the stubborn family jaw clenched tight.

"Good morning, sister. Look who I ran into." Jack kissed Virginia's offered cheek, but she dismissed him with the barest glance, electing to keep her gaze trained on Hallam.

"Lady Orkney," Hallam managed to say with a slight condescension of tone to his words.

Jack braced himself for trouble as Hallam stepped close to Virginia with his hand extended, but she did not extend her own to their old friend and neighbor. Instead, his sister dusted her clean fingers with a rag.

"My lord, so good to see that you still know the direction of

London. Perhaps you could consult a map again to find your way home to Parkwood. I have heard your mother only has a dim recollection of your features." Virginia laughed. "She mistook a gardener for you just last month."

Hallam stepped back. "Mother's eyesight is failing," he growled. "What would be your excuse for confusing Orkney for a gentleman?"

Jack winced.

Hallam had disliked the man Virginia had married even before the damage was done. With Orkney dead and unlamented, Hallam didn't bother to hide his disapproval. When would Hallam learn that these tactics would not gain her trust? Virginia had a stubborn streak a mile wide and particularly disliked any reference to past mistakes. It didn't help that she and Hallam were very similar creatures in that respect.

She finally looked up with a scowl for Hallam. "At least he knew how to present a respectable image in public."

"Oh, I know how to dress—and undress too," Hallam challenged. "I could show you my expertise. Privately."

Virginia gasped; her gaze bore holes into Hallam.

"Glad to see I have your complete attention," Hallam grinned. "Have you enjoyed the season? Have you kept the London shopkeepers in wages with your extravagant purchases?"

Virginia's eyes narrowed. "Tell me, my lord, does it take long for you to remove the cobwebs and dust from your person before you leave Oxford? Do the half-wits you boast of teaching do it for you as part of their tuition? If not, perhaps it is the clothes themselves. You are aging badly. The moths have been busy."

———•———

Constance retreated a step along the gravel path, startled by the intense expression on Hallam's face, a look that hinted he might just shake poor Virginia. Given that her person stood somewhat central to the conflict, Constance took that step in the hope of clearing the marquess' path to rescue his sister, should rescue be required.

Hallam set one hand to his chest. "Why, Lady Orkney, I had

no idea you took such an interest in my figure. I am flattered. Perhaps you should take care of these little matters for me, since I am clearly incapable. You can even help remove my boots later if you like. Such capable hands and such a generous heart."

The swarthy Lord Hallam looked Virginia over quite wickedly, until Constance grew uncomfortable. Her friend's face turned a fiery red, but she returned his appraisal, pivoted on her heel with a loud snort, and returned to the house.

Constance very much wanted to follow, but instead she took another discreet step toward Jack. At least Jack seemed in a happier frame of mind. The marquess' grin reminded Constance of the man he used to be. A nicer man than he'd become.

Hallam's gaze followed Virginia's retreating form. When she disappeared from view, Hallam grinned triumphantly. "First skirmish and she quits the field. I could win this round, Jack." The older man rubbed his hands together in anticipation.

"That wasn't a retreat. Surely you don't believe she's done yet," Jack replied.

When Jack tipped his head in Constance's direction, as if attempting to remind Hallam that he was rudely ignoring her, her skin heated.

"Now, where were we?" Hallam came forward and took her hand to bow over. "Ah, yes—the lovely Miss Grange."

"Lord Hallam, such a pleasure to see you again."

Beside her, Jack stiffened. Hallam's name was on the top of the list, but if Jack thought she could set her cap for a man like Lord Hallam then he was a bigger fool than she supposed.

"You are looking well and all that. Grown up as much as can be hoped for."

"Thank you, milord," Constance replied, still trying to decide if she was pleased to see him again. She thought not. She really didn't care for his arrogant ways with Virginia, even if he enjoyed unsettling her friend.

Hallam linked Constance's arm through his and led her toward the open doors of Jack's study—a place she thought would be off-limits. Constance caught Jack's eye and she raised an eyebrow in inquiry, curious if she should excuse herself.

Jack shrugged.

When they entered the study, Constance dropped Hallam's

arm and gazed about her. The masculine room, filled to the brim with curios and books, reeked of Jack's cinnamon scent. She took a deep breath and her tension fell away as she took a seat.

Her gaze lifted to the marquess as he crossed the threshold. With the sunlight streaming in behind him, her breath caught. The man was too handsome for her peace of mind. He blinded her.

A sudden half smile twisted his lips. Her heart fluttered.

"I tell you, Jack, this latest lot of students are even more dim-witted than the last. Lord Muster's son still believes the world is flat. Obviously the result of his upbringing. But his comments send the whole class into an uproar, and it takes an hour to settle the boys."

Unnerved by Jack's sudden smile, Constance wrenched her gaze away from him to Lord Hallam. He'd almost looked pleased with her.

"Yes, it is difficult to change a wrong opinion," Jack replied. "I commend you for your patience and perseverance."

"Oh, I gave up on changing his mind. The lad simply cannot fathom that things might not be the way he was told. The next time I cross his father's path, remind me to congratulate him for having a genius for a son. He deserves to believe that lie for making a mess of the boy's mind."

Jack dropped into the empty seat beside Constance, laughing at Hallam. "That should be interesting to watch."

Despite her earlier confusing thoughts, she relaxed. With Jack so close, she would not worry about appearing foolish in front of the far more intelligent baron. Hallam would center his remarks on Jack, leaving her free from the burden to make polite conversation.

"Taverham left London last week to scour Kent again," Jack remarked.

"Is he still searching for his wife? I do hope Miranda has a good excuse for her disappearance," Hallam grumbled.

The Marquess of Taverham's wife had disappeared on the night they had wed, eight or so years ago. According to Virginia, Taverham had been searching for Miranda ever since. To Constance, the tale sounded wildly romantic and scandalous in equal parts. Like everyone else, she had wondered why the new bride had run away from such an obviously good match.

"I have always believed she must. It was just so damn odd where the fire started," Jack said, but cast a surreptitious glance sideways. "She could have easily slipped away in the chaos."

Their gazes held and a strange warmth raced across Constance's skin. Flustered, she glanced down at her lap.

"Yes, you've said as much before. The more important question is why disappear at all?" Hallam scoffed. "She is a marchioness, not a scullery maid. She has a responsibility to produce his heir."

"That wasn't the only reason Taverham married her. He seemed to truly care for her."

Hallam laughed. "God, you've turned into a romantic popinjay behind my back. Next minute you'll be spouting poetry. Who is she?"

Jack sighed. "Never mind. What brings you to London?"

The conversation swiftly turned to other matters, and both men appeared to forget Constance sat among them. Or so she thought. Jack stood to pour drinks, brandy for himself and Hallam, Madeira for her. Their bare fingers brushed as the offering changed hands. Lightning rippled up her arm and she had to concentrate on the fine glass in her grip. When Jack reseated himself, his shoulder was a scant inch from her own.

"Has Virginia wearied you of Town life yet, Pixie?" Hallam asked abruptly.

Constance smiled, setting her untouched drink on an elegant side table. "Not yet. She hasn't wanted to venture out much at all."

Hallam pursed his lips but kept his opinions to himself.

Beside her, Jack stirred, shifting position until he sat with one arm draped across the back of the settee. Her unease returned. That cinnamon scent he wore was really becoming a distraction. It made her hungry for something sweet.

"You shouldn't coddle the woman," Hallam said suddenly.

Jack leaned forward, his arm dropping across Constance's back. She stiffened, but Jack didn't appear to notice where his limb had fallen. "I won't have her rushed."

Clearly, the men were discussing Virginia's fragile emotional state, but what could Hallam know of it? Why would he know more than she?

Hallam lurched to his feet and strode to the window, the angry movement forcing Constance back into her seat and farther into Jack's embrace.

Jack's arm curled about her shoulder. She blushed, thinking how scandalous a simple, comforting embrace between them was now. As a younger woman, she'd never given his occasional affection another thought. He was Virginia's brother. She trusted him.

Constance wriggled her shoulders, hoping to dislodge him. But Jack failed to notice. He slipped his fingers onto her skin at the base of her neck, the rough pads chilling her. Her heart sped up a notch.

While his breath stirred across her ear, he drew burning, hot lines on her back, down to the top edge of her gown, and then back up again to her nape.

"What are you doing?" she whispered.

"Teasing you," he promised.

Her gaze flickered toward Lord Hallam, but the baron appeared lost in his own contemplations. He did not notice Jack's actions. Constance struggled to find a way to reorder her senses, but the marquess' questing fingers blocked her every attempt. He was intent on teasing her, knowing she wouldn't react for fear of appearing loose in front of Hallam.

Jack drew sweeping circles on her skin, his touch so light she yearned to end the tickling. She twitched her shoulders again, leaning forward, and his fingers stopped moving. But they lingered a long moment, then slid downward.

The marquess slipped the tip of his fingers under the muslin and tugged her back into her seat.

Apparently, the marquess had decided upon another way to torment her. She had never known him to be improper. He must be trying to cause a scene that would embarrass her in Hallam's eyes. Tears gathered at how hard the process of finding a husband she could live with could be if Jack spent every waking moment tormenting her.

Did he truly dislike her that much?

Despairing and more than a little upset, Constance was glad Hallam all but ignored her. She emptied her glass, but decided to stay a few minutes beyond that. She couldn't live with a man like Hallam and she was determined to scratch his name from the list today. She excused herself, but was sure that Jack's gaze burned into her back all the way to the door.

Chapter Six

———◆———

A procession of servants entered Constance's bedchamber the next morning, struggling to see past their burdens. Horrified, she raised her hands to her cheeks as the gowns piled up on her bed, and then more and more wrapped packages appeared, growing to an alarming level over the chaise. With all that had happened in the last few days, she could not believe she had failed to cancel an order that would send her further into debt.

"Oh, wonderful, your dresses are here too," Virginia exclaimed, rushing through the door and looking around her with far more enthusiasm than Constance felt.

"Yes, they certainly are." This was dreadful. She didn't know what to do. She couldn't stand to be in debt to someone her friend patronized.

"Come along, let us have a look. I cannot wait until you can wear them out! I'm ashamed to say I am heartily sick of that yellow muslin you're wearing." Virginia approached the bed and picked up a ball gown in soft green silk. "Oh, this is divine. I should like to see you wear this to the Huntley Ball. The color and style are perfect for you."

Constance held her tongue as Virginia rushed over and held the ball gown against her body. She wished she could agree with her, but her mouth had grown dry. Constance tried swallowing to loosen her tongue, but it didn't help.

There were more dresses on the bed than she had ordered, and she hadn't ordered anything that needed to be wrapped in a small parcel. Obviously, the modiste had made a mistake and sent another lady's order instead.

"Are you not pleased?"

Constance summoned a happy smile. "Virginia, this isn't my order. There are twenty gowns on the bed. I just counted them."

"Of course it is your order. Madame would not make a mistake." Virginia shrugged aside Constance's fears as she pulled another gown from the pile. "See, I remember this one. I specifically asked for the little capped sleeves to be an inch longer. I must say, the fine lace edging was a good choice."

It couldn't be her order. She couldn't afford all this. Constance closed her eyes and sank back into the chair behind her, trusting that it was where she remembered. "But what about the parcels, Virginia? I didn't order anything that required wrapping."

"They are a puzzle. Let us open one and find out what they contain."

By the sound of rustling paper, Virginia had snatched one up.

A deep throat cleared behind her. "Virginia, before you start squealing over Miss Grange's bounty, perhaps you should organize tea. I'm sure Miss Grange would appreciate it."

Finally, the voice of reason. Constance turned her head toward the balcony doors and glimpsed the marquess leaning against the far railing, watching her latest disaster unfold.

"You think of everything, don't you? I shall be back in a trice," Virginia promised, almost skipping out the door.

Jack would help her return what she could—and hopefully suggest a way to pay for the rest. Constance dragged herself upright and out of the chair. "This is terrible! I forgot to send a note to cancel the order. Help me fix this."

"There is nothing to do except to store the gowns until you wear them."

Constance stepped out onto the balcony, stopping a few paces from the marquess. Freshly scrubbed, pristine in the early morning light, he didn't look as concerned as she expected. In fact, he looked smugly satisfied again.

"But I didn't order this many. Certainly none of those parcels. I dread to think of the disappointment suffered by the lady waiting to receive her purchases. How shall I proceed?"

"You cannot return them. They have been paid for."

"By whom?"

He sighed and glanced up at the sky. "Does it matter?"

"Yes, it matters. I cannot slide further into debt. Who knows when payment will be demanded? Virginia did not pay for these, did she?"

He glanced down again. "No. It was not my sister."

Constance's pulse raced. If he was certain Virginia hadn't paid, then that would mean he knew who had. And if he knew, then Jack had paid the bill.

This was the absolute worst news. "I will pay you back."

"Did I confess that I paid for them?" Jack asked, but a gentle smile tugged his lips upward. "I would never admit to such a gross breach of etiquette publicly." The marquess folded his arms across his chest, drawing her attention to the way his elegant, dark coat pulled tight on his upper arms.

She set her hands to his folded arms. "I must make repayment. I cannot accept such an act of charity."

"Must you be so difficult about every little matter? Surely you wish to be comfortable, to blend in with the society around you. It will make Virginia happy, even happier than she appears today. My compliments on your success with her, by the way, you have surpassed my expectations."

Despite the situation, Constance preened a little at his praise. Jack didn't hand out comments like those lightly. Unfortunately, she couldn't bask in his approval for long. "My lord, I cannot tolerate this."

"Did I misunderstand that you had decided to acquire a husband this season?" Jack crowded her, warmth fading from his features.

Constance clutched her skirts as her palms grew damp and shrugged. She didn't want to discuss the matter with him, of all people. Especially when she didn't want to think of it herself.

Jack gripped her upper arms. "Your chances of success will be greater if you appear as though you belong. You have the necessary breeding and deportment to succeed if you are dressed appropriately. You cannot continue to wear such inferior gowns."

"It is too much to accept."

Jack shook her. "Once you have your choice firmly snared within your web, then you can mention the unfortunate state of your financial affairs. If you do your work well enough before you tell him, he may not back out of the arrangement."

When Jack put it that way, it sounded so calculated, so cold. Could she really do what he assumed? "Perhaps he will love me and not care a whit about the money."

"Better make sure the one you snare has the funds to pay for you first, before the fool falls in love," the marquess bit out, and then he cursed under his breath. "Give me the list."

"Why?"

"If I am to help you I will have the final say on who you wed. We will put about that you remain my ward. The gentlemen must court you with my approval." Jack's scowl proved he had little liking for the task. "We cannot have you wasting your energies unnecessarily. Making love to someone without the blunt to settle the debts would be unwise."

Constance's face flamed at his words. "No, thank you. I don't require your assistance."

"Stop talking nonsense. I'll get it myself." He strode around her, entered her bedchamber, and crossed to the door. He pushed it closed, locked it, and then turned back in her direction.

Seeing Jack in her bedchamber rooted her to the spot. What was he doing?

He showed her the next moment when he crossed to her desk, rummaged through the papers in the top drawer, and removed the list Virginia had written. His hand lingered over her letters from Cullen, but he pushed them aside, along with her belongings. He made a furious swipe at a quill, jerked the lid off her inkpot, and bent over the paper.

Jack's serious face twisted into a series of scowls and downright ugly expressions that frightened her.

Constance edged closer to the doors. "What are you doing?"

"Be quiet," he warned, glancing toward the locked door. "I am culling the unfortunates without sufficient funds for your purposes." He spoke low. She moved to stand at his shoulder to hear him better, watching as he scratched off three names without a moment's hesitation.

"Don't do that." She reached forward to grab his hand. "I told you I don't need your help. I would appreciate it if you listened to me, for once."

She braced herself against the back of the chair to pull his hand away from the paper, but he slipped from her grip and laced his fingers through hers, trapping her in an awkward position over his shoulder. She couldn't move. Draped as she was, she could only stare at the large hand dwarfing hers.

Reluctantly, she turned her face toward his, supremely conscious that her breasts pressed tightly to his broad shoulders. There was not a trace of padding inside the coat as far as she could tell. The heat of him branded her breast through the thin gown, and she blushed at the scandalous image they would present if anyone found them like this.

The marquess' face flushed with color and his blue eyes widened. That couldn't be a good thing. She squirmed to get away. Another outburst like yesterday could mean her doom.

Jack didn't release her, but turned his head fractionally, nostrils flaring as he drew breath. "I will listen when you talk sense, Pixie." His voice whispered across her cheek.

Constance blinked. The marquess hadn't called her by her nickname in years.

He tortured her for a moment longer before practically throwing her from him. She staggered to find her balance, wrapped her arms across her aching chest, and stared at the floor.

"There has to be peace between us, for Virginia's sake," Jack forced out. "It appears her heart is set on finding you a husband. That has given her purpose again. I will not go against her wishes. But she is aware when we argue behind her back."

The sight of the marquess so discomposed stilled the cutting retort she wanted to utter. It wasn't *all* his fault that they argued. They both wanted Virginia to be happy again. But it was hard to keep up the charade of polite acquaintances when, the minute Virginia turned her back, they were at each other's throats.

"Are you willing to help me find a husband?"

"If you cease fighting with me over every little thing." The marquess shifted on his feet, appearing uncomfortable again. "If that is what you desire, then yes, I can help find the right husband."

"Thank you," Constance whispered. "I will try not to fight with you anymore."

The marquess slapped his hand over the hilt, fingers scrunching it into his palm, and hurried out.

———— ✦ ————

"Ooh, that man is the most insufferable, arrogant, blind idiot," Virginia fumed as she paced back and forth in her sitting room.

Constance had found her not ten minutes ago, and she was still waiting for the woman to calm down enough to answer a question rationally.

"Forever boasting his intelligence and belittling the poor students. Assuming women only know how to shop. Ooh."

Apparently, a lot had happened since Virginia had left to get the tea.

Constance settled against Virginia's bed. "What has Hallam done now?"

"I'll tell you what he did. He said that he could not contemplate how I had time to drink tea when there were so many other pressing matters that required my attention. He thought I should run out and arrange for the replacement of his wardrobe. As if I care that the cuff of his left sleeve is beginning to fray, or that the fabric of his waistcoat has become so worn it's begun to shine."

Virginia threw her hands up in disgust and turned away, missing the astonishment Constance couldn't hide. She had noticed neither defect in Lord Hallam's appearance this morning. But clearly Virginia paid more attention to Hallam than Constance did.

"It is a pity Hallam is such an impossible man," Constance observed. "The woman who marries him should expect sainthood as recompense for putting up with his outrageous outbursts. How could you imagine I would want to marry the man?"

Virginia's steps came to an abrupt halt. She spun to stare at Constance. Her foot began to tap, a good indication that she contemplated an unpleasant thought. "You are correct. He is only passionate about his books and studies. I should have learned to ignore his words long ago. Forgive me for suggesting him. He would make you miserable."

From what Constance could discern, Hallam was passionate about everything he did—including teasing Virginia. Constance was certain a purpose lay behind it. Why else would he go to such trouble to antagonize her friend?

She waited as Virginia pulled herself together, trying not to think of her own confrontation with the marquess. She was still shaking. If she did not know better, she would think she was falling ill.

"I am sorry. Your first week in London, I wanted everything to be perfect. My sorry self included."

"Oh, Virginia, there is nothing for you to be sorry about. I came to have a look at your gowns."

Actually, Constance had come to Virginia's room to get away from the mountain of gifts in hers. She was so confused by the situation. An unmarried woman shouldn't accept gifts from a man. Society would leap to the wrong conclusion and assume she was his mistress. Nothing could be further from the truth of course. The marquess had shown her nothing but polite, and occasionally angry, conversation. He'd never had that kind of interest in her.

But a part of her wanted to accept the gifts with no thought to the consequences. If she'd ever had a brother she might have received such generosity and thought nothing of it. She really didn't want to appear out of place by Virginia's side.

Jack still hadn't explained the size of her debts, but considering he had taken the list of prospective husbands, he would know who to weed out and who to keep. Still, the thought of letting Jack help her find a husband was almost as depressing as searching for one. Money was an ugly reason to prepare for matrimony. And, as Jack mentioned, she would have to make love to the man she married. That thought almost caused her to lose her breakfast.

Virginia turned to her gowns, admiring each one before the maid put them away. Like Constance, there was also a pile of parcels for Virginia to unwrap. She did so with enthusiasm. "I never know how he manages the feat, but he always purchases just the right item to make my gowns perfect."

"The marquess exerts himself to choose these personally?"

"I think he and Madame du Clair have an arrangement." Virginia's eyes twinkled at the thought.

Constance's stomach revolted again.

"Oh, now, do not take that the wrong way. I know it sounded dreadful, but he isn't having an affair. I simply meant that, at a later time, Jack will visit the modiste and together they add to my order. Look, do you see this gown? Do you remember it?"

"No," Constance confessed.

"I didn't choose this. Jack picks out at least three gowns each year without my advice or permission and Madame delivers them with the rest. No matter what I say, he won't stop. I gave up arguing about it years ago because his taste is excellent. Let's go see what is in your room."

With great reluctance, Constance followed Virginia back to her bedchamber. As a maid displayed them, Virginia commented on each, considering what trimmings would compliment them. "My, my, Jack has a very strong opinion of what you should wear. These are perfect for you."

She blushed at the impropriety of having a man choose her gowns, but she couldn't say she hated his choices. Unfortunately, he had doubled the size of her order. The parcels contained items to match: shoes, fans, reticules, and gloves. Items Constance had given no thought to.

"Oh, this is one you simply must open yourself." Virginia sank down amid the rustling papers at Constance's feet and placed a heavy square parcel in her hands.

Constance eyed the box suspiciously. "What is it?"

"Open and see."

Trembling with a new burst of anxiety, Constance tore the brown wrapping paper to reveal a hinged leather box. She dug her fingertips into the join, lifting the lid slowly.

Nestled inside on blue velvet was a single bright gem, strung on a fine gold chain.

She gulped. "This is paste, isn't it?"

"Will you feel better if I say it is? I don't really want to lie to you."

Constance closed her eyes. The gem couldn't be a diamond. But when she cracked her eyelids open again, she couldn't truly believe the stone wasn't authentic. Constance rested her fingertips on the cold stone. She let them slide away. This she should not accept. "He must take it back."

When she went to close the lid, Virginia's fingers were there—slipping the chain from its hooks, undoing the clasp, and encircling her neck with it despite her protests.

Virginia settled the stone into place over the fabric of her gown. Once she was wearing the new styles, the stone would lie between her breasts.

"As usual, my brother has excellent taste. You aren't going to argue with him again about the gifts are you?"

Constance turned around quickly, but slumped at the way Virginia grinned.

"No. I promised I wouldn't."

"Good, you wouldn't believe what it feels like."

"Like not being able to close a book," Constance recited, remembering Jack's earlier words.

"Ah, he has been honest with you. It's about time. I was getting sick of interfering between you pair. When I think how well you once got along…" Virginia shook her head. "Do say you will keep the gowns and other things. It makes him happy to spoil us."

Constance tried one last appeal. "Virginia, you know how it would look if anyone found out. I will look like a kept woman. I couldn't bear the scandal."

"And who would I tell? My brother is nothing if not discreet. Look how well he has managed to hide this future wife of his. I have not heard a whisper of her name or even met the woman. The man knows how to keep a secret. He's done so for years."

"I thought you were already acquainted with her?"

Virginia scowled. "He is being a beast about it and tells me nothing. Besides, I am hoping that word of your elegant presence on his arm will bring her out into the open at last. If my intended was dancing about during the season with a very pretty woman constantly on his arm, I would hurry myself to London quick smart. Either the woman or her relatives shall come running to confront my brother. I just hope to be around to identify them."

"You're planning on using me as bait?"

"That is such a terrible way to describe it, but, yes, I suppose I am. Do you see how desperate I've become about the matter? If only he would speak of it to me, but he is annoyingly closemouthed. He even went so far as to deny the betrothal existed, but I know better. Our father confirmed the arrangement before he died. He just didn't share the woman's name. But there is a lovely benefit for me—I get the advantage of having your company while I await the opportunity to find out who she is at last. Can you imagine a greater happiness?"

Constance pressed her hands to her face, aghast at her predicament. She refused to become involved in any scheme that might irritate Jack further. Her presence was burden enough.

Chapter Seven

———— ✦ ————

Preparing for her first London ball was a nerve-racking experience. Constance gripped the sides of her ball gown and then chastised herself. She did not want to wrinkle the deep blue silk, but still, she fidgeted with the neckline. No matter how she tugged and pushed, she could not hide her physical assets. Her breasts looked about to spill out of the gown. One inelegant stumble and society would know far too much about her.

"You look beautiful," Virginia complimented from her spot by the door. "The gentlemen will have a hard time keeping their eyes from you. I told you my brother has excellent taste."

Constance blanched. In the confusion of ordering, she hadn't remembered one dress from the next. Had Jack chosen this gravity-defying ball gown? She quickly considered whether she would have enough time to change, but the marquess had already sent up a note asking them to hurry along. She couldn't delay.

"You look lovely, too. Pink is a wonderful color for you. On me, it looks hideous."

Grasping her courage along with her evening reticule, she moved away from the mirror's startling reflection. Virginia watched her with a fond smile. Did she really not care that her brother's choice of gown threatened to make a scandal all its own?

But Virginia merely adjusted the chain around her neck and then touched her cheek. "Come, my brother is impatient to be on his way. They are waiting for us in the library."

Determined to keep the evening on a festive note, Constance refrained from uttering her fears aloud. Virginia appeared content for the first time since her arrival. She didn't want to ruin her friend's pleasure in the evening.

But Constance frowned. "They? Is Lord Hallam attending the ball with us? I thought he had little interest in London society."

"Who can understand what Lord Hallam thinks? He has it in his head to join our party. I do hope he has done something constructive with his appearance. At least, I hope he possesses a decent set of evening clothes."

"I am sure he will have done his best," Constance assured her. But the comment about Lord Hallam intrigued her. Virginia's reactions and contemplations were unconsciously done, but she had a much deeper interest in the gruff man than she cared to acknowledge.

"At least I can count on Hallam to frighten away the dull and dim-witted. Lady Huntley has a rather broad circle of acquaintances, I'm sorry to say. I cannot believe Jack agreed to attend this event as our first. He doesn't often associate with the Huntley's. Aside from pleasing your mama, which I think there is little chance of anyway, I wonder if there is a connection to his future bride. We must keep our ears and eyes open."

Constance rubbed her wrist as she pondered Virginia's suggestion. She'd rather not become involved in the siblings' squabble. "Virginia, what if your brother learns of your plans to uncover her identity? You do remember I cannot keep a secret from him, don't you? He will know the whole of your scheme within minutes."

"It will serve him right for keeping his own counsel," Virginia insisted. "Come, you look perfect. We have a husband to find for you. The gentlemen shall be struck blind by your beauty and will be pounding on our door on the morrow."

"Is it possible to feign illness and stay safe within Ettington House instead?"

Virginia chuckled softly. "Not a chance my dear friend."

Assaulted by doubts, Constance descended the stairs, her slippers making little noise on the treads. By halfway, she had managed to push her worries aside. Virginia might need her support tonight amongst the hundreds of guests sure to attend the Huntley Ball. She didn't like crowds and there would likely be many acquaintances to renew.

When the last few stairs came into view, Constance raised her gaze and found herself mesmerized. Jack and Lord Hallam were not waiting in the library at all, but were standing at the bottom step, watching their slow progress with widened eyes.

Jack was just too beautiful for words. The dark evening suit, white stockings, shirt and cravat, offset by a silver-headed cane he held loosely in his hands, created a dazzling picture that stole her breath.

Hallam let out an oath that broke the mood and Jack spoke sharply to him.

"Forgive me, Miss Grange. Perhaps those were not the correct words to express how exquisite you both look this evening. I am quite overcome."

Hallam bowed extravagantly, but Constance wasn't fooled. He liked behaving badly. The few days she had spent in his company had opened her eyes. She suspected he behaved as he did for no other reason but to force Virginia to react to him.

Constance managed a weak smile and tried not to stare at the marquess. No man should be so handsome. Jack handed his cane to Parkes, exchanging it for her wrap. With a faint quirk to his lips, he moved to enclose her in it.

Gloved fingers slid beneath the fine material, ghosting over her skin as he extracted a loose curl trapped beneath. He ran his fingertips over the clasp of her necklace and settled it where it should be. As his hands left her skin, one finger swept along her jaw to her chin, forcing Constance's gaze to lift. The blue of his eyes was so bright she had to blink or suffer blindness.

Uncertain of what to make of Jack's caress, she hastily looked toward the others. Virginia and Hallam were turned away, conversing in whispered, furious tones. While she watched, Hallam drew closer to Virginia but she backed up a step, her eyes widening with what Constance thought might be fear.

As Constance prepared to intervene, without even a by-your-leave, Jack secured her arm and led her forcibly from the house, almost pushing her into the carriage.

Jack waited until Pixie settled then took the opposite, rear-facing seat. "I would suggest you do not become involved in affairs between Hallam and my sister." Pixie opened her mouth to argue, but Jack held up his hand. "Two can play at matchmaker."

"Hallam and Virginia?"

He nodded. "They should have married years ago," he whispered.

As Virginia climbed inside, Jack grabbed her hand and pulled her to sit beside him. He refused to let Virginia cling to her friend all night. When Hallam entered, he filled the remaining space beside Pixie with his bulk, but his legs stretched to touch Virginia's skirts.

The awkward journey lasted no time at all. No one spoke. Pixie twisted her hands nervously and Virginia attempted not to touch Hallam, who appeared oblivious to her distress but was, in fact, surreptitiously watching Jack's twin.

For his part, Jack was trying to avoid thinking. His knees bumped Pixie's with every sway of the carriage, and a healthy dose of lust was not making his task easy. He hadn't imagined the blue gown would have such an overwhelmingly arousing effect on him. But that gown, and the view he had unwittingly afforded himself, was going to torture him all night.

By the time they reached Huntley House, Jack had his inappropriate lust in hand. Years of navigating society had forced him to learn to control his emotions, to hide his real thoughts from others. Hiding them from Pixie, however, was uppermost in his mind.

It didn't matter that his hand tingled when he helped her out of the carriage. She was not for him, and apparently he was not for her either. Tonight he needed to make everyone believe he was still acting as her guardian.

As they flowed up the steps in Virginia's wake, Jack risked squeezing Pixie's elbow in the hope of soothing her. By the way her hands fluttered about without purpose, she was anxious about her first London ball. She had no cause to be nervous. She would win society over with no trouble. All she needed to do was smile and be her best self. It might be vain to think it, but his presence beside her would do the rest to ensure her popularity. Jack's friends were never snubbed.

Arriving on his arm to her first London ball would make society take notice too. She would be considered, at first, as a potential future marchioness. Society was keen to see him conquered, but he had a plan for managing their expectations. He wouldn't dance with her and, after tonight, he would keep his hands to himself.

He chose not to think overlong on the other matter—her plan to hunt for a husband. Self-torture had never been a favorite activity.

As they followed Virginia and Hallam into the throng, Jack nodded to acquaintances, smiled and made the proper introductions. Pixie drifted beside him, her hand a light pressure on his arm at first. But as the crowds thickened, Pixie drew closer and his senses spun. By the time they'd made a circuit of the room he damn near trembled like a tuning fork. He barely produced an acceptable greeting to anyone else and was very glad when Virginia settled her mind to linger near a set of doors where they might be cooled by any breeze.

Pixie released a nervous sigh. Hoping to take her mind off her worries, Jack leaned closer. "I'm glad to see you're wearing my gift tonight."

———◆———

Constance swayed as Jack's words permeated her overwhelmed mind. She couldn't believe he would mention her acceptance of a gift where anyone could hear. And she hadn't accepted it—it was a temporary loan as far as she was concerned. He would get it back as soon as she didn't need it. He laid a gloved hand over hers on his arm and held her steady. The noise inside the ballroom was nearly too, but his words had cut through her anxiety as swiftly as a hot knife through butter. "Virginia insisted."

Jack was mean to tease. As soon as Constance got him alone, she was going to kick his shin so hard that he'd have to hop on one foot for a week of Sundays. Smug little smiles might make him appear younger, but they painfully reminded her that once upon a time he'd been her friend.

Constance glanced about the Huntley ballroom, cooling her

temper as she viewed Lady Huntley's taste in décor. The high-vaulted chamber was only marginally less imposing than the entrance to Ettington House. Lady Huntley, who'd made her come-out with Constance's mama, had smiled at her warmly, eyed her up and down, and probably recorded all the necessary details for the next month of letters.

The countess had purred when she had taken in Jack's black-clad figure beside Constance. Constance suspected it was a coup for a London hostess to have the marquess attend her function so early in the season. Lady Huntley smiled at him, made all the right noises, but Constance doubted Jack even heard half the woman's fatuous greetings. Something told her he was not truly paying attention tonight.

Jack scanned the crowd around them but seemed to rarely acknowledge others. Constance did not really know him anymore, but she was grateful for his reassuring presence at her side. The arm beneath hers flexed occasionally, causing tingles to shoot up her arm with every movement he made, but he didn't glance her way again for a good long while.

As they stood at the edge of the ballroom, a fine-boned blonde swayed back from her group of acquaintances, trying, it seemed, to attract her escort's attention. The girl's bouncing manner appeared urgent. Could this be his intended bride? Constance tried to turn Jack's attention in that direction. Jack resisted her gentle tugs, instead turning her to the opposite side of the throng.

A few moments later, there was a parting of the guests. Across the room, a ginger-haired Adonis waved and then moved to join them.

Jack dropped her arm as the gentleman smiled. "Daventry, didn't expect to see you here so early. May I present Miss Constance Grange? Miss Grange, you have the rare privilege of an introduction to the Earl of Daventry. If you had fussed before your mirror any longer, you might have missed meeting him altogether."

Constance blushed and tried to ignore Jack's accurate assumption of how she had spent her time before joining him. She let Lord Daventry take her hand. "Lord Daventry, it is a pleasure to meet you." She recognized the name as one of her potential suitors.

"Hmm, you are Ettington's ward from Sunderland, aren't you?"

"Lady Orkney is a very great friend of mine," Constance asserted, uncomfortable with the lie Jack wished to spread about her. He had paid for every item of apparel on her body, but there were limits on how large a brand she would bear.

The earl winked. "Oh, I like the fire in this one, Ettington. Good choice. It is a pleasure to make your acquaintance, Miss Grange."

He wasn't a bad-looking fellow, and he appeared to have an easy manner about him. Could she be so lucky as to find her spouse on her first night? Jack caught her eye and the scowl he sent made her tremble. She was fumbling for something to say when the earl cleared his throat.

"If you will excuse me, I see Lady Montgomery is waiting somewhat impatiently. She has promised me a view of something extraordinary this evening."

Jack appeared to shake himself. "Enjoy yourself, Daventry."

Lord Daventry winked at Constance again. "I most assuredly will."

The way the earl laced his words with a deep, masculine rumble set her aback. She watched him leave, puzzled by the hint of eager mischief in his tone. Uncertain what to make of him, Constance stored his name in her memory. She would ask Virginia about him later.

The fair-haired lady stood close again, and Constance smiled a greeting. She didn't know her, but the woman seemed very keen to approach. Thinking to be obliging, Constance turned her steps in that direction. The marquess set a hand to her back, catching hold of her gown. He turned her forcibly toward Virginia's retreating form and moved her in that direction.

"You don't own anything but the dress, my lord," she hissed the minute she could be positive she would not be overheard. "Stop shifting me about with it."

"Then don't be difficult. You don't need to make the young lady's acquaintance."

The cold tone got her hackles up. She would have argued against his decree except a friendly looking gent was bearing down upon them in a great rush.

"Ettington, a damned relief to find you here. Where the hell have you been?"

"Here and there," the marquess evaded, smiling kindly at the younger man.

He was very nice to look at, even if Constance had to look up a long way. Inches taller than Jack, but by no means the better looking of the pair, the young man's glance instantly offered friendship.

Jack prodded her toe with his ridiculous cane and she blushed, caught in her bold appraisal. He was probably carrying the thing because she had all but said he was ancient. He wasn't old, just terribly stuffy. She'd hide the blasted cane in the attic the first chance she got.

"Viscount Carrington, may I present Miss Grange? She is an old friend of the family, if you recollect."

"I don't believe I remember the name. Welcome to London, Miss Grange."

"Thank you, my lord. It's a pleasure to meet you as well. Have you been here long?"

"Ten minutes is too long without your company." Lord Carrington flashed a charming smile until Jack leaned across to whisper in the gentleman's ear.

Carrington's smile grew, and then the viscount burst out laughing before turning back to her. "I rescind my earlier bland greeting. It is a very great pleasure to make your acquaintance. I look forward to hearing of your adventures firsthand. Ah, I see my party has returned. Do excuse me."

Still chuckling, he sauntered off.

Constance couldn't help but frown after him. She didn't have adventures. Nothing exciting ever happened in Sunderland. She glanced up at Jack. His smug, self-assured expression was back in place. Fear assailed her. "What did you say to Lord Carrington?"

The marquess tugged her along. "Oh, I just mentioned your name."

"My first name?" Constance stopped.

"No, your nickname." Jack smirked. "It was only then Carrington remembered what he already knew about you."

"And what was that?"

"Frogs."

Constance's stomach dropped. "What about them?"

"Surely you remember the day you got angry with me for not taking you out riding. You snuck into my bedchamber while I dined, then crammed slimy frogs into my best riding boots."

"You told people about that?" Constance gaped at him.

"Of course. It was the highlight of my visit." Jack chuckled, placed her arm back on his sleeve, and forced her to keep moving.

That prank had been the hardest to accomplish, but she had aimed at making him angry, not amused. It was one of the first instances she could recall that she hadn't understood his reaction.

"I was only seven. Do you think you could avoid telling people such things about me? I do have a purpose for being here tonight." Constance raised a hand to her face, appalled to have such a long-ago event brought up.

"I've told only my friends about the shocking things you used to do, and besides," Jack's good humor vanished, "Carrington is to marry. But if he wasn't, he cannot afford you."

Constance pushed down her discomfort. She didn't know how to respond. It appeared as if he was looking to protect his friends from her plan to marry for money. He must hate helping her.

They were halfway to joining Virginia when a sultry, feminine voice hailed her escort. An angry curse crossed his lips, but he turned without taking Constance with him.

"At last, a chance for pleasurable conversation. I was considering the merits of organizing a picnic on the Thames next week. Care to join my party, Ettington?"

Constance peeked around Jack's broad shoulder, but instead of the blonde she had expected, a dark-haired older woman leaned toward him, eyebrow raised seductively. At least Constance thought she meant it to be seductive. From Jack's reaction, it was hard to tell.

"I have no interest in sailing on the Thames," Jack stated bluntly, frost lining his every word. "Lady Darraby, may I present Miss Grange?"

The lady ignored Constance. "Come now, my dear marquess, surely you agree that a bit of adventure now and again improves the season. Even the most innocent of carriage rides can be quite stimulating."

The woman sidled closer, but then she winced and her glance fell to the floor. Although Constance couldn't see, she was fairly certain Jack had just used his cane to keep the woman at a distance. She hid a smile as Lady Darraby took a half-step back. Apparently, the cane had some merit—he should keep it.

"Of course, but I see nothing worth putting myself out for," Jack replied coldly. "Good evening."

Constance wanted to applaud him for being so direct. Lady Darraby's face flushed at the rebuff, and then her gaze turned to finally take in Constance's presence. Lady Darraby's glare impaled her.

Jack led Constance around the older woman, but her senses prickled as if she had an archery target pinned to her back.

"Ignore her."

Jack negotiated a tricky maneuver to avoid a lurching lord. By the scent of him, the man was deep in his cups.

"You're very good at this," Constance replied.

"I have had a lot of time to practice," he murmured, tucking Constance snugly into his side to avoid another physically expressive guest.

"You don't have to be in London. You could always stay at Hazelmere. It's lovely there in spring."

"It's too quiet to stay there all year round. Winter is bad enough." Jack's arm beneath hers grew rigid. "Are you trying to suggest that I should go away?"

"No. I didn't mean that." Constance grasped for the words to avoid another argument.

"So you want me to stay?" he pressed.

Constance didn't answer. Jack's question confused her. He couldn't be comfortable with her in his home and certainly couldn't want to spend time with her while she searched for a husband. Yet, if she asked him to leave, she risked offending him.

They reached Virginia's side and joined the conversation. After Constance was introduced to Lord Archer, she fell silent, watching Jack as he conversed with the short, rotund man many years his senior.

Archer leered in Constance's direction several times, and Jack, while appearing restless to anyone else, moved until she could barely see the other man. She studied Jack's broad shoulder for the second time tonight. He was very nice to shield her. Archer was revolting and old enough to be her father. She didn't want men of his ilk peering down her gown.

After a few minutes of less-than-enthusiastic conversation, the man took the hint, gave her one last stare, and departed.

Jack turned to look at something over her head. "Watch out for Archer. He has sticky hands as well I've heard."

Being short had distinct disadvantages when speaking to Jack. He was so much taller and she had to lift her chin high to meet his gaze. His clenched jaw worried her, as did the tightness about his eyes as he tried to hide his reaction from society.

She almost set her hand upon his arm, but then he did something she was not prepared for—his glance fell straight into the open neckline of her gown.

Constance blushed from head to toe as a wry smile tugged the corner of his lips. She raised her hand to her chest, fiddling with the diamond necklace for scant comfort.

"I do believe I might be envious of a hunk of rock."

She couldn't misunderstand Jack. But he saved her from a response by rejoining the conversation going on around them. Constance tried to gather her scattered wits, unsure how she felt about Jack ogling her breasts. The knowledge didn't make her feel quite as bad as she had expected.

Chapter Eight

———◆———

Nothing irritated Bernard Hallam more than attending a London ball. He hated them. Why was he enduring this torture again? The heat, the competing perfumes masking the stench of unwashed bodies, the sniveling debutantes striving to appear unique when they all looked the same—all of it got on his nerves, and he longed to leave.

He did know why he was here, of course. Virginia was no longer wearing black or even half-mourning. His shock upon seeing her tonight had been profound. He'd not expected her to wear mourning forever, but to see her dressed in pink again stirred his blood.

Virginia received far too many appreciative glances for his comfort. Yet what could he do about them? She was a beautiful widow, and widows were the number one pleasure in a rake's appointment book.

Lord Archer greeted them and smiled too often at Virginia. The man's wife was somewhere around, probably availing herself of a gentleman desperate for a tumble.

Bernard understood the desperation, but there was only one woman he had ever wanted.

Unfortunately for him, Virginia wanted nothing to do with him.

The way Lord Archer kept glancing at Virginia's chest made Bernard long to hit him just once. But striking a fellow gentleman at a *ton* entertainment would surely displease Virginia. He clenched his teeth and settled for scowling at Lord Archer.

"Lady Orkney, might I trouble you for a moment of private conversation?"

Score one point less for the idiot. Virginia, a stickler for the proprieties, wouldn't meet privately with a married man.

"Lord Hallam is privy to most of our family's affairs, milord. There is no need for private speech. How may I help you?"

Bernard stood straighter as she mentioned him. That could only be in his favor. He tried not to gloat.

Lord Archer glanced at him awkwardly for a moment, then muttered, "Perhaps some other time," and then he withdrew.

Once Archer had gone, Bernard leaned closer to Virginia's ear. "You do realize what that bald badger was going to suggest, I hope?"

"I am not stupid, Bernard, even if you like to think so. I have been dodging those sorts of suggestions since the funeral." She cocked her head to the side. "*At* the wake, too, I think. Wearing colors again has not been the universal flag of surrender most gentlemen assume."

"They suit you better," Bernard blurted out.

Virginia froze and drew away from him. "Thank you."

Impressed that he had managed a compliment without thinking about it too hard, Bernard smiled. He wasn't very good at them, and he'd not had time or inclination to practice before but they seemed to have an effect on Virginia.

She fidgeted. "A drink. I do believe I am thirsty, Hallam."

Damn, she had dropped the use of his first name rather quickly. Perhaps he should practice being nice more often. "Is there any particular beverage you might wish for? Something cold, or something to warm your insides, perhaps?"

That came out a lot dirtier than planned. He was trying to charm her, not have his head whacked by the nearest vase.

Her brow furrowed. "Cold, I think."

So far so good. She had missed, or ignored, his double-entendre. Bernard held out his arm to escort her to the refreshment table. When he passed her a glass of wine, her hand shook a little. He looked away until she had downed it, and then handed her another. Judging by her consumption of a third glass, she had not missed his double-entendre after all. And he still had his head.

Feeling surprisingly buoyed by his success, he steered her back toward her brother and Miss Grange. At least with them, Virginia would be free from propositions.

———◆———

The bed shook, and Constance groaned as the bright light drenching her bedchamber pierced her lids. Carefully, she opened her eyes to find Virginia's face hovering above hers.

"Good morning, sleepyhead," Virginia exclaimed.

"It can't be morning yet. Tell the sun to go back down," Constance moaned. She had suffered the worst dreams last night and needed a few more minutes of peace. All sorts of twisted visions had plagued her. She needed time to shift the lingering unease. The marquess would never visit her in debtors' prison, but her foolish mind had conjured up horrid examples of how the man would sneer and laugh at her misfortune from the other side of a locked door.

"Nonsense. You cannot sleep the day away. We have a great number of callers expected. I am gratified by how well you were received by the *ton* last night. So many of my acquaintances commented on your pretty ways. Come along, time to get up."

Virginia whipped the covers from Constance's body.

As the cool morning air cruelly struck her legs, Constance scrambled into a seated position, and pulled the nightgown over her toes to keep herself warm. "What time is it?"

"It is a little after eleven. My brother thought I should let you sleep in, so I have already broken my fast with him and Lord Hallam." Virginia reached out a hand to straighten Constance's hair and let out a sigh. "You have such energetic hair."

"Oh, I'm sure it looks a fright this morning. I forgot to braid it." Constance dragged her hands over the wild curls, frowning in confusion. "Actually, I cannot remember coming home. What time did we return?"

"I think it was around four," Virginia said. "You were very tired."

Constance shrugged off her confusion and slipped out of bed, beckoned by the thought of cool, clean water to drink. She shivered at the draft sweeping into the room from the open balcony doors. "Amazing. I don't even remember climbing the stairs. I must have been sleepwalking."

"But you didn't climb the stairs. Jack carried you."

"Oh." Constance lost her grip on the jug and splashed water over the nightstand. She replaced it carefully and hurried to mop up the spill.

"I did think Hallam might have offered but, as usual, he has no interest in anything but himself. I am afraid he won't make a very nice husband," Virginia confessed. "Had your heart changed toward him?"

"Ah. No." She heard the soft scrape of book and looked up to find Jack peeking around the doorframe leading to the balcony. Constance hurried to slip on her wrapper. "I can assure you, Virginia, Lord Hallam is not on my list." Constance skirted the bed and approached the door, but there was no sign of the marquess outside now. She let out a relieved breath.

"I think that might be for the best. There are many more gentlemen to consider. Why don't I organize some breakfast for you while you wake up properly? I'll return to keep you company while you eat. Back soon."

Once Virginia waltzed out the door, Constance slumped on the bed. She couldn't believe Virginia had convinced Jack to carry her into the house. That was too great an imposition.

"Ahem." Jack's voice broke into her thoughts. When she looked up, his broad shoulders were blocking the light. "Are you going to sit about in your nightclothes all day? There is a matter we need to discuss, and we have only a short time before my sister returns."

"I cannot dress while you are standing there. Go away."

He mumbled something she didn't quite catch. Then he cleared his throat. "Very well, come and see me in my study in one hour."

The door creaked behind Constance as the little upstairs maid hurried in. Caught and embarrassed by it, she turned back to the balcony doorway, but Jack had already vanished. Lord, he could move quickly when he wanted to. She shrugged off her irritation and sat down to breakfast. Ham, cheese, and eggs—her favorite.

Virginia flew into the room a few seconds later and regaled Constance with her latest argument with Lord Hallam.

"Can you imagine him thinking that I would prefer to speak with Lord Archer? He truly is without sense."

"I think Lord Hallam is very right to be concerned about you. You are a widow, after all. Mama hinted once that gentlemen were harder to repulse once there was no man around to protect her. You are lucky to have a brother, and you have Lord Hallam too, it seems."

"Yes, but he is so overbearing. At breakfast this morning, he commented on the size of the portions on my plate. I cannot imagine that it is any concern of his what I eat."

"Maybe he wants it to be," Constance blurted out before she had time to reconsider. Watching the pair of them circle each other was vexing. Although Jack had warned her not to interfere surely a nudge couldn't hurt. She glanced at Virginia and smiled hesitantly. "I apologize. It is none of my business, but I think Lord Hallam has more than a passing interest in your welfare. Perhaps he should be at the top of *your* list."

"Do not be ridiculous," Virginia exclaimed. "I don't have a list. I'll not marry again."

"Why not? You could finally do something about Lord Hallam's wardrobe. The shocking lack of quality seems to bother you a great deal." She thought a moment. "Perhaps we could both find husbands this season."

Although Constance was mostly teasing, there was a great deal of truth in her statement. Virginia was wealthy enough that she could set her cap for any man she wanted.

Virginia set her hands to her hips and glared.

"But he likes you," she countered. "And I think you care about him far more than ever I could."

"I do not!" Head high, Virginia swept from the room.

"Oh, Virginia." Sighing, slightly ashamed of pushing a notion that clearly went against what Virginia planned for her future, Constance finished her breakfast alone and vowed never to bring the subject of Lord Hallam up again.

"You wanted to see me?"

Jack lifted his head from the daily newssheet and slid his feet from the desk with a thump. He had to give Madame du Clair credit. Pixie no longer looked like a girl fresh from the schoolroom. The new style exposed the maturity she already possessed, not to mention teased him. He had a great deal of trouble raising his eyes from the firm swells exposed by the lower-cut bodice.

"Kind of you to join me so promptly. Please, take a seat." Jack would keep the desk between them for this chat. Contrary to popular opinion, he wasn't made of ice, and appreciated the benefits of fashionable dress as much as the next healthy male.

"You said you wanted to discuss the list."

"Yes. Given what I know, I have crossed off the names of those insolvent, those about to wed, or those recently married. Virginia's list contained a few unavailable gentlemen. After making a few enquiries, I further trimmed the list of men known for their poor reputations. Men I know to be cruel to their servants and others."

Jack glanced at her and wondered if she would complain. Her brow scrunched tight. He almost laughed at how comical she appeared. She seemed poised to argue. He drew out the new list and slid it across the dark partner's desk.

"As you can see, the list is smaller." Jack's eyes lingered as Pixie shuffled forward in her chair to take it. Her posture exposed a great deal more than she realized, and Jack suffered another stirring of arousal that proved impossible to suppress.

Thank God he had chosen to remain behind the desk.

Reluctantly, he pulled his gaze away from her skin. He hadn't decided if he wanted to pursue her for his own, regardless of his body's reaction.

"Were there any other preferences I should have taken into account?" Like age or arrogance. She'd made it plain those traits were disagreeable already.

"Gamblers," she whispered holding the note as if it were a live, wriggling snake.

He was pleased with her proviso and stretched out his hand for the list again. After a moment, she passed it back. He scratched lines across another ten names. "Generally, those gentlemen are successful, but as you said the other day, luck has a way of deserting gamblers."

When the note passed back again, he waited for her questions to start or for her to remember her abhorrence of older men. But Pixie did not say a word.

"Is something the matter with the remaining names?" Jack asked, his irritation growing.

"How can you ask me that? I'm in an impossible situation no matter what I do."

"Choosing a spouse is not a matter to take lightly, I grant you. But this is what you claim to want now rather than marriage to that Brampton fellow."

Her cheeks colored.

"Since I franked a letter to him I assume you conveyed your change of heart concerning that misalliance."

"It was never a misalliance." Her blush deepened. "But I wrote to him and informed him my situation was not as I'd believed it to be when he proposed."

"Good." He smiled quickly. "If he cares for you at all you'll have a letter back protesting that the lack of Thistlemore mattered little."

Jack did not expect a letter of that nature to be forthcoming and Pixie squirmed a little as if she knew not to expect it too.

"What can you tell me about these gentlemen?" Pixie asked, running the paper between her fingers, warping the straight edge into ruffles.

"I will start with Lord Daventry. You met him last evening," Jack murmured, uncomfortable with this role. He did not want to tell tales on his friend, but it was necessary in this case.

"He appeared in a hurry to be elsewhere," Pixie remarked.

Jack opted to tell her the truth. She might not like it, but he was not going to sugar coat the characters of any of these men. "Daventry had arranged to meet his mistress at the ball last night. Within perhaps half of an hour of meeting you, he would have had her secluded someplace private, and would have been enjoying himself."

"Oh."

"He is a lusty man. Completely unrepentant of his lifestyle,"

Jack said. When Pixie's shoulders slumped, he added, "I don't imagine he would be an easy husband to manage. He would have trouble containing his pursuit of pleasure. I have my doubts if he could remain faithful without love."

Constance shook her head. "I need money to stay out of debtors' prison and a man with a strong character to endure my mother. If my husband cannot love me how he chooses to spend his time will not be for me to comment on."

Jack's jaw dropped. Would she marry only for completely mercenary reasons? "What is in it for you then?"

"Perhaps children. It is the only thing of value I bring to a marriage—my potential as a brood mare." Pixie's head dropped.

Stunned by her thinking, Jack circled the desk and pulled a chair next to hers. Pixie would bring much more to a marriage. How could she believe otherwise? Although he debated the wisdom of becoming more involved with her, he touched her arm and let his fingers slide until they encountered bare skin.

So soft.

A part of him—a growing part—wanted to pull her close. Only his head reminded him of her dislike, that she thought him arrogant, old, and unfit for consideration.

Jack let his fingers caress her arm and, then took the paper and tossed it onto the desk.

"Have you known Lord Daventry a long time?" she asked.

"His townhouse is across the street," Jack murmured. What he didn't add was that Daventry was older than him by several months. There was no need to bring age into her decision. She wanted a wealthy husband above anything else.

"Then cross his name off. You would be the one to know his character better than I could judge."

Ignoring her immediate demand, he let his hand slide upward, felt the tendons beneath his fingers and squeezed. "You give yourself far too little credit, Pixie. Any man would be lucky to have you for a wife. You would lighten any husband's day."

Life with Pixie would not be serene, but it would be interesting, and alarmingly informal. He squeezed once more, then snatched up the blasted list and, with great pleasure, removed Daventry's name.

Chapter Nine

———◆———

Constance hastily pulled her fingers back from Mr. Scaling's tight grip, and then turned to greet his pinch-faced wife. Virginia seemed perplexed with her visitors, but greeted them with the barest hesitation.

Mrs. Scaling regarded Constance coolly, looking her over from head to toe with a critical eye. Constance kept her head level and turned to greet the woman's daughter, determined to ignore the insulting behavior—only to find the younger woman giving her the same scrutiny.

After the charitable thoughts she had felt the night before for the fair-haired girl, Constance couldn't understand her behavior now. She had done her best to maneuver Jack in her direction, but moving the marquess was like moving a mountain.

Virginia gestured toward chairs, and Constance was unsurprised to find herself seated as far from Virginia as possible. She would laugh, but thought better of it. She could not do as she wished in London. She settled herself to display patience while Mrs. Scaling dominated the conversation.

"I am so sorry we have not been able to see more of you this past year, Lady Orkney. Have you been plagued by many inconveniences recently? I do trust they will be of short duration?" Mrs. Scaling asked, with a hopeful lilt to her voice.

Constance wondered if she was the inconvenience Mrs.

Scaling spoke of, but turned as a maid brought the tea tray, ignoring the implied insult. Surely, it was just her imagination.

"Not at all, Mrs. Scaling. I have been keeping very busy, and have seen no less of my friends than I'd hoped for."

There, a direct hit for Virginia. Mrs. Scaling held her tongue, but her daughter stepped in to claim her share of the conversation. "Is your brother expected this morning, Virginia? I had so hoped to ask his advice on a small matter. I understand he is something of an expert in the field."

Constance blinked that Miss Scaling used Virginia's first name so easily. She had not been aware the pair were that well acquainted.

"I am not my brother's keeper, *Miss* Scaling," Virginia said in a tone as cold as the sea in winter. "The marquess has many varied appointments I am not privy to," Virginia replied. "Would you pour the tea, Constance?"

Luckily, she did it flawlessly, even with every eye upon her. Miss Scaling received her cup last, and the look she sent Constance dripped venom.

"And you, Miss Grange? Do you know the marquess' plans today?" the blonde asked boldly, ignoring the strangled twitter from her mama.

Constance could not believe the girl's gall. She was directly challenging her presence in the house. She did not like Miss Scaling's insinuations one bit, although she had feared assumptions like these could happen.

"Lord Ettington does not confide in me at all," she confessed with a casual shrug. "Why would I know more than his dear sister?"

The chit smirked. "I did not think he would." Miss Scaling reached up to pat her perfect blonde hair. When she reached for her teacup, her smile suggested she had heard the best news.

Constance looked between Virginia and Miss Scaling, and then saw it. Virginia was blonde. So was Miss Scaling. Could Miss Scaling be Jack's intended? Would Jack choose a girl whose likeness resembled his sister's so closely?

Constance almost gagged, but she made herself sip her tea until the unladylike urge passed.

Mr. Scaling caught his daughter's eye, and then shook his head in warning.

No, it wasn't possible that Jack could have chosen this forward girl as his future bride. Jack would align himself to a family that would likely bring disrepute one day.

She turned her attention to the large portrait of Jack's father hanging across the room. The late marquess was dressed in the old style of wig and powder, making it impossible to see any resemblance between Jack and his father. It always drew her eyes when she sat in this room. The late Lord Ettington had a kind face, and the portrait had been painted very well. Today, his eyes seemed different though, almost alive. A shiver of shock swept her as one winked.

"Miss Grange, it was, in truth, you we came to call on," Mr. Scaling said in a booming voice.

Constance wrenched her attention back to the visitors.

"I believe once you read this note you will understand my interest in seeing expedient attention to the matter." Mr. Scaling spoke with businesslike efficiency, and Constance's heart considered stopping. She took the note but did not bother to read it. She expected only bad news anyway.

The voices around her grew muffled and eventually the Scaling's went away. But the loud thump of the drawing room door closing made her jump.

Virginia surged forward. "What on earth is that?"

The thick wad of parchment in Constance's hands dragged her spirits lower. "More trouble, I fear."

Virginia wrapped her arm about her and addressed the room. "You can come out now, cowards, it is safe."

Constance jumped again as the late marquess' portrait issued a small clicking noise and creaked open to reveal Jack and a grinning Lord Hallam hiding behind it. Of all the sneaky ways to avoid meeting the Scalings, yet hear every word. At least Jack had the sense to appear embarrassed.

"Bravo, Virginia, you routed the toadies in no more than twenty-five words. Very impressive," Hallam enthused.

Virginia rounded on him, leaving Constance to face the marquess alone.

He didn't say a word, but he did take the papers. Desperate for something other than debt to think about, she peered past him and got a closer look at the tunnel.

"Where does this go?" she asked, curiosity spurring her on.

"Back toward my study and to other parts of the house," he confessed.

Constance bit her lip. She wanted to ask if she could go in, if he would show it to her, but she did not want to risk rejection.

"Do you want to see?" Jack was watching her with an understanding smile.

Secret passages would be high on anyone's list of adventures and he should already know of her love of strange and new experiences. "You would show me?" she asked.

"Anything. Always remember that."

Constance blushed. He wasn't cruel, and an open doorway was an invitation, of sorts.

Jack showed her the location of the opening catch in the drawing room and on the inside of the tunnel. He held out his hand and led her into the gloomy passage, closing the door behind them. Constance could not see much at first and was a little wary of the musty smell.

"Don't be afraid, Pixie. I'm here." Jack pulled her to his side and she breathed deep, calming instantly.

"Thank you," she whispered.

"The tunnel contains several flights of stairs. We go down, then up to my study. Another flight of steps goes upstairs to the family rooms, and then farther on up to the top floor."

Constance nervously clenched Jack's hand tighter as he led her away from the pinpricks of light seeping around the now closed doorway. The passage walls were very close, and she was more than grateful for Jack's presence.

When they stopped, Jack raised her hand to let her feel the latch, pulling her tight against his side and just in front of him. Constance's face heated as her body brushed his. It was confusing how many times she blushed around Jack when she never had before.

"Only family knows about these passages, so be sure to check the spy holes carefully before opening. We try to keep them secret, but I think Parkes knows, and my valet might too. Make as little noise as you can, or you'll sound like mice in the walls. We both know Cook goes into a tizzy about them."

"I remember she ordered a search of Hazelmere that took

three days."

"Perhaps you won't drop mice in my hat this visit." Jack's lips brushed her ear as he spoke.

She squirmed at the tickle of his breath. "I honestly thought you might have liked to see them." She turned her head an inch and his lips touched her cheek.

"A mouse is very nice, but why did you leave so many in my room?" he asked, still whispering against her skin.

"I can't recall. I was very young then."

The way his breath struck her skin sent her pulse racing greater than any fear ever had. They remained locked like that until Jack slid his hand to the side of her face. He cupped it and then directed her head to a peephole. She could see Jack's study, and the room was empty.

She savored the feel of his warm hand on her face before depressing the latch. The door latch clicked open, and she stumbled out. She had not realized they had been plastered so tight together. Constance struggled to her feet without assistance, seeking to compose herself.

Jack stepped around her and locked his study door, granting them privacy. The bright room spread light into the tunnel, illuminating the beginnings of steps beyond the doorway.

"Where do they go?"

Jack's face shone with perspiration. He swallowed before answering. "They lead to my bedchamber."

"No wonder you seem to disappear every night." Constance complained. He did seem to disappear anytime she wanted to speak to him of late.

"I'll show you the houses other secrets some other time. When you're ready and don't have more young men expected to call at any moment." His voice sounded aggrieved. "Let us see what this is," Jack muttered, pulling the thick papers from his pocket to spread them across his desk.

With his back to her, she let her eyes linger on his silhouette. He might be all muscle beneath that coat. He certainly didn't pad the shoulders. Her fingers tingled with the desire to touch. Flushing at the memory of his breath against her skin, she was reminded of another puzzle. Why did they argue so much?

Dismissing the moodiness of the man, she stepped up beside

him and glanced down at three neat pages with a precise column of numbers marching beside each description.

"He's bought your mother's debts," Jack muttered angrily. "Now why the devil did he do that?"

Constance didn't care for the why. She only cared about how much it would cost her in the end. "Please tell me how much I owe now? I cannot bear not knowing."

Jack surprised her by slinging an arm around her shoulders. "The total now stands closer to thirty thousand pounds."

If not for the tight grip he had on her shoulders, Constance would have landed on the floor. This was beyond bad. It was hopeless. She fought the instinct to cry and allowed him to lead her to the settee.

Once she sat down, he pulled her head tight to his shoulder. "This debt crosses more names off the list, Pixie. There would only be three gentlemen who could repay the debts without creating more financial difficulties for themselves and even then they might have misgivings concerning your mother's spending habits."

It took Constance a couple of tries to speak. "I understand. Who are they?"

"Blamey, Bridges, and Abernathy."

"Do you know them?"

"Not well. They are a good deal younger than I, and obtained their fortunes through trade."

Constance nodded, her cheek rubbing against the soft wool of his coat. Was it wrong to want to stay here, hidden from the world? She very much wanted to. Constance could stand to inhale the calming cinnamon of the Marquess of Ettington for the rest of her life.

A large hand settled on her hair and reminded her she was being inconsiderate. She had taken up enough of Jack's time. "Thank you, my lord. I appreciate everything you have done for me." She stood, not daring to glance at his face.

She jumped as Jack settled his hands on her shoulders. "Don't do that. I will still help you."

Shaking her head, she didn't bother looking at him. It was better not to voice the doubts she had. There were only three men who could afford to pay her debts. That meant she had only three chances to keep them out of debtors' prison.

If none of them liked her enough to marry her, they were doomed. "I should return to Virginia."

"Of course."

Despair ebbed as the darkness swallowed her and Jack inside the tunnel. When Jack shut the door, he reached for her hand and pulled her toward the drawing room. Constance resisted. Panic over her situation gripped her.

He pulled her into a loose embrace. When she clutched at his coat, he tightened his arms about her. "Shh, Pixie. Everything will work out, you'll see."

It was nice of him to be so optimistic, but Constance couldn't believe him. His arms loosened and when he caught her hand again, she allowed him to lead her back to Virginia.

She stepped down the passage carefully, conscious of her hand in Jack's, the strength of his grip never faltering. His thumb brushed across the back of her hand, and she blushed in the dark. When Jack stopped, she bumped into him. His hot breath struck her face and neck, forcing another blush to race over her skin. She fought it.

At the portal, she looked through the peek holes carefully, checking for new guests before releasing the catch and stepping through the gap behind the painting. Virginia and Hallam were speaking by a rear window in low tones, so she turned and shut the doorway, trapping Jack in the room with them. She studied his bent head as he checked her long skirts for cobwebs and hard-to-explain dust on the dark material. Again, the irrational urge to lay her hands upon him surfaced. Blushing, she turned away.

"Do you ever wonder what it might be like?" Jack asked, standing directly behind her. She jumped as his fingers brushed across the back of her neck.

"I beg your pardon?"

"If only." He backed away. "Forgive me."

A knock sounded on the doors and she turned to face the next set of guests.

After exploring the secrets of Ettington house, the afternoon grew tedious. The strain of appearing cheerful in the face of ruin was very hard to do.

Today, Constance had seven gentlemen callers, each sure she would be pleased to drive in the park, attend the theater, or some other thing. Her answers depended on the shake of Jack's head. Most often, it was negative. Unfortunately, not one of the callers was one of the three she needed to meet.

Jack stayed with them for the afternoon but later excused himself to attend to a caller of his own. She was half glad to have him leave. Her callers invariably brought their sisters, who gazed at Jack in a manner that made her feel ill. Did all of London view him as a walking pastry? They flattered, they simpered, and on more than one occasion, Jack had caught her eye in an accusing manner, as if saying, "Look at what you are putting me through."

It puzzled her that no one else appeared to realize he was betrothed. It was not a new event. He had been betrothed for an age. And what had he meant by "if only?" If only what?

Lord Carrington called, bringing his sister, Miss Ryall, with him. At least she hadn't stared at Jack. She was an intelligent, witty girl, and Constance quite liked her. The Earl of Louth arrived as they were leaving, and the tension in Miss Ryall's manner during their conversation intrigued her. Constance knew almost nothing about Louth, but she wondered how he could be so blind to the girl's interest in him. Louth spoke earnestly to Carrington about a horse before they departed, but he did watch them leave. Perhaps Louth was not blind after all.

Lord Wade brought his aunt, a stern-faced matron, who inspected them and the room through a lorgnette before grunting in what Constance assumed was disapproval. Lord Wade, a narrow fellow a little older than Constance, seemed a pleasant enough visitor at first.

"Can't imagine why Ettington allows Louth near his sister, given his reputation," Wade sniggered next to her, low enough for his voice not to carry.

"Why should Lord Ettington not receive him?" Constance asked, puzzled.

"Well, since you are not long in Town, I daresay you've not heard his nickname. Believe me, when you hear it, I can promise you it most certainly is true. Oh, but then again, a fresh country lass like yourself is probably earthier than most would admit. Let us say, in the farming of beef, it is important to have one to continue the herd."

Lord Wade's sly smile revolted her and Constance wished Jack would return. "I beg your pardon."

"A bull, my dear. That is what he is said to be. Every inch, a bull."

Constance's skin heated in horror. She stood to move away from Wade but his low laugh at her expense rumbled behind her back. She took a turn about the room, conscious of speculative gazes following her, but didn't glance around. She feared Lord Wade or Lord Louth would be watching.

When Wade and his aunt took their leave, Constance sat with a sigh, hoping no more visitors would appear to take their place. But the door to the drawing room opened once more, and Constance braced herself for more empty pleasantries. However, her glance revealed Jack's return. She breathed easy again.

Chapter Ten

———◆———

Constance slid legs over the side of the bed and sat with her feet dangling high above the floor. No matter how hard she tried, she could not seem to fall asleep tonight. With a sigh, she lowered her feet to the floor and stood still beside the high bed.

Perhaps a glass of water would help. She stumbled across to the bureau as the moonlight disappeared and poured a glass of water once the thin light returned. The water was cold and quenched her thirst. But thirst did not seem to be the reason she could not sleep.

Outside, the moonlight flickered between the clouds above, painting the room in patchy light. She pressed her head to the glass pane of the door and twisted it from side to side, restless but unsure of what to do.

In her own house, she would wander the halls and find a book or activity that needed her attention. But she had no work to do. Her letters were finished, her reading done. She could take a trip down to the library and fetch a new book, but she was hesitant about roaming this house at night. Lord Hallam practically lived in the library and Constance had no desire to converse with him alone in the middle of the night. He would probably produce a lecture about her choice of book.

She placed her hand on the latch, and pushed it open with the slightest of groans. That needed fixing. She would have it seen to tomorrow. But then again, it was not her house.

The night air was cool on Constance's face and, although she should go back for her wrapper and slippers, she left them behind. She crossed the cold, gritty tiles barefoot, breathing deeply of the night air, and sighed at this little bit of freedom. London was so very dirty, and the abrasion under her toes made her miss the country even more.

She leaned against the balcony's railing to look over the night-shrouded gardens. Even without the clarity of day, they were very pretty. She would love to go down, to walk on the paths and grass, to lie upon a blanket to gaze up at the stars. However, when she looked up at the sky, she saw no stars. The clouds had thickened until almost no moonlight shone through. The romantic in her whispered that it was a night to share with someone you loved.

"Having trouble sleeping?" a deep voice asked.

Constance spun to face the house. Jack sat in a low chair just outside the next room. "Oh, you startled me." Her voice came out as a squeak and she scowled—mostly at her own panicked reaction.

"My apologies. I did not mean to frighten you," he whispered.

"How long have you been out here?" Constance asked in a steadier tone, pitched not to carry far.

"A while," he answered.

The deep, rumbled response only increased her tension. As he reached down, picked up a glass, and took a long sip from it, her heart thudded. Blast. She turned and faced the garden. "It's pretty out here, Jack."

"Yes, it is now, certainly."

She struggled not to grin at the compliment.

"Why can't you sleep?" he asked. "Were you dwelling on your flock of suitors today? It was an impressive turnout. I believe any young woman would be pleased."

While the words themselves were commonplace, irritation laced Jack's tone. Although unsure of what had upset him, Constance was a little pleased. She liked good conversation. Admittedly, Lord Wade was neither her version of good company nor conversation, but the other visitors were not all dull.

She turned to face him again, leaning back against the wall.

"You make them sound like sheep," she admonished. "Yes, I did enjoy the visitors today. Miss Ryall is a sweet girl, and I greatly enjoyed meeting her."

"You handled Miss Scaling very well."

The respect in his voice caused a rush of heat to sweep her cheeks, and she preened just a little. "Yes, well, when you have had to deal with my mama's twisting tongue as long as I, you learn a trick or two."

"Yes. Your mother is unique," he agreed, then stood and crossed to her side. "What did Lord Wade say to you?"

His direct question surprised her. She had hoped to forget the vulgar incident altogether.

"It was nothing of any great importance," she assured him. "I would rather not repeat it."

Jack placed his hand on her shoulder and held her still. "Did he insult you?"

The cinnamon-sweet scent of Jack and brandy filled her senses. How much had he consumed to sound so aggrieved? "No, he said nothing about me, or Virginia, for that matter. He's just a nasty man, best forgotten."

"Pixie, allow me to decide if I need to box the man's ears or not." His grip on her shoulder tightened. "You're a guest in my home. I will not have you insulted in it. I would prefer to know now what he said before I am forced to look at the pasty-faced weasel again."

She glanced up in alarm, then laid her hand on his chest. "It was really nothing, Jack. Please don't do anything rash."

"Pixie, what did he say?"

Constance looked into the stubborn-set face above her and gave in. "He just told me a person's nickname."

There. That left a lot out of the conversation, but told him what he might most want to hear. Hopefully, he would be satisfied.

"Louth's?"

Or perhaps not. "I believe that's who he meant, yes."

"No lady should have to listen to that. I apologize for allowing the man into the house. I had thought him harmless. Louth thought something unpleasant had occurred. He's very used to seeing the signs, poor bastard." Jack's head twisted away, but his hand remained on her shoulder, a warm, comfortable weight against her skin.

"I take it it's true?" she asked carefully, only mildly curious about Jack's friend.

"Are you interested in Louth?" Jack attempted to back away, but Constance curled her fingers into his dark waistcoat to keep him still.

"Good gracious, no. What a ridiculous idea."

"It's not so ridiculous. He is a good man," he assured her.

Jack's waistcoat slipped from her grip, but Constance caught it and held firm. "His name is not on the list. You said I shouldn't waste time."

Jack swayed forward. "So, you're keeping strictly to the list?"

"What other choice do I have?"

"There is one other option you haven't considered, Pixie," Jack whispered.

She peered up at him. No one had voiced an alternative to marriage. If he had a suggestion, she certainly wanted to hear it. "Tell me?"

Darkness hid Jack's face, and he was silent so long she wondered if he would answer. "There is always life on the high seas."

Constance used her free hand to thump his chest. He laughed softly as she rubbed her hand over him, aiming to soothe where she had struck.

Jack was quiet for a while. "By the way, my appointment book is in my study, on the third bookshelf from the bottom, at the end closest to the fireplace. Just in case you need to find me someday, of course."

Constance nodded but stifled a yawn, finally tired and ready to sleep. Unfortunately, she didn't want to leave Jack yet. She thought they might be friends again, since he had used her nickname—and she even had permission to look at his appointment book. *Take that, Miss Scaling.*

She dropped her head against his upper arm and breathed deep, letting his cinnamon scent lull her. He must have little packets tucked into his pockets—he always smelled so good. Another yawn broke free and this time Jack noticed.

"Come on, off to bed with you now, Pixie." He nudged her, but she kept her head burrowed against his arm. He chuckled.

"Am I going to have to carry you there again, little one?"

"I am not little." She hated when anyone called her that and glared at him in the dark.

"Yes, you are," he said, tapping her nose with a long finger. "You are exactly the height a little Pixie should be. Perfect, in fact. Now, run off to bed. If you wake up the household, I will not be held responsible."

He was lying. If they woke up the house, there would be hell to pay. Jack had already spent a scandalous amount of time alone with her and she was standing here in only her nightgown, unwilling to leave. Constance tugged on his sleeve.

In the dark, she couldn't make out his expression, even when he lowered his face to her level. Grateful for his support during such a difficult time, she pressed her lips to his cheek in thanks, and then darted to her room as if he would do the unthinkable and chase her.

———— • ————

Jack weaved through the crowded ballroom, keeping an eye on Pixie as he juggled two glasses of champagne. Even from this distance, strain had dimmed her smile. As her dance concluded with Mr. Abernathy, he followed her progress to Virginia and Lord Hallam anxiously.

He had not one reasonable word of objection against Abernathy, except he had the irrational urge to shove him away from Pixie. Abernathy was still wet behind the ears. Pixie needed more than a boy. She needed a man. Abernathy touched her arm as he spoke, and the flash of a charming smile irritated him.

Miss Scaling joined the pair and Jack cursed. How the devil did the scheming chit discover where they were going each evening? Considering tonight was a very late decision, he could only conclude she had made an arrangement with a member of his household to reveal their destinations. The thought left a sour taste in his mouth.

When he reached the edge of their group, Miss Scaling turned toward him. "Ah, there you are, my lord, we were wondering what could have kept you."

Thinking to ignore the girl, he attempted to step around her to deliver the champagne, but she stumbled, falling against his chest. Her unfettered hands made a swift examination of his person as she slowly pushed back. Around them, voices rose in shock at their intimate contact, but with his hands full, he was powerless to push her away.

Salvation came from an unlikely source. A quick hiss of metal sounded to his right, then a shriek, and all eyes turned in that direction.

"Oh, goodness gracious," Constance stuttered. "I am so sorry, so terribly sorry. I had no idea Ettington's cane contained a sword. I've managed to slice your pretty dress. Here, take it, my lord."

Pixie thrust the cane at him, blade still extended, and reached for one of his champagne glasses.

Miss Scaling backed away in horror.

"What the hell are you doing with that?" Jack growled, glaring at Hallam, who should have still held it.

"What was I doing? What about you? What kind of man runs around with a weapon at a ball?" Pixie looked around at the sea of male faces, but each one of them grinned.

"Attending balls was a dangerous activity," Hallam murmured. "Every gentleman needed to be prepared or face the consequences."

"I asked someone to hold it, not try to skewer society."

Pixie's hand shook, spilling champagne to the floor. "I didn't know it contained a sword. I was admiring the silverwork when the blade appeared. I should have known you wouldn't believe me."

Pixie pushed her glass toward Lord Hallam and rushed off through the crowd. Jack felt like the worst lout in history. He hadn't meant to sound so aggravated that she would flee from him. Pushing the other glass into Hallam's hand, Jack retracted the sword then turned his gaze to his sister. She would know what to do.

Virginia scowled, muttered, "You owe me again," so only he could hear, and hurried after Pixie.

Lord Hallam and Mr. Abernathy remained.

"You really shouldn't flash it about, Ettington." Lord Hallam laughed.

Abernathy chuckled. "Oh, I don't know. I thought that went very well." The young lord looked around him. "At least Miss Grange got the lady's hands off you. Very quick thinking on her part, I must say."

"She did not do it on purpose," Jack protested. But she must have read his mind. He had been wishing for the cane the moment Miss Scaling turned toward him.

"Either way, a very resourceful woman," Abernathy enthused.

Jack wanted to groan. Abernathy couldn't be smitten after just one meeting. It took years to appreciate Pixie. And he was only now coming to realize that.

———— ◆ ————

Constance sat down at the dressing table and pressed her hands to her flaming cheeks. At least she felt more tired than she looked. Just now, she could contemplate curling up on that sofa by the wall and hiding from society.

Mr. Abernathy had stepped on her toes at least twice during their dance. Her feet ached from the encounter. She reached down and slipped off her shoes to rub her toes. Although her anxiety grew every day, she couldn't stop dancing. She simply had to spend time with these men.

She didn't want to think about the fool she had just made of herself with Jack's cane. And of course, she had done it in front of Mr. Abernathy. Constance had never seen a bladed cane before. She'd almost sliced Miss Scaling in half with it. And Jack, well, he'd yelled at her in front of half the *ton*. That would not help her reputation at all.

As she slipped on her shoes again, the door opened and Miss Scaling swept inside, resplendent in her pale pink frothy gown, albeit a little sliced. The material was so light that her nipples were visible. Ghastly dress. One designed to leave nothing to the imagination.

Miss Scaling scowled at Constance, but kept to her side of the room. She had a maid stitch the rip Constance had made, then shooed the girl away as soon as it was done.

"Are you going to finish me off now that we are alone?" Miss

Scaling asked.

"Of course not," Constance assured her. "It was a complete accident. How should I have known the marquess' cane contained a sword?"

"How indeed? Strangely, I believe you. The marquess would never confide in someone like you. I am sure he sees you as a servant available to carry things for him. You should remember that your services will not always be required, and that things have a habit of changing."

Miss Scaling reached into her reticule, drew out a small perfume bottle, and dabbed the liquid to her wrists. Constance watched her, fascinated. She had no idea what was going on in the girl's mind, but it clearly did not represent Constance's reality. What was the woman suggesting?

Constance wrenched her gaze away and lifted her hands to her hair. Some pins were working loose and if she did not fix them now, the entire lot would fall down her back. While she worked, she kept her head down, working by feel alone to secure the mass.

"Here, let me help you. You missed a lock."

Miss Scaling tugged on her hair, but then the cold of liquid sliding down her back and beneath her gown made Constance gasp.

"Oh, I am so sorry. I must have forgotten to cap the bottle."

Constance turned, the noxious scent of lilac assailing her. She gagged. It was sickly, and her dress stuck to her upper back. Constance suppressed a shudder. When she glanced at Miss Scaling to swear an apology was not needed, she found that Miss Scaling appeared to be holding in a laugh.

Had she done it on purpose? Oh, of all the mean tricks to play!

She'd be incensed if she didn't now have a perfect excuse to leave, with or without Virginia. She could not possibly stay, smelling as she did.

Standing unsteadily, her whole body shaking in anger, Constance faced Miss Scaling, but the door opened and Virginia waltzed in.

"There you are, my dear. I came as soon as I could but Mrs. Scaling detained me on the stairs. I was afraid I might have missed you altogether. Whatever have you been doing in here for so long?" She paused to sniff the air and then waved her fan before her face. "Dear God, what is that stench?"

"A clumsy accident with perfume, Virginia. It is nothing of importance," Miss Scaling answered for Constance, looking contrite and apologetic, then slipped out the door without a backward glance.

Once she was gone, Constance spoke. "Virginia, I'm afraid I will have to leave early. I am drenched in perfume and I think it is going to require a bath and a good airing for this gown to remove the smell."

"It does smell very sickly. How did this happen? You don't normally wear that scent."

"It isn't mine," Constance said through clenched teeth. "I believe Miss Scaling poured the whole contents of her bottle down the back of my dress in retaliation for my mistake."

Constance gathered her things and faced her friend.

"You believe?" Virginia asked with one eyebrow raised.

"Under the ruse of helping me with my hair."

Virginia covered her nose. "Lets get you home. Oh, that smells terrible. I much prefer your own scent."

"So do I. It reminds me of springtime."

"I don't know where you acquired it, but it suits your personality to perfection," Virginia said, walking toward the door.

Constance stared after her. That was odd. The perfume had first arrived for her sixteenth birthday, and a replacement bottle had been hand-delivered at Christmas, and again on her birthday, every year since—always with a note penned in Virginia's hand. Why couldn't Virginia remember sending them? Was her memory affected too?

Chapter Eleven

———— ✦ ————

"I hate this. I absolutely hate this," Virginia muttered, twitching her dress this way and that.

Virginia should not be upset that her brother had organized a private dinner with his closest friends, yet she had fretted all day.

If Constance hadn't snuck down to peek at the dining room, she would be far more uneasy, herself. None of the invited guests included Constance's three potential husbands, so she could relax and be herself tonight.

Since Constance knew who was seated where, she guessed Virginia knew, too. Hallam was directly across the table from her friend. He would be impossible to ignore. After Constance's blunt suggestion yesterday, Virginia had been attempting to avoid Hallam. Constance sympathized with him. Virginia had turned as cold as ice toward him, and his eyes showed puzzlement. Like Constance, Hallam must have thought he had a chance to woo her, but Virginia's manner now proved otherwise. Constance should not have said a word, and if she could apologize for meddling without embarrassing Hallam, she would.

Tonight Virginia would have little choice but to look in his direction for the whole of the meal. Since Hallam's gaze devoured Virginia when they were together, his behavior in a small gathering of acquaintances would be noticed.

If her dress was any indication, Virginia was well aware of his interest. The hideous orange silk Virginia had chosen would repulse most men.

"You are being ridiculous," Constance said bluntly.

Virginia stopped in her tracks to stare at her. "I am not ridiculous."

"In that dress you are. What were you thinking? Do you want to embarrass Jack in front of his friends?"

"They are my friends too," Virginia muttered, yet continued pacing.

Constance looked over at the pile of crushed gowns littering the floor. "Exactly. And as a friend, I want you to look your best. That dress just isn't it. The neckline is higher than mine. You're a widow, not a debutant," Constance reminded her. "Do you really think he will be put off by an ugly dress?"

"I don't know what you are talking about, but I suggest you stop," Virginia warned.

Enough was enough. She'd already made a mess. "Hallam watches over your every move. You cannot tell me you do not know this."

"Please stop before you make a fool of yourself."

Constance let out an exasperated huff. "He likes you, Virginia. You should at least think about it. You're a widow—you don't have the same rules anymore."

Constance strode over to her wardrobe, ignoring Virginia's huff as she looked over the remaining selections. "My word, what a beautiful color. When did this arrive?"

"Last week."

"Oh, it's gorgeous."

"If you like it so well, perhaps you should have it," Virginia snapped.

Constance pushed the dress back into place and turned to face her friend. Virginia stood stiffly, looking away from Constance and the wardrobe brimming with beautiful clothes.

Given Virginia's posture, she was likely wearing a tightly bound corset under the hideous dress too. Constance decided to find out. Virginia attempted to bat her hands away and drew herself up proud—an easy thing to do when squeezed between whalebone.

"I do not appreciate your interference, Miss Grange."

"That is just too bad, Lady Orkney." Constance smiled sweetly, using Virginia's hated married title to distract her. She had promised never to speak it, but sometimes exceptions had to be made.

While Virginia's mouth hung open inelegantly from shock,

Constance attacked her gown. In two flicks, she managed to untie the sash. She grabbed two handfuls of dress high at the back, and tugged hard.

As she suspected, it was an old dress. The stitching was no match for her determination. She pushed the shredded gown from her shoulders before turning her attention to the corset. "While the gentlemen may appreciate your enhanced bosom, I think you are too beautiful to have need of this torture device."

Ignoring Virginia's strangled "no," she pulled on the ties that bound her. Virginia dragged in a full breath as she tossed it away. Satisfied, Constance left her there and went back to the wardrobe. Instead of the pink silk she pulled out a blue, and redressed her swiftly.

Virginia was still in too much of a state of shock at Constance's treatment to react. Perhaps not even the strictest of governesses had handled her this way before. It would do her good.

When Constance was done, she turned her friend to face the mirror.

"I cannot believe you just did that," Virginia said, glancing at herself in the mirror. Her eyes were wide.

"You're welcome."

"I was not thanking you," Virginia informed her.

"I know you wanted to, but the words escaped you," Constance said brightly, pleased that her friend did indeed look better now. "Shall we join Jack and his guests? We are very late."

"Yes, but…"

Constance was anxious to greet everyone, and there was a Miss Birkenstock alone downstairs with a roomful of men. Given her reported shyness, Constance doubted the girl would be enjoying herself. Of course, Miss Birkenstock would have her grandfather's protection, but she might be making eyes at the marquess as the other debutantes did. The idea rankled.

Could Miss Birkenstock be Jack's elusive future bride?

Constance reached for Virginia's arm to hurry her from the room by force. "Come on, dearest, I am very hungry."

———— ✦ ————

To Constance's way of thinking, Jack's dinner party proved to be a high scandalous affair. He did not appear to follow current etiquette in any way, and if word of this dinner got out, his reputation for disdain would crumble.

Constance met the timid Miss Birkenstock and could not find any indication of preference from either Jack or the girl. He was polite but distant—a perfect host, anxious to ensure his guests comfort. He appeared friendlier with the grandfather than the girl. After an anxious few minutes, Constance dismissed Miss Birkenstock as a potential bride and decided to let Virginia worry over who Jack's wife might be. After all, Constance was nothing but a charity case to the marquess. It wasn't right to spy on him in his home.

A great deal of bantering flowed over the dining table, and Constance sat in stunned amazement for the first few minutes. Why had Virginia been so nervous about tonight? This was fun. The most fun she'd had since coming to London actually. When Jack's leg bumped hers, she caught his wink and laughed aloud in delight.

Alcohol had loosened his tongue, and the gathering was noisy and absolutely fascinating to listen to. Jack sat at the head of the table, to Constance's left. He didn't remotely resemble the man she thought she'd be sitting beside.

He was foxed. He laughed loudly, talked frequently, and smiled a great deal. It was the most fun she had seen him have in years. Jack leaned her way often, describing what she did not fully comprehend, and frequently touched her leg beneath the table with his knee.

"I see our servants have picked up where they left off." Jack nodded to where his valet and her maid stood in the background making eyes at each other.

"I don't think she ever stopped," Constance confided, turning her head toward Jack and almost bumping noses.

"So glad to make the servants happy," Jack whispered. "How was your dessert?"

Constance giggled as his breath tickled her skin. "Delicious, thank you. Cook has done you proud tonight."

"It is all in the details—she has my mother's diaries to work from." Jack stopped, a drink poised before his lips. "You know I am not capable of this level of mastery."

"Well, I thought I had misjudged you," Constance confessed,

touching his leg beneath the table. She liked talking to him again. It was almost as if they were friends again and that was a very good feeling.

"You know everything about me," he whispered in her ear. A blush heated her cheeks. "In fact, I would be very happy to hand such matters over."

She turned her face to his and her breath caught in her throat. There was something about Jack tonight that drew her to him. She wet her lips. "Will you finally let Virginia run your home?"

His gazed dipped to her mouth and his lips twitched in a smile. "No. She needs her own life. I had thought to give them to—"

"Yes," she whispered when he paused. Her heart raced. Dear god that man should smile more often, but was he about to reveal the name of his betrothed or something else entirely? It almost seemed like he was flirting with her, which could not be right.

"I say, Miss Grange," Daventry, seated on her other side, interrupted suddenly.

Constance blinked and faced the earl quickly. "Yes," she sputtered guiltily.

Daventry smiled cheekily at Jack. "You don't mind if I borrow Miss Grange for this do you, old boy?"

Jack smiled tightly. "Not at all. I have no grounds to monopolize her in conversation."

Daventry pulled her into his conversation, a discussion of the latest crop of debutantes and although she did have opinions to share she felt inexplicably uncomfortable that Jack had now fallen silent. She glanced over her shoulder to find him frowning into yet another glass of spirits.

His gaze lifted and then Jack brushed her thigh again under the table.

———◆———

Bernard toyed with his wine glass as Virginia spoke to the Marquess of Taverham to the exclusion of all others. She was doing a fine job of ignoring him tonight.

Frustrated, he turned to his dinner partner. "How has the

young lad from Bruton Street settled in, Miss Birkenstock?"

Since the charity was her favorite subject, he could depend upon Miss Birkenstock speaking for some time. Perhaps it would distract him from brooding over Virginia's continued snubs.

The girl responded as he hoped, and as she was speaking, he gave her half his attention. Miss Birkenstock was pretty, intelligent, and very dedicated to the orphans. Though it was not an interest he shared strongly, he did contribute to the charity.

"I must say, you are looking quite lovely tonight, Virginia," Taverham remarked, his voice warm and full of praise. "Bringing Miss Grange to London appears to have been very good for you. I am glad Jack agreed."

Virginia's face flamed at the compliment, and Bernard forced his eyes to leave her.

But they fell on Lord Daventry—watching Virginia.

The burn of anger flared in his chest. The earl had an insatiable appetite. If Daventry placed one hand, or anything else, on Virginia, he was a dead man. He supposed shooting his friend was in bad taste, but really, once Daventry had gotten through with any woman, there was almost nothing left of her.

Daventry whispered to Carrington, who in turn glanced at Virginia. The admiring light to the young man's gaze infuriated him too.

One of them would have her. One of them would win her affections when Bernard had been chasing them all his life.

Enough of this torture—he was leaving tomorrow. No, the day after. He needed to find a new valet first.

Bernard pushed back and left his fellow diners gasping behind him. He'd start packing his books tonight.

———— ◆ ————

Virginia breathed a sigh of relief when Bernard returned to the drawing room. Lord Daventry and Lord Taverham had cornered her for the last half an hour and she was running out of polite things to say. She excused herself, then headed for where Bernard stood speaking to Agatha Birkenstock. She caught the end of their conversation and heard Bernard arranging a meeting.

Virginia's step faltered, but years of training allowed her to give nothing away that she'd overheard.

"...at ten o'clock. Thank you."

Bernard bowed and ignored Virginia's approach in favor of heading for the brandy.

"Isn't it wonderful news?" Agatha Birkenstock exclaimed. "Lord Hallam is in need of a valet before he returns to the country. Richard should suit him very well."

Bernard was returning home?

Virginia could not get her head around the idea. He rarely went home. He always returned to Oxford. Unnerved by his decision, and the fact he'd not informed her, Virginia sought him out. Bernard sat nursing his brandy by himself, but gazing away from the guests.

Given his slumped posture and weary expression, Virginia blinked in astonishment.

Nothing ever crushed Bernard Hallam's confidence once he set his mind to something. He had defied his family and his peers to teach, ignoring their disapproval.

Nervously, she sat beside him.

Without a word, Bernard passed over his brandy glass.

Their fingers brushed innocently as the drink changed hands, yet he curled his fingers into his palm as if that touch affected him. That fleeting brush reminded Virginia that she always felt safe with Bernard. She took a small sip of his brandy and handed it back.

The brandy soured in her belly as Bernard deliberately avoided touching her fingers.

She frowned, suddenly uncertain. "I understand you're going to Parkwood soon."

He leaned back, crossed his legs away from her, and scanned the room. "Yes, the day after tomorrow."

Not to be put off by his tone, Virginia stared at him. "Why?"

"Some things must be given up," he finally admitted.

She gasped. "You're not leaving Oxford?"

"I am. I tendered my notice last month," he said. "Mother can no longer manage the place without me."

Virginia clenched her hands together as her emotions churned. "Yet you have stayed in London with Jack all this time?"

"I thought there was something here that I wanted—

something that might need me too. But I seem to be causing more discomfort than good. I will return home."

Virginia's heart raced with panic. Could he be referring to herself? "You never give up on anything. Why now?"

Bernard grimaced, gaze turning to the far side of the room. Taverham and Daventry watched them. "If I were a betting man, I would say that the odds are not in my favor. There are much more distinguished gentlemen about who would suit a marquess' sister."

Virginia panicked. She wanted no greater friendship with Daventry or Taverham. And although she had intended to repulse Bernard's advances to avoid confessing her terror of intimacy, she hadn't thought about how he would react. There was something in his tone that made it sound as though he would never see her again, which was ridiculous because his estate marched alongside Hazelmere. Yet in reaching for peace, she had wounded him with her coldness and fears.

The brandy's heat curled in Virginia's belly and a flush built up her chest. She did not want him to go. She felt safe with him. She trusted him. She needed him.

"Don't go," she blurted out, unable to stop the words from spilling from her lips.

Beside her, Bernard uncrossed his legs, and turned his body to face hers. His knee brushed her thigh. "Are you certain?"

Virginia stood on a precipice. How she answered would affect the rest of her life. Bernard Hallam was not the kind of man to engage a lady in a casual affair. She knew his character well. He would want to walk about with her on his arm, and he would not care how society perceived any indiscretion.

Bernard's attentions were sincere and if she agreed, they would be a permanent part of her days. He would want marriage and the intimacies between lovers. Yet he cared for her wellbeing. He would leave her in peace if she wanted it, but that thought made her quake.

Virginia nodded.

Bernard passed her his glass. "Take a drink before you fall apart on me."

Although amusement tinged his words, she ignored it and drank down a mouthful. She had just agreed to let Bernard court her and probably more. Her hands shook around the glass, and she swallowed another mouthful. He touched her lightly on the arm and took the glass. In her panic, she'd emptied it.

———— ◆ ————

Jack struggled to focus as Hallam poked his head around his sitting room door. He looked nervous. Amused with this turn of events, Jack settled more comfortably to wait for the inevitable discussion.

"Care for some company?" Hallam asked, pouring himself a drink.

Jack was too foxed to refuse, so he waved him over to the opposite chair. Apparently, he had enjoyed his own dinner party to excess. Unhindered by society, he had indulged in a way he wasn't used to: food, wine, spirits, and Pixie.

Raising his glass, he gave a silent toast to his inspired and somewhat devious seating arrangement. Pixie, within easy reach all night, had savored every bite of food—and Jack had enjoyed watching her do it. Outside his home, that kind of attention attracted gossip, but he trusted his friends would be discreet.

Hallam drained his glass and refilled it, then took Jack's half-empty tumbler and filled it to the brim. Hallam must want something very badly. Jack knew what that was.

The glass wavered before Jack, but he took a mouthful and struggled to focus on the other man. "What do you want?"

"Virginia."

Jack chuckled at his friend's honesty. "My sister insisted when we were seven that I was not to consider myself her master. And do you know, I don't care for another bloodied nose at my age."

"I think she agreed."

"Well now, that changes everything. Go get her." Jack waved his arm toward the door in encouragement and splashed his drink across the floor. "Just don't hurt her."

"That is the last thing I would ever do."

"But is she the only thing you want?" Jack pressed, suddenly clearheaded. "If you run back to Oxford, you will make her unhappy."

"Your sister is the only thing that matters," Hallam promised, and then drained yet another glass.

"Just as well."

Hallam grunted and lifted his attention to Jack, boring holes into his head. "When did you become enamored with Pixie?"

"God knows, but it is damned inconvenient," Jack replied, slouching in his chair once more. "And it does not matter in the slightest."

"Doesn't matter—are you mad? The chit likes you."

"She might like me now, but she doesn't want to marry me. Didn't even make the damned list," he grumbled, dragging himself upright and heading for his empty bed.

"She appeared very comfortable with your hands all over her tonight," Hallam remarked as he followed a few steps. "You could easily change her mind."

"Why does everyone say that?" Jack asked as the walls wavered. He swayed a moment until Hallam caught his arm.

"You could ask," Hallam pressed as he walked Jack toward his large bed.

"And get laughed at. I think not." Jack turned shook off his grip. "You know, I always wanted an older brother. Congratulations, and welcome to the family."

"Perhaps you should seduce her," Hallam suggested as he pushed at Jack's chest.

Jack fell on the mattress and the room spun. "I'll think about that tomorrow—when I'm sober."

Chapter Twelve

———— ٠ ————

"For God's sake, when was the last time you saw a tailor?" Ettington demanded.

"A while ago." Bernard adjusted the cuff yet again as the new clothes resisted molding to his body. "What does a scholar need fancy clothes for?"

"I think you frightened Mr. Kemble witless," Ettington muttered. "If I had known you were going to growl at him so much, I would have sent you elsewhere. He's sure to levy a tax on me."

Bernard grunted as pain lanced his backside. He reached for his drink. "He should be more careful with his pins."

"He is perfectly capable when given a subject that stands still and does not fidget as you did today," Ettington argued. "At least the size of your order will comfort him tonight."

Bernard could not think of a socially acceptable reply he could use in White's without fear of expulsion, so he took a long, calming drink to avoid a response.

He had just spent an obscene amount of money to replace his entire wardrobe.

Initially, tensions had risen when the fussy Mr. Kemble had handled his existing clothes using just two fingers. There had not been that much wrong with them.

The tailor had stripped him bare and replaced every article, while his friend, Ettington, sat by, supporting his aching head and trying not to laugh. Watching Ettington's struggle had left Bernard even more irritated.

When the pins had pricked him...well, it was better not to think about that moment, or the ones after. If not for Virginia, he would not be torturing himself like this.

He swallowed his drink quickly. Virginia had particular grievances about his attire, and if he wanted her to take him seriously, then he had to look the part of a committed suitor. That meant a good tailor, and a valet to dress him. He adjusted the cuff again as Ettington barked out a short laugh.

"Come, are you fortified enough to face my sister?"

"One more, I believe." Yes, one more barrel should do the trick.

"All right, one more. But she will have to see your finery at some point."

Bernard signaled for refills. "What did you decide last night? Are you going to pursue your Pixie?"

"Damn, I was hoping I had dreamed that conversation." Ettington looked green.

"The chit was looking for you at breakfast this morning," Bernard murmured, but was unable to restrain a smile.

"My head wasn't good company," Ettington groaned. "How is Virginia today?"

"Looking just a little seedy too," Bernard said. "She gave herself a large shock last night. Are you planning to attend the Malvey ball?"

Bernard needed a plan that might progress his relationship with Virginia, something where his lady might feel adventurous enough to risk a kiss.

"The masque? We have not decided. Our next engagement is the theater tonight. Beyond that, we have no firm plans. Do you want us to attend?"

"Perhaps." Bernard thought a moment. "You are doing it again you know—speaking for your sister."

"Actually, I was not just speaking for Virginia. Miss Grange has an agenda of her own that must be catered to."

"You don't sound pleased."

Ettington shrugged and Bernard decided to let the matter drop. He didn't care to aggravate Virginia's twin. Ettington could handle his own courtship.

But Bernard needed to tread carefully with Virginia. She seemed easily frightened and had a complex sense of decorum. He twirled his drink around the glass, and an idea struck. It was not quite the gentlemanly thing to do, but he could always get Virginia drunk. Not to get her into bed, but to get her used to being touched—just enough to let her guard down. As it was, she flinched every time he made an attempt.

Bernard placed the empty glass down on the table and stood. Better to get this over with sooner rather than later.

———◆———

"And there is no hope?"

"None at all," Constance confessed. "The head groom believes it will collapse before the first mile, so it will have to be replaced, but…"

"Oh, I am sorry," Virginia interrupted. "Perhaps…perhaps you could borrow one of Jack's if the matter comes up. I cannot imagine why it should, however."

"I cannot always be going about in the marquess' carriages. It does not seem right," Constance told her.

Could she admit again that she did not like receiving charity? There had been another parcel delivered for her today, a heavy, embroidered wrap perfect for an evening when the air was cooler. Just the night before, Constance had admired Miss Birkenstock's wrap and longed for one just like it. Apparently, Jack could read her mind.

"It is not an issue of what is right, but what we are happy to do. I would hate to think we had chased you away so soon. Please reassure me there is no rush to leave us?" Virginia's eyes shadowed with concern.

"No, I cannot imagine leaving yet," Constance promised, but dread settled in her belly. "We have still too many things to do."

"Like finding you a husband?"

"There is that." Actually, the idea of finding a husband had become an agonizing venture to imagine. Constance had given serious thought to debtors' prison as a less painful alternative.

Although, running away to sea, as Jack had suggested, did have some merit too.

"I hope my brother is treating you better," she continued.

"Yes, of course he is. He has been very generous. I could not, in good conscience, ask for more." Constance turned away. Jack's friendly behavior was terrifying because she could get very used to receiving it.

"Do you know that any other woman would do just that? He would never refuse you. You should be pleased."

"Virginia, I do not wish to quarrel, but your brother has been far too generous as it is. I should not impose on the marquess and you know it."

"Pixie, I believe my brother is your friend as much as I. He would not put himself out as much as he has if you were ever considered an imposition."

"I don't belong here, Virginia. Heavens, I almost skewered Miss Scaling in the middle of a ballroom. I have become a menace to society."

"Nonsense, you did Jack a great service. That chit had her hands all over him, didn't you see?" Virginia asked. "Just be who you are, Pixie. That is all we want."

Constance looked off toward the house and spotted Jack at his study window. Some of her surprise must have registered with Virginia, for she looked to the house, gestured for her brother to join them, and dragged Constance over to meet him.

It was strange, but whenever she lifted her head lately, Jack watched her. He was probably checking to make sure she wasn't getting into more trouble.

As he approached, Virginia dropped her arm. "Just in time, my dear. Do excuse me. I must return to the house for a moment."

"That was subtle," Jack mused aloud. But he collected Constance's arm and strolled away from the house.

Her heart fluttered when Jack's hand settled over hers. They ambled along the paths, heading toward a shaded garden seat. When Jack gestured for her to sit and then joined her, she couldn't be more surprised. Although they sat in companionable silence, Constance was glad for the time to get her mind to function properly again. Strolling about on Jack's arm, when there was no need, confused her almost as much as the scent of him did.

"What do you think of the place?" Jack asked, keeping hold of her unresisting hand. It was so delicate compared to his.

"I think it's lovely," Constance stuttered.

———— ◆ ————

Jack studied her with a mixture of fascination and dread. Everything she did and said had to be examined. He already knew a great deal about her, but he had never considered that one day he might want to wake up beside her and fall asleep there too. It would take him a little time to reorganize his thoughts, until the idea was as comfortable as breathing.

He drew in a sharp breath, scenting her perfume on the air. "What does the garden need, Pixie? You have an excellent eye for this kind of thing."

She bit her lip as she looked at the grounds. "More color and a few more garden beds."

"Where?" he pressed, bumping her shoulder with his.

Before he could give serious consideration to the matter of wooing Pixie, he had to convince her that she was wrong about him. They needed to make it through a day without arguing. It would not be easy, but he had the advantage of knowing her tastes very well. She had a fine eye for gardens, and when she hesitantly pointed out her locations, he committed them to memory. Work would start first thing tomorrow.

"Will there be any statues needed in your improvements?" he asked, determined to draw all her visions out today.

"Perhaps, but I should not advise you on which one."

Jack studied her lowered lashes, the dark smudge thick against her cheek. At first glance, he had not noticed how straight they were, but they were in complete opposition to the curly hair on her head. He could not wait to see the wild mass loose again.

He shrugged off the unruly thought and squeezed her hand. "Just one? I thought a pair might be nice. But not a saintly couple, if you please. I have to live here too."

Constance bit her lower lip again and Jack really wished she would let it go. The plump flesh, dimpled by her teeth, pouted as red as wild strawberries.

"Would you care for Aphrodite and Hercules?"

"My own personal Aphrodite? Certainly." Jack glanced at the rapid rise and fall of her breasts and ignored the sensation of heat rising, along with other parts. "You may choose the hero you like best."

"Jack, I really shouldn't."

A foolish smile slipped free as his name crossed those strawberry-red lips. Now that he was not simply the marquess to her, matters could progress. He couldn't bear to have her "my lord-ing" him forever.

"And the house? How do you like the house?" he pressed.

Her lips pursed in thought and he glanced away, lest he find out if they tasted as good as they looked.

"My bedchamber is lovely, thank you. So is the rest of the house." Her mention of bedchambers reminded him he had to remain on his side of the balcony, and not stray too often to her side. He might mention locking the doors, just to be safe. "Is there anything you would have different?" he asked, sure that she would mention the hunting trophies in the dining room, but she did not. Her gaze fixed on where his hand still held hers, his thumb rubbing over her knuckle.

"My door to the balcony is a little creaky," she admitted.

Jack squeezed her hand and sat back. Here was his opportunity to mention locking the doors, but before he could get the words out, he spotted a meeting across the garden, and held his tongue.

———◆———

Virginia glanced up at the sound of footsteps on gravel and let out a strangled "Oh." Bernard looked so very…neat.

He stopped a few feet away and held out both of his hands in supplication. "Does my lady approve?"

Squinting in the sunlight, Virginia pursed her lips and considered him warily before she approached. Bernard looked very different from this morning. Very fine, indeed. Gone was the scruffy and outdated coat. He dressed as well as any Corinthian. He must have visited Jack's tailor.

She walked around him in a small circuit, pausing directly behind his back to admire his broad shoulders. His head snapped around to follow her movements. The cut of his starched collar bit deep into his neck, but he held his head there until she moved again to stand before him.

"Well?" Bernard demanded.

"How difficult were you for the tailor?" she asked, unable to flirt and confess how grand he looked. She was more comfortable with their acidic banter.

"He was amply compensated."

"Oh, the poor man." She laughed, yet anxiety tightened his jaw. "You'll do."

Those few words relaxed him so suddenly that he seemed to bend in toward her. Virginia stepped back, bumped the bench, and sat hastily, struggling for breath. He paused a moment then sat down beside her. Close. She stiffened in panic.

When he came no closer, she forced her body to relax. To blow out the breath she held. He was not even touching her.

"What did you do this morning?"

"Oh, I called on Aunt Augusta. I had an invitation to take tea," she blurted out, confused and unsure of what he expected now that he was holding up his end of the bargain.

"Just you?"

"Just me." Virginia swallowed over the memory of her uncomfortable audience with Aunt Augusta. The Dragon Aunt was not happy.

"What did she bleat about today? Getting Jack married or getting you your own house?" Bernard asked.

When he leaned against her shoulder, her heart thumped a little faster. "Both, actually," she admitted. "My aunt does not believe Pixie is a fit guest to accept into Ettington House. She's refused an introduction and asked me to send her packing. I haven't the heart to mention this to Pixie, since she is so sure she doesn't belong already."

"I would not do that if I were you. Jack may not like bending to the dragon's wishes on this issue. He is very fond of Pixie."

"Well, of course he is. We have known her forever. He would

never be cruel to a friend of long-standing."

"That is not quite what I meant, love." Bernard shifted his leg so their knees touched. "My dear, he is very, *very* fond of Pixie. You would break his heart if you sent her away."

Virginia touched his knee, but her breath churned painfully in panic. "Jack cares for her?"

"More than words can describe. Only the blind cannot see it," Bernard assured her, but she had to shake her head a few times before she believed her ears.

"But he has never said a word, never hinted that he has deeper feelings for her. How extraordinary."

"Ah, I see you have been blind too. He has never hinted because he has only just come to consider the matter. You should know a man rarely thinks far enough ahead to envisage his future wife. Cheer up. At least you like Pixie. She will make an excellent sister-in-law."

Virginia tried to wrap her mind around the image of Jack and Pixie together. They fit. She could easily picture them together, married with children about them, grown old and at peace. They would create a happy home. Virginia would never be uneasy with Pixie as Jack's wife. But what about his betrothal?

She drew in a shaky breath and dared to hope Jack could marry for love. His life would be filled with laughter, and she'd not worry for him as she often did.

Her only concern now was how Jack would get out of his betrothal. His intended's family was sure to demand significant compensation for breach of promise.

"I can hear that clever mind of yours working from over here," Bernard whispered, amusement softening his tone. "What are you thinking of with such serious attention?"

"I am relieved that Jack has chosen such a worthy woman."

"Only if she admits she loves him in return," he murmured, still regarding her with his dark-eyed stare.

Virginia squirmed and looked down, unable to hold his gaze a moment longer. She had never known how to react when Bernard stared at her like that. "Do you believe her indifferent?"

"I believe Pixie confused. But she is Jack's concern, not mine. I have my own personal matter to deal with, and she is all I can handle for the moment. She takes up all my thoughts and energies."

Virginia could not help it—she blushed and stammered out something incoherent, then froze when Bernard's fingers grazed her back.

"Do not fret, Virginia. It is not widely accepted that I am a patient man, but for you, my patience is endless." He removed his hand and sat forward, resting his arms on his knees.

Virginia fought to steady her breath. "Thank you. I appreciate it."

"Don't thank me yet. Wait until we have shared a bed before you decide if thanks are in order."

Virginia spluttered and turned on him. "If this is how you speak around women, then it is no wonder you have not married. What a fine display of tact."

"That's my girl—all fire and brimstone. I merely wanted to forewarn you that I have not taken a woman to bed in some time. It is possible that I've forgotten how it is done," he replied.

Virginia could not help it. She laughed. "Oh, I don't believe that for a moment."

He turned earnest dark eyes on her and Virginia's merriment died. "Four years, one month, and a few days."

Virginia gulped out another "Oh," and looked down, attempting to count back that length of time.

"The night we last danced," he supplied with a shrug.

"We argued, if I remember correctly, at my betrothal ball."

"That we did," he said sadly. "You were right, though. I was being an insensitive ass. I hope the vase you threw at me was not a sentimental favorite."

"No, not at all." After half a minute of silence she added, "I hope none of the shards hit the woman you were making love to?"

Bernard chuckled. "No, the lady was unhurt. Your aim was fairly accurate, given your degree of anger."

"I should apologize, I suppose."

"Not necessary. Your spectacular display of temper, and the reason for it, gave me something to think about other than my musty books."

Chapter Thirteen

———◆———

Jack sank into his seat with a groan. As much as he usually enjoyed the theater, tonight he was restless. Perhaps the rainy weather outside had dampened his enthusiasm. Perhaps it was being stared at by most of the *ton* while they pondered his every action. Couldn't they find something else to do?

But truthfully, his unease stemmed from the dark-haired Pixie sitting beside him, who had waved so happily to the box opposite. Had she waved to Viscount Carrington or Miss Ryall, his sister? Both had waved back.

Her excited smile forced Jack to bite back an oath. He liked Carrington. Truly he did. Only when he smiled at Pixie, danced with her, or talked to her, would Jack gladly strangle him. Carrington wasn't on the list of suitors, but he appeared to be becoming her friend. Jack hated that. He scanned the room as he attempted to suppress the urge to slay his competition for Pixie's affections and watched the musicians settling in to play.

Across the theater, he spotted Lord Blamey. There was very little to recommend Blamey. Plain, brown hair, round, unremarkable face, and clothing without a hint of ostentation. He was certainly not a compelling candidate for Pixie to tie herself to but he had enough money to meet her immediate needs.

If Jack was asked his opinion, and he doubted he would be consulted again, he would declare Pixie too good for Blamey.

Music echoed around the chamber and he turned back to the stage. He had no right to grumble about her pursuit of a husband. After all, it wasn't as if he had decided to enter the running himself. He liked Pixie, but marriage? Again, he wasn't sure he was ready.

Jack glanced around again. His friends, the Earls of Louth and Daventry, had made an appearance tonight, accompanied by two gaudily dressed light-skirts.

Daventry was in his element. He loved to shock. In front of the *ton's* astonished eyes, he appeared to be making love to one of the women. He leaned over to whisper in her ear and when she bent her head to his neck she appeared to be feasting on him.

Louth's companion was draped over his lap. When he slid his hand over her rump, the crowd's whispers increased to a roar.

Jack envied his friends' freedom to do as they pleased. Jack couldn't embarrass his sister by behaving in the same manner. But the theater could be so much more enjoyable if he could dabble with a dark-haired Pixie perched on his knee.

Jack was in trouble. There were a million ways his imagination suggested to prove he could be a superior partner. However, all required Pixie's cooperation. He didn't like that she thought of him as old and crusty. He would have to prove to her that he could more than keep up.

A gagging sound broke into his thoughts and he dragged his gaze back to his companions. Virginia and Hallam sat at the front of the box and spoke only to each other. At least it appeared they had finally stopped fighting. He felt incredibly good as a result. Jack wasn't subjected to Virginia's random and often extreme emotions, and he could concentrate on analyzing his own for a change.

That contemplation was turning into a bigger puzzle every moment because Pixie's future featured heavily in his thoughts.

That strange grating sound happened again and he turned farther to find Pixie choking.

Alarmed momentarily, he soon realized that she was struggling to hold in her amusement.

"Drop something," he muttered out the side of his mouth.

She did. Her fan tumbled from limp fingers and, after fumbling around for it and laughing quite heartily, she raised a serene face once again.

She had such an animated way of living. Jack found her antics fascinating to watch. Yet he could only converse with her freely in his home, and then he was always conscious of hovering servants.

"How silly of me to drop my fan," she apologized.

"I am glad to see you have found it."

"It was just next to my foot. I do hope it isn't ruined."

"Miss Grange, if the poor fan is ruined for the benefit of hearing your unabashed laughter, I would be happy to arrange a dozen replacements," Jack promised.

He knew an excellent place to purchase fans. Should he purchase a similar fan or find something more remarkable? He opted for the latter.

"I shall have to decline," she whispered. "No more charity, my lord."

Jack shook his head. He had not considered she might take his gifts as an act of charity. It was not that at all. He cursed himself for yet again underestimating the woman's stubborn streak. Oh, but she could get under his skin and work him into a frenzy of confusion in moments.

Jack didn't pity her. He gave her things because he liked to take care of her and wanted her to be happy. She had him wrapped around her pinky finger and the moment she realized his weakness, he feared he knew how it would go.

Marriage. God help him.

"My dear, you really shouldn't think the worst of me all the time." Jack turned, catching her embarrassed expression before she hid it. "I find great enjoyment in knowing that you wear or carry an item I purchased with your taste specifically in mind. If it was charity, I wouldn't notice you wear my necklace every day."

Frustrated, he dragged his eyes away from her pert nose and glanced across the theater. But his thoughts churned uncertainly. Could this feeling of lust and desire that plagued him when Pixie was near be more? He enjoyed taking care of her but did he want to do it for the rest of his life. Given their contentious past, would she even consider him as a suitor?

A disturbance caught his eye and he turned his head toward the movement. Another box was filling up with new arrivals—including Miss Scaling and her parents.

Somehow they had managed to follow him again.

Jack clenched his fist. He had wanted just one evening with Pixie without having to be on guard. Miss Scaling was intent on throwing herself into his path. He had hoped he'd misread the signs of pursuit but it was clear the woman was seeking to claim his affections. Well, perhaps not his affections, but she did have her eye on his title. Her ambition was preposterous.

The woman he married had better care more for him than his consequence.

The theater darkened and the performance began, keeping Jack free from further inspection. Miss Scaling's constant appraisals made him feel like the last piece of meat at the market. But all thoughts of the enterprising chit faded from his mind when a feather-light touch ghosted over his clenched fist. He forced himself to stretch his fingers.

———◆———

Society was blind as well as stupid. Tonight's performance confirmed it. But not the performers on stage—it was the audience itself Constance found fascinating.

The entrances of Lords Daventry and Louth were great acting designed to repulse the puritanical sector of society, but the courtesan glued to Louth's side appeared uneasy and uninvolved with his apparent groping. The girl kept her face turned away from the crowd, and Louth's hand, while appearing firm on her rear, never moved. Was she a servant dressed up for the role? When the lights dimmed, they put distance between themselves to watch the performance on stage.

Lord Daventry had his hands full of a tiny blonde woman and was oblivious to the action around him. Constance hoped he would take his form of entertainment elsewhere before he got too carried away. Given what she'd learned of him, she could not believe she had left his name on the list as long as she had. He might be a nice enough fellow, but she did not want to be pawed at like that.

Lord Carrington had waved to her earlier and was now speaking to a pretty redhead beside him. She couldn't help but think he was acting too. He was entirely pleasant and he waved at a great many ladies. Constance had noticed him nodding in Louth's direction before turning to speak to his sister. Miss Ryall ignored whatever he said and kept her eyes fixed on the stage. With Virginia and Hallam in the front row, it was difficult to see into the pit. She could only see small portions of those below, though once, she thought she spied the ginger-headed Mr. Abernathy in the crowd. But the next time she risked a glance he was nowhere to be found. The spectacle of the theater was interesting, there was no doubt about that, but she could not bear to live in this world for long.

More than ever, she wished she didn't have to choose a husband who had buckets of money to cover her family debt. Constance scrubbed her gloved hand over her knee, wishing she could marry for love. Marry someone who didn't care that she occasionally made a fool of herself, as she had with Jack's cane.

Jack should be embarrassed to be in her company, but since she often erred in his presence, he appeared to have grown reconciled to her blunders. The marquess was remarkably tolerant, and for that, she couldn't help but be grateful.

When Miss Scaling made her grand entrance, Constance bristled. The girl stared at Jack far too long. The foolish girl had no notion of subtlety. Jack stiffened, obviously very aware of the girl's scrutiny and, no doubt mortified by such bold behavior, his fist curled. Constance would like nothing better than to let her know she had no chance of winning Jack with those kinds of tactics. Miss Scaling would never be the kind of woman Jack needed.

He needed someone who adored him. Someone who could make him smile or, better still, laugh. Miss Scaling didn't stand a chance. Constance fervently hoped that his future wife had that ability.

Constance glanced to the side and smiled at the marquess, but he sat rigid and unsmiling. Hoping that no one could see, she carefully slid her hand over Jack's clenched fist and brushed her fingers across his knuckles. She would not like him to miss the performance because of Miss Scaling.

His long, slow breath brushed her ear as she diverted his attention. With the light gone, darkness covered them in seductive intimacy. Surrounded by thousands, yet only aware of the people close, she sighed as Jack pressed his shoulder against hers. She didn't restrain the grin that crossed her face as she pressed her own shoulder into his. She settled back into her chair, content.

The players moved on the stage and she watched, impressed by an art she had never mastered. She had barely mastered being the respectable Miss Constance Grange. Attempting to be anything or anyone else more was beyond her ability.

Jack's arm moved, and a bare hand pressed over hers. Constance relaxed as his warmth seeped into her, but instead of withdrawing, as he should, he turned her hand, laced their fingers tight together, and settled their joined hands between their chairs.

————◆————

Constance strolled along beside Virginia and tried not to wonder why Jack had held her hand through the first act of the play. It wasn't that she found his touch unwelcome, but it wasn't right. He had a woman ready to become his wife, and she had allowed him to take liberties belonging to her future husband.

Even worse, she was wicked enough to have enjoyed it.

As she'd followed Hallam and Virginia from the box, Jack's hand had settled briefly at her waist, his thumb stroking firmly over the small of her back. She didn't want him to get the wrong idea about her character, so she'd hurried to catch up with Virginia and put more distance between them.

But even now, she shuddered at the pleasure that small intimacy had brought her. In time, she would grow used to a man touching her. Her husband would have that right. What she needed to do now was focus on the three men on her list and gain their attention—not the unavailable marquess'.

In the halls, she met Viscount Carrington and his sister, Miss Ryall. Carrington was all that she remembered him to be, charming and witty, with a ready smile for his acquaintances. Miss Ryall enthused about the play, but her eyes darted around the crowd.

"Miss Grange, I trust I may call on you tomorrow at three. I would like to make my future wife known to you."

Behind him, Miss Ryall made a face.

Constance struggled not to laugh. "Oh, no, I am so sorry, but I have a prior appointment tomorrow. Lord Blamey is calling to take me for a drive in the park. Perhaps another time?"

Constance spied Miss Scaling across the room. The girl craned her neck, trying to catch Jack's eye again, but Jack kept his attention on the viscount.

"I shall gladly delay my call until a later time if you will promise to tell me the news of your interlude with Blamey," the viscount pressed. "I am starved for interesting adventures."

Constance didn't like the sound of that. "I make it a point never to gossip, my lord. If you will excuse me, I think it must be time to return to the box."

Across the room, the gentleman Virginia had pointed out as Lord Bridges smiled a greeting. She couldn't think of a way to speed up the process of meeting him, so she smiled back and turned to Virginia. Except Virginia wasn't there.

Alarmed, Constance tried to find her, until Jack's hand brushed her lower back.

"Hallam has already taken my sister back," Jack whispered close to her ear.

Oh, the way he smelled was remarkable. Needing more, she twined her arm through his and let him control the speed of their return, more than gratified he wasn't swift about it.

Halfway to their destination, she caught a glimpse of pink skirts caught between the folds of a curtain. Someone was hiding ahead of them. If she had to bet, Miss Scaling lay in wait. The woman had a peculiar fondness for the color. She seemed to wear nothing but that exact shade everywhere she went.

Unwilling to contemplate Miss Scaling's frantic handling of the marquess again, she pulled Jack aside and slipped them into what she hoped was a storeroom.

"Do you possess the power to read my mind?" Jack growled close to her ear. "I was just considering this very thing."

Startled by the deep husk of his voice, Constance glanced up. "You saw her too?"

"Who?"

"Why Miss Scaling of course."

"Oh, of course." Jack tugged her into his arms and pressed her firmly against the door so that it couldn't be opened. "Lets stay like this until she gives up and returns to her own box."

Alone in the heavy darkness, she pressed her hands against his chest and tried to think of a reasonable explanation for what they were doing if someone discovered her in his arm. They could not of course admit the marquess was hiding from another lady. How terrible would that sound?

Constance brushed her hands upward and the rapid pounding of his heart drew a smile to her lips. This was wrong but it felt wonderful.

Suddenly lightheaded, she rested her cheek against his chest and held onto him a little tighter.

She deserved to go to Bedlam.

———— ◆ ————

"Damn," Jack whispered. "You're not making this easy. Are you all right?"

"Yes, I'm fine," Constance whispered.

Jack laid his cheek against her hair and sighed. The dark mass was soft and his mind imagined the strands draped across his pillow. Desire surged instantly.

Definitely a problem he didn't need right now.

When Pixie clutched the lapels of his coat, Jack lifted his head and looked down at her face. He could not see much beyond her ear, so he raised one hand to her face. He lifted her chin. Unfortunately, darkness hid her green eyes and he had no idea of her mood. But he was determined to seize any opportunity to unravel his feelings for her.

Her grip on his coat tightened. Jack eased himself away from temptation and opened the door a crack. The hallway was clear as far as he could see, and there was no sign of Miss Scaling in her pink gown. They needed to return before the gossips noticed their absence. Thinking to whisper into her ear, Jack bent a little, but before he could speak, Pixie pulled his head down and kissed him on the lips.

Jack froze.

Then she was gone. Through the door and hurrying for his box before he could fully appreciate her soft lips on his.

Damn. Jack shut the door and counted to one hundred.

Shock was a wondrous thing.

Every secret wish, every stored-up hope collided in a rush of pure exhilaration. Pixie had kissed him.

Kisses did not signify a sisterly affection. He had a sister, and she had only ever kissed his cheek. Lips were something else entirely.

To be sure he was in control again, Jack counted another hundred before he stepped into the corridor.

Luckily, he encountered no one and slipped into his box and his chair without drawing much attention. Pixie had turned her face to the stage and took no notice of his arrival, but her hands wrapped tight around her fan.

Jack did not trust himself to touch her again, so he sat and concentrated on the remainder of the play. He tried very hard to suppress his body's reaction to that gentle kiss. And especially, he tried to keep from grinning like a lovesick fool.

Chapter Fourteen

---◆---

*D*on't panic, Pixie. Don't panic.

No matter how many times Constance repeated those words, she didn't feel any calmer. She couldn't blame her agitation on her pursuit of a husband. Although she was painfully nervous about spending time with Lord Blamey, that was not the reason for her fears. Constance had a much larger problem.

Saints preserve me, when will I learn to think before I act? Constance paced around the room, picking up small objects, cleaning them with a fine linen handkerchief, and then meticulously returning them to the precise place they had sat before. So far, she had circled the room twice. She didn't know what to do, and she didn't know how to forget what she had done.

Last night she had kissed the marquess.

Like the coward she was, Constance had taken breakfast in her room. She could not face him and behave normally. She was sure she wouldn't swallow a bite. The little food she had managed to choke down from her breakfast tray had settled painfully in her belly. She hoped it would not make a repeat appearance in the near future.

Constance pulled the cloth between her fingers. She still didn't know what had come over her. One minute she was a rational and sensible young woman. The next, a wanton lightskirt. Being so close to Jack overwhelmed her. The pressure of his gloved hands against her back mesmerized her, the thud of his heart was music to her fingertips. The blasted man had no right to scramble her wits like that.

Constance swung around and continued her pacing, remembering the brush of Jack's lips against hers. For one glorious moment, she had imagined that he wanted to kiss her back. Maybe she was lucky that he hadn't. She had hoped he did not taste of cinnamon, too, because if he did, she would have to forswear the use of it in her future home. Of course, she might not have a home to live in, but that was beside the point. The smell would eventually provoke painful memories. Kissing Jack might just be her biggest blunder yet.

His response had been so lowering.

There had been no more smiles, no more touches, and certainly no more holding his hand. Constance could freely admit that she missed all of it. At least she was honest with herself, even if the knowledge didn't provide a comfort. But what she should do about it was a mystery. Should one apologize for kissing?

Constance didn't know the etiquette about these matters. The greater problem was she had no one to ask. She couldn't expect Virginia to be sympathetic since she had practically thrown herself at her brother—a marquess, and an engaged man.

Constance slumped onto the thickly padded chaise and lowered her head to her hands. The prickling of an impending headache grew behind her eyes. No surprise, since she had trembled all night, afraid Jack would toss her out on the street for her presumption. Sleep had eluded her till very late, and when her maid had woken her, all her terrors had returned full force. Jack would be angry, and she couldn't blame him.

The door clicked behind her, and she turned, expecting the worst.

"Pixie, are you ever coming out?" Virginia asked.

Constance tried not to let her relief show. For one dreadful moment, she feared Jack had come. "Forgive me. I am a little sluggish today." Constance turned away to hide her embarrassment.

"Jack was concerned you might be ill. He sent me up to check. Here, look at me a moment."

Virginia turned Constance and her cool hand pressed to Constance's brow. She flinched. "Virginia, there is nothing wrong with me. I am simply fatigued."

Virginia's face was full of concern. "Your cheeks are pink and your skin is hot to touch. I think you could be getting ill. Shall I give your apologies to Lord Blamey?"

Constance turned away and toyed with the strings of her reticule. "It is nothing but the effect of a restless sleep. Don't worry so."

"Well, if you say so, but remember I will be expected to give a full report to my brother before you leave for your outing."

"Your brother is not my keeper," Constance snapped, yet regretted it as Virginia gasped.

"I know he has no claim on you, but he tends to feel responsible when we don't take care of ourselves. Forgive us for worrying about you."

Constance was the most undeserving woman in the world to snap at a friend. Virginia's contrite expression escalated her guilt. She had used Jack very badly last night and imposed upon him worse than Miss Scaling had ever done.

"Virginia, I didn't mean to quarrel," Constance apologized as she crossed the room. "As soon as I return from my outing with Lord Blamey, I am going to rest again. I hope afterward I will be fit company."

She didn't mention to Virginia that she would probably be packing as soon as she returned. Virginia would require a detailed explanation if Constance did.

Her friend hurried forward and gave her a hug. "Everyone is entitled to a display of bad temper now and again. Just remember we love you, and only want your happiness."

"I know, and—"

There was respectful scratching at the door and Constance crossed to open it.

"A caller for you, Miss Grange," the butler announced.

Trembling, Constance thanked him and fretted in silence while Virginia helped her don her dark blue pelisse and matching feathered hat. Together, they made their way to the drawing room to greet Lord Blamey.

"My dear, you look wonderful," Lord Blamey gushed.

Jack squinted through the portrait spy holes as the obsequious ass fawned over Pixie. In the light of day, he looked even plainer. His gray coat sat poorly over his less than muscular physique.

"My lord, it is such a pleasure to see you again."

He couldn't imagine Pixie would like Blamey, yet she seemed perfectly ready to be courted by this fool.

Blamey's thinning brown hair lay heavy over a patch of white skull, and Jack wished for a gust of wind to blow through the room. But with all the windows closed, it would take an act of God to get his wish.

"Oh, no, the pleasure is all mine," Blamey replied. "We have a lovely day for our outing. I shall be honored to have you beside me. Shall we go?"

Jack considered throwing up, but the tunnels were so hard to clean. When the door to the drawing room closed behind them and Virginia, Jack stepped into the room and strode to the front windows.

Blamey had jammed a conical top hat on his head, denying Jack the reflection of sunlight off his large skull. Teeth gritted as Blamey handed Pixie into a ridiculous high-perch Phaeton, he cursed under his breath when Blamey held her hand a fraction of a second longer than needed.

Hell, he didn't like Pixie being manhandled.

Blamey hauled himself into the carriage seat and slumped untidily beside Pixie. The tiny woman slid as far to the side as possible, and Jack leaned forward to see her expression. She looked uncomfortable. Did she fear falling out the other side? Why was he letting her do this to herself?

Perhaps last night might not have ended the way it should have. He hadn't trusted himself to do anything more than nod a good night. But in his bedchamber, locked tight in his desk, was the beginning of an important list. With a shaking hand, he had considered all the benefits of marrying Pixie. The reasons against had been few. It had been a troubling night.

A part of him still resisted. That part of him had wanted to talk to her this morning over breakfast and find any reason to tear up his list. Pixie's absence had sorely disappointed him and, as a result, he sent off two letters.

Later today, he had requested a meeting with his man of business to pay, anonymously, Pixie's debts to the tradesmen of her home village. The second letter's response would take longer to receive and he wasn't looking forward to it one bit.

Lord Blamey clucked the reins and then Blamey drove her out of sight.

"I thought you would have followed," Lord Hallam remarked as he stepped up to the window beside Jack.

"I considered it, but—"

"Come on, the horses are saddled. Your sister has had enough of my company for one morning. Come riding with me. If our paths happen to cross Pixie's, then so be it."

Jack looked at Hallam closely. "Why do you have such a particular interest in Miss Grange today?"

"I considered the benefits ascribed to the addition of siblings as a result of marriage," Hallam began, adjusting his new riding gloves over his knuckles. "It seemed to me that my best interests are served by ensuring the sister I acquire by marriage meets with my approval. Pixie is intelligent, well spoken, and Virginia already loves her as a true sister. I have no doubt Virginia would encourage me to encourage *you*. Just think of the familial bliss in that kind of future. Can you blame me for hoping to see that come to fruition?"

Jack choked. "God, you're trying your hand at matchmaking?" He would never conceive that his trusted friend's usual indifference had disappeared.

"I did warn you that I intended to make your sister happy." Hallam smiled. "This most assuredly will achieve that aim."

Jack did not know how to reply, but he did want an excuse to watch over Pixie. Hallam provided an easily explainable reason to be in the park.

———◆———

"My lord, have a care," Constance cried. Lord Blamey was a truly terrible driver. The gray threw his head to jerk the reins, helping to narrowly avoid the imminent danger of crashing headlong into the path of an oncoming landau. She was grateful for the horse's sense of self-preservation.

"Oh, pardon me, I didn't see that carriage there," he muttered, and dragged his eyes back to the path ahead.

Constance was relieved, but she didn't entertain the fantasy it would last. She had never encountered such a scatterbrained gentleman. He certainly shouldn't be responsible for managing a phaeton on London's busy streets. His gaze constantly darted around them in a most disconcerting way. Constance wasn't positive he even remembered she was squashed beside him, since he hadn't struck up much in the way of conversation.

Determined to fill the awkward silence, she risked distracting him to ask a question. "Have you been in London long, sir?"

Lord Blamey looked at her in surprise. "Oh, I have been here since the current parliamentary session began. I never miss a day."

Constance waited for him to continue, hoping he had more to say, but he turned his imperfect attention back to the horse and the surrounding sights.

"Do you enjoy all that society in London has to offer?" Constance pressed. "Do you attend the balls and the opera often?"

Blamey winced. "Some."

Constance shifted her gaze from the horse and looked at him properly. His gaze was pinned on an open carriage at the edge of the park. Lord Blamey stared with such fixed attention that Constance gathered the reins when he refused to heed her repeated warning. The horse, now assured of a competent driver, swiftly obeyed her commands. She brought the phaeton to a stop.

Lord Blamey looked at her with chagrin then retrieved the reins from her hands. They sat for a moment in awkward silence until a familiar voice hailed them.

"Blamey, good to see you again."

Heaven help her. Lord Hallam.

Constance couldn't think of a worse witness to her lack of decorum, but it was either grab the reins or allow the horse to swerve them into the trees.

"By God, Hallam," Blamey exclaimed. "Can't believe how old you look. Why, it must have been six years since I last laid eyes on you. I thought you were dead."

"Dusty," Hallam chuckled, "but not dead."

Blamey threw the reins and leapt from the carriage. Constance made a grab for the falling ribbons and hauled them tight, keeping the horse still as a boy scrambled to hold the gray steady. Assured that the horse was secure, Constance looped the reins and looked up, straight into Jack's eyes.

Don't panic, Pixie. Do not panic.

"You and your books," Blamey laughed, and turned his back on Constance in favor of continuing his conversation with Lord Hallam.

Jack frowned, his gaze shifting between Blamey and the horse. Then, uncharacteristically, he rolled his eyes. Was he thinking the same as she? *So much for Lord Blamey.* When Constance returned to Ettington House, she was going to scratch out his name.

She shakily returned Jack's regard, admiring how well he looked upon his horse. His mount was restless, but he held him steady with firm hands and a soft word. Was it wrong to admire an engaged man so much?

Two weeks ago, she could not have admitted such a thing. But she did see much to respect about the way Jack lived his life now.

Constance sat in her perch for an uncomfortable time, waiting for the lords to stop their reminiscences. As fine as the gleaming phaeton looked, she didn't feel safe at all. Her hands were sweating inside her gloves, and she adjusted her grip on the flimsy armrest.

Jack cleared his throat. "I say, Blamey, will you be attending the Sommerville party this afternoon?"

"Of course, of course. I attend every year."

Jack flashed a brief smile. "Then perhaps you'd best return Miss Grange to Ettington House. I'm sure she wouldn't want you to disappoint Lady Sommerville."

"Quite right. Quite right. Another time, Hallam."

Hallam chuckled. "I'm returning to Ettington House myself now. Perhaps we can continue our conversation as we go."

Lord Blamey puffed up onto the carriage, squeezed his broad backside onto the seat, and flicked the reins. He didn't remember to throw a coin to the scamp who had held the horse for them. But Constance did see a flash of silver arc from Jack's direction as the carriage drew away.

With Hallam guiding Lord Blamey, Constance did not once consider taking the reins.

When Ettington House loomed ahead, Constance drew a deep breath, relieved to be almost free of the misadventure.

Lord Blamey helped her disembark the phaeton.

"My lord, thank you for a pleasant afternoon."

"A pleasure," he assured her.

He climbed into the carriage, tipped his hat, then plunged into the traffic. He barely missed scratching the side of a stylish town carriage. The driver snarled out an indignant reply, but her erstwhile suitor was oblivious to it all.

Constance shook her head at his abrupt departure.

"I am very pleased to see you return whole, Miss Grange," the butler whispered as he held the front door open.

"Parkes," Constance whispered back, conscious of eyes watching their progress. "I would be very grateful for any warnings you might feel the need to pass on. I would prefer not to have another experience like that, if you don't mind."

"Very good, Miss."

Constance headed for the stairs and the quiet seclusion of her bedchamber.

The butler cleared his throat. "Excuse me, Miss Grange, but the marquess and Lady Orkney are expecting you to join them in the drawing room. Viscount Carrington has come to call."

She frowned. "Just the viscount?"

"Yes, Miss."

Although Constance would prefer to avoid Jack indefinitely, at least the charming viscount would be there to act as a distraction.

Squaring her shoulders, Constance pushed the door open and joined them.

Even though the space between them was greater than twelve feet, Constance was acutely aware of the marquess. Jack, still dressed for riding, lounged in his usual spot, doing his best to unnerve her with his silence.

Viscount Carrington, on the other hand, leapt to his feet. "I say, I'm so glad to see you return in one piece. The rumors about Lord Blamey's driving skills must be a gross exaggeration."

Constance settled herself across from the smirking viscount

and scowled. "Did it occur to you to warn me, my lord?"

"You can't imagine I would disparage a man of my own class for something as insignificant as poor driving. Half the *ton* suffers that affliction."

Constance fidgeted with the skirts of her gown. "Then it is a surprise there aren't less of you on the roads. The aristocracy must be on the brink of extinction."

Jack stared at her. He wasn't smiling, but he wasn't scowling either.

"Certainly not." The viscount bristled, but then his charming smile returned. "Although, I understand you may have made it your life's work to exterminate poor Jack here."

Constance opened her mouth and then closed it again. She couldn't argue that point because she had wanted, at some time or another, to pretend the marquess didn't exist.

"Carrington, watch yourself," Jack warned, sitting forward. "The pranks Pixie played on me in childhood are not to be repeated outside our circle. I believe she has developed other means of tormenting me."

Jack's eyes gleamed with devilry. He was talking about their kiss. The only problem was she couldn't tell if he was warning her not to or daring her to try again.

A further confusion was that Jack had used her nickname in front of the viscount. Flustered, she bowed her head. "I assure you, it won't happen again."

The viscount sighed. "Well, that is damned inconsiderate of you. The season has been quite exciting since you started going about. If I can't expect more adventures I shall have to find another way to brighten an otherwise dull year."

"Perhaps you and your betrothed could work something out between you?" Constance suggested.

The viscount's face lost its cheeky grin, but he very quickly had it back in place. "You never know. Oh, I almost forgot, Miss Penelope sends her apologies for not calling on you today. She apparently awoke with a dreadful headache and cannot make calls."

"Oh, that is horrible to hear. I do wish her a speedy recovery."

"You are very kind." Viscount Carrington fidgeted.

When Carrington took his leave, she was glad to see him go.

Yet the awkward silence left in his wake proved unnerving. She waited for Jack to scold.

Jack cleared his throat. "Was his driving really so bad?"

Constance lifted her chin.

Jack's blue eyes twinkled with amusement and his smile grew wide. "Tell the truth now, Pixie."

"There are no words to describe Lord Blamey." Constance raised her hands to her face and let the absurdity of the morning escape. She laughed. "Oh my stars. Spare me from another morning like this one. I don't think I have the strength to endure another carriage ride like that."

"Well, there is far more to a perfect gentleman than driving," Virginia offered. "There is a love of dancing, manners, and intelligence to consider. It helps if he can offer his heart as well."

Discomforted by talk of love, Constance changed the subject. "Are the viscount and his lady very much attached? Will they wed soon?"

Virginia clenched her hands together. "We are still waiting to hear of the date."

Jack and Virginia exchanged a long glance.

"Did I say something wrong?"

"No, not wrong, Pixie," Jack answered, sitting forward. "Although the viscount has arranged an admirable match with an earl's daughter, one that will increase his circumstances considerably, we are not entirely certain he wishes to marry the chit anymore. There have been some rumors about the match, but the date for the union seems no closer."

"Was she really unwell this morning?"

Jack grimaced. "I doubt it. Lady Penelope prefers to dangle Carrington on her arm, not the other way around. How he puts up with it I'll never understand. I wouldn't tolerate such treatment."

———— • ————

So far, so good. The way things were going, Virginia would have Pixie for a sister-in-law in no time at all. Her brother hovered over her friend, so obviously smitten that even a blind man could see how perfectly happy the union would be. Given the way Jack devoured Pixie with his eyes, an announcement of their marriage couldn't be too far away. She only hoped the potential scandal of his broken betrothal wouldn't distress Pixie overmuch. But Jack was not a patient man and was used to getting his way. Being sued for breach of promise wouldn't bother him in the face of marrying the woman he truly wanted.

Although she should be ashamed of her lapse as a chaperone, she couldn't be happier with developments. Between them, she and Bernard had hatched a plan to bring the pair together as often as they could. They had agreed to play to their strengths. Hallam would be blunt about his approval. Virginia would subtly point out her brother's sterling qualities and leave them alone at every opportunity.

When the doors creaked open to admit Lord Hallam, she let out a contented sigh. Now that he was behaving as she wished, she really could find no fault with him. Thank heavens he had acted to protect her brother's interests this morning and convinced Jack to follow the phaeton. Virginia had not wanted to raise an alarm, but it seemed that she should have given more credence to the rumors of Blamey's appalling driving skills.

Bernard thumped into the seat beside her, his large frame sprawled untidily. He wouldn't drink tea, but requested ale. He jogged his knee impatiently while waiting for its arrival.

Virginia contemplated educating him on the correct manners of a gentleman, but to be honest, she liked most of his rough edges. Not all of them, of course, but his unapologetic way of living gave her a thrill. That, and the words he whispered into her ear when no one paid attention.

She had never considered matters of the bedroom outside of it before, but he forced her to think about them—and to listen to him talk about them. Her only contribution so far was to tell him to be quiet in case he was overheard.

When Bernard shifted position, he brushed his hand over her shoulder, and then slid it down her back, lingering on her bottom. He squeezed.

Before she could stop them, memories rose—of pain, of terror, and of humiliation.

Virginia fought them, tried to delay the return, but they

proved far too demanding. Fear rolled through her mind of long hours bound in place, the taunting whispers in her ears, and the unrecognizable face of her husband, grinning in exhilaration as she cried out in anguish.

Her ears rang strangely, but she couldn't see beyond the memories. Voices called, but she couldn't understand. She gave in to the terror as the flush of wet heat scalded her skin. It was too much to take in all at once.

Chapter Fifteen

---◆---

Virginia swam up from confusion and chaos, glimpsing the white face of her dearest friend hovering over her head. Beyond her bed hangings, her brother, and beyond him, Bernard leaned against the wall with his gaze fixed on the bed.

Pixie pressed a cold cloth to her face.

"I'm all right," she whispered.

The door clicked shut and when she glanced over, the men were gone.

"What happened?" Pixie asked.

The raw pain still gripped her. Her memories were jumbled and terrifying. "I remembered my husband."

She closed her eyes to hide her pain.

Pixie wriggled forward and curled an arm around her, offering comfort. Virginia sank into her friend's embrace and let the tears fall. She had let herself forget so much.

The farce that was her wedding day turned her stomach. Virginia had been so happy. She'd planned to be the perfect wife.

"How did I get here?"

"Lord Hallam caught you as you fainted and carried you upstairs. He's been hovering at the door, too agitated to do more."

"It wasn't his fault." The fault belonged to her late husband. Bernard had just been the trigger that brought everything rushing back.

Pixie frowned. "Of course it wasn't his fault. Why ever would I think that? Hallam has been nice to you, hasn't he?"

She nodded but she didn't want to explain why Hallam was being so nice to her just yet, so she closed her eyes. If he couldn't even touch her without sending her into a panic they couldn't possibly have any sort of future together.

———— ◆ ————

"Would you like to talk about it?" Constance asked as Virginia let out a shuddering sob.

Virginia's eyes snapped open, but she stared at the ceiling for a long time. Constance did not like to rush her, but she worried about the lengthening silence. Her skin was pallid, her eyes dull. If she wasn't ill, then Constance didn't know what was wrong or what might make her cry in such distress. Did she miss her husband?

Constance knew very little about the late Lord Orkney. The rushed wedding hadn't afforded Pixie the chance to attend. She'd felt a little betrayed by the slight at the time but now she wasn't sure what was going on. When her friend's letters failed to mention him after the wedding, except to inform her of his death a month later, Constance hadn't pressed for particulars. Virginia spent years mourning at her brother's estate. She had secluded herself from everyone.

Virginia rolled into a ball as a large shudder racked her. Constance should not have asked. She should have left Virginia alone with her heartbreak.

"Orkney attacked and beat me," Virginia whispered.

What? Virginia's words cut through the room like an explosion, any thoughts of sadness burned away by anger. Orkney had hurt Virginia? It was impossible to believe it could happen, yet Virginia would never lie—not about something so important.

"Why?" Constance blurted out, unable to comprehend how a gentleman, described as mild-mannered in Virginia's letters, could be violent. All of Virginia's early letters had praised Orkney's warm and gentle nature.

"He was sick. He liked inflicting pain on his lovers," Virginia said in a rushed whisper. "I didn't know. I didn't know."

A tear fell down Constance's cheek at the thought. She brushed it away impatiently and wrapped her arms about her friend. "I should not have asked. I didn't know that about Orkney."

"No one knows. Jack protected me from the scandal, and from my husband afterward."

"It must be terrible to hold this secret so close. Do you want to talk about it?" Constance asked, reluctant, but determined to support her friend. When Virginia hesitated, she added, "Or should I fetch your brother?"

"No, I don't need Jack. He knows you're with me." Virginia scrubbed away her tears. "I could never understand why Orkney changed. I still do not. He said the vilest things. On…on our wedding night, he pounced on me—there is no other word for it. I never expected such fury. He had always been so gentle."

The shuddering breath Virginia took ripped at Constance's composure.

"He threw me on the bed, ripped my…ripped my clothes. He went crazy, biting and scratching. He held me down. I was so afraid, Pixie. I hope you never know how terrifying it is to be so powerless. He abused me so badly that Jack felt it in London, and he came for me. I am so ashamed that my brother had to see me in that state, but I doubt I would have survived more…" Virginia sobbed and curled into a tighter ball.

Tears streamed down Constance's face at the terror her friend had endured. She took a deep breath, struggling for control and awkwardly rubbing Virginia's back.

Virginia sniffed. "I remember Jack slamming Orkney's face into the bedchamber floor where he'd held me captive since our wedding night. I couldn't lift my head, let alone walk when I was released. I was so weak, in so much pain, I had to be carried from the room. Jack left Orkney bleeding on the floor, screaming that I was his wife, his property. If not for my injuries, my brother would have stayed behind to murder him. Poor Jack, he was drunk by the time we got home to Hazelmere and stayed that way. He had to numb the pain, you see. Sometimes we feel too much. I was confined to bed for three weeks. Three weeks of my life I cannot remember or ever get back."

"If he was foxed, who looked after you?"

It was not like Jack to neglect his sister. Someone else had to have seen and thankfully held their tongue.

"I...I am not sure I remember. It is strange too. The incident has never come up in conversation. I...no, nothing." Virginia's confused eyes were dry now but red-rimmed.

"You said Jack was beating Orkney, but you were watching. From where? Did someone else help you that night? Was Hallam with him?"

Virginia's eyes widened and she rolled away. "Oh, God. He was."

———— · ————

Jack paced his study, agitated because of his sister. A dam had just burst open and his heart beat far too fast. If not for Pixie's presence upstairs, he would be up there too. He poured himself a drink, hands shaking with the effort not to spill a drop, as Hallam came up beside him.

"Bad?"

Jack poured the brandy down his throat in one gulp and reached for the decanter. "Yes, very bad."

Hallam took the decanter. "You better let me do that. More in the glass is preferable to wasting it on the furniture."

As Jack raised his refilled glass to his lips, a wisp of color hovered at the door. Pixie moved into the room and directly to him. He wrapped her in his arms as she sobbed her heart out.

"Are you all right?" Jack asked, after giving her time to calm down.

She shook her head and burrowed deeper into his coat, her hands exploring his inner pockets to find his handkerchief.

"Virginia told me what happened," Pixie sobbed, wriggling as she wiped her eyes. "She told me everything."

Hallam's breath hissed out beside them, followed by a lengthy series of curses.

"Were you there, Hallam? Did you carry her from the house and bring them home?" Pixie turned in Jack's arms to glimpse Hallam's distraught face.

Jack kept hold. What Pixie saw would make everything

clearer. Hallam cared a great deal for a woman who'd married another. He knew everything that transpired the night Jack had almost lost Virginia to a monster.

"I was with Jack when he became ill," Hallam stated briskly. "We guessed Virginia was in trouble."

"*You* guessed. I thought it was my dinner," Jack replied, forever grateful for Hallam's clear thinking that night.

"Thank you. Thank you for taking care of them," she whispered.

Hallam nodded. "It was nothing."

"Not nothing. Virginia needed you, just as she does now."

"Has she remembered everything?"

Pixie shrugged. "She didn't say much, but perhaps you could fill in the gaps for her. You were with her, weren't you?"

Hallam nodded, turned on his heel, and stalked out.

"Are you matchmaking, Pixie?" Jack pulled her tight to him, enjoying the feel of her in his arms.

"Yes, well, I doubt I could make a career of it. What do I know about anything?"

Jack turned her and lifted Pixie's chin so he could see her eyes. They were red from crying, but so achingly familiar. "A great deal, I think. You bring sunshine just by being here. Everybody loves being near you, Pixie."

"I'm sure you can't wait to see the back of me," she whispered.

"Shh, don't say such nasty things. You're distressed." He rubbed his hand over her back soothingly. "I thought we had gotten past arguing over nothing."

Holding Pixie close demolished Jack's anxiety. Hallam would be with Virginia now. He had no doubts that Hallam would confess his part in the business at last, and there would be one less reason for tension between his sister and his friend.

Pressing a kiss to Pixie's hair, Jack committed himself to courting her. If she felt even the tiniest portion of the bliss he felt now, they could have a good life together.

Pixie's breath puffed warm through the fine linen of his shirt and against his skin. Nipples hardening, he berated himself. He really was trying to give comfort and it was bad form to get an erection in the process. But this attraction was too potent to ignore. Surely, she must feel it too.

"How did you leave matters with Blamey?" Jack really did not want to talk about him, but it might help to prolong this embrace.

"I don't believe he will call again," Pixie confessed. "And his absence won't bother me in the least. I'll be assured of a long life without him."

Pixie's hands settled at his waist, skimming under the bottom edge of his waistcoat. Damn, she could arouse him without trying. He crushed the urge to grind his hips into her, but he could not stop his breath from churning in and out.

"Perhaps Blamey isn't a good choice for a long and healthy life. Especially if you want to travel," he murmured. But the thought of bending down and kissing those soft lips proved very difficult to ignore.

"I would like to travel, but it doesn't seem likely."

Pixie drew small circles on his shirt with her fingertips, keeping time with his own hand movements across her back.

A rush of desire swept his skin. He gulped. "You will have to tell me where you would like to go. I'm sure something can be arranged."

"That is kind of you, but not now."

Constance twisted her head and pressed her cheek against his chest. He told his hands to behave as they brushed down the length of her back—kept away from the derrière he longed to stroke by a willpower he was surprised he had. When she drew in a great shuddering breath, his pulse quickened.

"You should get some rest, Pixie. It has been a long day," Jack murmured into her hair.

She did not answer. He leaned sideways to see her face and found her dozing in his arms. He nudged her. Her eyes flickered then shut again. She was faking. Amused, Jack picked her up and juggled her to reach the latch for the secret passageway.

"Where are we going?"

"I'm taking you to bed."

As soon as the words left his mouth, his desire almost blinded him. He couldn't act on it tonight. It was too soon. She had only just buried her past dislike of him. If he attempted to make love to her tonight, he was afraid she might laugh.

Since Pixie was tiny and weighed next to nothing, he navigated the tunnel easily without hitting her feet against the walls. He passed through his sitting room, out onto the balcony, and entered her bedchamber quickly, hoping no one saw them like this. Luckily, her maid was not in the room.

Pixie didn't speak as he pulled the balcony door closed behind him and tried to decide what to do. Put her on the bed alone or join her there? Perhaps he shouldn't ask himself questions.

At the bedside, he tried to be dispassionate about the situation, but he found it hard. She slipped her shoes from her feet while he pulled the pins from her hair, then he tucked her into bed, day gown and all, ignoring the desire to play with the dark strands of hair that spilled over her pillow.

Jack pulled the blankets over her shoulders and was surprised when Pixie grabbed his hand. She kept her eyes closed and that was probably a good thing. She would not see the erection tenting his breeches that way.

He leaned down, pressed his lips to her hair. "Thank you for helping Virginia. Your presence has made such a difference. I think she will be able to let go of the past and move on now."

He kissed her hair again, but she clutched at his hand tighter.

"Stay with me," she murmured sleepily, "until I fall asleep."

Jack could not have been more shocked. That was a dangerous thing to suggest, given his state. He was not sure he could trust himself to behave. The thought made him angry. He would prove his mind the master of his body.

"Just this once, little one." He brushed her hair away from the pillow and lowered himself on top of the blankets. "Lift your head."

He hoped this was truly what she wanted. The day had been so full of drama that she'd hardly know what she was doing. He wasn't sure *he* did.

When he had her settled in the crook of his arm, her back to his front, she pulled his hand around her and up between her breasts. Desire threatened to overwhelm him as she held his fingers close to her heart. The warmth of her skin, so provocative, so wonderfully tempting that he had to stroke his fingers just a little.

She didn't shriek, but grumbled in pleasure before falling fast asleep.

———◆———

Bernard scratched on Virginia's door and stepped in without waiting on a response. The room was cool and dark and he crossed the chamber, grabbed a lump of wood, and brought the fire back to life. Rubbing his hands, he sat back, and waited for Virginia to speak.

"How long were you with me?"

Bernard wouldn't lie. "Every day."

He stood and turned toward the sound of her voice. Virginia had curled up on the window seat, watching him come with firelight reflecting off her tired eyes. He slowly sat beside her, terrified of scaring her again.

"I should remember that, but all that comes to mind was being warm." Her glance flickered to the flames. "You are very good with fires."

"You don't enjoy being cold. It was the best I could do."

"Why is it that I can't remember?"

Bernard ran a hand over his face. "Your injuries were very bad. The physician ordered laudanum be given at regular intervals. You were hardly ever awake. When the potion wore off, you began to dream and thrash about. I was afraid you would aggravate your injuries so the fellow administered more until you were healing."

"You decided?"

"Jack was…he was not well, I'm afraid. He couldn't help you and it was tearing him apart. I kept him foxed most of the time. The duke approved wholeheartedly when he arrived."

"My uncle saw me?"

Bernard shook his head. "I would not allow him near you. I knew you wouldn't want him to see what Orkney had done."

Bernard watched her absorb that information. The press of her hand to her face was the only sign she was discomforted. He wished he could make this easier for her.

"I would rather that you hadn't seen, either," she whispered.

"Do you really believe I could stay away after I had glimpsed what that monster had done?"

He didn't get an immediate reply, so he left her alone for a few moments to think. He returned to his room, grabbed up a decanter of whiskey and two glasses, and returned to find her where he had left her. He poured two glasses then passed one to her.

Virginia took his offering, hands trembling, and sipped the amber liquid. When it was all gone, he kept refilling her glass until she started to slump.

Careful not to frighten her, he took the glass and crouched over her. He sat her up, then slid behind her back. Limp from the effect of the spirits, she allowed him to nestle her tight in his arms.

She raised her hands and they fluttered above his arms, as restless as little wrens until he wove them into his embrace. When her head nodded, he pulled her onto his lap, then took her to bed.

Since she was still dressed, Bernard loosened her gown and let it slide to the floor, ignoring the impulse to run his hands over her curves. He found her nightdress, and then stripped Virginia of her remaining clothes, putting her into the linen before she panicked.

Virginia's long pale hair splashed over his wrists as he removed the pins that held it as confined as she had kept her grief. When he pulled back the covers and urged her to lie down, she resisted. This was the difficult part. Despite the cold gripping the chamber, she had always fought against the bedding slipping over her. It was why Bernard had kept the room hot as she recovered.

"Hush, love," he whispered. "I promise you, you're safe with me."

Virginia stilled and her gaze rose. In the firelight, her brow puckered. "I remember that."

"I am not surprised. I told you as much every night."

She let him cover her, and Bernard tucked the blankets tight around her. Slowly, with great care, he lowered his lips and kissed her brow. She didn't turn away so he breathed out his anxiety and collected the decanter and glasses, removing all traces of his presence.

"Bernard?"

"Yes, my love?"

"Thank you."

Chapter Sixteen

———— ♦ ————

The carriage wheel hit a rut, tossing Constance sideways into Jack's shoulder. Blushing, she apologized and struggled to her side of the carriage bench.

"Nothing to forgive." Jack rapped on the wall of the carriage. "A little more care if you please."

The coachman grumbled and Constance hid a smile. The state of the road wasn't the driver's fault, but Jack always hated his passengers getting thrown about.

Across from her, Virginia appeared serene, but Hallam's face was one constant scowl. Just like Jack's. Neither man was happy to traipse about in inclement weather, and certainly not to a garden party. But Virginia had been adamant and so here they were, hoping the rain would hold off long enough for the event.

Jack folded his arms across his chest. "Are you certain we need to attend?"

"Pixie must be seen about Town if she wishes to be successful in her search," Virginia assured him.

Jack's expression grew pained. "I'm sure there are other events."

"A garden party is perfect, and you know it. So much less formal than a ball. Pixie will impress Mr. Abernathy and Lord Bridges, and have ample opportunity to sweep them off their feet. Leave everything to me."

Jack clenched his fists, but he didn't respond. Had he

rethought his commitment to helping Constance find a husband? Given her behavior of the past days, she couldn't blame him. She had not comported herself very well at all.

Constance's glance skated across the carriage to where Lord Hallam sprawled. The man's eyes gleamed with mischief as he watched Jack. That couldn't be good for anyone. She fidgeted, turning her fan over in her fingers, desperate for the nightmare of her search for a husband to end.

Could debtors' prison be all that bad?

Today was another opportunity to meet and impress the remaining gentlemen. She had two chances left before ruin. She had to do her best to impress. The carriage drew to a stop before the house so that passengers could disembark without suffering from the damp too greatly. Hallam struggled out first, holding out his hand for Virginia.

The minute Virginia faced away from them, Jack gripped Constance's hand tight. Since he rarely touched her in public, she looked up in surprise. His blue eyes were unreadable and she waited for him to speak. She thought he might, but he released her hand without a word and climbed out.

Constance had to take his hand again to alight from the carriage, yet there was no eager pressure in his grip, nothing to indicate excitement of any kind. Virginia linked arms with her, and they swept into the party before the men.

"Lady Beckwith, such a pleasure to see you today."

"Lady Orkney, and this must be the Miss Grange I've heard so much about. Welcome, my dear."

Constance did her best curtsey, but had to wonder what the lady had 'heard so much about' her. Had Jack told more tales? She glanced at him, yet he seemed less interested in the woman than Hallam was. His greeting was barely more than a grunt.

Constance was growing accustomed to Hallam's brusque ways. He was devoted to her friend, and that was all the recommendation she needed to forgive him his odd habits.

The damp lawns soaked her slippers though after two steps, but guests mingled in little clusters, appearing oblivious to the discomfort. If not for Virginia at her side, Constance would have turned back. She didn't want to mix with these people. She didn't belong.

When they stopped at the edge of the terrace, Jack paused too but turned away to join Lord Daventry. Although disappointed to lose his company, Constance brought her mind back to the task at hand. Husband hunting. She shuddered.

Virginia cleverly placed them within Lord Bridges' orbit soon after.

"So, you are Greedy Grange's daughter," Lord Bridges exclaimed. "I thought your name was familiar and now that I think on it, you luckily resemble your mother more."

"I beg your pardon." Constance glanced at Virginia, but she looked just as puzzled. Constance had never heard a nickname for her father before. Even though she did not like it, it did suit her late father's gambling habits. He'd never been able to walk away from a dare. "Do you have an acquaintance with Mother?"

The lanky man looked down on her from a great height. Constance had to lift her chin painfully to meet his gaze. Discreetly, she inched her body backward so it didn't hurt her neck so much.

"Your late father more than your delightful mother. We often played against each other as young men," Bridges admitted. "I've never met a man more prone to a bad hand than Greedy Grange. Never knew when to call it quits. Once, he even bet his horse, carriage, and the servants that went with it. Lost, of course, and had to walk home. Do you play?"

She remembered that particular carriage, and the servants that left with it. "No," Constance admitted, "not at all."

The lord's gaze held hers a moment then dipped. Appalled that he was obviously ogling her breasts, Constance took a whole step back.

"Well, I'm certain you're the lucky one in the family." His smile grew. "Some people have it and some don't. Lady luck shines brightly on my family. There's something in our blood that must be preserved."

"Of course," she replied. Constance considered Lord Bridges. Too tall, too obviously interested in her body, and far too happy to gamble. Jack had been wrong to consider him as a candidate. She'd prefer debtors' prison than to marry such a man. She didn't want a gambler for a husband, especially a man who believed luck lingered in the blood. What a ridiculous notion. One day he would learn that luck would abandon him and his family without mercy.

Constance nudged Virginia's arm gently. With a few more words, Virginia managed to leave Lord Bridges soon after.

"I'd never forgive you if you liked him," Virginia whispered urgently.

Constance offered a wry smile. "One left."

She turned to scan the gathering and saw Jack moving away. He paused beside a pillar and leaned against it. As she studied him, his gaze rose and raked her with such intensity that her cheeks heated. Somehow, she managed a small smile but his stare turned her legs to jelly. When she risked another glance, he'd disappeared into the crowd again.

She didn't know what to say to him. In retrospect, she should be ashamed of asking him to stay with her until she fell asleep last night, but it had been heavenly lying snug in his arms. When she married, she hoped her husband would be as agreeable.

If she married.

Given her dismissal of Lord Bridges, she had one gentleman left to encourage. Mr. Abernathy had seemed an agreeable man when they met at the Huntley Ball. And although he had witnessed her mistake with Jack's cane, he had appeared amused rather than disapproving. Constance lifted up onto the balls of her feet to look about. A recently wealthy gentleman with hair the color of carrots should stand out in the crowd. But with her height so limited, she hadn't spotted him yet.

Virginia nudged her side. "I see an old friend. Don't go anywhere without me."

Constance pulled her thoughts and gaze back to her circle with a start as Miss Scaling and Lord Wade joined the group.

She spotted a tall redheaded man in the crowd. Mr. Abernathy? Success. He was handsome. His pale skin contrasted starkly with the red locks on his head, and thick arched eyebrows framed green eyes that twinkled in conversation.

The crowd shifted and familiar blue eyes observed her. Constance blushed. Jack was speaking with Abernathy. She could only hope that he was saying good things about her, not relating more childhood pranks. Just to be certain, she would go and speak with the man herself.

Constance's toe caught on something and she tripped forward. For one horrifying moment, she teetered on the paved edge of Lady Beckwith's garden pond. She swung her arms and Lord Wade did make a grab for her, but instead of securing her, as she hoped, he fumbled and ended up pushing her away.

It could have taken only a moment to fall. It felt like an eternity.

Cold pond water surged over her face, muffling the sounds of horrified astonishment from the guests closest to her.

Miss Scaling and Lord Wade gazed down at her and did nothing to help.

Constance spluttered up to the surface and sank again, but strong hands caught hers and tugged. Dirty pond water splashed over Jack's pristine boots and legs. Gasps of shock echoed around them, and Jack even cursed. But then he removed his coat, slipped her arms in the sleeves, and wrapped her in it, unmindful of the damage she was sure to cause.

Around her, the sound of laughter drowned out the meaning of any whispered words. She wanted to die, to crawl away into obscurity, and see no one ever again. She lifted her gaze reluctantly at the repetition of her name on so many lips and found Miss Scaling standing very close. Not close to her, but close to Jack, a small smile playing on her lips as she gazed at Jack's profile.

Constance met Jack's gaze.

He was furious. His eyes flicked over those gathered and lingered on each laughing guest. He held their gazes a moment longer than might be comfortable, then reached for Constance's soggy, gloved hand. He wrapped it around his shirtsleeve and pulled.

Miss Scaling's face lost its smirk as Jack hurried Constance determinedly from the garden.

Constance stumbled as her wet dress tangled about her legs, denying her any dignity or grace in her exit. She kept her gaze lowered. She would not glance back again, but instead concentrated on her steps. Silence grew behind them, but the heavy thwack of her skirts sounded a counterpoint to her miserable exit.

Her trip to London was an abysmal failure and she wanted nothing more than to go home to Sunderland and wait for her jailors.

Virginia caught her other arm. Constance was grateful. As they made their way around the side of the house, a servant rushed ahead, hopefully seeking Jack's coach.

When they reached the front drive, Constance lifted her chin and glanced about miserably. Lord Daventry winked. Beyond him, a dozen of the most notable and wealthy members of the *ton* summoned their carriages too.

Constance was stunned at the degree of loyalty it conveyed. Somehow, she had made friends with important members of the ton. She wanted to giggle, but she feared she might become hysterical.

Jack urged her through the door of his carriage and she sat gingerly on the velvet seats, skirts squelching horribly as she ruined his upholstery.

Virginia threw a carriage rug over Constance's knees and then tugged off her wet, clinging gloves. "Did I see Lord Wade push you in, dearest?"

"He did not mean to," Constance replied, but she was not quite sure why she defended him.

Her teeth chattered as the carriage lurched forward.

"No, not Wade, but do you mean to tell us that Miss Scaling did not mean to hook your right foot with her left?" Jack asked, with some heat. "For God's sake, woman, do not make excuses for vulgar people. I saw what happened—all of it. I am sorry I could not get to you before you fell." Jack cursed and thumped the side of the carriage with his fist. He dropped his hand to his knee, tapped his fingers against it, and then stilled.

"I believe I shall have some fun," he said with a grin.

But Constance did not think that anyone else would enjoy it. Even slumped in her wet gown—miserable and embarrassed—the anger in Jack's voice concerned her. He would get revenge for her if she said nothing to stop him.

"Jack, it is not necessary. I lost my footing and fell. Please do not make me feel worse. I am not harmed in any way, just a bit more damp than I usually like." She tried to make light of it, tried to laugh at her predicament. Judging from the look on his face, Jack was aware of what she was trying to do.

He shook his head. "I suppose you mean to tell me next that Miss Scaling did not mean to pour a full bottle of perfume over your gown last week, either. Oh, yes I know about that." He arched a brow. "She has her black little heart set on embarrassing you, Pixie. I cannot stand by and allow this to continue. Who knows what she'll do next."

Constance said nothing as the carriage lurched on its way. What could she say to convince him and should she still try? Jack was right. Miss Scaling had set her sights on humiliating her. She considered Constance a threat, even when there was no need. Constance sank farther into her corner, conscious of the puddle forming under her, and buried herself into Jack's large coat.

When the carriage arrived at Ettington House, Jack escorted her inside, dripping water all over the entry foyer. Once the door closed behind them, Jack scooped Constance up in his arms and carried her up the staircase. She was grateful, since her knees were weak and her teeth chattered nonstop. Once at her room, Jack kicked the door shut and carried her to the hearth.

Constance shivered as he removed his coat from her shoulders. He ran his hands up and down her arms briskly then wrapped her in a blanket from the chaise. Wrapped tight against the cold, Jack held her until her maid arrived.

"Organize a hot bath and brandy. She's thoroughly chilled," Jack ordered.

Her maid's eyes rounded, but she hurried off to do his bidding, leaving them alone once more. Even though Constance was snuggled against Jack's chest, she couldn't get warm. She started to shake and buried her nose against Jack's waistcoat, seeking the greater warmth he radiated. His attempts to rub warmth into her back didn't prevent her teeth from chattering.

"You must promise me that you will be cautious around Miss Scaling from now on. Do not remain in her company for long, and never alone. She means to harm you. Promise me you will be on guard."

She nodded.

Despite her misery, the very real concern in Jack's tone reached her and she felt slightly better. He wasn't angry with her for the scene she'd just caused.

———— ◆ ————

Constance pushed the heavy covers down, only to feel them rise again. She pushed, but a deep, familiar voice rumbled in the darkness beside her, and she let them be.

"I'm hot, Jack."

"I know," he murmured into her ear. "You have a fever. Keep under the blankets and try to go back to sleep."

"What are you doing here?" she whispered. He shouldn't be in her room in the dead of night. She did not want to disappoint him by behaving improperly again.

"Your coughing was keeping me awake. Since I could not get back to sleep, I decided to keep an eye on you."

When he brushed her sticky hair away from her face, Constance leaned into his cool touch. "You don't have to, you know. I can look after myself."

"Shh," Jack whispered into her ear.

Constance rolled and encountered solid, silky skin.

She recoiled in shock.

While her mind struggled with the knowledge that Jack lay beneath the sheets with her, he wriggled closer and slipped his arm beneath her head. With her cheek resting on his bare shoulder, her senses ran wild. She breathed in, but the action caused her to cough. Her hands flattened on his taut chest, but she had no chance to explore. He captured her curious fingers and held them tight between his own.

When her coughing subsided, she pressed her head to his chest.

"Go back to sleep, little one."

Constance lifted her head. "I'm not so little."

Jack pressed her head back to his chest, and then hugged her tighter to him. "Of course, Pixie," he whispered. "You're practically a giant."

Constance smacked his chest lightly then closed her eyes.

She was too tired to debate the issue of her height at this hour. Besides, Jack was kissing her temple. Little light kisses that caused a contented lassitude to creep over her.

Her next memory was of Virginia's stealthy departure in the morning. She turned her head to the side. Jack was gone, but a dent remained in the other pillow.

Last night hadn't been a dream. But whatever his intent, she had certainly enjoyed his visit.

However, this morning she had another problem. She felt

dreadful. A chill had seeped into her bones and she ached all over. She reached for her handkerchief and sneezed, then buried herself back under the covers.

When the breakfast hour arrived, the housekeeper trooped in and out with honey tea for her throat, a hearty breakfast, extra firewood, and hot bricks in case she needed them. The little woman fluttered around the room so fast, Constance's head began to ache.

Jack strolled in not long after, impeccably dressed and sinfully handsome. "How is our guest this morning?" he asked from the foot of the bed.

"Not quite myself," she croaked.

Although Jack frowned at the news, a telling blush heated Constance's cheeks as she remembered sharing a bed with him.

"You seem flushed. Are you still fevered?" He paused beside the bed and brushed his knuckles across her cheek.

If it was possible to blush harder, she did. Try as she might, she could not look at him and forget he had held her against his bare chest. Or that she had snuggled against him shamelessly eager for his affection.

His eyebrow quirked upward. "Are you blushing, Pixie?"

Constance squirmed.

Jack rewarded her with a broad smile. He had lain down beside her. Why wouldn't she be embarrassed? She smiled hesitantly back, but started to cough again.

His smile faltered. "Virginia will return in a little while. She has some errands to run, but will be back to keep you company as soon as she can." Jack settled on the edge of her bed and pulled the newspaper from under his arm. "Would you like to hear today's news?"

While the servants bustled around behind his back, he read the paper aloud. But he skipped the society gossip. Her embarrassment was sure to have made the paper today.

Constance struggled to stay awake, but Jack's voice soothed her better than any sleeping draft. She drifted in and out of consciousness as Jack caressed her face, and once she even captured his strong fingers against her cheek.

Chapter Seventeen

———◆———

"**Y**ou're supposed to be resting in bed."

Constance gasped as Jack stepped into the stables, catching her where she was not supposed to be. "I wanted to check on Falentine. I haven't been riding in over a week and I am feeling just a bit guilty." Constance hooked her foot on the lower rail and raised herself up to reach her horse's ears. Falentine slanted her head and almost dislodged her from the fence.

Dear Lord, she had wished Jack's arms were around her as she fell asleep last night. When he had not come, her disappointment was intense.

Jack rested his gleaming boot against the lower rail beside her and Constance tried not to notice how his trousers pulled tight across his thigh. Ladies shouldn't think like that. But Constance found it very hard not to notice and admire how well he looked.

"No need to worry," Jack promised, settling his hand on her back to hold her in place. "The grooms have taken her out every day."

A larger head pushed close as Jack's horse demanded attention too. He indulged Lucarno with soft words and a good scratch, but quickly returned to touch her again.

Constance glanced at the grooms who began to shuffle their feet. "Ah, they didn't tell me that."

Falentine's velvety-soft whiskers tickled her cheek. Constance tucked her loose hair back out of reach of the nibbling horse, anxious not to let her graze on her dark locks. By rights, she shouldn't be running about with her hair down, but she had not wanted to put it up just for the ten minutes she needed to see her horse.

Jack turned his head to the grooms and they scattered. "Not surprising. They don't get many pretty visitors and no doubt wanted to extend your stay."

"Jack," she warned. "They meant no harm."

When Falentine nudged her again, Constance threw her arm around the horse's neck and squeezed.

Jack's warm hands closed about her waist and dragged her to the ground. "You shouldn't be out here."

It might have been her illness that made her sway into Jack, but whatever the reason, she really didn't care. She felt infinitely better in Jack's arms.

He secured her tighter against him with one arm, but the other rose to play with her hair. He twisted a long curl around his finger, and then unwound it before brushing the end across her nose.

Constance giggled and captured his hand.

Jack squeezed her tight then let her go. "I want you in bed immediately."

While he fumbled with her fallen shawl, Constance kept her eyes trained on her horse. That sounded nice, but only if she had Jack's company again. But he wouldn't. Not again.

A hot blush swept her skin, and she scrambled for something to say. "Did I thank you properly for the horse?"

"I believe so," he laughed. "You did crush my coat horribly."

Constance turned. "I'm sure it wasn't crushed beyond repair."

He cupped her face in his hand and his lips quirked. "Not beyond repair, but my valet did grumble. You need to return to the house now," Jack urged. "It is unhealthy for you to remain here long. Take my arm."

Grudgingly, she let him lead her back across the gardens. She *was* a little unsteady on her feet, but she didn't want to show it. Jack might get the notion into his head that she needed to be treated like a child again. She didn't think she could suffer that. Constance didn't like being ill, or confined to bed for that matter. It was so tremendously boring staring at the ceiling—no matter how many wicked cherubs graced it.

Jack opened the lower door and bade her to enter before him. As she stepped through, his hand settled against the small of her back again to propel her forward.

"Go upstairs and rest, little one," Jack urged. "When Virginia returns she will have plenty of news to tell, I'm sure."

"I hate being ill," Constance grumbled, but intended to take a nap just the same.

Jack cupped her face again and his smile grew wide. "It's a little hard to miss your dislike. Are you always this difficult to please?"

"No," Constance grumbled, not looking at him.

His grip firmed and his thumb brushed her lips, but then he turned and walked away toward his study without another word.

She watched his broad back disappear, wishing she could come up with an excuse to call him back. It was not often that they could talk freely, and she missed his company already.

Constance headed for the main stairs and resigned herself to a long and boring few hours staring at her walls.

"Lord Bridges to see you, Miss Grange," Parkes intoned solemnly. Surprised, Constance looked up and found herself facing the butler and Lord Bridges in the entrance hall. Given that she was on her feet and in front of him, she couldn't say she wasn't up to receiving visitors.

"Lord Bridges?" she asked, pulling her shawl tighter about her shoulders. "Forgive me, but I'm not entirely well today. I apologize that I didn't notice you immediately. A pleasure to see you again, my lord."

He reached for her hand, just as she clasped her skirts and bobbed a curtsy. Her head spun a little as she came back up.

"Yes, I had heard a rumor you were unwell, but I didn't expect to see you up and around. I understood you to be bedridden."

Constance chuckled and grasped the banister for support. "I escaped momentarily, but it seems I was caught in the end."

"I am in luck yet again. Might we speak in private for a moment? It will not take long."

"Yes, of course." She turned to lead him into the drawing room, dismissing the idea he'd come to propose as ludicrous. "How may I help you today, my lord?"

"A trifling matter." Lord Bridges chuckled softly. "An escape is often more successful when you have an ally. I am here to offer my assistance."

"I had no great plan for further adventure, I assure you. Just a short stroll to check on my horse then back to rest," Constance replied, leaving out the fact that the marquess expected her compliance and might think to check on her to be sure that she had indeed rested. That thought pleased her.

"Regardless of your supposed illness, you look as lovely as always," he promised.

He was a very poor liar. Constance knew she did not look her best. Perspiration made her brow itch but she couldn't wipe it away while he was in front of her. A flush of heat swept her skin so she sat quickly in an armchair by the drawing room fire and clasped her hands in her lap. "Thank you for coming to see me, my lord. You are very kind to visit."

She smiled and looked about her quickly. She should have summoned a maid to act as chaperone but she would not be with Lord Bridges long enough for impropriety?

"After the events of the other day, you must surely realize many men see you as an accident waiting to happen, but not I. I saw through your plan," Bridges chuckled. "It is a bold gamble indeed, but little digging ferreted out the truth you've been desperately trying to hide. Pretending to be in dun territory when you have the limitless resources at your command, eh? I commend you on an excellent ploy to garner sympathy from the ton and to weed out those without wits. Society assumes you are at death's door, but clearly you planned on having the last laugh on everyone."

Constance gaped at his speech. Had she heard him correctly? She was most definitely in dun territory. "My lord, I have little interest in fooling anyone. I *am* most certainly ill, and if you have no further business you must excuse me. I must retire. Good day to you."

"Not so fast." Lord Bridges raced her to the drawing room door where he locked it. "I am most certainly not done with you."

Jack smashed his way through the drawing room doors and found Pixie wrapped in Lord Bridges' arms. Given that she was fighting against his grip, Jack concluded that she didn't want to be there any longer than necessary. He crossed the chamber, pulled Pixie from Bridges' arms, and shoved the man away from her.

Bridges landed on a delicate chair and it collapsed under his weight, sending him sprawling to the floor in an untidy heap.

"Get up, you bastard."

Bridges scrambled to his feet and held up his hands in a poor attempt at defense. "I'm going to marry her."

"Like hell you will." Irritated, Jack stalked in to deliver a sharp blow to his midriff, and then an uppercut that sent him flying into a sideboard. Crystal decanters shattered as they hit the floor. "I'd never let a scoundrel have her."

Servants swarmed into the chamber and their presence put a stop to his murderous inclinations. "Get this filth out of my house."

"Gladly, milord," a footman agreed.

Bridges brushed his mouth with the back of his hand. "She wanted me. She did!"

Jack stopped. Never. Not in a million years would he believe that lie. "I suggest you rethink your statement on your way out or our seconds shall meet."

Bridges' jaw firmed, but he didn't retract his statement. He also didn't take Jack up on his challenge. The footmen forced him from the room.

Jack gave the destroyed drawing room a quick glance then went in search of Pixie.

"She fainted," Parkes called from within the library, and stood aside as Jack reached the table where Pixie's still form lay. "I caught her as she fell."

Given the way Parkes wrung his hands, it was obviously a new experience to rescue a damsel in distress. But Jack was getting used to coming to this woman's rescue. He never knew what would happen around Pixie, but he was learning he didn't care. "So much for her claim she never fainted. Thank you, Parkes."

Jack gazed at Pixie's face. It shone with perspiration. She should be back in bed. But the stubborn minx had refused to wallow. However, if she was not careful she could find herself in worse straits.

He leaned farther over her. Pixie still had her eyes closed and that worried him. He needed to see her awake.

He moved her skirts away from the table drawer and withdrew the vinaigrette Virginia kept there. Although Pixie looked good on his furniture and his mind leapt to doing other things with her on the sturdy piece, he worked the stiff catch open and moved the trinket toward her face.

"Don't." The word burst from her lips before he had even fully opened the vinaigrette.

Relieved, he dropped the vinaigrette back in the drawer and shut it. "Then open your eyes."

"Do I have to, Jack? I would very much like to remain invisible just now. This is not how I envisaged my day."

"Yes, you have to. Open them for me," he begged. When her green eyes slid into view, he drowned in the lush color for some time before remembering they were not alone.

"You see, Parkes, a job well done. Our thanks. Fetch a stiff drink and toss it down before you resume your post," Jack suggested.

The butler left the room, but Jack did not watch him go. He only had eyes for Pixie. The silence grew thick and he ran a finger across her cheek. "Are you ready to sit up?"

———•———

Constance gasped and scrambled up, but couldn't meet Jack's gaze. She should not have met with Lord Bridges without a chaperone. He would probably be mad at her about it, but up until today, Constance had never perceived a need to be so wary of gentlemen in the marquess' house. Illness wasn't really an acceptable excuse for missing the signs of danger.

Jack swept a hand over her hair as if to tame its wildness. "Did he hurt you?"

Constance shuddered at the memory of Lord Bridges' rough handling. Men like that were foreign to her. She'd always been protected. Constance shook her head quickly to reassure him she was unharmed. "Jack?"

"Yes, love."

"You will not fight him on my behalf." She was terribly worried about that. And especially about Jack. "You have my word I will not marry a bully."

The marquess sighed loudly. "I should teach him a lesson in manners but, as long as he holds his tongue about kissing you, and the proposal, I will let the matter of his lack of manners slide if you wish."

"Thank you."

"Bridges is no longer welcome to call here. I shan't let him near you again, love."

Constance nodded, but she was not really concentrating. She had heard an irregular word pass Jack's lips. He had called her love. Jack never used endearments. She dropped her eyes. Jack's hands touched her scrunched-up skirts. She wriggled in mortification and he helped to straighten them.

When she was respectable again, Jack placed his hands flat on the desk, but his thumbs rested on the edges of her skirts, his knuckles bloodied. Constance gently touched his fingers, carefully avoiding the raw edges. "Do these hurt?"

"Not yet," Jack told her. "But they will sting later when Cook cleans them. I won't say it wasn't worth it to trounce that grasping bastard."

Constance gripped his wrists tight. She did not like it when he was angry. When Jack moved his weight from his hands and they touched the sides of her legs, her heartbeat raced. She slid her hands higher up his arms. "I took his name off the list last night. I don't know why he called today."

His fingers pressed harder against her legs. "So you didn't ask him to kiss you?"

Constance shuddered. "Ask him to kiss me? Why would I do that? Bridges wasn't interested in me yesterday and I did not like his insinuations today. I was trying to leave the drawing room when he trapped me there." Jack rubbed her legs. The sensation mesmerized her. Her breath hitched. "He moved so fast."

"What insinuations did he make?"

"That I wasn't ill and was attempting to garner sympathy." She let her head fall. "I should never have gotten out of bed. I should never have been talked into coming to London."

"Shh, love. Don't overset yourself because of one foolish man," Jack whispered softly. Unfortunately, the motion of Jack's hands on her legs did not appear to calm *him*. His breathing quickened against her face and when he spoke again, his voice was deeper. "Desperation does strange things to a man."

"Desperation?"

"I learned yesterday that his situation is a fabrication. He lost a lot on the 'Change recently," Jack admitted.

"He said members of his family were born lucky. When I told Bridges I didn't gamble, he dismissed me out of hand. Why would he visit me today and suggest I am lying? I have nothing."

"He thinks you wealthy?"

"That's what he claimed."

Jack stroked the diamond necklace she wore and lingered where it lay between her breasts. "Perhaps this may have given him the wrong impression."

His littlest finger brushed the curve of her breast, and then dropped away as she froze.

Tears squeezed past her control and slid down her cheeks. "He thought I was rich because of a necklace?"

Now Constance could appreciate how truly horrible she was. She was pursuing men for the same reason. How could she blame Bridges for doing the same, although with more direct and improper methods of persuasion?

Would he have gone as far as compromising her to get his way?

She pressed her head into Jack's chest and tried not to think about what might have happened.

Her first deep breath drew in his scent and warmed her chilled soul in a way that amazed her. She had always liked being close to him, but she could not lie to herself that it was the same anymore. She moved her head off the cravat knot and diamond pin to rest her face above his heart. Jack's heart beat fast against her cheek and his body was so tense. Why was he still so angry? She caressed his arms, hoping to calm him.

When his lips grazed her brow, she smiled and enjoyed the sensation. Jack embraced her, caging her in warmth and security. She shivered in bliss.

Constance's lids fell, but Lord Bridges' face flashed before her. She snapped her eyes open as panic returned.

But it was Jack who held her tight. Jack whose scent surrounded her. And Jack's lips she wanted to feel against her own. She wanted to forget the ugliness of Lord Bridges, Miss Scaling, and the rest of the *ton*. Constance raised her face before Jack could kiss her brow again, and their lips brushed.

Her kiss startled him.

Jack stared at her mouth as her hands rose to his shoulders. He pressed his lips gently to hers. Their first kiss lingered sweetly, but he drew back to meet her gaze.

The blue of his eyes was dark and uncertain, but she was not. With her body so restless, Constance stretched up closer to Jack, inviting him to kiss her again.

He raised one bruised hand to cradle her face, brushing his thumb across her cheek, burning her with heat. Slowly, breathing harsh to her ears, he dropped his lips to hers, and kissed her. Not the way Bridges had attempted, but with a tenderness that stunned her.

She reveled in the heat of his pressing lips, clutching at his lapels to keep him close. Truth to tell, she did not want the sensations to end. Constance threaded her fingers into Jack's hair, holding him close.

His lips twisted to apply more pressure. When he kissed her again, sucking on her lower lip, she wriggled impatiently. With barely a pause, he dragged in a breath, slid his own fingers into her loose curls, and pressed his lips back to hers, eating at her mouth until she thought she might die. He drew back and she drew in a quick breath, desperate not to miss a moment of this exquisite torture. She had no idea that kissing could be so marvelous.

Bridges obviously had not done it the right way.

Jack's lips came back to hers and stayed a little longer this time, burrowing against hers as if he wanted to devour her. Constance liked the way he tasted. Dear lord, he tasted as good as he smelled. His arms encircled her and her silky gown helped her slide the few inches separating them and into his embrace. Legs touching, almost fused together, Constance tightened her arms about his neck and pressed close.

Suddenly, Jack wrenched away. "Tea tray," he warned. He dropped one last fleeting kiss to her lips before stepping back and slightly behind where she sat, leaving Constance to wiggle off the table on her own.

Chapter Eighteen

———— ◆ ————

The library at Ettington House was one of Constance's favorite rooms. The book-thick walls muted the sounds of the world outside, the dark mahogany soothed her. Standing just inside the chamber, Constance gazed at the thousands of tomes above her. Jack and Virginia combined couldn't read them all in their lifetimes.

Her friends were both gone from the house and Constance was restless. All because of Jack. If she had been busy, going to parties and making calls, she would have been able to push these troubling thoughts aside. Everything could have gone back to normal.

However, Jack had been adamant that, due to her illness, she must stay inside and recover. His insistence postponed her pursuit of her last potential suitor and she fretted over the delay. Constance needed the distraction of Mr. Abernathy to keep her mind off the marquess.

He had indulged a whim by kissing her. No doubt triggered by his anger at Lord Bridges. But he had no real intentions toward Constance—not with his betrothed waiting for him. Jack was just trying to make her forget and feel better about Lord Bridges' attack.

And it had worked. She hadn't thought of anything much but Jack's lips touching hers.

Struggling to bring her mind back to the present, Constance

looked out the front window. Carriages rattled past, intent on some activity, but it was no use. She searched for the marquess' carriage among them. Chastising herself, she moved away and slid her fingertips over the smooth mahogany reading desk—the place where Jack had kissed her, held her close with such an insistent grip. The passion in Jack astounded her.

Nothing he did made sense anymore.

Constance sank into a low chair, her spirits sinking with her. Jack had become a very complicated man, a puzzle she had no hope of understanding.

Reaching for a book to redirect her thoughts into safer, calmer waters, she traced around the pattern of gilded vines with her finger and then the central motif pattern. Constance could not quite make out what it stood for—perhaps a flower.

Inside, the same red, trailing vines graced the cream endpapers. The book was titled *Les Manières de L'Amour,* and while Constance's French was not as perfect as it could be, she settled more comfortably into the chair, placed the pillow on her lap to hold the book, and opened it to the first page, expecting to find a challenge in the French novel.

It took several minutes for Constance's brain to comprehend what she held in her hands. The finely drawn and hand-colored pages depicted scenes she could not have anticipated. Scenes she should not be looking at.

Constance trembled. What wickedness was this?

She glanced at the door. Luckily, she was still alone. She turned the page and found yet another image, similar to the first. Then turned page after page.

They were all of a kind. It was a book depicting all the ways and positions to make love. Good gracious, there must be sixty pages.

Constance snapped the book shut, a blush burning her skin. How could Jack have such a scandalous book in his library where anyone might find it? She peeked again, but the book opened to another page and her mind refused to believe that a lover, a husband, would expect a woman to do that. Was it even possible or comfortable?

Constance twisted the book this way and that. Yet, no matter the angle, it still amazed her. Had she truly thought she could marry? Thinking of the gentlemen she had met this season, she hesitated at doing any of those things, with any of them. No, she absolutely refused to.

The front door opened and Jack's and Virginia's voices echoed in the entrance hall. Panicked, Constance closed the book, and then left it exactly where she had found it.

Hopefully, no one would suspect that she had seen the scandalous thing. She crossed the room, picked out another book, and pretended to read about arranging flowers.

But both her mind and her body thrummed because of those images. She grew hot, restless, and she patted her flaming cheeks with sweaty hands.

"Parkes, have you seen Miss Grange?" Virginia asked.

"Not recently, my lady. Shall I summon her for you?"

"No, Parkes. She is probably upstairs resting again. I'll peek in as soon as I change."

Virginia's footsteps faded up the stairs as Jack's heavier tread disappeared toward the back of the house. His steps were slow and measured. He was calm today, she thought with relief. Since the pond incident, his steps had been hurried and loud as he moved about the house most days.

Constance looked toward the scandalous book again. It was calling her. It beckoned her to learn all that it could teach. Constance almost laughed aloud. She had only just learned kissing. Kissing was very good, thrilling. She wanted—no, needed—more kisses.

She stopped pretending to read and sat back, thinking hard about the book and about Jack. Might he have done all the things depicted in that wicked book?

The thought worried her. It was his house, and very likely his book.

———◆———

Constance managed to secret the wicked book upstairs later that night. Despite the fact she had danced two dances with Mr. Abernathy at the evening's soiree, she had barely thought of him. And he was not the reason she couldn't sleep now. She held the page toward the candlelight and studied the pose. Certainly not ladylike. She doubted she could permit any of them, but the book had given her a tantalizing glimpse into her future.

Of course, she did not believe that only married couples behaved like this. She was not that naïve. But this new awareness proved a real distraction. She had not been able to concentrate on dinner, and had blushed harder when Jack had questioned her health. If he only knew the naughty thoughts swirling around her head, would he be ashamed to know her curiosity had been stirred by erotic images?

Constance accepted that men's minds turned readily and easily to sex. She had not realized that a woman was as capable of the same thing. She found herself watching Jack's movements, wondering what he looked like beneath his clothes. Of course, that caused a surge of embarrassment, and to excuse her high color, she'd coughed heartily.

Jack did look very good stripped of his coat. The curve of his rear, firm and well-muscled, encased in trousers drew her eyes. His broad back tapered to a trim waist. He was certainly strong enough for position thirty-four.

Constance leaned back, raised her legs high, and separated her knees. No, the space was still not wide enough. She parted her knees farther. A pillow replaced the man and she wrapped her legs around it. Constance groaned. It would bring Jack so shockingly close.

Constance hugged the pillow to her. Jack, Jack, Jack. Her mind brought her continually back to him. He was the man she imagined in bed with her. But it wasn't possible—she couldn't have him.

Rolling to her front, she shoved the pillow away and wriggled up the bed, reaching for the book again. The next page was very similar to the last, except the man was standing. Constance wriggled until her bottom neared the edge of the mattress. Yet it didn't seem right. She twisted back to the page, saw her mistake, and wriggled closer to the edge. When she twisted to view herself, her nightgown bunched at the top of her thighs and exposed white legs spread wide. The sight shook her, excited her. She pressed her head back to the mattress and panted.

The images in the book and her own imagination had inflamed her. But she had no idea what to do about any of it.

Blushing, she rolled face-down into the mattress and groaned. She was depraved, wicked, and so very confused.

A knock sounded at the bedchamber door.

"Yes?" she managed to squeak out, struggling to right herself.

"Is everything all right, Pixie?"

Jack's voice.

No, it was not all right. But she could not answer truthfully. Jack would never understand. Constance tried to think of a plausible lie. But none came to mind before the doorknob turned. Why hadn't she thought to lock it? Jack's fingers appeared around the door and then his concerned face.

"I am fine, really, Jack. Just having trouble sleeping, is all."

He paused at the door, his fingers pressed white against the dark wood of the door. "Perhaps, if you blow out the candle and actually got under the covers you might sleep better?"

Constance squirmed then realized her knees were bare and visible. She hastily tucked them beneath her nightgown and pulled the blankets over her lower half. "You are right, of course. Forgive me for disturbing you."

"You were not disturbing me." He seemed about to leave, but he glanced back at her once more. "You groaned. Is something vexing you?"

"Only a small matter."

"I would be only too happy to help, if I can."

Constance fidgeted, the hard edge of the book digging into her calf. She ignored the pain. Jack could not learn she had it. He was ridiculously proper sometimes. She risked a glance down. The book hid enough beneath the covers that Jack would never see, yet she squirmed with embarrassment. She had just spent the better part of an hour imagining Jack in this very bed, doing a great deal more than sleeping with her.

He looked wonderful in candlelight. Then again, he looked amazing in daylight. He looked altogether different, relaxed, yet tense at the same time. The ways that Jack might help her made her head spin.

———•———

Pixie fidgeted on the bed. She was up to something. The messy bed covers proved just how restless she was. The hills and valleys of coverlets couldn't hide, however, that her nightgown was gathered at her knees, or that the ribbon at her breast had come loose to expose a tantalizing expanse of skin. And one freckle.

That spot caused more mischief in Jack's mind than he realized at first. Blood swirled and pooled in one place, expanding his body in a way he had been fighting since they had kissed days ago.

Although Jack had judged her too sick to take things further, he was eager to explore just how well they might suit each other. Given their combined reaction to chaste kisses, he shuddered to think what it would be like to delve his tongue past those strawberry lips. He already knew a lot about Pixie—she was as hungry for kisses as he.

As she shifted restless, her nightgown parted further and exposed the plump curve of one breast. Jack's breath hitched. What he wouldn't give to press his lips there. He hastily raised his gaze, only to find Pixie's face flushed amid the halo of dark curls.

She bit her lip.

"I would give anything to know what you are thinking right now."

When her blush deepened to scarlet, Jack's muscles locked briefly, and then he was moving deeper into the room. She could not possibly be thinking along the same lines as he.

Her eyes dropped to the bed.

Jack didn't need the reminder of where she sat. "Shall I snuff the candles for you?"

"I can do it."

But Jack had already pinched her candle out, leaving firelight to illuminate the room. Pixie rose on her knees, and when he stepped closer to the bed, she hastily shoved the book she'd been reading fully under the covers. He touched her flimsy nightgown, rubbing the material between his finger and thumb.

Pixie's breath caught, her eyes widened.

When he touched her cheek, she swayed into his fingers with a breathy little moan.

Jack could not think of being proper. He could not make

himself leave her side.

When Pixie's eyes dropped to his lips, his erection throbbed. Leaning in, he drew in a deep breath. The scent of her perfume and another, deeper scent assailed him. He clutched her arm and she met his gaze. Firelight reflected off eyes glassy with passion. He dragged in another large breath. The unmistakable hint of aroused woman lingered on the air.

He forced himself to resist. He couldn't act on his desires yet. The existence of her suitor list, and his exclusion, still rankled. And there was one last name to have dismissed. He wouldn't be happy until Pixie gave up her ridiculous plan to marry for money. He meant to prove by deed, by word, and by patience how good it could be between them.

Jack pressed a kiss to her temple. "Sleep well, little one."

Jack retreated quickly. Yet the expression on her face was priceless. Her pout almost made him cross the chamber and take her in his arms again. But he didn't dare. He doubted he had the power to stop twice. He would join her on the bed and, in his current state, he would be hard-pressed to stop himself from taking things a great deal further than kissing.

Chapter Nineteen

———◆———

Constance placed her heeled slipper on the gravel drive, struggling to keep her balance. Jack had relented and grudgingly agreed she was well enough to attend a ball. And not just any ball—this was the annual Malvey masquerade she had heard so much about. She was so excited she almost danced without music.

The house before her was ablaze with light. Small fires lined the curved driveway, while moonlight streamed down from a clear sky to illuminate the gardens but leach away the colors. It looked like heaven. She couldn't wait to slip inside to experience the decadence she expected.

Virginia tugged Constance toward the house, her spirits high too. They had sipped champagne as they bounced along London's streets, gems flashing as they giggled like girls over the silliest things. It was good that Jack and Lord Hallam had decided not to accompany them for the short carriage ride. That stuffy pair would not have appreciated their antics during the trip. However, they had promised to meet them in the ballroom and be surprised by their costumes.

There was no receiving line, but champagne-bearing footmen waited on the broad front stairs, directing guests. When Constance and Virginia passed through the entrance hall, she caught their reflection in a large mirror and had to look twice. Virginia's pale pink gown was so fine it appeared transparent.

The sheath hung from a noose of diamonds and flowed loosely over her body without further ornamentation. Defying convention, Virginia's blonde hair hung to her waist, covering her back and parts of her ready to burst from the tiny bodice.

Constance's own outfit was eye-popping. Two tiny gold chains were all that stood between her and complete exposure. Sheer drifts of gold silk hung from her shoulders and gathered beneath her bust then fell to her feet. She shimmied the fabric around her legs as she looked about, enjoying the decadent slide across her skin. She looked like a gold butterfly about to blow away in a strong wind, but she flowed with the tide through the crowded house.

Virginia gripped her hand tight in anticipation.

Constance did not recognize herself behind the safety of the mask and prayed no one else would. As they entered the ballroom already swarming with costumed guests, eyes turned toward them expectantly. Appreciation glimmered behind the masks, and courtly bows and curtsies were exchanged, but no one hailed them as yet.

Sipping champagne, Constance looked about at the other revelers. She and Virginia were not the most flamboyantly dressed. She spotted no one she recognized, and concentrated on balancing in her high-heeled shoes, a necessary novelty due to the length of her frail, dress. She lived in dread of tearing it with a misplaced step.

When they moved deeper into the crowd, a voice hailed them, not by name, but with pretty words of poetry, and Virginia paused near a tall, dark stranger.

"What visions of delight I behold,
That makes a man feel bold,
To slip an arm around a pretty thing
And…"

The man spoke the last line directly into Virginia's ear and she swiveled to face him, letting go of Constance's arm. The caped, masked man touched Virginia's arm, caught up her fingers, and placed a kiss on each knuckle. He looked to be making love to her hand.

Virginia sighed and the desperate edge to it surprised Constance. The man touched Virginia's face and nudged her mouth closed before tugging her in the direction of the dance floor.

Constance made a move to follow discreetly, but hesitated. The air around the pair was alight with desire. She had no wish to interfere with Virginia's enjoyment of the evening.

A hard presence fitted against her back. Fingers stroked above the gold cuff on her upper arm. Constance slapped her hand over the borrowed treasure and anxious, glanced toward Virginia's retreating form. Her friend had stopped and was watching her. Virginia smiled broadly, nodded and turned away, following her handsome escort through the crowd.

Strong fingers wrapped over her protective grip and another hand took away her champagne. Constance could barely breathe she was so excited, so hopeful of what she'd discover if she turned around. Once a footman took the glass, the man curled his arm around her body. "You take my breath away, love," Jack whispered.

She breathed deep. His firm grip held her in place, but her pulse thundered in her ears. She slid her fingers to the back of his hand and when she found metal, she traced over the top.

The top was plain.

Disappointment thundered through her that she had imagined hearing Jack's voice until the hand turned to reveal a cabochon ruby set into the thick gold band. Jack had hidden it in his palm, to keep his identity hidden from everyone.

Only then did she raise her eyes and turn. Jack smiled down at her, his blue eyes twinkling in amusement behind a mask. She breathed his name and his grip tightened. He leaned in, bending his head to brush his forehead against hers.

"You seem surprised." Jack's face split into a grin. With lace at his throat, he looked like the portrait of his father in the drawing room, but with a mask instead of face paint and wig. He looked nothing like she expected.

The crowds melted away as she stared up at the gorgeous man she had known forever.

"Can I stay in your company tonight, Pixie?" Jack asked.

"Don't you have someone to meet?" Like a mistress? It was the perfect setting for a scandalous dalliance.

"I already found you. You look delicious." Jack's breath rushed over her neck and she shivered deep inside. His voice stroked all of her desires and a few she had yet to discover.

Constance swallowed. "You look wonderful, too. I cannot believe you kept your father's suit. It looks so good on you."

"And my mother's dress fits you to perfection, as well." His expression changed. "Have you grown taller?"

"High-heeled shoes," Constance explained.

A pleased smile flashed across his face. "I cannot wait to see those on your legs." Jack's voice dropped lower and caused gooseflesh to rise over Constance's body. "Come, let us find somewhere quieter to watch the spectacle the *ton* will make tonight. I want to talk to you."

"What about?" Constance asked, almost afraid of a reprimand about her daring appearance.

"Everything. Anything. I don't care. I've been dying to whisper in your ear all season."

His confession astonished her. She had no idea he hadn't said exactly what he wanted already.

Constance glanced about. She could spend the whole night alone with him at this ball without risk to her reputation, as long as they were not recognized.

Judging by the laughter around her, the tone of the gathering was lowering rapidly. There would be a lot of gossip about Town tomorrow, and from behavior that was far more scandalous than just talking. She might need a protector before the night ended. Virginia was otherwise occupied and she had no idea of when she might return. Besides, would anyone believe that the cold-hearted marquess would attend this scandalous masquerade?

Jack brought his lips to her ear, and his fingers twined through hers. "This way, my little Pixie."

She shivered as his lips brushed her skin, but let him lead her away from the ballroom. They moved slowly through the crowd, hands joined, while all around them raucous laughter rang out. Lady Malvey's ball would undoubtedly be an outrageous success, if it did not end up an orgy she suspected. A great number of guests had sampled the free-flowing champagne and stronger spirits, and the laughter was boisterous and utterly overwhelming.

The crowd was thick around the base of the stairs and Constance clung to Jack. He glanced at her, moved his arm around her, and directed her up the stairs before him. While Constance held her skirts clear of the steps, Jack curled his fingers about her hip, keeping her steady. Constance's pulse leapt.

When she reached the top, Jack's arm encircled her waist and they walked away from the overcrowded area. "This is better. Your dress could cause a riot and I might have trouble protecting you from all that."

She glanced up at him and smiled. "I don't like being pushed around by strangers."

Jack squeezed. "Far better to be pushed around by me then?"

Constance opened her mouth to speak but shut it quickly. She didn't want to argue about his bossy ways. She just wanted one short hour of peace with him.

Jack found a secluded place by the marble balustrade, hidden from most eyes by a wide column. By the time they stopped, Constance's skin was so flushed and tight that she had to fan herself to cool off. The air stirred the curls draped across her upper chest and Jack's nimble fingers slipped them back with the others behind her back.

The way everything dimmed when he was near and when he touched her, she may as well have been blind. Struggling to control her instinct to do something foolish, Constance turned to admire the ballroom below.

The dance floor looked chaotic from their vantage point. The small orchestra in the corner was no match for the crush of people before them. They were playing a waltz, but the dancers were not dancing it. Thanks to the freely supplied drinks, the dance floor was almost at a standstill.

Jack's arm slid possessively across her back and curled tight over her hip.

Constance gasped, as surprised by Jack's actions as she was by the man wearing a walrus head, grasping the breasts of a large-busted woman on the floor below.

"Lord Hobart has made an excellent start on his evening, don't you think?" Jack laughed into her ear. "But I believe he could be more discreet when entertaining his mistress. The woman hitting him is his wife."

Constance laughed with him and looked for the next act of decadence.

"Not everyone in the *ton* behaves as you would expect, Pixie," Jack whispered, sliding his fingers up and down her side. "We each have our temptations to manage."

She had known the ball was famous for scandal, but she hadn't quite imaged it was filled with sin too. Constance would have a lot of news to leave out of her mother's letter this week.

In the distance, she spotted Virginia. She, too, was not dancing the waltz. She appeared to be standing still, gaze focused on her dance partner. Virginia cupped his face. Even from this distance, she could see a shudder pass through the stranger. That touch was all the encouragement needed. Virginia's partner kissed her in the middle of the dance floor, surrounded by hundreds of members of polite society. Some of the observant even cheered.

Beside her, Jack muttered something she could not understand. She asked him to repeat it.

"I said it was about time."

He laughed, settled his hand more firmly at her waist and inched her closer.

"But your sister is going to…" she blundered, but he only smiled.

"Fighting can conceal other desires, Pixie," he whispered. "Virginia and Hallam have better things to do tonight."

It took a moment for Constance to catch his meaning. "No? That was him?"

"Oh, yes." Jack chuckled and wrapped both his arms around her waist.

"Ah, there goes Lady Malvey, making a very large spectacle of her departure," he muttered darkly. "She causes a scene every year, but next week she'll begin planning the next party."

"Some people like attention, some don't." She glanced around quickly. "If we are unmasked tonight—"

"Trust me, Pixie, no one will recognize us tonight and if they do it will not matter in the slightest."

She hoped he was correct.

When Constance glanced around Jack, trouble headed toward them. She froze. An unmasked Lord Daventry approached, a masked lady hanging on each arm. He shouldn't pay them the least attention, but the fear remained. Would Daventry recognize Jack? Would he stop and speak to his friend?

For a moment she thought they were safe, but then Daventry's smile grew wide as he looked them over on his way past. He winked at her.

Constance turned to Jack and his lips twisted in a rueful smile as he ran his hand along her ribs.

"He recognized us?" Constance shuddered at both the thought of detection and the pleasure Jack's fingers evoked. "Surely anyone else could?"

"Don't worry about Daventry—he can't abide gossip."

With Jack sliding his hands over her back and neck, teasing her with the light touch of his fingertips, it was hard to concentrate on being worried. When he drew lazy patterns across the bare skin of her shoulders and down, over her dress, she had to twitch her shoulders.

"Ticklish, are you?"

"Not really," Constance lied. If he knew the truth, she would stand no chance of avoiding further torture.

Jack's other hand toyed with her fingers until she could stand it no longer and she made a grab for him. She traced the lines on his palm to each of his fingers, examining the texture of his skin in detail. The crowds below faded away. She found a scar he had received from swordplay as a younger man and stroked the fine hair on the back of his hand up to the cuff of his sleeve.

All the while, his undivided attention and his hot breath ruffling her hair thrilled her. The hand at her back moved, long fingers curling in onto her belly. She let Jack turn her toward him and she ran her hands from his wrists along his coat sleeves to his upper arms.

Disturbed by the pose, Constance fiddled with his sapphire cravat pin.

When Jack tugged her hips, she fit her body along his. His groan made her shiver. She had not meant to misbehave tonight. She meant to watch others rather than participate. But she was obviously better at wickedness than she thought. She had never felt such a heady rush as Jack swept his hands over her possessively. She didn't want him to stop.

Suddenly embarrassed, she pushed against his chest. "There

are a lot of people moving this way."

"Hmm, I think you might be right. Perhaps we should go somewhere else."

"That might be a good idea." The words had barely left her mouth before he swept her off her feet, took the necessary steps to the closest door, and ducked them inside.

As the door closed and locked, Constance's ears rang from the lack of noise and the stillness of the dark chamber. Jack carried her across the room and sank into a high-backed chair by the window, settling her on his knees. She had sat on his knee before, but only as a small child. Yet it seemed so very different to do it at the age of one and twenty. His long, hard-muscled legs cradled her and his hands held her tight against him.

It felt right. Thrilling.

With Jack, everything created a twisting tension she couldn't get enough of. His lips pressed to her forehead, his breath tickled her skin. It was a fatherly kiss really, and she frowned. He was not her parent—she had never thought that.

Constance turned her face to him.

Moonlight illuminated his features as he held her gaze. "What are you thinking, Jack?"

"I'm thinking about your shoes. May I?"

Constance nodded, but butterflies assaulted her.

Jack ran his hand down her leg, grasped her ankle then covered her foot. He touched down to her toes and voiced a deep, appreciative groan. His fingers slid back up her leg very slowly. "Lovely, just lovely," he murmured.

Constance blushed, unsure of how to react to his words. She tracked his hand as it slid over her hip and settled at her waist again. When it moved higher and paused under her breast, her breath seized.

"What do you want from me, love?" The deep gravel of his voice sent chills racing along her limbs.

Constance squirmed on his lap as confusion and desire warred within her. She shouldn't allow him liberties but she wanted so much more still.

She licked her lips. "Will you kiss me again?"

"Any time you wish," he whispered.

Jack cradled her face and aligned her lips to his. Like the first time, his kiss began gently, but Constance still gasped at the sensations. He returned his lips more firmly, twisting his head to deepen the kiss. The masks touched and she pulled back to remove hers. Jack tugged his off as well and threw it away.

Without the masks to hide behind, Constance lost a little of her courage. She shouldn't be doing this. Jack shouldn't be letting her experiment on him. But Constance was powerless to say the words to bring them back to proper decorum.

He slid his fingers into her hair, brushing his fingertips across her ear and sending fire down her legs. His hand firmed around her head and then he began to kiss her again with greater passion.

If she thought she knew anything at all about kissing, Jack disproved her assumption in the next moment. His tongue tickled her lips and she gasped, opening her mouth at the unexpected sensation. He took advantage of her response to sweep his tongue into her mouth and the flavor of him exploded her senses.

Jack tasted of cinnamon too.

He claimed her mouth, exploring, controlling. She couldn't get away and she couldn't get enough. He ate at her mouth, sending her pulse racing. Constance's world shrank to where she touched Jack. He was her favorite smell, taste, and touch.

On instinct, she darted out her tongue to touch his. Jack groaned and withdrew, opening wide to let her explore. Constance tasted him, flicked her tongue across his, and reveled in the sweetness of his kisses.

Kissing Jack was beyond anything she had ever expected. His hands were moving on her body, fingers flexing and kneading as they kissed, melting her into puddles of longing. She explored his face with her fingertips, feeling the unique contours of a man she had thought she knew, but clearly had a lot to learn about still.

———— ◆ ————

Jack almost disgraced himself when her hands cradled his head. She wanted him, wanted his kisses, and he set about teaching her how to kiss thoroughly. He groaned as she became more aggressive, actively plundering his mouth with her tongue, sucking on his lips, and using her teeth to bite down.

His wicked Pixie was voracious in her passions.

Jack got a firm grip on her hair and sought control, but she was enjoying her first taste of desire so much that he only succeeded in arousing himself to greater heights. Her dark hair was gloriously soft over his fingers. He wanted to feel the whole of it sweep his bare skin.

Pixie resettled herself so she straddled him. Jack grasped her hips, stunned by her desire and how far he had led her toward sin. He wanted her desperately, but not here, not at a masquerade where any indiscretion might be uncovered. He had to stay in control. She had only asked for kisses.

Not that she needed much guidance from him.

Fighting desire, he lifted his head. "Don't wriggle so much when we kiss, love. I need to get you back out of the room without ruining that gown, remember."

Jack's voice came out as a lusty growl, and he hoped he didn't frighten her with his desire.

He tried to pull back, to regain control of their passion. But instead of complying, Pixie kissed him harder, pressing against him as her passionate nature took complete control of their encounter. Her fingers raked through his hair, massaging his scalp, holding his lips tight against hers. She clutched his shoulders and breathed the same air. If she kept this up, he would take her here upon the chair.

Jack cupped her breasts. The firm flesh was the perfect size and settled within his palms as if they belonged to him. Desperate for more, he brushed his thumbs over her pebbled nipples, and then pressed a thumb in.

Pixie stilled, finally aware of where his hand had wandered.

He kissed her again, but let his thumb drag off the hard point slowly.

She whimpered when their lips parted. "Jack?"

He pulled her head to his shoulder and held her tight. "It's called passion, my love, but we had best stop now. I do not want to ruin you in this house."

Constance ground her head into his shoulder and panted. He could fully understand her difficulty—he hadn't been prepared for the depths of their passion either.

When he thought she was calm enough, he stood and took

her with him, letting her slide down his body, a sweet torture that fuelled his desire all over again. As her feet touched the floor, Pixie's knees buckled. He caught her fast against him, pleased by Pixie's dazed reaction.

When she was steady at last, he reluctantly slid his hands from her crumpled gown to straighten his clothes. In her excitement, Pixie had undone the buttons on his waistcoat, pushed his coat back, and made a mess of his cravat. He looked down at himself ruefully. Well, he had wanted her to undo some of his buttons, but it appeared that she went a bit further than he had initially anticipated.

When he was as neat as he could hope, he pulled Pixie into his arms again, and swayed with her in the moonlight. Her hands fluttered over his chest, but soon settled. They couldn't stay this way much longer so he kissed her one last time, secured their masks in place, and led her back out to enjoy the rest of the night's entertainments.

Chapter Twenty

———◆———

Virginia placed her hand in the stranger's, caught by the dark fire in his eyes— determined to keep those eyes gazing on her tonight.

Virginia forgot her responsibilities to Pixie. Forgot she stood in a ballroom of society's finest in favor of her masked suitor's attention. The warmth of his gaze obliterated all her doubts. He tugged her toward the crowded dance floor, his gaze never leaving hers, a devious smile playing at the corners of his mouth.

When he dragged her into his arms, she tensed at the power of his hands. He could use them to hurt her if he wanted to. She should be afraid, or at least cautious, but those eyes, those hands, that scent, calmed her as nothing else could.

Bernard Hallam held her. He was her safe haven, her harbor. The dance floor was a crush of bodies that jostled them ever closer together, making it impossible to dance. Virginia let herself fall toward him, certain that he was the safer choice in this mass of throbbing humanity.

The hard arm around her back held her tucked into his body, twisting her away from dangers. She took a deep breath of his scent, and then closed the space between them, touching her body to his, reveling as his warmed her through.

Virginia's mouth grew dry. The champagne had made her thirsty.

When she licked her lips, her partner stopped so still,

appearing mesmerized by her mouth. Amazed by the reaction, Virginia did it again, then exalted as the full weight of Bernard's attention focused on her lips. The hand at her back dragged her the remaining distance. She had not thought they could be any closer. How wrong had she been?

Bernard branded her from breast to thigh. His warm breath caressed her cheek. Virginia flushed and lifted her arms to encircle his broad shoulders. He was all solid muscle beneath her fingers and her nipples ached under the thin gown at the thought.

Her body had never behaved this way before. It behaved with a will of its own—one she could not reason with. Only her mind was amazed, and thanks to her consumption of champagne, its voice was muted and dim.

The overwhelming heat of him, the scent of cigar and sandalwood, the possessive way his hand traveled her back, should have shocked her. But Virginia did not care. All her attention was poised, focused, as it had never been before. Bernard gave up his hold on her back and slid one hand directly down to her derrière while the other cupped her face. There was no room to move, nowhere to go, no reason not to stay. .

They swayed to the music, mesmerized by each other.

Bernard slid his fingertips over her jaw almost reverently. "Do you know that you have become more beautiful to me every day that I know you?"

She pressed her fingers into his hard shoulder muscles. "And you have changed, Bern. What has happened to you these last years? I thought you led a quiet, indolent life at Oxford. Have you taken up boxing?"

"Not boxing. I row twice a week, or I did," he informed her, his tone conveying his pleasure at her curiosity. "I will have to find a new amusement when I return home."

"Why are you still here? You do not like London. You do not like dancing, either. Yet you have been in London for weeks now. I could never imagine you in such a venue before. You always said that masquerades were pointless," she accused, struggling to find a point to her argument.

"They *are* pointless—if you don't know who you are with. I am here to dance with you. I only dance with you because you like it."

"Bernard, we have not danced together in years."

"Far too long, indeed."

While they spoke, he kneaded her derrière, his fingers sending waves of pleasure to her core. Virginia allowed it, but breathing normally grew difficult. She focused on his lips where another smile played—a smile she was not familiar with.

When he came no closer, disappointment thundered through her. Yet if she wanted things to change, to go forward, then it would be by her choice alone. Bernard would never push her. He would only take what she freely gave.

The fingertips on her face stilled. "I would never hurt you, Virginia. I could not do to you what he did. If the bastard wasn't knifed by that thief, I would have done the deed myself."

Virginia drew back, searching his eyes. "A part of me was afraid you had."

He shook his head. "I never left your side until you were strong enough. But he was dead by then, and I lost my chance to avenge you."

Virginia's eyes misted with tears. She shook them away and tightened her arms about his shoulders. He had cared for her and kept her secrets. Virginia's heart beat a proper beat this time. He was the truest friend she'd ever had. She raised one hand to his face and scratched against the light stubble on his jaw.

Bernard kissed her gently, but it was an awkward kiss. Virginia was still startled and half afraid to trust again. He must have known it too because he smiled gently and tried again. They kissed and this time it was heavenly. Perfect. Everything a kiss was supposed to be. The last hint of her hesitation broke away. She leaned into him and let him take over.

They had never kissed before—not once in the fifteen years of their acquaintance. As their lips brushed, a jolt of unexpected lust flowed through her, knocking her world into shambles. Bernard released her face, to stroke the curl of her ear, and then settled at the base of her skull. His lips firmed and applied more pressure, but he drew back as cheering swelled around them.

He rested his head against hers. "Come away with me."

Virginia panted hard. She felt so light. Free at last of her cares. "I thought I already agreed to that?"

She did not expect to be able to tease a lover, but she could behave no other way with him. They had always tormented each other, but his lust-filled glance made her heart race.

"I want to make love to you. To show you how good it can be," he begged.

As much as she wanted to agree, she feared there would be more pain like last time. "What if I can't accept..." She couldn't finish her explanation, too embarrassed to admit to the complaints her husband had hurled at her head.

However, he nodded as if he understood. "Pleasure only. I promise to make it good for you. Trust me?"

Hope flared in his eyes and she dipped her head in agreement.

Bernard moved them through the crowd quickly, keeping Virginia close by his side, protecting her with his size and aggression when anyone blocked their way.

Virginia was used to Bernard's arrogance, and she relaxed about what was to come. She knew him, even if there was an unfamiliar mood radiating from him. It might have been within him all along, but she had not witnessed it before. He excited her. It was as if she was seeing into his soul at last.

At the edge of the ballroom, he turned them down a long corridor and opened a door halfway down. He drew her in with him, locked the door, and pocketed the key. A fireplace glowed brightly, but she had no time to think before he pulled her into his arms again. His breathing beat roughly against her face. She should be afraid. Her mind screamed in fear, but thanks to her consumption of spirits, her body refused to listen.

A slight tremble flowed into her from Bernard. Was he nervous too? She shifted her long hair back behind her shoulders and Bernard's strangled gasp betrayed just how much he liked what he saw. His breath caressed her chest. Her nipples hardened to painful points as he gazed down at the flesh she had exposed to the firelight.

He kissed her lips again, and then drew back. His hands lifted to her face, caressing and seeking, slipping her mask past her eyes then letting it fall carelessly to the floor. His fingers ghosted over her hair, careful not to disturb it from sleekness, but his lips pressed to her temple then moved to the corner of her eye.

In the dim glow from the fireplace, she could not see clearly, but his black-masked face intimidated her. She slid her hands up to remove it then she traced over his lips, across his cheeks, over his nose, and up to his thick, dark eyebrows that had always fascinated her. She brushed her fingers over each one, smoothing out the short hairs with her fingertip. Virginia ran her fingers into the sides of his hair where the first touches of gray had appeared in the wavy locks. Her nails rasped over his skull, and he groaned heavily.

He would not hurt her. He was a teacher, her friend. He could teach her not to fear a natural thing. His thumb rubbed against her lips, and she kissed it as it passed. He stilled, then pressed his thumb against her mouth again. Virginia parted her lips, sucking on him instinctively. Lips touched again and his tongue tickled hers, then his mouth sealed to hers as he kissed her open-mouthed. His tongue invaded her in a possessive surge, shocking her to her very core. She struggled with the idea, the sensation of Bernard in her mouth, and tasted the exhilaration of him.

He taught her to accept his tongue, to kiss him back, to use her tongue to excite them both. She pressed her body to his as a torrent of sensation and mutual pleasure surrounded her.

Virginia did not feel them moving until her back hit the wall.

With the wall to support her, Bernard used both his hands. He devastated her. His hands swept her front to caress her breasts through the gown. Bernard squeezed, grasped, and stroked until her nipples peaked painfully. He rubbed his thumb across one nipple, and she moaned.

Bernard's primitive response thrilled her. He squeezed and rubbed her breast with one hand while the other cupped her bottom. He lifted her feet from the floor, pressing his erection against her core urgently.

The sheer strength of him stunned her. Virginia had never once considered that a lover could pick her up so effortlessly, as if she weighed nothing at all. He was totally in control. Bernard could do anything to her, just as Orkney had. She swallowed down the panic that threatened to overwhelm her, but Bernard must have sensed the change.

He lowered her feet back to the floor and gave her space, but he never stopped kissing her.

Virginia was grateful for the slight reprieve. Kissing Bernard was intense. She had no idea how to cope with her responses to him, let alone deal with the unwanted reminders of her husband's cruel treatment.

Cool air caressed her legs as Bernard raised her skirts. The brush of his trousers against her bare skin set her heart to pounding, but in a way that she sensed would only get better. With the panic gone, she pulled Bernard's body against her, flushing as the rough wool caressed her bare legs.

He rubbed her thigh and she curled a leg around him blindly.

This is what she should have felt with her husband. Not pain or humiliation. Passion.

Virginia looked up into Bernard's dark face and rejoiced.

He smiled, teeth flashing white in the firelight. "You are not afraid any longer?"

"No. I understand better now," she admitted, pulse thundering in her ears. The mix of cool air and his warm hand about her leg increased and added to her excitement.

"Good," he grunted, and adjusted his grip. "This is what lovers do…to ease the ache here." He slid his hand over her curls and gently cupped her sex.

Virginia gasped as he rubbed with firm pressure.

When she flexed her hips into his hand, Bernard was the one to moan. "Ah, my girl, I'm going to make you burn."

He moved his hand and she felt the tickle as his fingertips parted her folds. He gently explored and, to her embarrassment, a tremor shook her body. She gasped for air as he lingered between her legs, spreading her desire over her aching cleft.

A long moan escaped her lips, catching on a sob as he probed her flesh harder, sliding up to find and caress a point that made her shudder.

He swirled his fingertip around the sensitive nub and she pressed her head back to the wall, fighting for something, panting in short gasps in a counterpoint to his motions. His finger dropped lower and pressed inside. She'd expected pain and found nothing but pleasure. Her hips flexed and he grunted aloud before moving his finger in and out with firm strokes. Bernard's lips branded her neck, sucking hard on her skin, matching the noises he made with her wet lower lips.

His hand left her and Bernard fumbled with his breeches. Soft, burning skin touched her inner thigh. She had only a moment to prepare before he wrapped his hands around each of her thighs and lifted her high against the wall, legs spread wide.

Virginia squirmed at the loss of close contact, but he settled against her skin as his length nudged her entrance

She met his gaze as he slowly lowered her onto him.

He let her body weight slide her down, pressing into her possessively, inch by hot inch. Virginia expected to feel pain, but there was none—just pressure and deep, throbbing pleasure as he joined with her.

A flush of heat ran up her body. Bernard was so hot inside her. When she thought he was done, he flexed his hips to bury his whole length to the hilt. Some hidden instinct made her roll her hips, settling him deeper.

Bernard hissed out an exultant "yes" at her gyration. He yanked her skirts away, repositioning her against the wall, and kissed her roughly. She gripped him tight with her knees and clung. He flexed his hips, drawing out of her completely.

Virginia moaned in protest and was relieved when he slammed back in and out again.

Blood pounded in her ears and a dull roar was all she could hear besides Bernard. She loved it. Loved the feel of him, the steady push and pull of him inside her. She moaned again, higher, desperate. Bernard wrapped her legs around his waist, and pleasure built as he changed the pace, thrusting faster and harder. Virginia's head bounced against the wall heavily once, but she was lost in sensations she had never expected. Overwhelmed by his absolute domination.

She tried to look at him, tried to focus her eyes on him, but she was crawling out of her skin, blinded by lust, and a need greater than she had ever known. Her body clenched. She screamed and her body shuddered. She bucked against Bernard as tremors racked her body, but sobbed when he withdrew. He shouted her name as hot liquid splashed against her thigh.

In the aftermath, Virginia hung pinned against the wall as Bernard heaved in gasping breaths. She was so stunned she couldn't think. She wrapped her arms tight around Bernard's broad shoulders for support and knew she'd never be afraid again.

Chapter Twenty-One

————◆————

To Constance, Virginia looked like a cat that had fallen in a vat of fresh cream. Virginia reclined in an armchair, both legs draped over an arm, as she ate a peach—mellow and introspective. Clearly, a great many things were on her mind. Constance did not require incessant conversation, but she hoped they might speak at some point today.

One way or another, Constance would leave London very soon. But before she left for debtors' prison, she still had a chance to convince Mr. Abernathy she might make him a suitable wife. He was the last gentleman on her list—her only chance to avoid ruin.

Her behavior last night had been a mistake of mammoth proportions.

Jack might be the only gentleman who truly knew her, but he wasn't available. Their relationship could not progress beyond friendship or carnal pleasures. Yes, he had taught her to kiss, but he had also made a promise to marry another. She could not keep kissing Jack just because he was close at hand, even if he was exceptionally good at it. She had never heard of friends kissing forever.

Kissing either led to matrimony or scandal and a broken heart.

If she wanted to explore the startling feelings that had stirred within her, she would have to find someone else—a husband. Yet the thought of kissing anyone else was repulsive. She was quite certain she could kiss Jack whenever she wanted to and enjoy it thoroughly. She just could not allow herself to do it again.

She was ashamed by what she had asked of Jack, but, in truth, he should have said no. He should not make himself available to kiss anyone that asked.

Constance glanced at Virginia's neck again. Virginia might have done a good job with her cosmetics, but there had been a red mark on her pale skin last night and she could still see it now. Hallam had given her a love-bite. Constance wanted to giggle. Who would have thought the stuffy man had it in him to be so outrageous?

Another sigh rattled up from her heart. She was so confused. After their kisses, the front of Jack's breeches had appeared tighter than usual. She had made Jack desire her with her outrageous behavior.

He is betrothed, you fool.

Oh, but the things Jack could do with his mouth made her shift in her chair. How would she ever face the woman he married?

Oh, yes, I agree. Jack is a wonderful kisser. Constance rolled her eyes. That would probably be the first words to spill past her lips, too. She shuddered. What was she thinking to ask Jack to kiss her?

When she married, or when Jack married, could never see him again and trust herself to behave?

Probably not wise.

Disappointed and feeling very low, Constance slumped in her chair. The Jack she liked was the private man who knew all the naughty things she used to do and laughed about them with her.

That man had become her best friend.

Constance raised her hands to her hot face as the memory of his large hands cupped over her breasts filled her mind. Her nipples tightened.

He was the lover she wanted.

Last night Jack could have ruined her, but instead, he had kept a sane head about him and ended things before it was too late. They had been carried away on a tide of desire and it was perfectly understandable now why it had happened. Their good sense evaporated once they were alone together without a chaperone.

Constance stilled. Given the liberties she had allowed last night, Jack would know how badly attracted to him she was. How doubly embarrassing. Jack may even suspect that she thought of him a bit more than was proper. Dear God, he might think she even loved him and he would be right.

Constance closed her eyes as her heart began to pound painfully.

She couldn't fall in love with a betrothed man. But she feared she had.

"Is everything all right, Pixie?" Virginia's voice startled Constance out of her thoughts.

"Of course, everything is wonderful. Why do you ask?" Constance managed to stutter out, desperately wishing she had a fan to cool her face. *Was this really love?*

"Your expressions have just run through a dizzying array of emotions. What are you thinking about?"

Constance fought for control over her flushed face. "Nothing. It is nothing. How was your peach?"

Was she in love with Jack or in lust with him?

"Delicious." Virginia frowned at her obvious change of subject. "I forgot to ask, did you have a nice time last night?"

Constance shuddered. *Definitely in lust with him.* She could never tell anyone how she had truly spent her evening. Not even Virginia. "Yes, I had a wonderful time. Although, judging by the reports in the newspaper, I will have to deny attending that ball to anyone who asks me about the event."

"It was a bit wicked, wasn't it? I am so glad Jack decided to let us go. He promised to look after you and I trust he was attentive enough."

She nodded. He'd been very attentive. Protective and funny. She'd never enjoyed herself more. But was that love? Trying to forget Jack for a moment, Constance quirked an eyebrow. "And did you enjoy your evening?"

"As a matter of fact I did," Virginia confirmed. Virginia grinned shamelessly and looked down at her fingers. She looked like a woman well pleased with her life. Happy content. Was she in love with Hallam at last?

Her expression filled Constance with curiosity. "Virginia?"

"Yes, Pixie."

"Can you tell me what it is like?"

"What *what* is like, dearest?"

Constance traced the pattern on the upholstery nervously. She hoped Virginia would not be scandalized. "Making love."

When silence followed her words, Constance feared Virginia was too shocked with her. Constance yearned to know how it felt to be intimate with someone you loved.

"It was wonderful," Virginia replied, her voice a breathy rush of sound.

Constance lifted her gaze, hoping she would say more.

Virginia's skin had pinked, and she brushed her fingers along her jaw. "It was not at all what I had feared it would be like. The last time hurt a great deal. However, with Hallam, the experience was nothing short of bliss. I think I am not explaining myself very well. It is hard to put into words."

"There is a book I have seen, in the library," Constance blurted out. "Not really a novel, but pictures…pictures of people making love. Was it like that?"

"I have not really read a great many books in this house." Virginia smiled. "I do not believe ladies can learn everything they need to know for marriage from books anyway. I certainly didn't. The sensations are so very different, so very hard to express. All your thoughts, your whole self turns toward the man. At least, that was how I felt. For you, it may feel different."

"Why different for me?"

"You won't have the same fears that I had. Last night was a great relief for me. I—I worried that I was damaged. That I would not be able to enjoy what everyone else feels with their husbands or lovers. But it was nothing short of wondrous." She paused and smiled again. "When you go to the marriage bed, there will be nothing but joy for you. I promise."

"Do you think you will marry again?"

Constance may not be able to marry the man she loved, but Virginia could. She was almost certain that Virginia loved Hallam, and he certainly displayed possessive tendencies about Virginia. But Constance was uncertain whether Virginia had considered remarriage in her current frame of mind.

"I never thought to marry again," Virginia answered, yet a

blush flooded her pale skin with brighter color. Virginia was lying. She *had* most definitely thought of it.

"Virginia, if I wanted to attract a gentleman, what should I do? I have little time to convince Mr. Abernathy of the merits of proposing." Constance would need every scrap of help she could dredge up.

Virginia frowned. "Abernathy? But I thought you'd forgotten all about him."

"You know I cannot. There are debts to be paid. I must bring him up to scratch. He is my only hope."

"That is not true and you know it." Virginia shook her head. "I am sorry but, as your friend, I don't believe I should help you with Abernathy. He's not right for you," Virginia insisted.

"But Mr. Abernathy is a perfectly acceptable gentleman and it was you who made me consider him," Constance pressed. "What could I do to win him over?"

"You should talk to Jack before you do anything rash, Pixie," Virginia pleaded, and Constance wondered why she was so sure Jack could help. Jack was the reason she needed to speed up the process of courtship.

"I'm not an infant. I asked you, not Jack. I thought you wanted to help me?"

Virginia dropped into the chair beside her and gripped her hands. "I do. You're my best friend. As close to me as any sister might be," she pressed. "But I just think there are matters you should discuss with my brother before you try any desperate tricks to win over Abernathy. Promise me you will talk to him today."

Constance nodded reluctantly, but said no more. She did not like to lie to Virginia, but the truth was just too horrible. She had to stop depending on Jack. Although Virginia appeared crestfallen and stood to walk about the room, Constance hardened her heart. She'd have to win Abernathy's affections without assistance.

———◆———

Jack stood just outside his sister's sitting room, heart tumbling in distress. He probably should not be listening in at doors, but he liked to hear Pixie speak. But damn that bloody list. Why hadn't she given it up yet?

After last night, she shouldn't have any doubts about where her future lay. She belonged with him. They had both experienced the rush of astonishing desire building between them.

Anxious, he retreated down the hallway to a concealed space beside her door, waiting to say good morning. He was determined to start his day with Pixie's kisses. Then, he was going to talk her into forgetting Abernathy and take her out in his carriage. It was time to make his intentions public. But kisses were necessary first. Heady kisses where he forgot everything but the woman in his arms. He really did need her.

Jack did not have long to wait. Pixie's light footfalls headed rapidly toward him, and he snagged her as she flew past. He dropped his lips to hers and kissed her for all he was worth. She kissed him back as he tightened his arms around her.

When her hands were clawing through his hair, he let go of her lips to speak. "I missed you." Jack pressed a trail of kisses up her neck, stopping when he reached her ear.

Pixie squirmed without any real strength behind her protest, his hair firmly held by her tiny hands. "You can't do that."

"Why not? Didn't you miss me, too?"

Jack gave her no time to respond because he was kissing her again. He could not stop.

Pixie struggled to speak around his mouth and he had to pause. "Well, there is someone else to consider."

Their warm breaths twined between them, binding them closer together. "What the devil are you talking about?"

She pushed against his chest. "I shouldn't be kissing you."

"But you do it so very, very well." Jack kissed her again, wrapping Pixie tight against him, touching the delicate softness of her skin. Tangling their tongues until he had her undulating against him, her hands clutched the sides of his head. He opened his eyes. Her dazed expression made him smile.

"I did notice that. But it has to stop." She contradicted herself by kissing him. God, this little bundle of mischief amazed him.

"Don't ever stop," Jack told her and groaned as her lips found his ear. Oh, lord, but that was her teeth on him. Jack's arousal soared and he started taking steps toward his bedchamber.

"I'm sorry. One of us has to do the right thing and it's going to be me." Pixie was saying one thing, yet Jack could vouch for the ferocity of her attraction to him. He was ridiculously pleased.

"You don't mean what you are saying. You want to keep kissing me." Jack nipped at her neck again and headed south toward her gown's neckline. Just a little lower and he would touch the beginning of her breast with his lips. As his back hit his door, he reached for the handle, but Pixie skipped out of his grip and out of reach.

Her eyes were wide and filled with anguish. "I couldn't live with myself. Surely you can understand."

"No, I do not understand, Pixie. I want you." Jack spoke as firmly as he could, without shouting it for all to hear.

She backed up another step, shaking her head. "It's just because I'm close at hand."

Male voices from the floor below froze them where they stood. They both glanced down the staircase. Just out of sight, Parkes was receiving a caller. From the sound of it, Mr. Abernathy was here and asking to see Pixie. Jack looked at her in annoyance. She could not choose Abernathy over him.

The butler's heavy tread advanced up the staircase. Pixie backed toward her bedchamber door and escaped, leaving Jack alone to face his servant.

"Excuse me, my lord. Do you perhaps know where Miss Grange might be found?"

"Her bedchamber," Jack growled.

"Of course. Thank you, sir." Parkes started to turn away, but looked back. "Shall I have your valet return to your chambers to assist you?"

Jack glanced down. His clothes were a fright. "No, that is perfectly all right. I can manage on my own. What does Abernathy want?"

"He is here to take Miss Grange out in his carriage, I believe."

"Wonderful, just wonderful," Jack muttered as he stalked back into his room to straighten his own clothes.

———◆———

Mr. Abernathy's driving skills were a vast improvement after Lord Bridges' dangerous display. He was pleasant company, handsome to look at and, above all else, comfortable.

Constance was utterly bored by the time they reached the entrance to Hyde Park.

Joining the ranks of society in search of diversion, he circled the park, paused to speak to acquaintances, introduced her when required, and spoke about himself and his family with an open, friendly manner.

Overall, Mr. Benedict Abernathy was perfect for what she needed—a wealthy man able to afford her current debts—but she felt not one spark of attraction flow between them.

"Were you, by any chance, at the Malvey masquerade last evening?" Abernathy asked as they took a tight turn.

"No," Constance confessed, lying through her teeth. They had all agreed to deny attending. "I retired early."

For a moment he appeared disappointed. "Lady Orkney made a wise decision."

"I've always enjoyed a good story. What did you see?"

Abernathy scrunched up his face as if he had unpleasant memories. "There was far too much corruption for me to repeat, especially to a lady. I was extremely shocked by some behavior I witnessed."

Abernathy would be shocked if he learned that Virginia might have been one of the more daring guests in attendance. Constance was tempted to tell him, just to see how he reacted. "Did you stay long?"

"No, I circled the dance floor, bumped into an old acquaintance I recognized, and left early."

"Ah," Constance replied. He would have missed the fireworks and singers later in the evening. After kissing Jack, those had been the highlight of her evening. Jack had held her in his arms, whispering into her ear for the remainder of the night. Thanks to him sharing his confidences, she understood a great deal more about the *ton*. And after listening to what he had to say, most of them should be ashamed.

Constance summoned her best smile. "Are you in London for long, sir?"

He chuckled. "No. My sister is to be married shortly and we

are here only to spend an obscene amount on her trousseau while we wait for the happy day to arrive. Our house is at sixes and sevens over the arrangements."

"I believe that is the case with most wedding days." Constance was impressed she had him talking about marriage so soon into their outing. "Can you imagine the pleasure of your own?"

Abernathy looked grim a moment, then his lips quirked into a sad smile. He didn't speak immediately. Had she blundered? Perhaps she shouldn't show too much interest in weddings.

He drew in a large breath. "I think, perhaps, I won't marry."

Constance's mouth grew dry. "Oh, why ever not?"

Abernathy's expression grew pained. "The usual tale, I imagine. I lost my heart to an angel, but she fluttered her wings and flew away."

With a toss of his head, he threw the emotion aside and concentrated on the horse.

"I'm sorry."

Mr. Abernathy nodded. "So was I."

Constance looked away, blinking rapidly to hold back her tears. The poor man sounded heartbroken. If she had known of his past disappointment, she might never have pursued him.

Constance slumped a little. She didn't know if she had the fortitude to pursue a man with a broken heart. His words hinted that he wasn't over the woman, his angel, and it might take more skill than she possessed to turn his thoughts in her direction.

By the weary set of his shoulders, he dwelled in the memory of his lost love. If she looked in the mirror one day, would Constance see that self-same pose confronting her?

"You appear tired today, Miss Grange. Are you entirely recovered from your illness? I would not like to have Ettington take me to task for keeping you out too long. I understand you are very dear to him."

There it was—the first subtle suggestion linking them together. Before long, society would whisper loud enough to ruin her chances of making a respectable marriage. Humiliation would run her out of London faster than the creditors could chase her.

She rolled her eyes dramatically. "Sometimes the marquess forgets he isn't my guardian any longer."

"Well, I imagine you know him better than I. However, I

should return you before you catch another chill. I wouldn't like to lose the man's good opinion."

As wealthy as Abernathy appeared to be, he clearly wasn't strong enough to stand up to Jack. He would certainly have no chance against her mama. "Thank you, sir. I do think I feel a headache coming on."

Abernathy clucked the reins and turned for the park gates. "You should have said something sooner."

Despondent and at a loss for what to do, Constance sat quietly as the carriage turned for Ettington House. The lie she had just told brought heat to her cheeks. She hated lying and was very quickly coming to despise herself. London had corrupted her from the honest woman she had thought herself to be.

Clenching her hands together, she pasted a contented smile on her face but inside, she quaked. Aside from Abernathy, there was no one else. Did she have the skills necessary to turn a damaged heart in her direction? Could she do such a cold-hearted thing?

Ettington House loomed ahead—temptation waiting behind those impressive doors. Fearing another encounter with Jack, Constance was quick in alighting from the carriage, said goodbye to Abernathy on the street, and turned for the steps.

Parkes stood waiting.

The butler took one look at her face and drew her inside. She didn't speak, and thankfully neither did the butler because if he offered one word of inquiry about her drive, Constance feared she'd weep.

Once she gained her bedchamber, she locked the door, drew the curtains, and crawled into bed. Abernathy had been her last chance. He'd told her a great many things about his life, but all she remembered was that his hands were a little smaller than Jack's and that he didn't smell as nice.

Rolling onto her stomach, she slid her hands under the pillow and pressed her burning cheeks into the cool linen. Her hands encountered a hard object.

Curious, she struggled up and opened a small alabaster box. A pair of diamond earbobs rested on red velvet and glittered in the weak light. They matched the necklace Jack had already given her.

Snapping the lid shut, she pushed the box away and let herself give in to a hearty fit of weeping.

Chapter Twenty-Two

———•———

After two near misses with poorly managed phaetons, Constance and Virginia entered Hyde Park on horseback and rode along Rotten Row. Since they hadn't managed to get out on horseback since Constance's arrival, she was relieved to spend some time away from Jack.

Try as she might, she couldn't seem to avoid him in the house anymore. He had even caught her before she went riding—twirling her through an open door and kissing her senseless amongst the clean linens.

Given the cheeky smile Jack had given her when he let her come up for air, Constance thought he would try it again. That was why she had to leave. If she remained in London, Jack would forget his responsibilities to his betrothed. She did not want to be some kind of sordid distraction society whispered about. He had made a promise to another woman. Constance was only in the way.

Of course, now that she realized she loved Jack, her situation was grim. She couldn't honestly dredge up any interest in securing a husband. She wasn't the woman to mend Abernathy's broken heart. She'd burned the list this morning, tucked away the gifts she would leave behind, and begun to plan to return home on the mail coach.

Today's ride was her farewell to her horse too. Falentine

would stay with the marquess. She couldn't bear to sell the mare to cover the debts, so she would let Jack take Falentine back where she would be well looked after.

The Row teemed with eager riders. They occasionally paused so Virginia could introduce her to other acquaintances, but their greetings were thankfully short. Every rider was keen to keep moving. However, she could not escape the sensation of scrutiny and longed for privacy. There were too many eyes watching, eager to see her made a fool of again.

She and Virginia kicked their horses to a canter, letting the ever-present grooms follow along. Having the marquess' liveried servants trailing behind added more discomfort to her day, a constant reminder of how spoiled she'd become. Little luxuries, servants to fetch and carry out her every whim, would become an unpleasant memory to torture herself with in Fleet. The thought of debtors' prison chilled her, but she wouldn't let her grim future spoil this day.

As they approached a bend in the broad sweep, Constance spied a body of water—the Serpentine, she supposed—and a group of riders milling just off the track. She recognized Miss Scaling, her mother, and Lord Wade watching riders file past. Mrs. Scaling waved and good manners gave them no choice but to slow their pace.

"What a surprise to see you, Lady Orkney," Mrs. Scaling greeted Virginia, but she did not acknowledge Constance's presence. "Now we are guaranteed a splendid ride."

Virginia inclined her head, but didn't speak. She caught Constance's eye and nodded toward the path. Constance urged her horse alongside Virginia's dappled gray, but inside she fumed. This was to be her first, last, and only ride in London. She didn't want to share the moment with rude people.

As they rode along at an elegantly slow pace, Virginia's horse grew agitated by the unfamiliar horse crowding her other side. Falentine danced aside to give the gray room and Constance watched anxiously until Virginia settled the high-strung gelding.

But while she wasn't paying enough attention, Miss Scaling smoothly drew her horse between them and Constance found herself separated from Virginia. When Lord Wade's gelding joined her other side, Falentine began to toss her head, unhappy with her new companions. Wade's gelding nosed her mare in a most uncomfortable way, and Constance had no choice but to back her up.

"I say, that's a very fine piece of horseflesh," Lord Wade noted, turning his mount to follow.

Given that none of the party had deemed her fit to speak to before, Constance bristled at the abrupt statement.

"Is that a touch of envy I hear, Lord Wade?" Her tone lacked civility, but she failed to care. "I cannot expect you to be familiar with a horse from Lord Ettington's extensive stables, given your limited acquaintance with him. Excuse me."

She directed Falentine away from the Scaling party and looked for her groom. She was done with trying to fit in. She didn't belong and never could.

Virginia twisted in her saddle.

"Pixie, what's keeping you?"

How to answer that without sounding pathetic? Constance didn't know and had no wish to explain in front of strangers.

Miss Scaling, perhaps sensing that Virginia was planning an escape, backed her mount so its gray flanks butted Falentine's head. At the touch, Falentine shied and the gray lashed out with its hind legs, grazing Falentine's foreleg and narrowly missing Constance's riding habit.

It was all too much for her mare. Pushed and bullied by unfamiliar horses, Falentine threw her head then bolted. Constance cursed as the mare took the bit between her teeth and left the well-ridden path, heading for the green parkland beyond.

Virginia cried out, but Constance could not answer. She was too busy ducking low branches. All her concentration focused on her panicked mare as she plunged on, abruptly turning for the Serpentine.

Constance tightened her grip on the reins and tried to regain control. No matter the trick she used, she made little progress beyond a slight turn. With the Serpentine on her right, trees dotted everywhere else, Constance started to panic. She was unfamiliar with the park, but a stand of trees came into view directly ahead. Constance used all her weight on the reins, but she was unsuccessful.

The foolish horse was going to get them killed.

A shout reached her ears, and then the pounding of hooves drew closer, but could not risk a look. The mare was not tired and those trees were not getting any smaller. A snort at her side told her another horse had caught up.

Jack's stallion, Lucarno, drew level and advanced on the mare's head. He and his horse bumped, attempting to control Falentine's wild flight. The mare turned, but found another horse caging her in.

———•———

Jack cursed the mare. Trust Pixie's mount to grow into a contrary beast. Jack pushed his horse slightly ahead of Pixie and reached for the halter. Using Lucarno's bulk and his hands on the bridle, Jack got control of the horse by pulling Falentine into a long, slow circle, careful not to cause Pixie to slip from the saddle by a sharper turn. Both horses were blowing at the change, no doubt disappointed to stop their flight.

When they had slowed to a walk and finally stopped, Hallam walked his ugly gray in to take Falentine's reins. Jack dismounted, swept Pixie from her saddle, and crushed her against his chest.

She could have been injured—he could have lost her. His heart pounded so hard he thought he heard double. "What the devil happened? You could have been hurt."

He squeezed her again, and then worried for her ribs. Jack let Pixie go, pushing her to arms length to peer into her face. Her eyes were closed, but her hands gripped his forearms tightly.

After a moment's tense wait, listening to her settle into long, deep breaths, she opened her eyes. "I'm all right."

Although relief coursed through him, Jack turned away to examine the horse before anyone noticed him showing Pixie too much attention. Even in the midst of a near tragedy, desire turned parts of his body rigid.

The mare was heavily sweated and blowing hard. Jack soothed her with his gloved hands and started to check her over. As he ran his fingers along her front leg, Falentine flinched away from him.

Jack soothed the horse. "What happened, sweet girl?"

"She was kicked."

Jack whipped his head around in Pixie's direction. "And who was so ill-mannered as to kick at you, my love?"

As the last words left his lips, riders approached, and he turned as his sister, the groom and, calmly following some distance away, the Scaling ladies.

Jack swore. By the time he had finished expressing his irritation, Pixie's eyebrows were almost to her hairline. Now he understood. He could guess the *who* quite easily. Perfume, a pond, and now a bolting horse.

Despite his best intentions, Pixie was not safe gadding about London without him anymore. Her very life was in danger because he had failed to act—to prove to society that she was more than a mere house-guest.

She was his future, and if that meant publicly claiming her before she'd given up on the list, then he would. He would take steps today to show London that he did not possess a heart of ice.

Jack looked at Pixie.

A light sheen of perspiration marred her skin, her hair had lost most of its moorings, tumbling about her shoulders in chaotic waves. Yet he didn't think she'd ever looked lovelier.

Although he had wanted to avoid acting precipitously, he could no longer avoid it. Miss Scaling had better get it into her thick head that he had a very great interest in Pixie's welfare. If she were a man, he'd call her out.

Lucarno's head swung over Pixie's shoulder, docile and adoring, and she hung on his neck. Jack held his breath. With any other person, Lucarno would have tried to bite them long before this point. When Pixie let go, Jack pulled the stallion's head to him and tugged down. The horse obediently knelt.

"Oh, he will still do it!" Pixie cried happily, startled out of her frightened state by his horse's little-known trick.

Pleased, Jack mounted the stallion then held out a hand for her. This was going to be a very public rescue. Pixie walked to him with a little hesitation in her step, but he lifted her to his lap and waited while she arranged her skirts.

Jack tightened his grip on her waist. "Ready?"

Lucarno struggled to his feet, prancing about foolishly.

"Thank you, Lucarno," Pixie whispered, and then settled

against Jack's chest.

As a tremor raced through her body, Jack tugged her tight against him, gave her a little time to settle her breathing, and then turned his horse toward the closing riders.

"I am so sorry, my lord. I don't understand how she got away so fast," the groom blathered, fittingly embarrassed that something should have happened on his watch.

The fellow had but one job to do. Jack had employed him specifically to keep Pixie out of trouble.

"I am perfectly all right, sir. Would you be so kind as to relieve Lord Hallam of Falentine's reins and return her to the stable? Have Brown go over her forelegs," she requested, but a faint tremor betrayed her fright.

"Yes, both of you return home. Once Falentine has been cared for, I want to see you in my study," Jack snapped, unconsciously tightening his grip at Pixie's waist.

The servant paled. "Yes, my lord."

"Jack," Constance warned, digging her fingers under his to loosen his grip as they moved to follow at a slower pace, "there's no cause to scold your servant."

"He has gone soft, Pixie." Jack smoothed his thumb over her belly and her body lost some of its rigidity. A pity he couldn't say the same. With every jolt of horse's hooves to the ground, Pixie's hip nudged his groin. He was going to be in agony before they even left the park.

Pixie turned, trying to look at him, but her hat bumped his nose. "It wasn't his fault."

Virginia and Hallam flanked drew close, watching him and nodding in unison.

He sighed. "Get rid of the hat, Pixie, I want to keep my eyes."

When she removed it, he stuffed it between them. "I gave the fellow a list of instructions explaining how to keep you out of trouble, all of which he seems to have ignored." Jack grumbled, as Miss Scaling and her mother blocked their path back to the safety of Ettington House. "But enough of that now—we have unwanted company."

"Oh, my lord. Such splendid riding, such elegant horsemanship," Mrs. Scaling gushed, sickeningly eager, as always, to stay in his good graces.

Jack spared her no attention and kicked his mount to a trot. Miss Scaling turned her horse aside quickly but moved up beside Virginia and it annoyed the hell out of him that they would follow them from the park. The young blonde smiled with a pretty mix of innocence and calculated flirtation, but her eyes eventually strayed to Pixie's presence in his arms. Her glance turned cold and calculating. Pixie pressed into his chest, recoiling from the venom in her stare.

Jack dropped his chin to rest on Pixie's head. "I'm taking you home."

Pixie sighed deeply. "Yes, home is where I long to be too."

Virginia beamed at him.

———◆———

Unsure what to make of Virginia's sudden happiness, Constance kept her eyes on the Scalings' party. She didn't trust them.

"Come along, sister. We'll be late."

Virginia soon joined them but glanced around the gathering crowd.

Word of Jack's behavior would spread, and Constance shuddered at how society would perceive her current situation. Jack's betrothed would certainly hear of it.

"We look forward to seeing you at the Frampton soiree tonight," Mrs. Scaling called after them. A ripple of interest passed through the crowd, but neither Virginia nor Jack acknowledged her words. Hallam's horse fell into step beside them, but Jack kicked his stallion and headed for the park exit.

Even amid the bustle and noise of London's chaotic streets, Constance felt very safe. But she wasn't fool enough to forget her ease had a lot to do with the strong arm wrapped tight around her middle. She could breathe now, and when she did, she drew Jack's cinnamon scent deep into her lungs, hopeful this last breath would sustain her.

Jack's arm tightened, tension evident in how close he held her against his chest. He was not relaxed at all.

"You frightened me very badly today, Pixie," Jack admitted as they turned up Park Street, taking a detour to avoid the more congested route toward his home.

"Well, I did not do it on purpose, so I don't see how you can be angry about it. It wasn't my fault."

She raised a hand to rub her brow. Her morning had not gone as planned. She'd wanted one last pleasant day before she left. Miss Scaling had ruined it.

Jack's arm tightened into a possessive squeeze, and then he relaxed. "Have you not learned a new excuse yet, love? That has been your reply for any misadventure for the past few years," he cautioned. "It's time to find a new one."

His breath tickled the back of her neck and she struggled to maintain some decorum. "Well, I've always thought the old excuses were the best. It is important to have your own traditions."

"Speaking of old, you frightened me out of ten years of my life today. A decade I could not afford to lose since I am almost a relic to begin with."

Constance frowned, surprised by Jack's attitude toward his age. She hadn't thought he would pay attention to her hasty words. Privately, she thought he was the perfect age—old enough to understand the world, but young enough to still laugh at it. Except he hadn't done a great deal of laughing lately. His situation with Virginia has sobered him quite a bit.

"You're not old, Jack. You may be eight years my senior, but you're a long way from needing spectacles and a nursemaid to bring you gruel for every meal." She laughed at a sudden thought. "And besides, a sword cane is hardly an affectation of an old man. Have you had a great need of it in Town?"

"Husband-hunting debutantes," Jack admitted sadly, but amusement laced his tone. "You can never be too careful with your virtue."

A great pity Jack hadn't taken it to the Malvey masquerade. "At least you don't have to use your fists too often these days."

"I know you feared I was becoming too much of a hot head, but believe me, I find very little reason to thrash my fellow man," Jack promised. "Except perhaps where you are concerned. For you I could commit murder."

Constance turned. Jack looked rather serious about that. It was a very odd confession too. She had been very ready to wash her hands of him four years ago. Virginia's long-lettered protests had persuaded her that, while not cruelly intended, Cullen had provoked Jack. But all of that discussion had taken place within private letters that should not have been shared.

Constance gulped. "Has Virginia shown you my letters?"

"Not exactly."

She had written very harshly of Jack at times, and wished to slide from the saddle and disappear.

"I am very glad I wrote nothing shockingly private in them." Another lie. She had poured out her hurt in those letters, strongly protesting against Jack's high-handed ways.

"I am sorry. I did not mean to pry. I was concerned about how you were getting on up there. I took my role as your guardian very seriously, despite your mother's protests."

Constance faced forward again as she considered those letters carefully. A small thing had been puzzling her for years and she meant to find out now. "Did Virginia develop an interest in farming and agriculture in the last year or have you been dictating to her?"

Jack's lengthy silence behind her back unnerved her. Now that she thought about it, the tone of the letters had changed too. She had thought that marriage might have accounted for the formality, but a shocking idea was forming, and it had some merit. "Have I been corresponding with Virginia at all?"

Gentlemen did not write to unmarried women unless they had an understanding. Jack had one, just not with her.

"Yes, of course. I mean, no, not precisely. Sometimes." Jack's chest swelled behind her and his hand fidgeted at her waist. "When Virginia's situation changed after marriage, I kept up all her correspondence, including yours. I regret not informing you of Virginia's true circumstances, but I could not put her situation in a letter. Given your mother's habit of gossiping, I couldn't risk my sister's reputation. If you require one, I most humbly beg your pardon. I would not have you unhappy."

That was quite a confession. Jack had been writing her letters for years and she had not been able to tell the twins' handwriting apart. Although she couldn't know for certain which letters he'd penned, they'd all contained words of deep affection, and had all but begged her to come to London too.

Constance blushed. "I looked forward to receiving those letters, Jack. And, yes, I did need the help and guidance you sent. Thank you for thinking of me."

Jack's sigh rattled through his chest. "I shall have to admit now to impatience at receiving yours. You are a very tardy correspondent, Pixie."

"Virginia would have forgiven me."

"My dear sister will forgive you anything. But I have to tell you, the lengthy delays between letters made me worry."

The gloved hand at her waist tightened, and she hesitantly covered his hand with hers. "Did you send me perfume for my birthday, and at Christmas, too?"

Jack drew in a large breath and slowly let it out. "Another impertinence, but I love the scent on your skin."

Chapter Twenty-Three

———◆———

"**M**iss Grange!" Cullen Brampton's anguished voice cut through the pleasurable daze in which Constance rode, and she looked down to the pavement beneath her. There, waiting on the front steps of Ettington House, stood her former betrothed.

The marquess' butler, in the act of closing the door, froze in shock—and this time his expression was clear. He did not care for Cullen, and that puzzled her. Everyone liked Cullen. Well, everyone except Jack.

"Good afternoon, Cullen. When did you arrive in Town?" Constance called, and then instantly regretted her familiarity. This was London, not Sunderland. She should not embarrass Jack by behaving as a hoyden in public.

"Just this morning. Here, let me get you down."

Lucarno danced away from Cullen's approach, forcing Jack to work to calm him. After her scare this morning, Constance's heart was very quick to race again. But she found herself just as soothed by the marquess' whispered words across her neck as the horse was. By the time Lucarno was steady again, Constance was sure that her own dazed reaction to Jack was visible to all around.

"Step back, Brampton," Jack ordered as a groom ran to his horse's head. "Your kind of assistance is not required."

Jack passed Constance her hat and swung off, but immediately turned to wrap his hands around her waist. She floated from the saddle to the ground, but could not miss how irritated Jack was to see Cullen standing next to them. Gripping his forearms, Constance whispered her thanks.

Cullen quickly moved to offer his arm.

"It is good to see you, sir," Constance told him as she fiddled with her sadly squashed hat rather than take it.

"And it is very good to see you. Be happy, I have come to take you home."

Constance's head snapped up and she stared at him in confusion. "Home?"

Cullen held a thick letter with her name scrawled large on the facing side and then his arm. She shook her head. Letters never contained good news. When she didn't take either, he frowned. "Your mother sends for you. She rightly feels you have dallied in London for long enough. I have my carriage ready and waiting to depart within the hour."

Why would he speak to her as if nothing had changed? Had he not received her letter?

Virginia and Hallam drew up and dismounted. Constance quickly performed the introductions. Pleasantries done, Virginia took Constance's arm, tugging her toward the house. "A public discussion will draw a crowd," she whispered out the side of her mouth. She turned away. "Mr. Brampton, I am sure you will agree to join us inside," Virginia called to him.

"After you, Brampton," Jack muttered harshly.

Jack's response seemed to needle Cullen. He swiftly moved to take Constance's other arm to escort her up the stairs. Strung out between Virginia and Cullen, all of Constance's nerves bristled.

Once inside Constance passed the butler her sadly dented hat and then turned on Cullen. "I cannot return to Thistlemore with you. I am so sorry that my mother sent you on a fool's errand. She should not have sent you."

"Come," Virginia urged, leading the way into the drawing room.

Cullen caught up her arm and directed her to a settee, then took up all the space at her side. "The only foolish thing was coming to Town in the first place. You should be at home awaiting our marriage."

Virginia gasped and Constance winced. Clearly, Jack hadn't

told his sister about the betrothal either.

"Did you not receive my letter?"

"I've received no letter."

"That's a lie." Jack insisted. "It was delivered into his hand by my own man."

Virginia grasped her brother's arm and dragged him toward a window. Hallam, however, stayed exactly where he was.

"It was so obvious you forced her to write that letter that I could not believe a word of it," Cullen complained. "I'm here to save you from him."

Cullen took her hand and squeezed.

Hallam growled, settling into a chair opposite. "Mind your manners, pup. Miss Grange needn't be mauled."

Constance clenched her hands together in her lap. "I wrote that letter myself, Mr. Brampton and I am sorry to say I meant every word. I cannot marry you."

Cullen blanched. "Constance, what is the meaning of this nonsense? You can tell me the truth."

Constance winced. "The truth is I must decline your offer of marriage. The circumstances that I felt sure of when I originally accepted your offer no longer hold true. I cannot, in good conscience, marry you."

Cullen gaped at her. "But what about our plans for Thistlemore?"

"Thistlemore will survive, perhaps with a different vision for its future than we expected." Constance peeked at Jack across the room and he nodded. He would keep her home. He would keep his word never to kick them out, too. "I apologize, sir, for the inconvenience."

"Apologize? Apologize!" Cullen screeched. "Your mother will certainly have something to say about this."

Hallam cleared his throat and stood. "I believe it's time for Mr. Brampton to take his leave. The subject is closed for discussion."

Cullen scowled. "I am still charged with taking Constance home. We will leave first thing tomorrow. Go and begin your packing."

Constance bristled. "I cannot travel alone with you, and you well know it. I will make my own way home."

Traveling alone with him in a carriage for that length of time would ruin her reputation. Of course, given all the kissing she'd practiced on Jack, her reputation was already a little worse for wear.

Cullen looked like he wanted to argue again, but Jack took her declaration as an opportunity to throw his oar in. "Miss Grange has had an eventful morning, Mr. Brampton." Jack's smile never faltered as he turned. "Parkes, be so good as to see Miss Grange's guest to his hat. He is leaving. Now."

Cullen glared. "How dare you. You are no longer her guardian to say what she can or cannot do. You will not bully me about either."

"Is that so?" Jack advanced and Constance quickly put herself between the two men.

"I do thank you for calling on me, Mr. Brampton," Constance whispered. "Please give my regards to my mother should you see her before I do."

Cullen didn't look happy, but he did take his leave with a promise to return tomorrow.

Constance twisted her fingers until Virginia prompted her to look at her letter.

Instead, she turned to glare at Jack. "Did I ask you for your interference?"

"No," Jack grumbled.

"I want to remain on good terms with Cullen and his family. They are my neighbors and were almost family to me."

"Be glad it was only an almost," Jack muttered, settling into a chair. "I thought the idiot would have learned his lesson last time we met not to cross me."

"You mean when you thrashed him for no good reason?"

"Oh, I had a reason for the pleasure, believe me," Jack argued, surging out of his chair to pace to the front windows.

"I doubt that."

Jack growled. "Pixie, you were halfway up an apple tree. The little sneak was looking directly up your skirts."

"He did no such thing," Constance protested.

"Of course he did—why do you think I thrashed him? Do you truly believe I would waste my energy on that worthless excuse of masculinity? I told him to stay away from you. I warned him what

I would do if he behaved without honor toward you again. I had caught him hanging from the side of your house the night before, peeking into your bedroom window one night. Did you wonder why I ordered the rose vine removed? It wasn't damaging the house."

That silenced her. "What!"

"Miss Constance Maria Grange," Jack said with deadly earnest. "You really shouldn't climb trees without first adding drawers to your undergarments. He was standing directly beneath you with a rapt expression plastered all over his scabby face. He didn't believe my threats. And as your guardian, it was my job to protect you from your own lack of foresight. Looking after you seems to be my lot in life."

In the silence, the only thing she heard was the ringing of Jack's departing boots. Constance could not make herself look up. Her face was flaming so hot with embarrassment.

Another set of boots departed and a swirl of muslin overlapped her knees as Virginia hugged her.

———◆———

Jack tossed the last of his drink back and let the masculine peace of his club calm him. He was so stupid. Pixie hadn't known about Cullen's spying. God knew what else Cullen had been up to in Jack's absence. Jack had always disliked Cullen Brampton, but since Pixie's parents had included Lord Clerkenwell as part of their circle, Jack had suffered his presence when his family had visited. Given Brampton was Clerkenwell's heir, the man seemed attached to the little rat.

Catching Brampton spying on Pixie, however, had added completely new levels to his dislike. No gentleman behaved that way. The image of Pixie married to that scar-faced scoundrel set his guts to churning. Jack was marrying Pixie, whether she realized it or not. And then he'd see if Brampton's interest in friendship remained. He doubted it. But he still had to convince Pixie that he was her perfect match.

The chairs on either side of him creaked, and a pair of glossy boots and another set of knees impinged on his vision. Jack raised his head.

Lord Daventry watched him, eyes alight with amusement, but Lord Hallam appeared deadly serious. Jack seized a whiskey glass from a passing waiter, and tossed it back.

Daventry raised a brow. "Why the devil aren't you married yet?"

Since his friend rarely meddled in other people's affairs, Jack was surprised by his question. "I don't know what you are talking about."

Daventry glanced about them, and then sat forward. "Well, I will tell you what I see. I see two friends making each other miserable. What do you think you're doing? You had her at the Malvey ball, didn't you?"

"I did not attend that one." A few men moved in their direction. Jack scowled and they thought twice about joining them.

"Don't talk rubbish," Daventry grumbled. "I recognized you both. I do walk around London with my eyes open. You had her, man."

"She does not want me, Daventry. She has a list of potential suitors," Jack admitted.

"A list? I hope that slimy toad on your doorstep a short while ago isn't on it. I thought Parkes was going to shoot him when he wouldn't go away." Daventry sighed. "Her eyes follow you, Jack. One day someone will see it and make a joke about it. She will be so mortified, she'll return to Sunderland and you'll lose the chance to start your marriage the right way."

"Daventry, you really should shut up."

A look of disapproval crossed Daventry's face. "Are you going to make her your mistress?"

Before he could prevent it, Jack had curled his hand into a fist.

Daventry noticed and laughed. "I thought not." He smacked Jack's shoulder, making heads turn toward the sound. "Offer for her. Quickly. My nerves cannot stand the suspense."

But what if she refused?

Jack glanced at their silent companion. Hallam grimly held another glass. He looked uncomfortable. He wanted something, and Jack knew Hallam hated asking favors. "What is the matter, Hallam?"

"I had a letter from my mother's companion this morning. Mother's eyesight has failed completely."

"Damn," both Jack and Daventry muttered. Lady Hallam was a decent woman; neither of them wanted this for her.

"I have to return to Parkwood. She should not be left alone to manage the estate with me here. My bags are being packed, and I will leave this afternoon."

"I'm sorry, Hallam," Jack said. "Have you told Virginia?"

"No, not yet. I will tell her this afternoon. How long will you be staying in Town?"

"We will be home as soon as I can arrange it," Jack offered. He would not rush his courtship of Pixie just so Virginia could be free of her chaperoning duties. "As soon as I can."

———— ◆ ————

"What are you doing in here?" Constance asked as a maid rammed Jack's appointment book back into the shelf and spun about.

If Jack had not specifically mentioned where he kept it, she might have ignored the maid's activities. The girl looked ready to burst from her skin.

"I was just practicing my reading, miss. I did not mean to neglect my duties. If you will excuse me, I had best get back before I am scolded." The maid curtsied and made to leave, but Constance was having none of that. She kicked the door closed with her foot. The little maid yelped.

"I don't believe I dismissed you." Constance leaned against the door. "That wasn't just any book. How long have you been spying on the marquess?"

The maid gasped and drew back in horror.

Constance tipped her head to the side as she inspected the maid. She appeared no richer for her activities. "I have often wondered how Miss Scaling always knew what entertainments the marquess and his sister were attending. You have been telling tales, haven't you?"

Constance waited out the silence until it stretched to the breaking point.

"Please, miss, don't tell the marquess! He will dismiss me for sure," the maid pleaded.

"Lord Ettington would be well within his rights to dismiss you," Constance agreed. "He values loyalty above all else."

"I know, but I had no choice. My mother and my brother work for them. They would have tossed my family out with nothing if I hadn't done as they demanded. Mrs. Scaling is a demon in disguise."

The little maid wept and Constance stayed firm only a moment longer. The girl deserved a good scare, and there was a fiendish way to deal with this mess.

"Sit down."

Constance pulled the bell to summon the butler, and the maid wept all the harder. When Parkes arrived and Constance told him what she'd discovered, he was so angry she thought he might burst something. However, when she explained what she wanted done, the butler was beside himself with glee. He ushered the maid out the door.

Constance ran her fingers over the elegant script in the appointment book. Jack was not going to be writing to her anymore. When she pushed him away, she would give up all hope of continuing their friendship. Her heart ached.

She looked at the scratched-out names and the circled one, and she smiled.

At least she could do this for him to repay him for his kindnesses. The maid would report only the first crossed-out name. The Scalings would have a name that Jack had written in the appointment book, but not the event he would attend. Unless he changed his mind, their paths should never cross.

If the Scalings dismissed the maid's family from employment, they would approach Jack's butler about a position. With luck, Jack wouldn't turn them away once he knew the truth. All around it was a good decision. The maid was young and foolish, but she was good at her job. If she was dismissed out of hand, they would only corrupt another member of the staff. It was a perfect revenge, subtle, yet with a nice sting in the tail. The Scalings should be chasing Jack's shadow for some time.

The front door slammed, and booted feet ascended the stairs. Lord Hallam's tread if she were not mistaken. Uninterested in what he was in a rush over, she wandered up the stairs to see if Virginia was ready to go out, but at her door, Constance hesitated. At the moment before her knuckles would have touched the bedchamber door, a bed frame creaked and the low-pitched murmur of a male voice carried through the door. Constance backed from the door and, as quietly as she could, fled downstairs.

That had been just a little too close for comfort.

With nothing to do but wait, she took refuge in the library, watching the world outside through the far window. Jack's carriage returned and he stepped out of it with a parcel tucked under his arm. Curious, she sauntered to the library doorway to spy on him. Jack did not see her. He swept through the hall and took the stairs two at a time, leaving behind the scent of a cigar. Constance enjoyed the view. Jack's legs were truly worth watching.

The butler discreetly coughed into his glove. "Lady Orkney regrets to inform you that she will not be making calls today, Miss Grange."

He handed her a note, and Constance was both surprised and annoyed by the hastily penned apology. Hallam was leaving. Constance was not going to stay in the house while Virginia and Hallam said their goodbyes. They might not come out for hours.

"Thank you, Parkes," Constance replied, keeping her tone light. "Could you inform the stables that I am ready to go out?"

"You're going alone?" the butler questioned, and his query surprised her.

"I am going to tea, Parkes, and will take a maid if you will fetch one." She shrugged. "Nothing bad ever happens at a tea party."

Chapter Twenty-Four

———◆———

"It is a pleasure to see you, Lady Marchmouth. I am so sorry, but I must convey Lady Orkney's apologies. She is suffering a headache and has remained abed today." It was not a complete lie. By the time Constance returned home, she expected Virginia to be exhausted.

"It was so good of you to call and inform me personally. Please, won't you join us?"

"Thank you."

Lady Marchmouth encouraged her to sit in a nearby chair, introduced her to the other women present, and pressed tea and biscuits on her with a smile. "I, myself, am always in excellent health," she promised. "Marriage is a great cure for many ills. It is such a shame that she became a widow so young. She must still be deeply distressed over losing Orkney in such tragic circumstances."

Constance tried to come up with a diplomatic response and could only think to incline her head. Lady Marchmouth looked elated. Botheration. The woman would scramble that into nonsense and twist it until Virginia was close to death, pining for her late husband.

"It is such a pleasure to see you up and around again. Have you recovered completely, Miss Grange? I understand the marquess was most attentive during your illness." The lady was fishing for anything that might lead to more gossip, but Constance knew her type—she was just like her mama. A sugar-coated schemer.

"Actually, I saw very little of the marquess while I was ill. I was confined to bed by the doctor's orders." She held the viscountess' gaze without flinching.

Finding nothing scandalous in her words, the lady settled into a happy gossip about other people. When they touched on Agatha Birkenstock, Constance sipped her tea to hide her grimace. They concluded that she had set her sights for a very highly placed gentleman. They even hinted at a future duke.

Lord Carrington's engagement was commented on, his betrothed praised for her elegant manners. They voted him the most agreeable man in the *ton*—always so obliging to dance with absolutely anyone irrespective of their position in society. That sounded mildly insulting since Constance had danced with him several times herself. But she knew better than to let a reaction show.

"Lord Wade happened to be collecting a pocket watch that he left for repair and saw the whole transaction. Only this morning, too," Lady Marchmouth gushed. "Deep red stones set in a crust of fine diamonds. Astounding piece, he said. Far too rich for a mistress to wear, he must have decided to marry at last."

"They say he has spent a small fortune these last weeks," another lady piped up, eager to share in the news. "New carriage, and a house in Bath too. He never quibbles over the cost, you know. You can't call him cold-hearted any longer, the way he spends his blunt, can you?"

The ladies swooned over the still unnamed gentleman's good taste as if he was more than mortal while Constance cringed in horror. Nothing remained a secret in London for long.

Then she remembered that Jack had returned home with a parcel tucked under his arm just this morning, and that he was the man society called cold-hearted. He had ordered a new carriage recently. Did they mean him?

While her stomach lurched with agitation, she could not show it. Constance concentrated on pressing her knees together and scrunched her toes in her shoes to keep her anxiety contained.

As she listened, not one of the ladies claimed to know who the lucky woman was, but speculation was rife. They all agreed that

Miss Scaling had the upper hand in terms of dowry, and it was thought she was on good terms with Jack's sister.

If only they knew the truth.

The second favorite, and one that almost made Constance lose her poise, was Miss Agatha Birkenstock. She could not believe it. Yet, Jack was unfailingly polite to Agatha, and he had called her by her first name at his dinner.

They would make a perfect couple. She was tall, slim, and elegant, if a little nervous in society. With her blonde hair to complement his, Jack's offspring would be just as handsome.

Constance's eyes prickled at the perfect pairing and she glanced down. She could not cry here. So she forced her chin up, pasted an unaffected smile on her face, and prayed it would fool those around her until she could escape.

Traveling home in the marquess' smallest town carriage, she sank into the seat in despair, pulled a folded quilt across her knees, and wrapped her cold hands in it. She should never have listened to the gossip. Jack's life, wife, everything, was none of her concern. Yet she wanted to see with her own eyes if the parcel had contained that necklace. But to see it meant that she had to enter Jack's suite of rooms.

Ettington House was quiet when she returned. Hallam had already left for Parkwood, and Jack had gone out again. It was the perfect time to appease her curiosity.

Constance stood in the hall near Jack's room and hesitated. She had never been in a gentleman's bedchamber before. How shocking could it be?

The door leading into Jack's room was heavy and closed loudly behind her. Constance winced at the noise, and then looked around. She was in a sitting room. The fire was out, but the room was warm from the sun shining through the tall windows. She had expected a heavily masculine room, but instead she found it light, airy, and comfortable. Two long couches faced each other before the fireplace and a low, empty table sat between. Bookcases lined the walls, but were strangely barren of books and curios.

At the end of the room stood another doorway and she stepped toward the opening cautiously. Inside, she breathed deep. Jack. The room smelled of him.

In its center was a huge bed with ornately carved posts and red silk patterned hangings with the family crest. There was another doorway at the foot of the bed. A glance inside revealed a dressing closet, the domain of Jack's valet. Every stored article was neatly laid out. Row upon row of black. She could not see the parcel yet, but she really didn't want to start opening drawers to find it.

There was one room left, the farthest from where she had entered. She turned the knob, hands trembling, and stepped inside. Constance stopped breathing.

In front of her, on every surface, was a wealth of riches. A crystal chandelier hung from the ceiling. Silks and lace covered every chair. An antique screen hid a large bath, big enough for two.

Constance swallowed past the lump in her throat. She gravitated to the elegant dressing table by the window. Silk stockings and garters lay beneath a blue velvet box. A red velvet box lay upon that. Constance's gaze swept the room again, and she fanned herself with her hand, fighting a flush. Against the wall sat traveling cases embossed with the family crest on black lacquered wood. Every single item in the room spoke of permanence and looked pristine.

She reached for the red box and opened it. A diamond-encrusted ruby necklace, bracelet, and ring lay on a plush, satin cushion. She snapped the lid closed, dropped it to the table, staring at the room's contents again without really seeing them.

This room was waiting for the next marchioness.

Constance gazed around her in horror. She had made a grave mistake coming to London. She had come between Jack and Agatha. She raised her hands to her lips and tried to breathe. Everything in this room would suit the girl. She deserved adoration like this.

A single tear slid down her cheek before she could stop it. Constance backed out of the room as a strangled sob burst free. She couldn't see. She stumbled out the door, not stopping when she gained the hall and turned blindly for her own room. Inside, she collapsed to the floor just inside the closed door and allowed her heart to break into little pieces.

"Agatha, it is a pleasure to see you visiting today," Jack told the shy woman as he sat down in a hard chair across from his sister.

He was, in truth, looking for Pixie, but his quarry had done a very good job of hiding. Jack caught glimpses of her skirts as she ducked out of sight, but by the time he reached that spot, she was gone again.

"Thank you, my lord," Agatha smiled. "I was just telling Lady Orkney about the orphanage's youngest charge. We have taken on a very young child, just a few months old, and I am quite enamored with her."

"Did Miss Grange go out, Virginia?" Jack asked, wondering how he hadn't known.

"No, she is finishing up a letter. I expect her at any moment," Virginia told him with a knowing smile and turned back to Agatha. "What have you called her?"

While the pair chatted, Jack cursed under his breath. Well, if his sister knew he had designs on Pixie, there was no chance of surprising her with the good news he would marry.

Pixie arrived just as the tea things were laid out. She took a cup quickly but seemed distracted from the conversation. She only managed the barest of civilities to Agatha and sat a little apart from the group, letting Virginia do all the talking. She held her teacup loosely in her hand but she didn't drink it.

He smiled at something Agatha said and responded without too much thought, still glancing discreetly at Pixie. As if feeling his eyes, she straightened a little, and her free hand fluttered to her stomach. She put her cup down with a clatter, apologized, and dashed from the room.

Jack looked at Virginia, perplexed, but when he made a move to follow, she shushed him and had him stay with Agatha. It was then he realized that he was alone with Miss Birkenstock, in a chamber with a closed door. With a murmured excuse, he put his cup down, and strode to the door to have Parkes summon a suitable chaperone.

Jack remained in the front hall until a maid arrived, and then went above to find the ladies. Virginia was standing outside Pixie's door, knocking and asking to be let in. There was no response and the door wouldn't open. Virginia looked at him anxiously then disappeared behind his bedroom door, no doubt heading for the balcony to access Pixie's room.

Jack gripped the doorframe and pressed his head to it. But he heard nothing from within.

Virginia returned a bare minute later. "Pixie said she felt ill all of a sudden, but is feeling better now. She's going to rest for the rest of the day." Virginia glanced at the door then shrugged. "I'll return to Agatha and pass along Pixie's excuse."

Jack waited till Virginia had disappeared down the stairs then headed for the balcony himself. But her doors were locked against him, the curtains drawn tight. What the devil was going on now?

Jack returned to his study. He supposed he could go find the housekeeper's set of keys and let himself into her room, but he would rather keep their liaison private until he proposed. Maybe if he gave her a little time she might come out on her own.

His butler entered his study an hour later and stood patiently on the other side of his desk, disturbing him from the plans he needed to make for the wedding. "Yes, Parkes?"

"Miss Grange has requested a tray in her room for luncheon. I thought you might prefer the same, my lord."

So much for talking to her. "Thank you. Has there been any response from my uncle?"

"No, my lord. But I did speak to His Grace's housekeeper earlier and believe he is expected to arrive the day after tomorrow."

At least his uncle wasn't here to witness him making a mess of his courtship. The duke was well acquainted with Pixie and would probably laugh at Jack for requesting his presence for a wedding without securing her acceptance first. It seemed only fair to give his uncle advance warning. He was growing older and disliked surprises immensely.

"My lord, if I may, I wondered if I might share an observation with you."

Puzzled, Jack nodded. "Of course."

"On the day Miss Grange attended Lady Marchmouth's at-home, I heard crying in the house."

"Crying? I assume you dealt with the maid who had her heart broken by one of the footmen."

"It wasn't a maid crying, my lord. The sounds were coming from Miss Grange's bedchamber, and I have noticed a certain distraction in her manner since then. I believe she has become unhappy."

"Oh." Jack had detected a tendency toward lower spirits lately, but he hadn't pinpointed the exact moment of the change. Pixie rarely cried. "Did you mention this to my sister?"

"No, my lord. I know you prefer not to rely on Lady Orkney. I thought Miss Grange would have brought her troubles to you, given enough time, but I have just overheard that her maid is preparing for Miss Grange's departure."

Jack stood. "I beg your pardon. Is she packing?"

"Not yet, sir, but the maid asked for one of the smaller trunks to be brought down tomorrow," Parkes replied. "Given you've not requested a carriage made ready as you would usually, I thought you might be interested."

Virginia swept into the room, and Jack had the butler relate Pixie's recent request again. She appeared perplexed.

"Did Pixie say anything about the Marchmouth at-home?" Jack asked.

Virginia frowned. "Not a word, come to think on it. Do you think someone was horrible to her there?"

Jack tidied up his scattered papers before his sister noticed and dropped them in a drawer. "I don't know, but something has upset her. What gossip is circulating around Town?"

Virginia threw herself into an armchair. "Well, there is talk about some jewelry you purchased yesterday morning. It is rumored that you're about to pay off your mistress and marry."

"I don't have a mistress."

"Just as well. Pixie doesn't care for them any more than I do."

Parkes coughed, and made to escape, but turned back on the threshold. "Oh, there is one other matter, my lord. Miss Grange might have invaded your bedchamber that day too. I recall the door being left ajar and since you are particular about your bedchamber I berated the upstairs maids. None of them admitted to it."

Jack raked his fingers through his hair. "Miss Grange has access to the whole house. But how far into my rooms did she go, do you think?"

"As far as the marchioness' boudoir—that door was open, too."

Parkes fled. Damn, she might already know about his wedding gifts. What else had Virginia said? Then Jack remembered the last part of Virginia's gossip. Society should barely know his plans for Pixie yet. "Whom am I supposed to be marrying?"

Virginia threw her hands up. "The gossip for the last few months has been that you will wed Miss Birkenstock. I know, I know, you are just being kind, but you are rarely kind without reason. There was some gossip, initially, about Pixie's presence, but it is generally thought that you have no time for her."

"Like hell," Jack exploded, pacing the room.

"Perhaps Pixie believed the gossip?"

Jack was stunned. Everything made sense. He really ought to go upstairs and paddle her little behind. "Damn her foolishness. No, damn mine. Virginia."

"Yes, dear?"

"I have no intention of marrying Agatha. I have a fondness for her, but as far as it goes, I am not at home when she calls. Is that clear?"

Virginia's answering smile lit the room.

"Oh, and one more matter. Make sure Pixie's traveling cases have been misplaced. We need to have a discussion and I can't do that if she runs away."

"Brother, you are making a mess of this," Virginia chided, but she rose, skirted the desk, and pressed a kiss to his cheek. "Remember, we are promised to attend the Jamison ball tonight. I will make Pixie attend, but you must put things right tonight. And be sure you get rid of the other woman too."

Virginia hurried out the door. He shook his head. No matter how many times he promised he was unencumbered, Virginia still didn't believe he wasn't already betrothed.

Chapter Twenty-Five

---◆---

"If I drew pleasure from inflicting pain, Miss Grange, I believe I would take you across my knee and give you the spanking you deserve," Lord Daventry murmured with a smile totally at odds with his words.

His voice cut through Constance's misery like a knife. "Lord Daventry?"

Shocked to a standstill on Lady Jamison's ballroom floor, she glanced around, but no one appeared to have heard his threat.

"Take my arm, Miss Grange," Daventry ordered, still smiling, but his tone was far from pleasant.

She did not understand what had changed. Daventry had never put himself out in either pleasure or vexation before. Yet he watched Constance closely now and, judging by the postures of the society closest to them, they were beginning to draw attention.

Constance placed her hand on his arm. Daventry covered her fingers and used firm pressure to keep her hand in place as he escorted her off the dance floor and away from her chaperone.

"Miss Grange, I believe I shall show you a little play. I know you enjoy the theater, so you may find our little dramas entertaining. I can assure you that from where I sit, it is all painfully real, and could be dealt with in a few simple words. Perhaps you have seen part of the play yourself, and not fully understood?"

Constance struggled to keep up. Had Daventry finally gone mad? Could an excess of pleasure disturb the mind?

Daventry stopped by the refreshment table and handed her a glass of freshly poured champagne. Constance sipped hers, still unable to move away. With Virginia out of sight, she longed for the dubious safety of Jack's company across the room.

Daventry's gaze flowed over her, lingering on her breasts and mouth. He caught her hand in his. "Are you still untouched, Miss Grange?"

Constance's skin flushed. "Of course, Lord Daventry," she replied, attempting to step back. "Release me."

"Not just yet. Our play is just beginning."

"What play?" But he didn't answer. Daventry deposited her unfinished glass on the table, then strolled a few more steps taking her with him. Yet his gaze swept her body almost as if he were undressing her.

Constance squirmed. She did not like this game Lord Daventry was playing, but they were still in a crowded ballroom. She was reasonably safe for the moment.

"Take a look around you, Miss Grange. Take a good look at all the people you are acquainted with and watch what they do. You would be surprised what people reveal when they let their guard down. When they think no one is watching they are at their most honest."

He steered her toward a large pillar and placed her in its shadow. "Take Lady Wallis, for example. Can you tell the man she has her eye on?"

Lord Daventry's breath tickled her cheek, an unpleasant sensation she discovered. She shuddered but turned in Lady Wallis' direction and watched her converse with her staid husband. Before long, the lady's eyes did drift, in Jack's direction.

Then the slender Lord Wade passed Lady Wallis, and her gaze stroked *him*.

"Yes, the lovely lady is not averse to a man of more trim and muscled dimensions than her husband. Look again. What else can you see?"

He was determined to torment her but she gritted her teeth and looked around them. Of course women stared at Jack. He stood in conversation with Agatha and Mr. Birkenstock across the dance floor. His gaze flittered around the ballroom continually, never resting on any one face for long. Not even Agatha's. The girl watched her grandfather and Jack speaking, but her gaze flickered across the dance floor, not quite at Constance and Lord Daventry though.

Constance turned her head to her right. Lord Carrington lingered nearby. He was gazing at Agatha from beside another pillar, a frown creasing his forehead. That was certainly a surprise. Agatha and Carrington were watching each other. When she thought about it, Carrington often joined in on her conversations when Agatha was near, but the girl usually excused herself soon after.

"Fascinating, is it not?" he supplied, reading her mind. Obviously, he saw much more than she usually did. "Keep looking."

Daventry's hand touched her upper arm and she jumped. When she turned her head, she found him closer than was comfortable. If she protested the liberties he was taking she risked drawing unwanted attention. If she stayed here with him much longer, people would begin to whisper. The earl was playing her for the sake of his own twisted amusement. A prickle of anxiety swept her skin and she returned her gaze to the center of the ballroom.

Jack had left the Birkenstocks, but had halted a few feet from them, directly across the ballroom floor. He was staring at her and only at her. Constance gulped, suddenly nervous.

Daventry's finger dragged along her upper arm and he whispered into her ear, "Take my arm."

Jack's jaw clenched.

"Trust me, Pixie. I have no designs on your pretty self," Daventry whispered when she hesitated.

She should not trust him, yet she was curious as to what he was about. She placed her hand on his arm and chose not to look at where Jack was standing again.

Daventry wound them through the throng, pausing to exchange flirtatious comments with several women. By the time they reached the ballroom entrance, Constance had overheard a great deal more flirtatious comments than she wanted to. The man was obsessed.

Once in the hallway, he pushed Constance against a wall. She yelped at the harsh treatment. But he merely stood beside her, arms loosely laced across his chest, waiting for something.

Jack barreled through the doorway a moment later, radiating aggression and panic.

Daventry smiled. "Ettington, old man, so good of you to join us."

Jack pivoted, and his blue eyes were as cold as ice. He saw Constance and relaxed a little, but his eyes returned to Daventry. She had never seen Jack so angry. He advanced a step, fists curled tight at his sides.

"Now, Ettington, no harm done," Daventry assured him with a confident and pleased grin. "Such a pretty girl, you cannot wrap her up in silk and not expect her to attract admirers."

Jack grasped Daventry by his cravat, slamming his back into the wall.

"Jack, stop." Constance glanced around the hall. They were alone, but the hall would not stay that way for long.

"Ah, but you see, Miss Grange, our Jack is not quite himself. Not when it comes to you." Daventry struggled to speak around the tightened neck cloth. "You could almost think he was dealing with poachers on his land. Ettington, you've forgotten I stick to my rules—never an innocent."

Red stained Lord Daventry's cheeks before Jack let go of the earl.

"There's always an exception." Jack drew in a deep breath. "Leave, before I do something permanent."

"Your servant, Miss Grange. Have a very pleasurable evening, Ettington."

As soon as he turned, Lord Daventry started whistling. The man was deranged. Constance glanced up at Jack and was surprised to find his eyes closed.

Thinking to return to the ballroom before her absence was noticed, she edged around the angry man. But his hand shot out and gripped her arm tight. She stared at it, then up at his face. Jack pulled her to him, placed Constance's arm through his, and started walking.

He placed his free hand over hers and held her tight. Despite the gloves, Jack's hands were hot. She kept her eyes lowered as he pulled her down the hall, past a few small groups of servants avoiding their duties, and around a corner to a part of the house she had never seen.

Jack's breath brushed her cheek a moment before he kissed her. Her mind spun as he assaulted her so passionately that she sobbed. Jack held tight to her and plundered her mouth, running his hands over her hungrily. As quick as lightning, her senses were on fire. She should resist his demands yet waves of desire threatened to drown her. She clung to Jack as if he was the only lifeline she had.

Jack kissed her again, kissed her as if he would never stop. But she remembered where they were and that at any moment they could be found. A scandal she could never live down was just around the corner.

She struggled against him.

He lifted his head a fraction, kissing her again, once, twice, lips softer, teasing. "Not Agatha, you little fool. You're the one I want."

He pulled her hard against him so they touched from breast to thigh.

Constance felt the rest of Jack, the hardness at the top of his thighs, straining against her belly. He lifted her from the floor, held her against the wall, his body pushing her skirts in between her legs. He ground his hips, making her blush as a thousand nerve endings erupted.

Constance sobbed, unable to help herself. Jack kissed her again then trailed his lips to the side of her face and down her throat. She instinctively rubbed her own hips into him and heard a tortured groan escape him.

He returned to her lips, stroking inside her mouth with his tongue. Constance's hands slid from his shoulders to his face. She drew him back to stare at him.

"You will ruin me," she warned him, hope threatening to strangle her. Would he risk exposure like this if he did not care about her? He had her pressed to the wall by his own body, her lips surely red from his kisses.

"Never, ever doubt that you are mine to kiss," he told her bluntly, grinding his hips into her again and making her gasp at the sensations he caused. "Stay away from Lord Daventry."

"Lord Daventry doesn't appeal to me." Constance twined her arms around Jack's neck, but her mind buzzed with the thought that Jack was jealous. She moved one hand to the side of his head, but he cursed.

"Damn gloves. I want to feel your hands on me tonight."

Constance did not dare remove them and lose the time she could be touching him.

Jack eased back, breathing hard, and let her slide down the wall. He crowded her, unable, it seemed, to let her go completely. She took a deep, steadying breath and slid her hands over his waistcoat. His heart pounded beneath and she looked back up into his eyes. "What are you doing to me?"

"Making sure you do not leave."

"I have to leave eventually."

"No, you do not. We have to talk. If you have heard the nonsense that I have a mistress, you are very much mistaken. I want you. I've already settled the debt with Mr. Scaling. The other outstanding notes will be repaid shortly."

She swallowed as his words sank in.

"Did you never think that I could afford you?" he asked, eyes flashing wickedly. Constance's head spun at his words. She couldn't answer that one. He brushed his thumb across her cheek. "Go to the ladies' retiring room. You look as if you have just been ravished."

Constance nodded and slipped her hands from his chest. She took a few steps away, but turned back, dazed. Jack's eyes were still on her or, more precisely, on her derrière. She blushed as he smiled wolfishly. Then he stalked her to the base of the staircase, watching as she ascended.

Moments later, she sat before a mirrored table and caught a glimpse of her face. It was indeed fortunate she had not encountered anyone on her way here.

Her eyes were bright, her cheeks were flushed, and her lips were as red as cherries. The skin of her throat looked red, too. She let out a shaky breath and looked down at her gown. Crushed, beyond all hope of appearing respectable. She looked like a woman well loved.

Constance could not help herself. She laughed, unable to hold in her excitement. She had been a fool to listen to gossip. Jack wouldn't lie to her. He had no mistress waiting in the wings. She brushed her lips with her fingertips and tried to control her smile, but her happiness could not be contained.

She twirled Jack's cravat pin in her fingers, flushing guiltily at the thought that she was looking forward to undressing the rest of him. A great weight lifted from Constance. It dimmed somewhat when she considered that Jack had repaid her obscenely large debts without discussing the matter first. It was far too generous of him. But Jack wanted her, desired her enough to lose his head in jealousy.

She ran her hand over her chest as she hoped, no prayed, that it might be so. If Jack loved her, she could bear the scandal of being his mistress.

Chapter Twenty-Six

———◆———

Virginia prowled through the ballroom, frantic but trying her best not to show it. How had she lost Pixie? She waved to Agatha, yet managed to avoid stopping and having to make conversation. Bernard was right. She should have gone home with him. All this insipid chatter was getting on her nerves.

She wanted to leave, but not before she located that little minx of a Pixie. She doubted her friend was in trouble, as she had seen no sign of the Scaling party tonight.

Virginia studied the thick crowd ahead. Dear God, Jack would be cross about losing her. Yet she hadn't seen him either, come to think of it. Perhaps they were together.

It was high time too.

At the refreshment table, she grabbed a glass and sipped slowly, pondering where to look next.

"What are you doing roaming this hell all on your own?" Daventry asked. "Have you lost someone?"

"Perhaps," she murmured.

Daventry laughed and held out his arm. "Or maybe you lost two someones?"

"Where are they?" Virginia asked, absolutely certain the earl knew more than she did.

"Ettington has just walked back in. My, my, he is a bit rumpled. And if my eyes don't deceive me, he's missing a cravat pin, too. Very messy." He laughed again, clearly delighted by the image.

For all her height, it was often advantageous to have a taller man around. "Can you see Pixie?"

"No. But he'll have sent her off to the retiring room by now. I imagine she's looking a little mussed as well."

"I had better go find her. Thank you, Daventry." She turned for the door, but the earl held her back.

"It is good to see you happy again, Virginia. When you see Hallam, tell him he has my admiration and congratulations."

Virginia blushed and moved on, shaking her head at Daventry's foolish insinuations. But as she climbed the stairs, she wondered if he was right. Was her happiness all due to Bernard? He would probably preen like a peacock at the thought and she still could not wait to tell him.

Virginia was so lost in her thoughts that she careened into Pixie at the top of the stairs. Taking in her bemused expression and rumpled appearance, Virginia turned her around and marched her back inside the retiring room. "You can't go out there looking like that."

Virginia ignored the blush staining her friend's face and straightened her gown, ridiculously pleased that her soon-to-be sister had fallen as hard as her brother.

Pixie clenched her hands together. "Perhaps I should go home?"

Virginia studied her friend's distracted state. Perhaps that was the right idea. She was bored anyway. Once Pixie was at home, Jack would undoubtedly continue his seductions in private.

Virginia was going to go home, find a bottle of something pleasant to sip, and lock her door. The less she knew about what transpired when she wasn't looking, the better.

———◆———

Spying was socially frowned upon, but watching Jack at his desk scratching notes on his papers fascinated Pixie. She took a deep breath and stepped into his study. Although she had retired a while ago, she had not been able to sleep. Jack's kisses had inflamed her body and mind, not to mention aroused in her a curiosity she had never expected to have. If she continued to think about the way he had brushed her body with his, she would get no sleep at all. She was too keyed up, too restless.

Jack looked up and smiled at her with real pleasure in his eyes. "I was about to come and talk to you. Having trouble sleeping again?"

Constance nodded.

Jack rose and circled the desk, sitting on the polished edge, and making his breeches pull tight across his thighs. "My fault?"

Jack held out his hand and Constance walked forward to take it, sighing as he pulled her into his arms.

"I'm glad to see you, too," he murmured against her hair.

He lifted her chin and kissed her, brushing his lips lightly against hers. They were nothing at all like his kisses at the ball. Jack had not been in control then, but he was now. He continued to kiss her lightly until Constance kissed him back more insistently. She moved until she didn't have to stretch to reach his mouth.

Running her hands up his arms to his shoulders then neck, she dug her fingers into his hair.

Jack's hands were not idle, either. He tugged pins from her hair quickly and caught the mass in his palm. "God, I love touching you," he whispered.

"And I love being with you." She framed his face with her hands and kissed him hard.

Constance gave up trying to think, letting him sink them down into the sweetest desire she had ever known. Their tongues brushed and tasted in maddening passes while their hands molded them together. He slid one hand down her spine, under the length of her hair, and very firmly squeezed her bottom, tilting her hips to bring her flush against the hard length of him.

———◆———

Jack released her mouth to take in more air. His breath was fast and loud to his own ears. Each time they kissed, he reveled in the heat rising off their skin. He wanted to strip the clothes from his back, strip her too, and continue this heady freedom. He wanted to kiss her without restraint. He kissed her jaw and worked his way to her ear before trailing his lips down her neck.

Jack traced a path from one freckle to the next, letting his breath tickle over her wet skin, making a promise to count each and every one usually covered by her gowns. Pixie gasped and wiggled in response then pulled his face back to hers with firm hands. She kissed him for all she was worth, dueling tongues and lips, hands and bodies, grasping and rubbing with delicious friction.

Jack stood, losing precious contact with her as he held out his arms. "I have always regretted not dancing with you. Shall we?"

Her dazed eyes widened with delight and she raised her hands to assume the waltz position. "I would be honored, my lord."

He growled. "No more 'my lord', thank you, Pixie. Address me as Jack, or darling, or anything else you damn well please, but not that ever again."

"Of course, sir. Anything you say, sir," she answered cheekily.

Jack bent to kiss her and then dropped a hand to lightly swat her backside. He shook his head. "My girl, what in the world am I going to do with you?"

Her smile widened. "Make love to me?"

Innocent, yet eager. Jack had never imagined he would want a woman this badly. He swallowed, held out his arms, and danced her to the door. He pushed her against the wood, dropped a hand, and flicked the lock. "That is something I have wanted to do for a while, Pixie. I was trying to be a gentleman."

When she smiled shyly, he made a promise to devote a whole night to dancing with her. He dropped his lips back to hers and in moments, their passion blazed between them. Thank heavens he had comfortable furniture in this room. They would never make it to a bedchamber. As they kissed, he scooped her up and moved to sit on the settee so that she straddled him. He ran a hand from her ankle, beneath her skirt, over the intoxicating feel of her silk stocking, and up to where he met bare flesh.

Uncertain if Pixie was aware of their change in position, he did not rush. So he waited, softening his kisses, running his free hand to the back of her gown, sliding his fingers beneath the fabric to caress her skin. He unhooked a button at the top and stroked his fingers over new territory.

Pixie finally drew back and opened her eyes. They were very dark green and she was very, very aroused. She looked at him with silent longing as he ran his fingers down to the next button. He popped it open.

Pixie's breath panted across his cheek. He moved his hand on her thigh, rubbing until he found her skin. He waited, giving her the chance to stop him.

When he undid yet another button, her fingers flexed in his hair. As more buttons popped, Pixie undid the knot of his cravat and removed it.

He slid his palm over her very bare rear, enjoying the silky smoothness of her skin and the gasp she couldn't hold back as she rocked forward at the sensation. Thank God she wore no drawers. Jack's fingers squeezed the firm globe he had fantasized about and Pixie whimpered. She dropped her mouth to his bared neck, bit down, and then kissed him better.

He popped three more buttons, sure that he could wrestle the material down to expose her breasts. When he eased her back from his chest, Pixie resisted a moment before giving him what he wanted. When her eyes locked with his, he placed his finger at the base of her throat. He ran it down the center of her chest into the valley between her breasts, then he snagged the front of her gown and jerked it down.

"Beautiful."

Constance exulted in the hungry look on Jack's face, and heard his rough groan as he lifted her, using his hand on her bottom to bring her breasts level with his face. As he took one nipple between his lips, fire shot directly to her core. Constance looked down at him, suckling at her breast, his hair disordered. This was right. This was where she should be.

She cradled his head, enjoying the feel of his mouth tugging and shaping her breast to please them both. The heat of his lips, the caress of breath over her skin, proved such exquisite torture that her body pulsed with longing.

He teased her nipple with his tongue.

Constance's breath hissed out and she squirmed, settling lower and tighter against him. Jack kissed his way to her other breast and she thrummed in anticipation. He paused a moment, his eyes open, and stretched his tongue to the pointed nipple. Constance squirmed at the teasing touch.

Jack chuckled. "Like that, do you?"

"Of course I do. You know I do," she replied softly.

His open-mouthed kiss swallowed her nipple and he tugged hard until she couldn't stop the sounds escaping.

"I think you will like this, too."

Instead of continuing his feast as she expected, Jack kissed her lips fiercely, and swallowed her surprised shriek as his hand moved to the curls between her legs.

He cupped her mound firmly, then parted her lower lips and stroked her aching flesh. She shuddered and he caught her moans with more kisses. Constance rested her head against his, breathing roughly while her body thrummed with desire. He kept his hand on her and stroked, spreading her wetness, running his hand down her back and driving her insane.

Constance shifted, struggling to use any of her faculties. His hand among her curls was maddening and created such a powerful ache. The invasion of his finger, she assumed it was one, made her want to push down. Jack appeared not to mind her restlessness and looked positively wild with his hands beneath her skirts. He was so very thorough at driving her crazy with lust that she could not help but voice her enjoyment.

Determined to explore him, she attacked the buttons on his waistcoat and pushed it aside. Next came Jack's shirt—the crisp material was no match for her determined fingers. She touched his bare chest. His warm skin was so very pale, with a light sprinkling of golden hair upon it. Constance gulped, overwhelmed by the sight. She ran her hands over smooth, lean muscle, outward to his shoulders, pushing his shirt away from the heat of his skin.

Jack dragged his shirt over his head then returned to giving her pleasure.

Her hands slid lower, running over the crest of his chest, past nipples, pointed and hard with desire, down his ribs to his waist. She curled her hands inward to find a thin line of hair that traveled lower. Curious, she traced the line of hair to his waistband, slipped sideways to the button, and worked it free.

Jack sucked his belly in. He ceased exploring between her legs and watched her fingers move over him. The folds of her gown obscured her view, but then he tugged at the material, pulling so her skirts hung behind her and out of the way.

He shuffled so she had better access. Her hands stilled. The outline of him, long and very impatiently straining against the fabric of his breeches, took her breath away.

He leaned forward to kiss her brow. "You don't have to continue. You could stop. I want nothing more than to pleasure you."

"That doesn't seem fair," she whispered.

"My wonderful, darling angel," he began, but didn't finish his thought.

He moved his hand again, stroking her, making her wetter, if that was possible. He kissed her neck and shoulder, then brought his other hand around to her breast and squeezed. He brought all of his attention back to her.

Jack was so focused that he did not appear to realize she opened the flap of his trousers, exposing him to the air and her eyes. Constance goggled. This was what made men so different.

She had seen the picture book. Jack was touching her as in page thirty-three. But if she reached out, she could perform number six. Jack had said he wanted to pleasure her. He certainly deserved the same.

Nervously, Constance touched him.

"Jesus, Mary, and Joseph." Jack's voice burst from his lips and he looked down.

"I'm sorry, did I hurt you?"

"Christ, no. Do it again, love." Jack kissed her hard. "Touch me again."

She ran her index finger along smooth skin and then grasped him firmly. He groaned.

"Your skin is so soft and hot, Jack. Am I doing this right?"

"I won't break. Hold me like this." He wrapped her hand around his length, but he hissed out a breath against her neck then settled to kissing along her jaw. He guided her hand until she understood what he enjoyed most. He showed her how to stroke, how hard to squeeze, and the pace he liked best.

When Jack released her hand, he returned his attention to her body, sending heat rushing to her face. This was nothing like the book. It was so much better.

Jack brought his second hand under her skirts and concentrated on driving her insane, his lips kissing anywhere they could reach. A short burn of discomfort pierced her pleasure haze and Constance thought he must have slipped a second finger inside her. But the incredible feeling of fullness as he pressed all the way in thrilled her, and then rubbed where she ached most.

Her body rocked against Jack's hands as she strove to get closer. She found Jack's lips and kissed him again, while he did something incredible to her body. Her breath caught, and then she sobbed, squeezing Jack's probing fingers as every nerve ending in her body shuddered.

All the way through, she held Jack's length in her hand, instinctively pulling and stroking until he bucked and groaned loudly, too.

Warm, slick stickiness coated her hand as she concentrated on trying to breathe. Nothing had prepared her for the pleasure of making love to Jack.

Although she sat perched on his thighs, legs spread wide, his fingers still buried deep inside her, she wasn't embarrassed.

She should be though.

As for Jack, he lay back on the settee, head thrown back. His blue eyes had closed and his lips parted as he breathed hard. He looked done in. Satisfied. She had to bite back a happy smirk at her achievement.

"I need to get you into bed before someone finds us," Jack said suddenly.

She winced as he removed his fingers from her body, then he reached for his cravat. He wiped off her sticky fingers first, then stroked up the long expanse of his bare chest, absorbing and cleaning away his release.

A tremor shook her leg, but she didn't want to move.

Jack's wide grin drew one from her. He lifted up until his chest brushed her nipples and kissed her, sending a warm glow all the way over her body. Making love to Jack defied description.

"Is it always like that?" Constance asked, puzzled and a little afraid that he did not feel as awed as she did. She would hate it if she could feel that way with someone else.

He kissed her nose. "No. Making love has never been that

good. I've always said that you were special."

"I thought you were just being kind," Constance said as she frowned at how easily her perception of him had changed. Had he always been so sweet to her?

He hugged her. "Kindness is not the only reason we're friends, love."

He stood, taking her with him, and then dropped her to her feet. She grasped his hips as he buttoned his trousers. When he bent to collect his shirt from the floor, she skimmed her hands over his smooth back. He grinned and shrugged his shirt over his head, hiding his body from her sight.

Her gown had slipped low and, without the buttons fastened, threatened to continue downward. Jack redressed her, a gentle smile crossing his face as he did so.

He kissed her lips. "Come on. Time to get you into your bed before its too late."

They walked to the door of the secret passageway together, Jack's arm around her shoulders. The doorway opened with a soft click. They climbed the stairs in silence and when Jack slid them into her bed, tucked the blankets tight around them, and kissed Constance's cheek, she wondered if now was the right time to bring up the change between them.

But Jack's heavy breath proved he'd fallen dead asleep the moment his head hit the pillow. She cuddled up to him and closed her eyes. Tomorrow was soon enough to find out what he expected from a mistress.

Chapter Twenty-Seven

———◆———

Jack stood before the mirror and wondered why he looked the same. He felt different—alive. His pulse pounded loud in his ears. Pleasuring Pixie had done that. He stirred at the memory of what they had shared last night. Dear God, it was the best fumble he had ever experienced. Pixie's responses were so natural, so erotic and instinctive, that they had indulged in mutual pleasure again this morning as they woke in her bed just before the sun rose. It was quick and frantic, both of them conscious that the servants would be stirring soon, but unable to part until the other was satisfied again.

Tonight would not be quick, tonight he would take her to new heights, take them both past the point of no return. Tonight he would have her bare and on her back in his bed, and nothing was going to interrupt them. Not even the house burning down around them.

Jack pushed his anticipation down as his cock swelled, focusing on his reflection. He grimaced. He was tired of black, tired of being haughty, unable to smile, unable to show any sign of being warm or caring. He'd rather avoid the ball and stay home, take Pixie to bed, and truly make her his.

He was already missing her.

Jack had only managed a short time with her after breakfast. Just a few kisses and a deep inhalation of her fragrance. He'd pulled her into his study, pressed her back against the door, and kissed her until she'd panted as hard as he. Only Virginia's querying voice had parted them. Since they had an appointment with the modiste again, Virginia had whisked Pixie away. Jack hadn't seen her since their late return, but after tonight's ball he would go down on bended knee and ask her to marry him.

Tomorrow, by special license, they would marry. Tomorrow, Mrs. Grange should arrive with his uncle for the wedding ceremony, and then they would move to Hazelmere, where he could put a stop to Mrs. Grange's incessant gambling. Jack had decided on a devious way to control his future mother-in-law: grandchildren—as many as they could manage.

With the effort to don the mask of the cold-hearted marquess, Jack arrived downstairs late, only to be informed that the ladies had left without him. God, his sister had such a bee in her bonnet about tardiness since Hallam had returned to the country.

Jack hurried after them, cursing Hallam's influence on his sister. By the time he arrived at Lady Rosthorn's townhouse, it was overflowing with the cream of London society and, quite naturally, every gossip possible.

As he stood beside the crowded dance floor looking for Pixie and his sister, expectant eyes focused on him. He ignored them, anxious to see Pixie again. She hadn't said a word about Abernathy, and Jack wanted to hear her say that she was done with the younger man and the stupid list.

Across the room, the inevitable cluster of women whispered furiously behind fans, all openly staring in his direction. He shrugged it off. He had better things to do than worry about their endless speculations. He moved on, spotting Miss Birkenstock in the crowd speaking with her grandfather. Her gaze flicked toward him, her expression disappointed, and then she glanced away quickly. What the devil could that be about?

"Good evening, Lord Ettington," a loud voice called.

Jack turned toward the voice, and found Mr. Scaling before him.

"It was," he replied, not caring who overheard his remark. There were some benefits to having a reputation for coldness—he could be dismissive when and where he chose.

Jack searched the crowd for Pixie. He did not want her to see Mr. Scaling standing with him. Pixie might return her attention to the debts. He'd repaid them all without her consent. He didn't want her to become prickly over how he should have waited for them to be actually married before he dealt with them. He enjoyed tussling with her in far more pleasurable ways.

Scaling cleared his throat. "It never ceases to amaze me how quickly secret alliances have a way of becoming known. I have asked around and it appears that quite a number of Miss Grange's debts have been paid by a mysterious benefactor. Care to enlighten me where the young lady acquired the blunt to do it? I was led to believe she would have to sell Thistlemore before any of her creditors got even a shilling in payment."

"Sell Thistlemore?" Jack asked, arrested by the gossip but trying not to show it. "Now who would tell you such a falsehood?"

"Let us just say that an acquaintance is eager for the property at any expense. He boasted over a drink or two that he almost had the property," Scaling remarked.

"And who would that be?"

"Oh, just a country lord and his whelp of an heir," Scaling offered.

Brampton, and his uncle? "I believe I can guess the identity on my own," Jack replied, grimacing as he considered. "Thank you for your candor but what is your purpose in telling me this?" Jack asked.

"Let us say my curiosity was piqued enough to investigate the matter and I believe Miss Grange was in danger of being duped."

"The matter has been taken care of," Jack promised, wondering what the devil was going on at Thistlemore that he'd missed.

"Don't thank me," Scaling protested. "Just let me know when the property comes up for sale. I am prepared to offer fair payment."

Rendered speechless, Jack could only stare. Did Mr. Scaling really think he would ignore what his daughter had done to Pixie and still do business with him?

Scaling bowed and walked away, leaving Jack with a dilemma. He should investigate why so many people were keen to acquire the property but he was also about to marry and had plans to take a long holiday with his bride. Perhaps one of Lord Daventry business contacts could look into the matter. He'd ask tonight but he was probably already sweeping some eager lady off her feet and into bed.

He should be doing the same. Jack turned to see Pixie, resplendent in green silk, bearing down on him.

A cross expression marred her beauty. "How did he find you?"

"The man is blessed with all the traits of a hunting dog," Jack replied, fighting the urge to bend low to kiss her cheek. It was best not to start anything here. Later, he would taste her properly.

"I may have overstepped, but I thought I had fixed the Scalings problem for you."

"What did you do?" Jack asked, falling into step beside her as she prowled the edge of the dance floor. The dress, another low-cut gown of his choosing, drew his eye, and he stirred as the stamp of her feet jiggled the smooth, creamy skin above the neckline. Jack envied the diamond necklace nestled between her breasts more every day.

"Oh, I stumbled over their spy, a housemaid, in the act of reading your diary," Pixie grumbled. "Poor girl has had the wits scared out of her for no good reason. I was so sure it would work."

"I'm sure you did your best." Quite frankly, Jack didn't care about the Scalings following him about anymore. He was too busy planning exactly how quickly he could remove Pixie from that gown when he got her home. He almost steered her toward the open balcony doors with the intention of finding a dark corner and slipping his fingers across her chest, burrowing beneath the fabric to touch her nipples.

"Well, I know you value loyalty and your privacy." Pixie's face twisted in distaste. "Her parents and brother work for the Scalings, but they had threatened to dismiss them if she did not turn traitor."

Despite the seriousness of her discovery, Jack wanted to laugh at her pique, and that destroyed his lustful thoughts for the moment. Pixie did not enjoy being thwarted.

"You know, it is entirely possible they simply wait outside our house and follow us," Jack suggested. "Getting information from the maid, or any servant, would only warn them where we were going ahead of time."

"They couldn't be that direct, could they?"

"It does appear to be Mr. Scaling's style," Jack mused. "What did you do about the girl? Did you dismiss her for me?"

"Of course not. It's not my place to order your staff, but her family might come to Parkes in search of employment in the future. Please be kind to them."

Jack smiled. It would be interesting to watch Pixie deal with the servant problems in the future. She treated her own as friends more than paid employees. "I'm sure something can be arranged. Perhaps we could speak of it later. Where has that sister of mine got to?"

"I believe she is conversing with Lady Rosthorn and her daughter by the terrace doors," Pixie warned him.

Jack groaned. Lady Rosthorn's daughter was unmarried. "Perhaps you should join her. I need to speak to Lord Daventry before he disappears."

Pixie's eyes widened. "Be nice."

"Of course I will. I'll tell you about my suspicions later though."

⸻ ◆ ⸻

Constance crossed the ballroom floor between sets, only to be intercepted by Lord Daventry. She glanced behind her, but Jack had disappeared from sight. "Ettington is looking for you."

Lord Daventry held out his arm for her to take. Humoring him, she allowed him to promenade with her.

"Well, it appears that his better half has found me instead," Daventry grumbled.

The whispers from the sidelines increased another notch louder. She wondered what all the fuss was about tonight. There was always something society squawked over. They had only gone a few steps more before Agatha joined them. Agatha linked her arm with Constance's free one and together they led her farther away from the whispers, behind a pillar, of all places.

"What is going on?"

"Nothing of importance. Stay here with Miss Birkenstock. I need to find Jack and bring him back in here to render an explanation," Lord Daventry fumed.

Confusing man. "All right, if you must."

When she turned to her companion, Agatha's face wore a worried frown. "Are you feeling unwell, Miss Birkenstock? Perhaps you should sit?" Constance looked around, but saw no vacant chairs, only curious, whispering people.

"We should stay here until Lord Ettington returns."

Hmm, that could take a while. Constance craned her neck but saw nothing of him. "Do you know what they are whispering about tonight?"

"Yes," Agatha said in a small voice.

"And."

"I don't want to say," Agatha whispered.

"I beg your pardon?" All this whispering was getting on her nerves, but Constance was more disappointed that Agatha's confidence was backsliding.

"I don't like to gossip," Agatha apologized, and looked down at her hands.

"Could you tell me then why Lady Rosthorn just turned her back on me and took Virginia with her?" Constance demanded, finding no further fun in the evening.

"Oh, dear," Agatha murmured. "That is not a good thing. Not good at all."

"All right, enough of this. Just tell what they're saying or I'll...I'll take a key from your pianoforte the first chance I get," Constance threatened. "An important one."

Agatha looked horrified. "You can't do that."

"Just try me." Constance crossed her arms in a mocking, aggressive stance.

Agatha didn't even crack half a smile. "You won't be cross with me? I don't have so many friends as to lose any."

"Just tell me."

"They are talking about the Jamison ball."

"The ball? Really? Did I make another social gaff and not notice?" Constance thought back over the evening, but could not remember how she could have offended anyone.

"Yes. I mean no."

"All right, I give up." This was worse than listening to a bad poetry recital. Constance glanced around them but could see nothing of Virginia or Jack yet.

"About Lord Ettington…"

Constance's head snapped around. "Excuse me?"

"They know about that night. That's what they are whispering about. They know about you and Ettington. They say you're his—" Agatha didn't finish.

But Constance understood.

She was a fool to have come tonight. Of course, any gossip about the marquess would spread faster than honey on a hot day. She had given up her respectability last night, but she did not regret one single minute that she had shared with Jack. "That was quick."

"It's true?" Agatha goggled, and Constance braced herself.

"I suppose it is. I should apologize. Lord Daventry never should have left you with me. And I should have had the foresight to stay away. Please, go find your grandfather. You shouldn't be in my company."

Constance went to pat Agatha's hand then thought better of it. "Excuse me."

"No," Agatha cried. "I know how hard it is to refuse an ardent suitor. I'm not going to leave you alone." She took Constance's arm.

"Agatha, I'm not going to be alone long," Constance promised, trying to extract herself from Agatha's grip. "I'm going to return to Ettington house immediately."

"Wait." Agatha clenched her arm tighter. "I'm coming with you."

"Agatha, you shouldn't. This will not help you, and your place is here. Mine isn't."

"I don't belong here either, but the marquess and his sister have always been kind to me. It is the least I can do." Agatha tucked Constance's arm through hers and hurried toward her grandfather. When Agatha told him she was ready to leave, he didn't quibble the haste.

Once they hit the open air of the city, Constance could breathe again, but she shook all over.

Mr. Birkenstock commandeered Viscount Carrington's hack as he arrived and poor Carrington stumbled about so dazed that he stepped aside without a word of protest.

Agatha and her grandfather were blessedly quiet for the journey to Ettington House. Although the older man's jaw clenched occasionally, he never brought up the subject of her scandalous behavior.

Yet as she stepped from the carriage outside Ettington House, it occurred to Constance that Jack might be irritated she'd left without him. However, Jack should have known society would not ignore a mistress, especially one displayed right under their own noses. She waved the Birkenstock's away and turned for the steps.

———◆———

Jack searched the ballroom again with his eyes and his control slipped. "Where did you say you left her?"

"Over in the corner with Miss Birkenstock. I don't see them," Daventry looked around, "or Mr. Birkenstock either. They must have tried to find you. We must look for them."

"Don't bother. She's not out there," Virginia informed him, scowling like a fury. "There's more hot air circulating in this room than can be contained in one of those atrocious balloons. Jack, what have you done?"

"A slight miscalculation, sister. Don't fret," Jack muttered. "Where is that woman?"

Daventry groaned. "Ettington, you are the most watched man in England. Of course someone worked out you favored Pixie, but please tell me you didn't actually forget to ask her a particularly important question?"

"I may have," Jack squirmed. As if he would make her his mistress. How absurd the gossips were to suggest it. "She distracted me."

Daventry and Virginia exchanged disappointed glances.

This mess was completely fixable. He just had to propose and announce the marriage.

Viscount Carrington joined them with a laugh. "Is there any particular reason Miss Grange just left the ball with Agatha Birkenstock and her grandfather? The girl seemed ready to faint."

"She left?" Jack winced as his sister thumped him.

"They appeared to be in a very great hurry too," Carrington offered.

Jack groaned aloud. "Now you can fret, Virginia. Daventry, see my sister home safely, but not for a few hours."

Chapter Twenty-Eight

———— ◆ ————

"Going ta spread your legs for the marquess again, are ya?" a slurred voice called out to Constance as she reached the front door of Ettington House.

Peering into the dark of Orchard Street, Constance could make out a slim form slumped against the house fence. She moved to better view the face and gasped. "Cullen? What are you doing here at this time of night?"

"Why so surprised ta see me?" Cullen dragged himself to his feet and staggered forward a step or two. "Told ya I'd come back. Ya should have listened."

Constance stepped back from his lurching gait. "Cullen, you shouldn't be here."

"Where else would I be?" Cullen asked, raising a flask to his lips and taking a long pull. "I only had one job to do and that was get you ta marry me. Don't think I want to, now that I know where ya been."

Cullen must have heard the rumors too.

His gaze raked her, but despite his words, he grinned lasciviously at her appearance. She drew her wrap tighter about her shoulders.

He had not even asked if the rumors were true. Just convicted her without proof, then come to taunt her for her weakness. And to think this man's opinion had held sway over her thoughts for the last year. If not for the money problems she had, she would have married him without knowing this side of him.

He did not make a very good friend. Jack had always asked her to explain her mistakes before he chided her for them.

Constance bit her lip, then moved toward the house and safety. "I think you should leave, sir."

"Sir, now is it?" Cullen lurched forward. "Why, you crafty piece of—"

Cullen never completed his sentence. Footsteps swiftly descended the stairs and a dark arm swung toward Cullen. Parkes' fist connected with his flapping mouth. He fell hard to the pavement. Two burly footmen caught Cullen's arms and dragged him off into the dark street.

"He'll just use ya till he gets bored and toss ya away, ya silly strumpet!" Cullen called loudly. "My uncle and I had plans to get rich from Thistlemore. At least you would have been respectable!"

"Don't listen to him, miss. Come inside."

Parkes led her, unresisting, into the house, throwing a scowl behind him at the door. Once inside, he took her shawl, gripped her arm firmly and ushered her upstairs. Outside her bedchamber door, he stopped and bowed low, conveying a respect she had not anticipated. Or deserved. "Don't think about that fool again. Some people cannot be happy for another's good fortune."

In a daze, Constance entered her room. She had expected to lose the respect of her friends when she became Jack's mistress. She just hadn't expected it to happen so soon.

———◆———

Jack took the stairs two at a time. Panic had long ago reduced his ability to think with any clarity. All he knew was that he had to get to Pixie. His butler's hurried warning had only served to heighten his worry. She would be humiliated by the rumors and by Mr. Brampton's loud and very public abuse.

He barreled into her bedchamber to beg her forgiveness—only to find it empty.

He grabbed a bedpost and swung around. She was gone. Despair threatened him a moment before he snapped out of it, pivoted, and hurried to his own door.

Once he got rid of his evening clothes, he would search the city for her. Jack rushed through his sitting room, and then moved to his brightly lit bedchamber.

His valet was not normally so thoughtful to light so many candles—not in spring—but the room was warm and welcoming. Jack ripped out his cravat pin and struggled with his cravat, letting the diamond pin lay wherever it landed. He rubbed his hand around his neck and tried to think where she might have gone.

"Did your valet tie it too tight, or did you grow tonight, Jack?"

Pixie's soft amused voice floated to him and Jack spun toward the sound.

She sat in a froth of white lace and silk, watching him undress, a twinkle in her eyes and a smile on her lips.

He staggered a few steps, overwhelmed by the relief of seeing her. A shocking lack of blood in his brain accounted for his inability to speak immediately.

After a moment, he managed to put together enough words to produce a reply that made sense. "Too much starch, I believe."

"Well, that can be easily taken care of."

Jack's brain was working now. "Will you speak to the housekeeper tomorrow?"

She laughed and his panic fled. "If you ask nicely, perhaps I could be persuaded to drop a hint or two."

"Well then, I had better do just that." Jack eyed her sitting there, moved toward his dressing room. "Give me a moment, and I will be right back."

———◆———

Constance was puzzled that things were not progressing quite how she had imagined. Although she sat alone on his big bed, she had hoped Jack would take that very large hint and come to join her.

When he emerged from his dressing room a moment or two later, Constance's heart raced. He was perfect. He had changed. His coat and waistcoat were gone. His shirt flowed free of the breeches on his hips, and best of all, no shoes or stockings—only bare feet.

Constance swooned at the sight, landing lightly on her back. Jack crawled up the bed after her. Delicious heat enveloped her as he hovered above, eyes twinkling with affection.

"My darling Pixie, I almost swooned myself to see you sitting on my bed." He swooped in to kiss her on the lips. "I'm sorry about tonight. Someone must have spotted us. As if I would dishonor you by making you my mistress. Come, sit up."

He pulled her up with him and sank to his knees beside her.

"What?"

"My dearest love, I could not bear it if you returned to Sunderland. Would you do me the very great honor of marrying me tomorrow, or is it today? I need you so very much."

Tears stung her eyes. "Oh, Jack. Less starch in your laundry is not a reason to offer to marry me."

"Forget the starch. I've been going mad. Please put me out of my misery. I want you so very terribly, little Pixie. I love you. Marry me. I want to spend the rest of my life openly adoring you."

Tears fell, clouding her vision of the man she loved enough to suffer the scandal of becoming his mistress. "Jack, I would love to marry you, but you know I can't."

His brow creased. "Why ever not?"

"I realize you've kept the connection secret, but you are betrothed," Constance sobbed. "All I can be is your lover."

"Ah, Pixie, I'm such an idiot. I did not realize you'd heard of that nonsense, but I swear it is not what you think. Look at me." Jack cradled her face. "I'm not betrothed, love. Not in any conventional sense."

Jack grasped her hands tight in his. "Our fathers were foolish men, and terribly addicted to gambling. Do you remember how they were together? All in or nothing. But in a moment of weakness, my father crossed the line of honor and agreed to something that I cannot ever condone. As payment for your father's debts, he acquired Thistlemore—and you."

Constance gasped. "What do you mean *me*? He bought me?"

"They traded you." Jack's face turned an ugly shade of red. "I learned of it when my father died and I burned the document immediately. Then I came to Thistlemore to acquire the copy in your mother's possession. She would not give it up easily."

Revulsion churned in her belly. "That's why she was angry with you?"

He nodded. "At first she feared that I would toss you both out once I had the document. The lease appeased her somewhat. We argued—until I eventually got my way. But I remained your guardian until you came of age."

"That's why she calls you a cold-hearted beast?"

"Well, it wasn't me who sold you," Jack argued.

"Papa said you were betrothed," she shook her head, unwilling to consider this was real. "He never said it was to me."

"There was no stipulation that I had to marry you. You were to be my mistress or my property."

The regret in Jack's eyes drew more tears. She squeezed her eyes shut over the humiliation her father had dealt her from the grave. "You didn't tell me. Why?"

"The whole agreement was an atrocity. I just wanted to forget that they could agree to such a thing," Jack confessed, slumping beside her and lacing his fingers through hers.

By his expression, he had lost respect for his father, and hers too. Not that there was much of Greedy Grange's life to admire, but Constance had liked Jack's papa. He had always been kind to her, and now she knew why. "I'm sure he meant well."

———— ◆ ————

Jack scowled. He did not believe that. He still harbored great anger at his sire for buying a woman. "My girl, you are far too forgiving."

Jack raised her hand to his face and held it there. "Tomorrow you will wish them both to the devil. I have thought that repeatedly for the last four years. So, was that a yes or a no to marrying me?"

"Yes, I will marry you. I love you so much it hurts."

Gathering the folds of her nightgown, Pixie turned toward him. She dropped the fabric and ran her hands up his chest to his neck, pulled his head to hers and kissed him soundly. She swallowed his groan as she flung herself over him.

Jack enjoyed her aggression. He kneaded her derrière, and then stroked the backs of her thighs, all the while devouring her with deep kisses. Nothing else mattered.

He broke the kiss, but kept her tight against him. "I have something for you."

Her eyes glistened in the candlelight and he didn't want to tear his eyes away. "It can wait," she said.

"No. This is too important." Jack produced a dainty ring that he'd been waiting to give to her. "I want to do this right. Give me your hand."

"Oh, Jack, I love it." She allowed him to push it on her ring finger, and she held it up to catch the light. "It fits perfectly too. How did you get the size right?"

"A man in love can do anything for his woman," he boasted with a wide smile and kissed her cheek. "It is the original partner to the one I wear—my mother's ring."

Tears glistened in her eyes again and she hastily scrubbed them away as she stared at the elegant ruby and diamond ring. Jack sighed and rubbed his nose to hers, relieved and excited to have finally claimed the woman he loved with all his heart.

Jack kissed her again, slow and hungry, and pushed her to the bed's softness. Hovering over her, Jack did his best to keep his impulses under control, but he couldn't help but try to kiss every part of her.

Lying beneath him, Constance's hands were busy. She pushed his shirt up over his head and attacked the remaining buttons on his breeches, loosening them from his hips. Soft hands glided over his stomach as he followed the trail of freckles to the neckline of her nightgown. Using his teeth, he snagged the ribbon that held it closed and lifted his head slowly, watching the bow loosen to expose more skin.

Pixie froze as he inched the garment from her shoulder and continued to kiss a path downward. His lips pressed to the soft swell of her breast and he impatiently slid the fabric aside, grazing the peaked, pink nipple with the stitching.

Pixie gasped and then her hand curled around his waist, pulling at him with no clear sense of direction. Her other hand swept a line of fire, following the contours of his body, rubbing against the grain of his chest hair until her fingers found his nipple. Desire burned as she strummed over the peak and he did the same to her.

Jack caught her gaze and held it as he lowered his lips to her breast. He took the hard peak into his mouth. Pixie froze again until he suckled. Her back arched. She pulled him down against her curves, bending him to her will and her body.

As he suckled, Jack inched her gown lower so he had clear access to both breasts. Shaping them with both hands, he changed sides and the moan of desire she breathed against his face was another distraction to master.

She gripped his hair and pulled him up until he lay hard against her. Pixie appeared voracious, but he was not going to blunder and rush. She was a tiny woman. If he remained in control tonight, he would not have to wait long to make love to her again.

Anxious to keep her aroused, Jack returned to her breasts. Pixie's hands wove into his hair and encouraged his ministration. But she undulated on the bed so much that Jack had to lift away, as blind desire clouded his mind. He let his lips slip from her breast slowly. She stared at him with lust-shrouded eyes.

He grabbed hold of her nightgown and worked the thin material lower; her chest heaved as he exposed her to her hips. When her dark curls peeked above the linen, he ripped the material away and pressed his lips to her belly. Jack let his mouth wander lower, randomly kissing newly found freckles and the hard edges of her hips. He could not halt his downward progress if he wanted to. He kissed his way down her leg, over her knee, took the arch of her foot into his mouth, and pressed a heavy kiss there.

Jack settled back on his heels and let his gaze travel along Pixie's perfect body. She watched him, breasts jiggling as she dragged in frantic breaths. He raised her other foot to his mouth, pressed lingering kisses from her heel to her toes. They wriggled, and he chuckled but continued his reverent kisses along her other leg.

———◆———

Jack was going to drive her insane.

Constance had never dreamed he would expose her like this. That he would carry out such an intense inspection before they made love. She had thought tonight would be more like this morning's frantic rubbings. Her heart raced just the same. But Jack appeared in no hurry as his lips branded her skin.

Constance fought to hold still and not let the moans she wanted to utter break free. When he reached her breasts again, she threw him over onto his back and held him down.

Constance needed a moment to regain her sanity, but Jack laughed at her audacity and pulled her to him, sliding her skin against the heat of his. Dear God, she'd never be cold again. She wrestled his hands back to the mattress and kissed his neck. He gasped as she kissed a path to his shoulder, down to his nipple, and then kissed them too.

The encouraging groans he uttered were supremely satisfying.

He escaped her clutches and cradled her head against his skin. She nipped and kissed her way lower, sliding over the ridges of rib and the muscles of his stomach.

When he pulled away, she grinned up at him. "Are you ticklish?"

"So it would seem," he admitted, a touch of humor in his voice.

Constance wriggled lower and used her fingers to follow the trail of hair that disappeared into his breeches. She slipped her hands under the waistband and carefully pushed his breeches and small clothes down to his thighs.

His moan was tortured as she ran her palm up and down his length lightly, teasing him and learning how to please him.

She helped him remove his clothes completely.

Finding herself at his feet, she grasped both and raised them for her inspection. He had big feet, nicely shaped toes and, to her amusement, he was extremely ticklish.

Constance giggled as he drew his feet away. "Just how ticklish are you?"

"Too ticklish, it seems. Come here."

"Not yet." She had a full view of all of his endowments, and what she saw made her mouth water. Images from the picture book caught in her mind and gave her a wicked idea. Grasping one of his restless legs, she lowered her mouth and kissed a curling path from the inside of his calf to his hip until her face was level with what she desired.

Before he could stop her, she pressed her lips against the smooth flesh. She had just enough time to appreciate how lovely his skin felt against her lips before he gripped her with both hands, and pulled her up his body.

Chapter Twenty-Nine

———◆———

Jack lifted her away from temptation and into his arms. How had she become so knowledgeable in such a short length of time? He wasn't complaining, except that her enthusiasm wasn't helping him remain in control. He arranged Pixie so she straddled him, letting her body rest a moment against his.

But Pixie was unwilling to be still. She wriggled as she kissed him, so he stroked between her legs. At his persistent touch, she moaned heavily into his mouth, and curled her arms tight around his shoulders.

He lifted her up and fitted the head of his cock to her entrance. "My love, this might hurt. I'm sorry."

Pixie met his gaze. Tousled as she was, she had never looked more beautiful. Her lips were full and well kissed. "Better you than anyone else."

Jack growled low in his throat as he eased her down. No one but him, ever. He used all of his control to take it slow, fought the urge to surge upward to impale her. She was a virgin, small, and bound to be incredibly tight.

Even with his controlled entry, she squeaked his name.

"Yes, love?"

"Is that it?" she asked, panting and digging her nails into his shoulder muscles, as if she needed an anchor.

"No, there is quite a bit more of me," Jack said through clenched teeth.

"Finish it, Jack. I think I am going to explode."

"As my lady desires," he agreed. There was no finishing between them, but he understood her. She was so aroused it was agony. Jack was absurdly pleased, and he pushed up with one hard thrust and held still as she gasped.

He was buried deep inside her—and he was home. Although his body craved friction, Jack remained still until she removed her nails from his shoulders. He kissed her fiercely when she turned her lips to his, and rolled her onto her back.

Pixie's eyes widened. "Oh, dear. I'm going to be a marchioness."

Her husky laugh drew him deeper. Jack held himself above her, grateful for the distracting conversation because all he wanted to do was move. "Damn right you are."

Constance wriggled beneath him awkwardly. "Oh, the *ton* is going to go up in flames when they realize."

"Talk about it later," Jack suggested as he pulled out a little then pressed in again, watching for a grimace of pain. When he saw none, he thrust again.

Jack began slowly, pushing down his own needs and letting her adjust. When her knees relaxed, he nudged in stronger, varying his thrusts, adjusting the angle until she breathed raggedly and she was with him again. He watched her eyes, but worried over the glazed look in them.

"Are you all right?"

"Yes," she gasped, wriggling her hips then pulling him closer with her hands on his ass. "Love me, Jack. Just love me."

"Forever."

With one arm bracing his weight, he caressed her breast and demanded her lips come back to his. Kissing made short work of his remaining senses.

When her sobs grew louder, he lifted her hips from the bed, encouraging her to wrap her legs higher around his back. When her feet touched his ass, he groaned and ground his hips into the cradle of her thighs. Pixie cried out as Jack pushed her over the edge and she dragged him with her. His whole body convulsed, and he let loose a groan of the deepest, earthiest gladness.

———◆———

Virginia lifted her pink skirts above the long grass and trudged her way to the stream. Of course, Bernard *would* be at the far end of his estate when she wanted to talk to him. It was a beautiful day for a stroll, but she was impatient and had quite another matter on her mind.

A tussock tripped her up, and she cursed it but kept walking until she found what she sought. She cursed when she saw Bernard dripping sweat over a chopping block.

She cupped her hands around her mouth to yell over the noise. "Did you scare away all the workers when you returned?"

Perhaps her greeting lacked the affection she felt, but she was hot and uncomfortable from the long walk, and fast losing her temper, which annoyed her more than anything.

Bernard dropped the axe but spoke before turning. "I'm not such a beast to expect them to work every minute of every day. I'm merely doing this for the exercise." Bernard turned and reached for a cloth to wipe the sweat from his face. "When did you get home?"

"This afternoon."

"Is Jack with you?"

"No, he and Pixie married yesterday morning and no longer require a chaperone. Tomorrow they depart on their honeymoon. Apparently, the list of places to visit is very long. I shall not see them for a while. I thought I should come and pay my respects."

"You saw my mother already?"

"No, I came to see you," Virginia ground out. He was just so dense for an overeducated man.

He froze then he moved away from her. "I need a swim."

He stalked to the water's edge, pulled off his boots and shirt, removed his trousers, and then dove straight in without a backward glance.

Typical.

His long arms propelled him away and out of sight. Virginia sighed, disappointed to be denied a longer view of all that muscled perfection. She settled next to his clothes to wait, lying down to watch the clouds go by; making shapes out of the puffy whiteness until they rained on her.

Bernard shook water from his hair again as she sat up. "Oh, don't do that."

"If your eyes hadn't been open, I would have thought you asleep. What were you thinking about?"

"Lots of things. How was the water?"

"Cold."

"Not that cold." She indicated his upstanding cock in amusement. "Is that for me?"

"Could be," Bernard chuckled. "If you're very lucky."

Virginia fought not to smile. She'd had a most enlightening trip home and armed with positively indecent knowledge, she intended to shock the man. She got to her knees before him. "What if I were to beg?"

His eyes widened slightly. "Well, if you really feel you must."

Virginia touched him, sliding her fingers over his thighs until he grunted. "I want children."

"To be above scandal, that would require a wedding. I had heard you were not keen to do that again."

She ran her finger from the tip of his cock to his balls. "I've changed my mind."

He groaned. "Congratulations, when is the happy event?"

He hissed as she tugged them. "Just as soon as I can arrange it. I would need a groom."

"No shortage of those lying about the countryside," Bernard offered, but he didn't voice any objection or encouragement to continue what she was doing.

He was not going to make this easy. Nothing between them ever had been. She wrapped her fingers tighter around his cock, prepared to ask the question that had hurried her from London as quick as she could go. "Bernard Hallam, would you do me the very great honor of marrying me? I want my children to be yours." To make her question all the more enticing, she began a lazy stroke with her hand.

"Well," he gasped. "Since you put such feeling into your request, I might be persuaded." He dropped to his knees. "I was going to ask you, you know. I have a ring in my bedchamber, waiting for you to come home."

"I'm home now. I missed you," she confessed as she wrapped her hands around his wet hips and squeezed. She kissed him. She simply couldn't wait another moment.

Bernard lowered her to the ground, kissing her all the while.

This was perfect—everything she'd ever wanted. When her legs were spread, and he was about to enter, he paused.

"When did you become so bold?"

Virginia twisted, brushing his cock with her curls. "My darling new sister gave me a wicked little book she found in the library at Ettington House. It was very edu...cational." Her breath fractured as he joined with her and she wrapped her legs around his wet thighs, running her nails over his damp skin.

"I think I know the book. What else interested you?"

Bernard rocked his hips and set up a gentle stroke that made her body sing. "Oh, lots of things. It's good that you're so strong. A couple of them require strength and concentration to achieve the appropriate angles."

Bernard groaned and nipped at her neck. "It's good that you want to marry me. I've been having a lot of trouble keeping my head around you."

She gasped as his hand closed on her breast. "You, Bernard?"

"Be quiet. Thank God I don't have to worry about where I come anymore."

He sped up his thrusts, turning their gentle loving into blinding passion. He groaned deep into her neck before she was halfway to finding her release, but she did not care. She would get to have his children. She would get to have him.

"I love you," Virginia whispered into his ear.

Bernard sagged his weight upon her then pulled out, flipped her over, and dragged her to her knees.

Virginia squirmed at the unusual position. "What are you doing?"

He positioned to enter from behind, and she gasped as he filled her. "Position four is a favorite of mine. You better not expect a small family, Virginia. I am not going to be patient about creating our children. I have a lot of work to do, and I always honor my promises. Christ, I love you."

He slid a finger into her curls and pushed her over the edge.

Epilogue

———— ◆ ————

"Jack, stop that." Constance giggled, swatting at her husband's wandering hands.

He laughed into her ear. "No. Wriggle a bit to the left."

Constance turned and swept her hands over his chest, admiring the cut and color of his new wardrobe. "We are supposed to be serious tonight. How can you laugh at such an important moment like this?"

"Easily, I have been hoping this day would come for years," he whispered. "Can we go in yet?"

"There they are. Now, you remember what you have to do?"

"I am the older party here, Pixie. I think I can manage one last performance." Jack tugged his waistcoat. "Did I mention how much I admire that gown? Can you wear it to bed tonight? I want to peel you out of it with my teeth."

"Jack, you have mentioned it several times already. Do you think you could keep your mind focused on the task at hand and not on lovemaking?" Constance asked impatiently.

Jack sighed, but Lord Daventry's bored voice interrupted their repartee. "If you two are done bickering like a randy married couple, do you think we could hurry this along? I have someone to meet."

Jack laughed. "Daventry, someday I hope you will fall in love so hard that you cannot see straight."

Constance giggled as the greatest rogue in London crossed

himself. It would require a very strong woman to take him on.

Constance nudged Jack toward the ballroom. "Off you go,"

When he was out of sight, Constance risked a peek around the doorframe to watch the effect he had on the ladies.

"I didn't get a chance to tell Ettington the news?"

"What news?"

"I sent a man up to investigate all this interest in your former home at his request and received very good news this very afternoon."

"What is it?"

"It seems that beneath the surface is a thick seam of coal." He grinned. "Perhaps half a mile wide and it is very likely it might connect to a property recently purchased by Lord Clerkenwell. That coal is going to make you both very rich."

Constance sighed with relief. No matter how much Jack might love her she'd felt guilty over the financial burdens he'd shouldered on her behalf. He would be repaid when the coal was mined. "That is very good news."

"I had hoped so," he said with a wink.

Constance cast a glance at her companion. "You were supposed to go in already, Daventry," she murmured.

"Ettington wasn't happy to leave you alone out here dressed like that. I'm here to make sure you remain unmolested until your entrance."

Constance laughed so hard she almost cried. "He left you— the man aiming for the title of *most debauched* —to guard me?"

"I don't touch married women, Pixie. He knows you are perfectly safe. Actually, you have always been safe with me. I never touch virgins, either."

Constance scoffed at his statement, and then took a deep breath of night air, desperate to regain her composure before she lost her nerve and stepped into the ballroom.

Absolute silence reigned when she was recognized. Constance knew exactly how she looked. Madame du Clair had clapped her hands with glee when she had requested this gown. This dress had originally been for Jack's pleasure alone, but they had both decided the red silk needed a larger audience and it went so well with Jack's wedding gift. She set her hand on the crust of ruby and diamonds at her throat, anxious that they still be there, then brushed a loose curl over her shoulder to show off the band of gold on her ring finger.

Jack stood alone, one hand held out toward her. She let all the love she felt for him shine through her smile and when she reached him, she slid her hand into his palm.

Very slowly, smile brightening his eyes, he raised her hand to his lips and kissed the symbol of their marriage and love.

A confused mutter swept the room then rose to a deafening roar. When they were sure everyone in the room had seen them together, they turned to look directly at Miss Scaling. Her mother and father stood in shock behind her.

Jack led Constance to her. "Have you met my wife, Miss Scaling?"

Jack's voice purred, anger rippling beneath in his tone.

The excited chatter of the *ton* died as they craned to hear every word.

"Your wife? No, that's not possible."

Jack scowled and drew Constance tight to his side. "I'm so sorry your informant didn't have time to tell you about the wedding. She and her family are on their way to one of my other estates, and no amount of bully tactics will ever induce a member of my household to confide details of my family again."

Miss Scaling glanced about her nervously. "Why would I do such a thing?"

"Why would you have so little control over your mount that it could endanger someone? How did Pixie fall into a pond, or come to be covered in that noxious scent you wear?"

An angry mutter began in the crowd and all eyes bored into Miss Scaling.

"Pixie? I didn't touch anyone called Pixie."

"Come near my wife again and expect to lose a great deal," Jack growled, and Miss Scaling did faint in truth.

Unsurprisingly, Lord Wade caught her.

Jack turned, a smile on his lips. "Now, where were we?" He wrapped his arms around Constance and squeezed. "I remember. This dress. Is it the most daring you ordered?"

"No," Constance laughed, draping her arms around his neck and stretching up to whisper. "The white one is transparent, even without damping with water."

"That does it." Jack hoisted Constance over his shoulder and slapped a hand on her derrière, but ignored her shriek of protest. "We're going home."

Constance struggled to see past her fallen hair as she choked on gasps of mirth. She had to use one hand on Jack's backside to hold herself up, and giggled helplessly at the shocked expressions left in their wake. She gave up trying to see and slapped her other hand on his other cheek. Jack's protest set her off again, and she giggled until he stopped her with his kisses.

———— ♦ ————

IF YOU ENJOYED CHILLS DON'T MISS THE NEXT DISTINGUISHED ROGUE

Broken

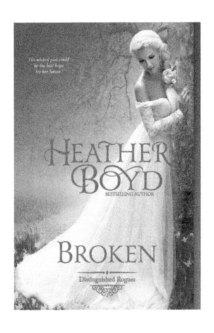

The Distinguished Rogues series continues with Broken as a wicked rogue's peace is shattered by the return of a face from his past...

Chapter One

Summer, 1813

Giles forced a smile to his lips to welcome Lord Winter to his country estate in Northamptonshire. "Winter," Giles called. "Welcome back to Cottingstone."

The newcomer shook his head. At least the old baron could pretend to look pleased that Giles had broken his rule about receiving a guest at Cottingstone Manor. But no, Lord Winter's face wore a perpetual frown, just like every other time their paths had crossed in London.

"Daventry." The older man's quavering voice, pitched somewhat lower than Giles', betrayed exhaustion. "The place hasn't changed."

Giles held out his hand. "You must be weary. Dinner won't be served for an hour, but I have some excellent whiskey to soothe you while we wait."

The baron crushed Giles' fist. "Brandy would be preferable in its place—especially today. But first..." Winter returned to the carriage.

Giles took a step back toward his butler. "Dithers?"

"I shall switch the decanters when I return to the house, milord," he promised.

"Do that, and ask Cook if dinner can be brought forward," Giles murmured. "Lord Winter doesn't appear in good health."

"I don't believe *his* health is the problem, milord," Dithers replied.

Without another word of explanation, the butler stepped back, leaving Giles to ponder to whose health he had referred. The baron traveled alone and often. His servants all looked a disciplined, healthy bunch. But they moved carefully on the carriage and didn't speak overloud. The horses were settled swiftly, too. Calm, efficient, eerie.

As Giles stepped out of the way of a burdened footman, a bloodcurdling howl erupted from beyond the house. Every man stopped and stared, not in the direction of the sound, but at the dark carriage they were unloading.

The steady pounding of paws heralded the arrival of Giles' ancient wolfhound, Atticus. Judging by the dog's speed and his whining agitation, something was seriously amiss with him. In fact, this level of energy from the hound was more than a little surprising. He had spent most of Giles' visit lying under his feet snoring.

Atticus skidded to a stop beside the closed door of the carriage. If the door had been open, Giles was sure the hound would have barged his way in. He ignored the restless horses and stunned attendants to haul his beast out of the way. The dog was heavy and determined to stay exactly where he was, but Giles managed to pull him aside.

Lord Winter stared at the dog, nodded, and then stepped into the carriage. When he emerged a few moments later, he held a body in his arms.

Atticus, generally so docile, whined and whimpered, straining against Giles in such a fashion as to cause alarm. Lord Winter adjusted the black-cloaked figure, and the bundle moaned.

Every hair on the back of Giles' neck rose. That was a woman's moan—one in great pain. He renewed his grip on the restless dog.

Lord Winter moved slowly toward the house, keeping his movements smooth. The grim set of his features showed just how much effort he expended not to jostle his burden. There was agony on that rugged face, too much grief for one man to bear alone.

With a hitched brow, Giles glanced at his butler, but Dithers revealed nothing. The butler scurried ahead to push the main doors wide and gestured Lord Winter inside. Giles followed, imitating the baron's quiet steps and keeping Lord Winter in sight.

Just inside the doorway, the baron stopped and bent his head to the bundle in his arms.

"Atticus." A voice carried to Giles' ears, eerily soft and pain-filled.

Giles only just managed to stop the dog from flinging himself at the woman.

"Atticus, come." Again, that voice called his hound, and a

pale arm slipped from beneath the black travel cloak to hang down limply.

Atticus whined, pulling Giles forward unwillingly. The dog reached the woman's hand, rasping his wet tongue against it. At first, she jerked back, but returned to rub the dog. Since Giles held the beast, he couldn't miss the shudder that vibrated through Atticus. Giles was stunned by the sensation.

"Atticus, heel." The woman spoke again, and Giles tensed as the voice tickled his memory.

The wolfhound calmed instantly, pulled free of Giles' slackened grip, and moved along with Lord Winter. Troubled, Giles followed them upstairs.

Once at the chamber, a nurse, who Giles only now noticed, pulled the drapes closed, ushering Dithers out with agitated flicks of her hands. Lord Winter lowered his burden to the high bed, removed the dark cloak, and pulled the blankets tightly around her.

From his position at the doorway, Giles noticed no more details of the woman, but her identity intrigued him. She knew his dog's name? What was Lord Winter doing driving across England with an ill woman in tow? Surely, he could have arranged some other care, rather than dragging her on what appeared to be a painful journey.

To his surprise, Atticus padded across the room and stepped onto the dais. Once on the bed, the hound nosed in close to the woman's hand. Surely Lord Winter would shoo him away.

But the woman clutched at the dog's shaggy coat, pulling him against her side with a soft sigh.

His guest said nothing as he joined Giles at the door, so Giles stepped aside to allow the baron room to pass. Winter looked over his shoulder once before closing the door on the woman, dog, and nurse.

"What the devil is going on?" he demanded.

"Not now, lad," Winter begged and turned away.

Giles stared after his guest in shock at his lack of manners then hurried to catch up. He rarely entertained guests for a reason. Giles liked privacy and peace at Cottingstone.

"I trust you had an uneventful journey," he asked.

Winter grunted and strode for Dithers who was holding a glass of brandy.

An hour later, not even spirits and a pleasant meal had sweetened his mood or made him more forthcoming. The food had been more than satisfactory, braised duck with plum sauce, followed by truffles and plum pudding.

The company at the table, on the other hand, had been poor.

Giles was fast losing his patience with the baron. Unease knotted his shoulders. The woman's voice nagged at the edge of his memory. She was a puzzle he couldn't solve. The man opposite offered nothing by way of explanation for her presence but stoically downed glass after glass of Giles' best brandy as if determined to forget.

The baron had aged in the last few years. Iron-gray hair graced the sides of his head and candlelight reflected off the top. The once proud Corinthian dressed with supremely dull taste, but, given his habit of constant travel, perhaps that was more a matter of practicality than choice.

"Never thought she'd survive this long," the baron began suddenly, staring into his glass as he swirled the contents around. "Been years more than I thought she'd have. Dragged her from one end of the country to the other in the hope of a cure, but it has all been for nothing. Quacks and charlatans. Every one of them useless."

Lord Winter poured another large drink with unsteady hands. "She was such a bright little thing, always ready with a smile. Full of life. A perfect angel." He shook his head as if frustrated by his own words. "I just could not bear to leave her behind. You have to be so careful with her."

Giles didn't respond, but he inched closer, intrigued by Winter's words to be sure he caught them all.

"Too many accidents. Too many mistakes. Her reaction to your hound was the first real response I've witnessed in years. I'd stopped believing she was there. It has gotten my hopes up again, but nothing good can come to her now. It's too late."

"I'm sure you're doing the best you can," Giles said, not knowing if he spoke the truth, but positive he should say something rallying.

"I wish I could believe that. No man should live longer than his child."

It took only a moment for Giles to review the Winter family tree in his mind. He reared back. "That's *Lilly?*" Giles jerked at his cravat, suddenly hot at the thought of her.

"Who else did you imagine it might be?" Winter's composed veneer blurred away fast under the influence of brandy. He sat forward, eyes alight with anger.

Giles had no answer other than the truth. "I was told your daughter died years ago, sir."

Lord Winter's face turned an ugly shade of red. "And who told you such a blatant falsehood?"

As a rule, Giles preferred to speak the truth, but in this case, he hesitated. He did not like to meddle between a man and his wife, but if Lady Winter had spread lies, the baron had a right to know. "I'm afraid your wife informed me, sir."

Lord Winter slumped in his chair, rubbing a hand over his face. When he looked up, the baron's face held pain. "What is a man supposed to do when the mother of his child would rather her be dead?" Lord Winter sobbed on the last word, rusty grief shattering the peace of the room.

In his entire life, Giles had never been in the presence of a crying man. Drunk, vomiting, or fucking, yes. Occasionally all three on the same night, but never crying. Where was one supposed to look?

Lord Winter cried like a man who had held back years of anguish. Giles sat silently, waiting uncomfortably for the storm to pass. Lord Winter shifted in the chair, finally turning his face away. The man surely had to be embarrassed.

Perhaps he should pretend he hadn't heard the sorrow. Giles rose from his chair, poured Winter another drink, and then moved to the window to look out into the stormy night. But his body screamed for flight.

Years ago, Winter's daughter had fallen from Cottingstone Bridge into the stream that ran, flood full, through the property. She'd only been a young girl at the time, and her injuries were so serious that their betrothal had been severed soon after. When Giles had crossed paths with Lady Winter wearing mourning black in London, she had spoken of her lost daughter with credible grief. But why would Lady Winter wish people to believe her daughter was dead?

He glanced at Lord Winter as several odd things about his behavior fell into place. Lilly remained unwell after all this time. Had Lady Winter given up home and rejected the burden Lilly's care would impose on her?

Behind him, Lord Winter blew his nose, then clinked glass against teeth as he took another drink. "I know my search for a cure cannot continue. I have to accept that, but I cannot take her home. Living at Dumas would certainly speed her death."

The baron paused to clear his throat, as if his words had suddenly stuck. Giles was half-afraid Winter would suggest he still marry Lilly. Surely, God wouldn't torture them both with such an ill-advised union.

"I have heard there is a place in Wales that might take her, a home of sorts. I have made plans to see it soon, but I do not believe Lillian can handle the journey yet. With your agreement, I would like to leave her here while I inspect the situation and make arrangements. She will be no trouble. It's why I pressed for the invitation to visit. You see, Cottingstone is on the way. If it is acceptable, I will return and take her there as soon as she can travel again."

Giles swallowed a sigh of relief, but panic still threatened. Giles had a well-deserved reputation as a rake and Lord Winter was so upset that he was not thinking properly. "You cannot mean to leave her in a bachelor household?"

"I know it is beyond the pale to impose on an old association. I would not consider it normally, but you see how she is. Travel is very hard on her; she can barely stand an hour in the carriage. If Lillian can rest here for a time, she will be stronger for the next stage of the journey. The nurse is capable of taking care of her. You need do nothing to entertain her. I hadn't initially intended to tell her where we are, but she recognized the dog and remembers this place, it seems. She said to thank you for inviting her to stay."

Giles caught his open-mouthed reflection in the night-dark glass and swiftly closed his mouth. Thank God his back was to Lord Winter. Giles hadn't expected her to remember him; he hadn't spoken to her since she was a child.

Try as he might, he couldn't think of an excuse that would have them both gone tomorrow but the obvious one he'd already brought up. Lord Winter had to know of his reputation. His presence could ruin any innocent woman's good name just by breathing the same air she did, no matter her physical state.

The baron must be barking mad to consider leaving his

daughter without an army of stiff-backed chaperones between them. It was the grief talking, Giles thought. Come morning, the baron would see reason and change his mind.

Giles made a noncommittal sound, turned to the sideboard, and poured himself a very large brandy. God, he was going to need it. When Lord Winter eventually bade him good night, Giles took his brandy decanter to bed with him.

The ghost haunted his dreams that night.

In brandy-infused visions, the white-clad girl glided round and round him as he lay back on his soft bed. He yearned for her touch, but she remained elusive, just out of arm's reach. Her soft whisper spoke to him of earthly delights she could no longer share.

Giles dared her to come closer, to spread her tattered soul over him, to ease the ache they both shared. A cold touch slid along his straining leg muscles. He breathed raggedly, begging her to come near, to keep her hands on him. Ghostly fingers brushed against his thigh and he groaned, kicking the remaining sheet off his body, overwhelmed by need.

Lightning cracked outside the manor and he woke with a start. He was alone, as if the ghost had never been. Flashes of light danced on the walls as he blinked away the remnants of sleep and sat up against the headboard of his large empty bed, breathing hard.

The memory of the ghost had plagued him the last two years, disturbing his dreams, invading his waking moments too sometimes. The little sprite had the instincts of a bloodhound and found him every time he dabbled in pleasure within the walls of Huntley House in London.

Tonight's dream was different. The sense of being together was strong, more like the moments she appeared in his waking hours. Present but apart from him. Her watchfulness added to his arousal, but she usually kept a distance. Only he dreamed of further intimacies.

Giles' laugh echoed in the empty, dark room as thunder boomed outside.

What folly. He lusted after a ghost—a dead woman.

About Heather Boyd

————◆————

Determined to escape the Aussie sun on a scorching camping holiday, Heather picked up a pen and notebook from a corner store and started writing her very first novel—Chills. Years later, she is the author of over thirty sexy regency historical romances. Addicted to all things tech (never again will Heather write a novel longhand) and fascinated by English society of the early 1800's, Heather spends her days getting her characters in and out of trouble and into bed together (if they make it that far). She lives on the edge of beautiful Lake Macquarie, Australia with her trio of mischievous rogues (husband and two sons) along with one rescued cat whose only interest in her career is that it provides him with food on demand and a new puppy that is proving a big distraction.

You can find details of her work and writing at
www.Heather-Boyd.com

·

Made in the USA
Monee, IL
13 January 2022

88859042R00166